Come Dark

Books by Steven F. Havill

The Posadas County Mysteries
Heartshot
Bitter Recoil
Twice Buried
Before She Dies
Privileged to Kill
Prolonged Exposure
Out of Season
Dead Weight
Bag Limit
Red, Green, or Murder
Scavengers
A Discount for Death
Convenient Disposal
Statute of Limitations
Final Payment
The Fourth Time Is Murder
Double Prey
One Perfect Shot
NightZone
Blood Sweep
Come Dark

The Dr. Thomas Parks Novels
Race for the Dying
Comes a Time for Burning

Other Novels
The Killer
The Worst Enemy
LeadFire
TimberBlood

Come Dark

A Posadas County Mystery

Steven F. Havill

Poisoned Pen Press

Copyright © 2016 by Steven F. Havill

First Edition 2016

10 9 8 7 6 5 4 3 2 1

Library of Congress Catalog Card Number: 2015949192

ISBN: 9781464205255   Hardcover
        9781464205279   Trade Paperback

Poisoned Pen Press
6962 E. First Ave., Ste. 103
Scottsdale, AZ 85251
www.poisonedpenpress.com
info@poisonedpenpress.com

Printed in the United States of America

For Kathleen

Acknowledgments

With special thanks to Kelly Gatlin, Andrew Smart, and Dr. James Hall.

Posadas County, New Mexico

Chapter One

"Your days are numbered, you little ignorant peckerwoods." Monty Schaffer stood with feet spread, fists tightly balled on his hips—an angry man ready to strike. But instead of striking, he unholstered his cell phone and hit number one on the auto dial, squinting hard as he struck the tiny key with a big, sausage-like finger.

The call connected.

"This is Miles Waddell."

"Miles, the little bastards tagged one of the cars." As if in sympathy, Schaffer reached up and touched the polished oak trim strip below the curved, tinted windows of the railcar, the fourth car in a line of five such custom units behind the slick narrow gauge locomotive.

Waddell sighed, sounding farther away than the mesa-top home of his *NightZone* development thirty miles to the west. "Just the one?"

Well, the one is bad enough, Schaffer thought. Waddell could be excused for going ballistic upon hearing of the latest spray painted vandalism. But the brakeman had learned long ago that Miles Waddell, the owner and sole fund source for the mammoth astronomy theme park project, *NightZone*, managed his blood pressure by taking things in stride. In the great universe of the developer's current challenges, a panel of sprayed-on wannabe gang graffiti didn't amount to much.

"Just the one." Schaffer stepped back and surveyed the incomprehensible design. "This is what them little bastards call art, I guess. I can make out a P and an F, with a whole bunch of shit and curlicues designs around 'em. Got a panel about six feet long, from the rocker panels up to the window trim strip."

He stepped closer and touched the offending design lightly with the tips of his fingers, then dug in a strong thumbnail. "Looks like enamel. Ain't completely cured. I'd guess they got in here last night, most likely. It's like there ain't enough regular railcars around on the main line that they got to target ours."

"*P. F. Patrullas de la Frontera,*" Waddell muttered. His mangled Spanish failed to sound the *ll* properly as a *y*.

"How'd they know we had company comin' today?" Schaffer asked. "This one's gonna take a gallon of Taginator."

"Yeah, well." Waddell clearly had other things on his mind this morning.

"Catch 'em in the act and shoot 'em. Leave 'em lyin' for the buzzards. That'll put a stop to it."

Waddell chuckled quietly. "That might not be the kind of PR that we want just now, Monty. The run this morning is more important, so how about taking that car out of line until we can get it cleaned up? Just go with the four today. That way we won't have to explain the vandalism to some reporter."

"You got it."

"All we can do is keep on top of it, Monty. If it happens again, don't let a single day go by before it's removed. For now, put it in the shed so they can't see you working on it. All the taggers want is the publicity."

"Yep."

"And take some good, clear pictures of the design before you scrub it off. I'll want to give a color copy to the SO first thing today for their files. Is Springer there yet?"

Schaffer lifted a hand in salute as the engineer in question walked down the line of cars toward him, taking his time, eyeing every wheel, grease fitting, brake block, and hose. "He's walking toward me right now."

"Well, sheeeeeit," Boyd Springer cursed when he saw the artwork.

"Miles is on the line." Schaffer held out the phone.

"Yup," Springer greeted his multimillionaire employer.

"Boyd, I told Monty just to kick the car loose and go with four. There'll be plenty of room. And don't forget…Frank Dayan gets first choice of where to ride, but don't let him see *that* car. I don't want to see it on Page One."

"Sure." As publisher of the local *Posadas Register,* Frank Dayan had supported the massive *NightZone* project since the first day, when former rancher Miles Waddell had announced his almost incomprehensibly grandiose plans for an astronomy-based theme park perched on the laser-flat mesa-top, away from the highway traffic of State Route 56, away from any community of ranchers, completely out of sight of tourist traffic.

The most charitable county residents thought Waddell a bit goofy at even dreaming of a three-hundred-fifty-million-dollar project, even though the funding came as the bulk of an inheritance. But savvy in ways that few could understand, Waddell was close to pushing the whole concept to fruition. He'd managed his enormous inherited wealth carefully. One of his important talents was being able to ignore criticism from skeptics.

The latest deluge of publicity had fired up just a week before, when assembly of the long-awaited radio telescope dish, an enormous bowl-shaped antenna sixty meters across, had progressed to a point where visitors could actually tell what it was. Trucks had spent weeks bringing the parts to the mesa-top, and now the towering dish could turn its huge ear toward the heavens.

At the moment, to be sure, the great dish was stone-deaf. But eventually the maze of computer connections would be finished, and the installation, funded by a California university, coupled with scientists in New Zealand and India, together with the National Science Foundation, would join a worldwide grid of similar facilities.

The dish was the only structure on the *NightZone* mesa that was not funded entirely by Miles Waddell. Instead, he hosted the project, donating the acreage for the radio telescope facility, and he had helped move it. But the radio telescope wasn't the sort of facility where visitors could peer into an eyepiece. The tiny whispers of microwave background noise from deep space were the target, less intense than the beating of a tiny moth's wings.

The legion of conspiracy theorists amused Waddell. They deluged the Internet with wild tales about what the mesa installation was *really* designed to do, but the developer refused to spend an instant trying to refute silly rumors. The giant dish was deaf to neighborhood conversations.

And certainly, the radio telescope was but one feature of the massive two-hundred-thirty-acre *NightZone* mesa project. Waddell's dream included the tramway that rose almost nine hundred feet from the prairie below to the mesa-top, a new hotel and restaurant topside, the battery of three sixty-inch telescopes linked to the giant screen theater, and on and on.

Everything except a small interpretive center and the train station were on top of the mesa, out of sight. A tourist could drive west from Posadas toward Arizona and the Mexican border and never know the facility was there. There was not a single sign or billboard that announced, "Turn HERE! See the Heavens! Moccasins for the whole family! Martian Souvenirs!"

And today marked the fourth shakedown trip by the *Night-Zone* narrow-gauge locomotive, a ride that would take mesa visitors from the village of Posadas westward thirty-seven miles through rugged Sonoran Desert country to the mesa-bottom, ready for transfer to the tramway ride to the summit.

Waddell had mapped every inch of the train's route himself, favoring impressive scenery rather than a quick, efficient route—affectionately calling it his "bird-watcher's route." He had included picturesque trestles over torturous arroyos, wound the route through rock-choked narrows, and even tracked to the north a bit to take in an oak grove-garlanded box canyon featuring one of the few live springs in Posadas County.

Rather than choosing an antique steam locomotive, Waddell had settled on an amazingly quiet natural gas-electric engine. The locomotive's appearance was designed with futuristic simplicity, its paint scheme a deep, midnight blue color that complemented the tawny colors of the prairie through which it passed.

Visitors did not drive to the top of the *NightZone* mesa—Waddell was adamant about that. Part of the park's mystique was that visitors had to *want* to go there, had to *want* to make the effort. This was no place for a casual, spur-of-the-moment drive-by. First the train ride out from the village, then the tram, then the wonder of the on-top facilities. Once on top, visitors would experience the vast dome of the night sky—no light pollution from the sweep of headlights, no dust on the county road, no fumes from traffic, no flatulent, blaring exhaust resonators.

Even most vendors serving the park would keep their trucks out of the area, using the train's single freight car for deliveries.

Ever the realist, Waddell knew that a daytime train ride and tour would not have the impact of a night spent on the mesa. But journalists had to see the details, and with any luck, they'd be back to enjoy the ambience come dark.

"And take it slow," Waddell reminded his engineer. "We don't want some silly accident with the train full of reporters and cameras. *Serene* is the byword." The first three trips, all without incident, had run unannounced, twice in daylight, once at night. This fourth trip was entirely for journalists, and had garnered considerable media attention, including a full-page spread in the big-city Sunday metro paper.

"I hear ya." Springer reached out and patted the car's gleaming, and now defaced flank. "We'll get 'er all cleaned up."

"I have a meeting with the architects next week. We'll take a look at siding in the locomotive barn on Highland, with doors at both ends. That way we can button her up when she's not on the tracks."

Springer nodded as if Waddell could see him. "The way you've got it all laid out, this train is going to drive her wheels off. She isn't going to get the chance to sit still very long." The admiration in his voice was clear.

"Let's hope not. Look, I'll be there in about an hour," Waddell said. "I'll do just a little meet-and-greet with the press. And I don't want any of them having the chance to photograph the vandalism, so boot that car off first thing. We don't need to give the little bastards any publicity. I told Monty that I wanted good, clear photos of the damage for our own file. And to make sure the sheriff gets a copy. And Bill, too, for that matter. I asked him if he'd come along on this ride. Nobody knows more about the county than he does."

"Knowin' him, he'll want to be up in the cab," Springer said.

"Then that's where he goes," Waddell added. "If he wants to sit out on the cowcatcher, that's the way it is."

Former Posadas County deputy, then undersheriff, then sheriff, then livestock inspector, then retired to a rich life of his own historical studies and fieldwork, Bill Gastner had been sidelined by a shattered hip. He had spent nearly a year coming to grips with what he called his new "bionic" hip joint, and seemed to be working hard at making up for lost time. Friends with Miles Waddell for years, Gastner had scouted the *NightZone* mesa thoroughly. Although the seventy-seven-year-old Gastner refused any sort of salary or remuneration, Waddell depended on him for advice and consultation.

Scheduling the train ride for this particular Friday was typical of Waddell's far-reaching sense of community relations, and the mesa-top astronomy development was not the only community attraction for journalists—and Waddell knew it.

Blazing their own trail of stardom, the girls of the Posadas High School varsity volleyball team had posted their sixty-fifth consecutive win on Thursday, the night before. The four-year string of victories included every championship on the books, a truly legendary performance by any standard.

No one had seriously expected the Posadas Jaguars to lose to their opponents, and sure enough, no astonishing upset popped the victory bubble. The Jaguars put another lopsided scorching in the record books. A few fans dreamed of the day that the Jaguars would take on opponents from the giant quad-A city schools from Albuquerque—even a simple, non-recorded scrimmage would serve.

Still, the excitement had been palpable for Thursday night's game, not tempered much by any sympathy for the opponents. The media would be in town for both the game and the *Night-Zone* festivities the next day. The team had scored a full-page feature in the Sunday metro paper the weekend before, with Waddell's locomotive and the rising *NightZone* project on display in another section of the same newspaper. The draw of the two events was obvious, and to make sure, special invitations for the Friday train ride went out to television, radio, and print media.

One of the narrow-gauge trestles crossed a picturesque arroyo spanning the Rio Grijalva, a bone-dry arroyo near one of the ranch roads. Media could station themselves there for a dramatic shot as the train whispered overhead. In case they ignored the opportunity, Waddell's staff photographer had already captured the photogenic moment from a dozen angles during the trestle's construction and the locomotive's first three trips, and eight-by-ten glossies had been distributed liberally.

The publicity had worked. Volleyball and *NightZone* were putting Posadas County on the map.

Chapter Two

The blue Volvo wagon slid into a spot in The Spree's enormous, freshly lined black macadam parking lot, sandwiched between an Oldsmobile and a white utility rig from Ace-1 Plumbing and Heating. The Volvo's driver's door opened and a young woman got out. Fifty yards away, coming up the aisle in a Posadas County Sheriff's Department Expedition, Deputy Thomas Pasquale grinned.

Stacie Willis Stewart stepped out from the line of vehicles and walked with the same roll of the hips she had fifteen years before when she melted hearts and sent hormones soaring at Posadas High School. She turned to check traffic and saw the Expedition idling toward her. She didn't pause, but twiddled her fingers—flirtatious fingers, Pasquale thought—in his direction. He grinned even wider and lifted a hand in salute. A twiddle, but no smile. Still too stuck-up for that, the deputy thought.

Deputy Pasquale hoped for a second glance and twiddle as the young woman walked toward the store, but like most of the other shoppers, she was no doubt eager to escape the heat of late morning.

As rarely as they had crossed paths over the years, it would be nice to imagine that Stacie actually remembered who he was. Fifteen years before, he had spent the entire year of B-Level senior high school English admiring the back of her neck. A dozen other boys in the class wished that they were lucky enough to sit so close to Stacie that they could inhale her perfume.

The intervening years hadn't lessened her appeal. Folks had assumed she was destined for New York, or even Hollywood, given her flawless face, husky voice, and perfect figure. How surprised they were when she chose to marry a small-town banker and then lock into a career of her own as an auditor with the Posadas Electric Cooperative. There were rumors, of course. In that respect, Posadas was no different than any other village.

She didn't look back as she disappeared into The Spree.

Too small for a Walmart or any of the other huge boxes, the village of Posadas had nevertheless attracted its first sign of boom. The Spree had been open less than a month, and already it was lauded and cursed in equal measure. Some concluded that the store had been attracted by the world-class tourist potential created by the new astronomy theme park southwest of town.

Not everyone was supportive. There were folks who found it fashionable to vow never to darken the doors of the new store, even if it meant driving to Deming or Las Cruces to buy what they needed.

Deputy Pasquale didn't dabble in politics. He didn't concern himself with thorny civic issues, like which box store might bulldoze lesser competitors out of business. He hadn't even lobbied for a passenger seat on the narrow-gauge train sliding out of town earlier that morning for its much ballyhooed public run out to *NightZone*. Maybe the sheriff would go. Probably not. Certainly the ebullient county manager, Leona Spears, would never miss such an event. Pasquale had seen the news crews assembled for their ride, had seen the two choppers parked out at the municipal airport.

In another stroke of good fortune, he had missed having to work the eardrum- and record-shattering volleyball game Thursday night, choosing instead the peace and quiet of an evening at home.

More exciting things than politics were on his mind…and when it came right down to it, more exciting things than watching the Lady Jaguars work up a sweat, or more exciting even than a glimpse of Stacie Willis Stewart.

An early-term sonogram clearly showed that Tom's six-year marriage to Linda Real Pasquale was about to produce not one child, but two—a his and hers set of twins. Linda and he, both with no siblings of their own, had tried without success to imagine what life was now going to be like with twins—and when both tots were dashing about as terrible twos. Often, they lay in bed now with Tom's hand comfortably resting on Linda's enormous belly, feeling for the first signs of territorial spats between boy and girl.

And they wondered about the years ahead. Was there a strategy to prevent the twins from becoming, in thirteen or so years, sullen, distant, parent-hating teenagers? Beyond that, when they grew up, what would the twins *do?* What would they *be?* Would the world still be a blue sphere in orbit?

Like with computers, would it be possible to trade the twins in for upgrades, if things went wrong?

Ever-practical, Deputy Tom Pasquale knew that the myriad diapers he was going to have to buy were substantially cheaper at The Spree than anywhere else in town. That mattered, even though his wife could enjoy paid maternity leave from the Sheriff's Department, where she was treasured as the department's only full-time photographer.

On this particular day, he wasn't after diapers, but the glimpse of Stacie Stewart wearing a white outfit of light summer duds was a nice bonus for a scorching Friday morning in September. Not that his eyes and heart wandered to pretty women as a matter of course, but who could *not* enjoy the view?

Even with newshounds flooding the town, even with everyone skipping with delight over the volleyball victory, working the day shift required inventive measures to chase boredom. Baked by the usual hot weather of summer's last gasp in southern New Mexico, an entire day shift could pass without a single radio call.

Were he given the choice, Deputy Pasquale would work the four-to-midnight shift, or even midnight-to-eight, when the world could be a different place. Midnight was when the action was—fueled by saloon traffic, bored kids, and family disputes, lubricated by alcohol or by drivers just too tired to keep it on the road. He'd even missed the solitary one vehicle accident the night before, when the driver had hit first a deer and then a utility pole over on Fifth Street.

With Labor Day now three weeks past, kids were enjoying yet another holiday on this Friday as their teachers tried to concentrate on some arcane subject that somehow warranted a full day in-service. That meant that a few teen thugs might be out and about, risking the exposure of daylight, and that could prove entertaining.

Even now, a photograph of the latest gang graffiti was clipped to his logbook. Deputy Pasquale recognized the work—a certain precision and talent evident in the presentation—that marred the polished wooden sides of the railcar. He didn't know the artist, but taggers didn't work in the heat of the day. Night creatures, they'd be nailed by one of the swing shift deputies. Who knew, though.

With the twins soon to arrive, his work schedule had been shifted around to days to favor domestic tranquility—a change that smacked of the Posadas County undersheriff's fine touch. Estelle Reyes-Guzman was perfectly capable of subtle adjustments of staff scheduling when circumstances warranted. Tom *wanted* to work nights, when stuff happened. The undersheriff *wanted* the deputy home at night to help Linda cope with the twins. The undersheriff won.

Undaunted, Tom found work to keep his eyes from going heavy-lidded with boredom. One of his tried-and-true remedies was to idle through parking lots—even at the high school—checking license plates of out-of-towners. With his usual department ride in the shop, he drove one of the older Expeditions, this one normally used by his wife, Linda, and he enjoyed the lingering smell of her perfume. The vehicle lacked an on-board computer. That meant a call to dispatch for each ten-twenty-eight, and he kept young Mike Estancia busy.

He had already checked the parking lot of the Posadas Inn, south by the interstate interchange. He'd cruised the on-street parking on Grande, including the Handi-way gas station and convenience store. He'd been instructed to "stay central" during his shift, within easy reach, instead of wandering the rural countryside.

Even with school not in session, he circled through the high school parking lot, since hiding a vehicle there was clever thinking. More likely was finding randy teenagers sweating away in the back of an SUV or crew-cab pickup. Twice before, during school hours, he'd discovered rifles left in the rear window racks of ranch kids' pickups, and in both cases sent the gun and the owner home to disarm before school officials could overreact. But this day, the lot had been empty of student rides. Five vehicles were parked in the staff lot.

The wants and warrants checks usually reaffirmed for the deputy that a surprising percentage of drivers were in violation of some motor vehicle law, even if just an unpaid traffic citation. Unless the hit was a felony warrant, Pasquale usually let it go after filing the information away. He could not bring himself to care if a motorist had an outstanding parking ticket issued in Salt Lake City or Dubuque.

So far, it had been poor hunting, and Pasquale was considering some radar work on south NM 56, the two-lane state highway that wandered from Posadas down to the tiny village of Regál and the Mexican border. Or the interstate was tempting, where high-speed traffic abounded. The sheriff wouldn't care if the deputy stopped a speeding reporter or two, but County Manager Leona Spears would, what with the county's hospitality on high alert this day.

The new store, The Spree, might turn a hit or two, although it was several blocks away from the busy interstate, with only the store's enormous red, white, and blue four-story-high sign to attract motorists.

Seeing Stacie Stewart was a bonus. A memory or two about a dream girl from his raging adolescence was always entertaining. He glanced ahead toward the store's automatic front doors, hoping for another glimpse. Pasquale's recollection was that

Stacie had managed to survive all the peer traps of high school, including his own wiles, and upon reflection the deputy realized that was a remarkable achievement. No doubt *she* had gone to the game the evening before. It would bring back memories for her, for sure. A mean spike, that girl had.

After graduation, Stacie went to Texas Tech to study something like corporate bookkeeping—duller than a day shift at high noon he thought. She'd earned her chops working for an oil company in Lubbock for a while, but then returned to her hometown to marry Todd Stewart, now the first vice president of Posadas State Bank.

In high school, the future banker had been a year ahead of Pasquale and Stacie Willis. Stewart, one of the BMOC at Posadas High, graduated second in his class and attended State in Las Cruces, leaving Tom Pasquale safe to ogle the back of Stacie's fine neck throughout his senior year.

Pasquale had seen Stacie Willis Stewart perhaps a dozen times during the three years after her return to Posadas and her marriage to the banker, always during informal "sidewalk" moments such as this one. And he'd earned a friendly twiddle of the fingers each time. Maybe she *had* been aware of his existence in that English class. But she had never made it a point to stop and chat.

An Illinois license plate drew his attention to the row of cars on his left, and he examined a charcoal gray Ford Fusion. The trim little sedan was obviously new, even showing the scab of glue on one back window that outlined where the dealer's price sticker had been. But its license plate was a veteran, old enough to be scarred with signs of wear and tear, including the characteristic horizontal dig left by the repeated hitching and unhitching of a trailer. No reporter's car, this.

Denting a license was neither unusual nor uncommon. Pasquale had done the trick several times as he hitched his motorcycle trailer to his older model Jeep, letting the trailer hitch slide a couple of inches forward, riding over the top of the ball, to smack into the license plate.

The Fusion didn't carry a trailer hitch and ball—not even a socket for a removable one. And the license plate location was far too high above the bumper, nestled just under the trunk release.

In New Mexico, drivers could take the old plate off a trade-in, keeping it for the new car. Pasquale had no idea what Illinois' practice was, but even if it were legal, who would be so cheap as to put a scabby old plate on a brand new car? Curiosity won out. Pasquale lifted the mike.

"PCS, three oh four. Ten twenty-eight on Illinois two baker thomas three zero five."

The radio fell silent. Dispatcher Mike Estancia was enjoying his first week working solo in dispatch after eight weeks with supervision breathing down his neck. Eventually he found the transmit bar. "Three zero four, ten four." He did not parrot back the plate number as he should have, perhaps still a little self-conscious about stumbling through the phonic alphabet.

While he waited, Pasquale continued on down the row toward the store, keeping the Fusion in sight in his wing mirror. Reaching the end of the aisle, he swung the Expedition in a wide circle, the all-terrain tires jerking and complaining on the hot pavement. He backed up along the broad sidewalk, far enough that he wouldn't block shoppers as they left the store. He parked ten spaces away from the Fusion. Not by coincidence, Stacie Willis Stewart's Volvo was also in view up the aisle—a pretty deep-blue late-model wagon with a bright yellow *New Mexico—Land of Enchantment* front plate.

"Three zero four, PCS. Illinois two baker, uh, thomas three zero five should appear on a 2002 Ford three-quarter-ton pickup, color white. Registered to a Clayton Bailey, Star Route 12, Cathay, Illinois. Negative twenty-eight."

Pasquale's attention snapped away from Stacie Stewart's Volvo. Every nerve fiber honed in on the Fusion. He let the Expedition idle backward a few feet. Slipping the compact binoculars out of the center console, he rechecked the Fusion's license, reading the number aloud several times.

He hadn't made a mistake—Illinois two baker thomas three zero five. "PCS, run that plate again for me." He repeated the tag number as he backed farther along the sidewalk so that if the Fusion's owners left the store, their attention wouldn't be drawn immediately to the cop vehicle.

"Three zero four, copy that. Illinois two baker thomas, three zero five."

In a moment, Estancia repeated the electronic computer news. "No wants or warrants," he radioed. Just a plate borrowed off someone's pickup truck, the theft—if that's what it was—not yet noticed. Pasquale pondered that for a few moments.

"PCS, three zero four."

"Go ahead, three zero four."

"PCS, find me the phone number for the sheriff's department that serves that area in Illinois." Silence followed. Had Estancia fallen asleep? Or had he expected the deputy to explain *how* to find the number?

In a moment, his tentative "Ten four, three zero four," followed. "Be a minute."

Pasquale settled back to wait. If the plate was stolen, the Illinois SO would know. There were all kinds of possibilities. He didn't have long to ponder that before his cell phone interrupted, jarring the peace and quiet with a ringtone that mimicked a Harley Davidson motorcycle revving and then accelerating away.

"What you got?" The three unadorned words announced Sheriff Robert Torrez, and his voice was hard to hear, little more than a hoarse whisper. The call surprised Pasquale, since it was possible to work for days—maybe even weeks—without any indication that Torrez inhabited the same planet. And the big man wouldn't show much interest in a license plate stolen out of Illinois.

Chapter Three

"Sir, we have a new gray Ford Fusion sedan in The Spree parking lot, and it looks to be carrying an Illinois plate originally tagged to an Illinois pickup truck."

"You talked to the driver?"

"Negative, sir. I would guess he—or she, or they—are inside the store."

"Huh." Just bubbling enthusiasm, but Pasquale knew Sheriff Torrez would sound the same way if the impending end of the world were announced.

"Negative twenty-eight, though. Maybe he just borrowed the plate off the truck for a few days for the trip."

"Check him out anyway. Pay attention."

"Ten four." *Pay attention? Was I not?* Pasquale thought. During his now-ten years total employ with first the now-defunct Posadas Police Department and then with the Sheriff's Department, the thirty-two-year-old Pasquale had managed enough bone-headed escapades to warrant a sharp supervisor's eye, but he'd also managed more than a handful of truly spectacular apprehensions—including one that had put him in the hospital with a bullet through the hip.

Apparently it took a long time to earn Sheriff Robert Torrez' unqualified respect. The man still treated Thomas Pasquale as if the deputy were a fresh sixteen-year-old. Pasquale took comfort in realizing that Robert Torrez treated most people that way.

The sheriff had terminated the phone call with nothing more to say, and Pasquale keyed the mike.

"Three zero four is ten six Spree, reference Illinois two zero baker, two seven five. You have that information for me?"

"Ten four, three oh four." Estancia transmitted the phone number for the Cathay County Sheriff's Department, repeating it twice. "And be advised we have a complaint of an infant locked in a vehicle, that location. The sheriff is responding."

In the radio background, Pasquale could hear voices, which meant that dispatcher Estancia was still holding down the transmit bar. "Sheriff Torrez is heading that way, three oh four," the dispatcher repeated.

"Ten four." He surveyed the parking lot, seeing only a handful of customers in transit to their vehicles, or in the act of loading purchases. Out on the sidewalk of Grande Avenue, a gaggle of half a dozen middle-school-aged kids moved southward, toward The Spree.

Simultaneously, the motorcycle ringtone inside Pasquale's cell phone roared again. Robert Torrez' voice was *still* unexcited and a near-whisper.

"Stay away from the car. I'm just around the corner. Be there in a minute. Go to channel three."

"Yes, sir."

Pasquale settled back and took a deep breath. With just the hint of possible action, his pulse had come awake. He switched the radio to the car-to-car frequency where there were fewer police-monitoring freaks, then gripped the steering wheel with both hands and pushed hard, squaring his shoulders. Through painful experience, he knew that his best course of action was to do exactly as the sheriff requested.

Before he had time to dwell on the "what ifs," he saw the sheriff's rolling wreckage, his long-of-tooth Chevy pickup, burble into the parking lot from the north side. The thirty-year-old truck, with its sun-bleached paint and large spots of gray primer, was the perfect undercover unit—had ninety percent of the county's population not been well aware of the veteran vehicle.

At the same time, three people left The Spree, heading in three different directions.

Across the lot, close to where he'd first seen Stacie Willis Stewart, an elderly woman stood by the open trunk of her Toyota sedan, frowning at her own cell phone. The Ace 1 Plumbing and Heating utility truck had left, leaving a slot between the woman's Toyota and Stacie Stewart's Volvo.

"Where's the Illinois car?" the sheriff's disembodied voice murmured from the radio.

"Third row, dead ahead. About halfway down toward me."

"Got it." His pickup truck idled down the row, and he regarded the Fusion with no particular display of interest. In a moment, he pulled up window-to-window with Pasquale's unit.

"Look, do you know Helen Barber?"

"Sure I do." Pasquale pointed. "She's standing right over there by her car. The Toyota with the open trunk." On numerous occasions long ago, the now-elderly and retired elementary schoolteacher had swatted then-second-grader Thomas Pasquale, had even shaken him until his teeth rattled. She bore him no grudge, but was certainly pleased to see him advance to third grade, yet another child in a long line of hyper, attention-deficit-disordered youngsters who needed to be outside raising hell, rather than cooped up indoors.

His truck already rolling, Torrez said, "She's the one who reported the abandoned child. I got an ambulance comin', just in case. Stay put here. If the folks show up at the Fusion, just detain 'em for a little bit until you get the answers."

"Sir, that Volvo…the blue station wagon right by Ms. Barber's Yote-tote? That's Stacie Stewart's. I saw her go into the store a little bit ago."

"We'll see," Torrez said. At the same moment, the flashing lights of one of the EMT units appeared, and as he kept watch for the owners of the Fusion, Pasquale glanced toward the action now and then, surprised to see the sheriff's pickup truck and the ambulance stop directly behind Stacie Willis Stewart's Volvo, partially obscured by other vehicles.

Did Stacie Stewart have a child? Pasquale couldn't remember, but why wouldn't she? A little dog yapped incessantly, and now Pasquale could see it leaping up and down in frantic excitement, locked along with the infant in the Volvo station wagon, seeing danger with all the strangers gathering around the car.

The brilliant sun could turn the insides of a closed car into a suffocating oven in minutes. Stacie Stewart had to know that. If she had hustled into The Spree for just a moment, she was long overdue back outside. And why not just carry the child in with her?

Pasquale knew that Sheriff Robert Torrez would pop a window without hesitation, either with a slim-jimmy for the door lock or, if necessary, with a swat with his window tool. He wouldn't wait for the owners.

A teenaged shopper exited The Spree carrying a single plastic bag. He walked across the parking lot toward Pershing Street, rubbernecking the commotion around the ambulance as he went.

Torrez, Miss Barber, and two EMTs clustered around the Volvo. Miss Barber held up a folded newspaper to shield the parchment skin of her face from the beating sun, then transferred the spot of shade to a target in the Volvo. Pasquale's radio squelched again.

"You saw Stacie Stewart go into the store?" the sheriff radioed.

"Yes, sir. Not too long ago. Just a few minutes."

"Go in and get her. We ain't waitin'."

"I'm on it." Pasquale lunged out of the Expedition and jogged along the sidewalk, past the displays of wheelbarrows and barbecue grills. Once inside, it was impossible to see more than a portion of a couple of aisles at once, and Pasquale strode toward the office complex on the west end of the store where a narrow stairway accessed the upper floor and the closed-in observation deck.

"Hey, stud." Tilda Gabaldon hadn't inherited height from the sheriff's side of the family, but Sheriff Bob Torrez' cousin looked as if throwing cartons full of stock around the storeroom would be no problem. She favored Tom Pasquale with a brilliant smile, highlighted by just a wink of gold. Tilda had been headed down the stairs toward the floor, and Pasquale paused. "Whatcha need, Thomas?"

"I gotta find Stacie Stewart. She came in the store just a few minutes ago. Like maybe ten?"

"Come on up." Tilda turned with Pasquale following, and in a moment they entered the long, narrow room with deeply tinted, slanted windows looking down on the store. A row of computer screens on the back wall showed the various views of the store's security cameras. "What's she wearing?"

"White," the deputy said. "White blouse, white slacks."

Tilda laughed playfully. "Like you'd notice, right?"

"I'm a trained observer and investigator," the deputy said with mock solemnity. "I notice things like that." Back and forth between observation windows and computer screens, they searched the store. "There are some dead zones still," Tilda said. "You know, like over there in automotive? What's the deal, anyway?"

"She left her baby and a dog out in the car," Pasquale said. "No problems, though. The sheriff is going to get 'em out."

"You know, it doesn't take long to overheat in weather like this." She looked worried. "We train the kids who go out to gather the shopping carts to *always* keep their eyes open for something like that. And there's the notice on the front door to remind shoppers *not* to leave kids unattended. People get preoccupied sometimes, though. Let's page her."

"Thanks." He watched the store while Tilda's voice boomed out on the PA. "Stacie Stewart, please come to the customer service desk." Tilda repeated the message twice, enunciating the name clearly. "I'll give you a holler if I see her first," Tilda said as Tom headed back downstairs.

Chapter Four

Dodging down one aisle after another, the deputy expected at every corner to come face-to-face with the young mother. Stockers sliced open cardboard boxes in one aisle, two men concentrated on handheld inventory computers in another, a scattering of shoppers ranged from an aging Elvis Presley look-alike to four more high-schoolers who flushed guilty when Pasquale hustled by, and a few housewives who glanced at him with interest. No Stacie Stewart.

Circling back along the store's perimeter to the south corner, he opened the door of the women's restroom a bit. "Stacie Stewart?" He was about to shout a second time when Tilda Gabaldon dug a knuckle in his ribs.

"Let me check for you," she said. While she did that, Pasquale scouted the men's room, inhabited only by a store employee with a mop bucket who looked as if he'd rather be somewhere else.

"She's not in there," Tilda reported. "Are you *sure* it was her who came inside?"

"Absolutely."

"Then take another swing through the store, up and down each aisle. I'll stay at the courtesy desk and watch that she doesn't scoot around an end cap somewhere."

This time, as he strode along the back wall, past the large bags of pet and bird food, he stopped at the *Employees Only* exit. The door yawned open against heavy pistons, and beyond, the back stockroom was mammoth sea of boxes, cartons, and laden pallets. Empty boxes were piled near a crusher, and a generous pile of empty wooden pallets sat behind those. At the opposite far end was a roll-up door, large enough to accommodate a delivery truck or forklift. Directly ahead of him on the back wall, another heavy steel door was marked with prominent stripes and signs, one just above the latch bar announcing that *Alarm Will Sound If Door is Opened.*

It didn't, unless it was a silent light now glowing on the control console up in the office. He pushed the door open wide and surveyed the fresh black macadam, so fresh it appeared liquid. The wave of heat collided with the cold front escaping from inside the store.

He counted eight black trash Dumpsters, a collection of three already-crippled shopping carts, and against the store's wall farther down, the forest of power poles and transformers feeding the store's huge electrical service. He saw no young woman walking out across the vacant lot between the rear of The Spree and the residential side street beyond.

Pasquale ducked back inside and closed the door, making sure it was secure.

"Sir, may I help you somehow?" A short, chubby man approached, his necktie loosened to give his blocky neck some room. "Tilda tells me you're searching for someone?" The name tag identified Paul Smith as assistant store manager.

"Yes, sir. A young lady named Stacie Stewart came in the store a few minutes ago. We need to talk with her."

"Ah. Well, it's doubtful she would have gone out this way. Her car's out front?"

"Yes, sir."

"She may have already come and gone then, Deputy."

"Not likely, sir. The sheriff is waiting out at her car."

"That's what the ambulance is about?"

"Yes, sir."

"What's the deal?"

"Child left in the car, sir. In this weather, it only takes a few minutes."

Smith grimaced. "Well, then." Smith pivoted, scanning the stockroom. As he did so, Pasquale's phone rumbled.

"You find Stewart?" Torrez asked when Pasquale connected.

"No, sir. We got people lookin'."

"Out back?"

"I checked there. No sign, sir."

"Look, the undersheriff is here. We're going to transport the kid. She's dehydrated, so we don't want to wait around. Estelle will meet Mr. Stewart at the ER. If the mother shows up in the next few minutes, bring her along. Don't just send her. *Bring* her."

"Yes, sir."

"Keep lookin'. She might have walked across the street to Tommy's or something."

Not likely in this heat, Pasquale thought.

"Did you check all the Dumpsters?"

The sheriff's suggestion drew Pasquale up short—not the heat or the smell cooking inside the Dumpsters, but the thought that in just those few moments, someone might have grabbed the young woman, clouted her unconscious or dead, and then stuffed the body into the hot tomb of a trash container.

"I'll do that right now, sir."

He reached out for the exterior door, then turned to look at the assistant manager. "The alarm is connected?"

Smith shook his head. "Not yet. That's on our 'to do' list. Help yourself."

Outside, the eight trash bins marched along the back edge of the macadam, bordering an unkempt, weed-strewn lot. The Dumpster lids opened with little effort. The first three units were still empty, and Pasquale worked his way down the row, carefully examining the refuse inside each. Hiding an adult body in any of them would have been unlikely. The containers weren't even a third full, and no large boxes wasted space, thanks to the store's compacter.

Smith watched the deputy, following him down the row of Dumpsters.

"Maybe somebody picked her up," he said. "But you said she left her baby in her car?"

"It appears that way. Kid and a puppy."

"Good God."

"If she's not in the store somewhere, that's the best bet…that someone picked her up." He slipped a small two-way radio off his belt. "Tilda, this is Paul. Any sign of the young lady?"

"No, sir. We have four people looking now."

"This is nuts," Pasquale muttered. "Other exits?"

"Not that she would have used. There's the one behind the employees' break room, where we have our meetings each morning."

"I need to see that."

"Sure enough." Behind the customer service center, past the public restrooms, a single door marked *Employees Only* opened into a long, narrow room dominated by two eight-foot folding tables placed end-to-end, along with a dozen or more chairs. A coatrack, coffee machine, and posters on a large bulletin board hid nothing. At the end, another door was marked *Exit,* and Pasquale pushed it open.

The heat flooded in, the sun so bright that he winced. Looking past the corner of the store, across the parking lot and Grande Avenue, he could see a portion of Tommy's Handi-way gas station, and beyond it, the scattering of other businesses south on Grande. By looking to the west, he could see the corner of Posadas Elementary School, the high school athletic field, and the apartments beyond Pershing Street that constituted much of the neighborhood around the school.

"She could have walked over to the school," Smith suggested. "You wouldn't have seen her."

"Maybe." Pasquale stood silently for a moment, his Stetson pulled so low that it touched the rims of his dark glasses. "Huh. Why would she do that? School's closed today." He nodded his thanks to Smith, then returned to the store, striding up the wide center aisle, winding his way through the many displays of gadgetry. Again, the store's PA boomed out the request that Stacie Stewart report to the customer service counter. At the front of the store, Pasquale paused to look back. Stacie Stewart did not appear.

The man with the Elvis haircut watched Pasquale, amused. He had been browsing through the real estate and automotive *PennySaver*s from the rack by the courtesy desk, and he kept two of the issues, rolling them to form a heavy tube.

"You lose somebody?" His smile showed what had to be cheap dentures—too straight, too white, too coarse. Before Pasquale could think up a noncommittal, polite reply, the man nodded toward the parking lot. "Trouble out there?" The ambulance was just pulling away, Undersheriff Estelle Reyes-Guzman's white Charger following close behind.

"Just another typical day in paradise," Pasquale replied.

"Ain't that the truth? Hey, here's the wife." He grinned at Pasquale. "Finally. Have a better day, Officer." The man straightened his shoulders, hiked his pants up over a modest pot belly, and joined "the wife" at the first checkout for fifteen items or less. His companion could have been his sister, glossy black hair cascading over rounded shoulders, short and dumpy. She filled out a dull white blouse and a light green skirt, both looking like something from the fifties. Her white anklet socks sagging down over sensible shoes. The woman pushed a shopping cart lightly loaded with a loaf of white bread, snack food, canned juices, and half a dozen packages of lunch meat.

With a last glance around the store, Pasquale slipped past the checkout and joined Sheriff Torrez on the sidewalk outside.

"Gonna have you stay put for a little bit." Torrez looked more like a disheveled rancher than the county sheriff. Two inches taller than Tom Pasquale's six-two, and starting to add a hint of padding around his girth earned by a pleasant domestic life, Torrez was dressed in his habitual uniform—trousers that might have once been blue jeans, a light denim shirt carelessly tucked, and a battered cap that announced Maynard Diesel. He was perfect photographer fodder, and County Manager Leona Spears would be irritated that on this day, with the media lurking about, the sheriff of Posadas County chose to dress like he had a part-time job at Joe's Oil and Lube. Of course Sheriff Bob Torrez had avoided riding the new train out to *NightZone*. He did not hang on fake bonhomie well.

Pasquale glanced across the parking lot toward the now-empty Volvo and felt an odd surge of relief that none of the little car's windows appeared to be broken.

"If Stewart shows up," Torrez instructed, "let us know ASAP. Bring her down to the SO first. She'll freak when she sees no kid, no dog. Anyway, Estelle is going to process this mess," he said it as if talking to himself. "She's got somebody from Children, Youth and Families comin' to the emergency room." He glanced at Pasquale. "Baby's temp was already a hundred and three. It don't take long." He shook his head in disgust. "And mama just walks off. Gonna have a soda somewhere with a friend, maybe."

"You want I should bring her to the SO rather than to emergency?"

"Yep. Maybe that'll encourage her to think twice next time."

Torrez drew in a deep breath, and nodded at the Fusion. "When the folks drivin' that show up, you might have a chat with 'em. Could be a dozen reasons for the old license, and we might not care one way or another. Right now, I'm more concerned with Mrs. Stewart, so you need to be here for a while in case she returns."

He regarded Pasquale. "Good catch on the Fusion, though. We got somebody comin' over to give you a hand. If both Stewart and the Fusion folks show up at the same time, you'll be busy." He almost smiled. "You talked with the SO in Illinois?"

"Not yet. I'm about to."

"I'll be interested to hear what they have to say."

"It's like…I don't know. It could be any number of things," Pasquale said helplessly. "And Stacie's kid? I can't see her doin' that, leaving the child unattended."

Torrez regarded Thomas for a few seconds, and the crow's-feet around his dark eyes deepened a bit. "You know her pretty well, do you?"

"No. I mean, I went to school with her years ago. I saw her get out of the car, walk into the store, and that was it. Like she just vanished."

"Yeah, well. She'll turn up. She's probably sittin' down in the women's clothes, tryin' on shoes or something."

"I can't believe she'd leave the baby and the dog in the car, though. I mean *everybody* knows better than that these days."

"You think?" Torrez almost smiled. "Is Linda doin' okay this morning?"

"Uncomfortable, but okay."

"Twins," Torrez muttered, and shook his head in commiseration. "Hey…" He jerked his chin toward the parking lot. Elvis and "the wife" were quick-stepping along the parking lot aisle toward their car. They stopped at the Fusion, and its lights flashed as they clicked the remote for the doors.

Torrez kept his expression friendly but disinterested as he stepped off the sidewalk and ambled toward them. The man was on the down slope past fifty, paunchy, with too much black hair on his head, waved and pompadoured in the fifties style. His wide black belt hiked tan slacks up on his watermelon gut so that he looked like a dressed bowling pin. Idiots on the lam, Pasquale thought.

Chapter Five

Slumping just a bit to make his height less intimidating, Sheriff Torrez walked with his hands thrust in his pockets.

"Hi, folks," he said cordially. The pair froze, he by the driver's door, she near the trunk. They may well have wondered who the big, shabbily dressed fellow might be, but there was no question about the sharply uniformed deputy sheriff who followed and then circled behind their car.

"Good morning. What can I help you with, sir?" The man thrust out his hand as he took a step forward. "Howard Swartzman. And my wife, LeeAnn." He spoke like a salesman, used to glad-handing. Torrez ignored the outstretched hand.

"I'd like to take a quick look at your license and registration, sir."

Howard Swartzman looked puzzled. "Here? In the parking lot?" He offered a silly grin. "Was I speeding?"

"I was hopin' that maybe you saw the young lady that came out of that blue Volvo there, behind you." The sheriff nodded in the general direction of the Volvo across the way.

Swartzman turned to look. "That little blue rig there? No. Can't say as I did. What's the deal?" He visibly relaxed.

"Just checking. If we need to contact you later, it'll help to have some personal information."

"And you are?"

"Sheriff Torrez." The big man didn't elaborate, and Swartzman looked nervously at Deputy Tom Pasquale, who said nothing.

"Well, sure. I have that. They're in the car."

"Maybe you'd get 'em. And I was kinda curious about your license plate."

"My…?"

"The plate on the back." He didn't move from his comfortable leaning spot against the front fender, but Pasquale did, standing directly behind the Fusion, taking time to examine the battered license plate. Sure enough, a number of dents and bruises marred the plate, from years of hitching and unhitching various trailers.

"Where are you folks out of?" Torrez asked.

"A long trek from Illinois, that's for sure." Swartzman pushed himself upright. "You got this conjugation goin' on here with that theme park, and we thought we'd take a look. See what the opportunities might be. Always a need for quality entertainment. But…" and he shrugged hugely. "If there's nothin' there, we're going to head on up to Vegas. You know," and he touched his long, well-oiled and coiffed locks, "all kinds of crazy things happen *there*."

Torrez raised an eyebrow. "Vegas, like in Nevada? What, you get lost or something?"

Swartzman grinned again. "Well, side trips here and there. Like I said, there's this new theme park we read about somewhere right in these parts."

"The conjugation." Torrez kept an absolute poker face.

"That's it."

"You're about five hundred miles off-course for Vegas."

"Our bucket list, you know. Neither the wife or I have ever been to Mexico, so we drove down to Juarez for a day or two. Weeellll…" and he drew out the word. "Don't need to do *that* again."

Torrez screwed up his handsome face as if thinking were a chore. "Cathay to Joplin to Juarez…that's a long haul."

For an instant, the remark didn't register, but when it did, Swartzman couldn't keep the apprehension concealed. *He* had never mentioned Cathay, that little farm town in Illinois, to this affable Mexican hick.

"So," Torres said slowly, "how well do you know Clayton Bailey?" He watched Swartzman's face, and the man's nervous hands.

Swartzman's expression went blank. "I…"

"He a neighbor, or what?"

"I mean…Clayton's a neighbor, back home." Swartzman's head wobbled as if he couldn't decide whether to nod or shake it. "He's all right, isn't he? I mean, how did you…?"

"Wouldn't know how *he* is," Torrez said affably enough. "We were just wondering how the license plate from his truck came to be on your car."

Swartzman looked confused. "You're with the police? I mean, shouldn't I see some identification?"

"Yep," but Torrez made no move to show his badge or credentials. "Deputy, go ahead and call in the VIN. Let's find out who owns this buggy."

"Yes, sir."

"Mrs. Swartzman?" Torrez said. "You want to come over here?" The woman did, walking as if she were on skim ice with nothing but black water underneath. She stopped a couple steps from the sheriff. "There's just fine. And sir, I'll want to see your license and registration."

"Now look here. This car's brand new," Swartzman blurted. "We haven't even had a chance to get the paperwork."

"Dealer gave you something, I guess."

"Well, sure."

"So, does the dealer back there in Illinois know you have this car?"

Swartzman's face fell. "Oh, come on now, Sheriff. He *better* know. I gave him enough money for it. Anyway, I work for him."

"For who?"

"I work for Jensen Motors in Cathay, Sheriff." He said it as if everyone would surely have heard of the dealership, and that upon hearing the name, the sheriff would nod pleasantly and say, "That's all we need…you have a good day, sir."

"Show me what you have."

Swartzman opened the front passenger door and eyed the glove box. He made no move toward it.

"Got something in there you don't want me to see?"

"This being New Mexico, I guess you're used to this sort of thing."

Torrez waited without comment, and Swartzman finally shrugged. "Look, I always carry a handgun with me when I'm traveling. You just never know."

"Illinois don't usually head the list of gun-friendly states. Take your time and let's see it."

Swartzman was between the car and the door, and a quick, hard slam would waffle him. Torrez moved so that he could rest a hand on the top of the doorframe, fingers flat.

With a grunt, the man slid down into the passenger seat, both feet outside on the pavement, his shins another tempting target for a door slam.

"Just the license and registration, sir. If that's where you're keepin' the weapon, leave it."

Swartzman's left elbow thumped on the center console as he leaned away from the passenger door. With his right he reached for the glove box. "Okay, well…I just didn't want any surprises."

The huge glove box carried the plastic envelope with all the vehicle paperwork—the thick owner's manual, the maintenance booklet, tire warranty, motorist's aid, and a tube of touchup paint. Swartzman sorted through the papers three times, then looked up bleakly at Torrez. The gun, if there was one, remained invisible.

"You know, the sales document is about that long," and he held his hands eighteen inches apart. "All the taxes and everything…the odometer declaration. The whole ball of wax. LeeAnn," he called, "what did we do with all the paperwork?"

"You're the one, genius boy."

"How helpful is that?" Swartzman muttered. "Look, Sheriff… maybe we can work something out, here."

"'S'pect we can," Torrez said helpfully. "How about a license, then. That ought to be easy enough." He watched Swartzman's hand near the center console, where the sheriff now expected to see the weapon. Swartzman's elaborately casual body English had pointed that way.

"Why, sure." He leaned to his right away from the console, and dug in his back pocket, finally finding the well-worn wallet. After a moment of shuffling with no results, he took a deep breath and sagged as he looked up at Torrez. "You know, this isn't my day."

"Nope." Torrez caught a glimpse of the little blue box and logo on the upper left of the laminated license. "Might be it's that one right under your thumb, sir."

"Well, jeez." Sure enough, he drew out the license, held onto it for a moment as if he just didn't believe it had reappeared, then extended it toward Torrez. "You're pretty sharp, Sheriff."

Torrez didn't take the license immediately. So many things of potential interest were going on here that he took his time, never losing his grip on the doorframe. "Missus, I'd appreciate it if you'd have yourself a seat out of the sun, over there in the deputy's vehicle." Making no complaint or comment, LeeAnn Swartzman did as she was told. Pasquale held the door for her, then gently closed her inside, alone with the air conditioning.

Torrez took the offered license and held it at a comfortable distance. "New look," he said. "New hair, anyways."

"Well, it's a wig," Swartzman whispered. "We're show folks, you know. Job-hunting, maybe even Vegas comin' up." He tried a weak laugh.

With the couple separated and contained, Tom Pasquale took his time calling in the license information, using his cell phone instead of the radio so the woman couldn't hear both sides of the conversation. After a few minutes, he left the SUV. The sheriff accepted the Post-it note from the deputy, keeping his right hand on Swartzman's door.

"Huh." Torrez frowned at the note as if the English language were his third or fourth idiom. "So."

"So what's the deal?" Swartzman asked. "We're all set? Just like I said?"

Torrez looked at him for a long moment. "We're kinda backward in these little towns, sir, so you'll have to bear with us." He held up one finger. "I'm going to ask you to step out of the car, sir."

"But I…"

"Let's do it." Torrez eased past the open door, holding it wide. He beckoned Swartzman out, giving the man the hint of a chance. With his right hand on the door, Torrez appeared vulnerable. Swartzman's left elbow was still near the center console and he took the opportunity. With one smooth jerk he snatched open the console lid and dove with his left hand for the revolver that lay beneath it.

He managed to touch the black plastic grips with his fingertips before his door was yanked wide and he found himself being lifted bodily. With one hand on Swartzman's belt and the other at the nape of his neck, Torrez slammed the man's weight forward. Off-balance and unsuspecting, Swartzman found himself driven face-first into the dash, his nose smeared into the GPS screen.

He yelped as Torrez then yanked him out of the car, spun him around, and slammed him against the roof and the center post so hard that he gasped. A deft twist, and Swartzman's hands were behind his back, the click of the handcuffs loud. "Pay attention to the woman," Torrez snapped at Pasquale.

Amid screeches of protest from LeeAnn, Pasquale pulled her into position with her face pressed against the security screen. He managed the cuffs, and gently pushed her back into the seat with a hand on her shoulder. "Just relax, ma'am." He closed the door on her squeaky protests.

The sheriff slammed the door of the Fusion, and with one hand against Swartzman's back between the shoulder blades, frisked him. One hand dove into a trouser pocket and came out with the car keys, which he tossed on the roof. "And what the hell is this?" the sheriff muttered. He pulled up the man's shirt, and the loud rip of hook-and-loop fasteners followed.

"See if Taber is available for transport," he snapped. Turning back to the husband, Torrez demanded, "So what is this?"

"What do you think it is?" Swartzman replied testily. He snuffled at the blood that had begun to leak from his nose, and glanced nervously at the huge cop in mechanic's clothes, apparently deciding that testy wouldn't work. "It's a false belly," he said reasonably. And sure enough, the man's own midriff was trim. "No need to go and get all violent. I was just going to hand you the gun, anyways. It ain't even real."

"Huh." Torrez didn't release his grip. "I know exactly what the gun is, my friend." He turned the girth enhancement belt this way and that. "Most folks want to get rid of belly fat." He reached out and tugged at the man's obvious wig, and it slid off to reveal a close-cropped thatch of dark brown hair, just beginning to show some sprinkles of gray on the sides. "A little more like the license photo now, huh."

"Look, Sheriff…"

Torrez interrupted him again. "So…we got this car here, who knows where it actually came from." He glanced at the note Pasquale had handed him, and held up a second finger. "You say you got it from Jensen Motors in *Cathay*, Illinois, where you say you work. And three, you got a license plate stolen from Mr. Clayton Bailey, also of Cathay. How am I doin'?"

"I…Look now…"

Torrez waited while the man mulled his options. Mrs. Swartzman sat quietly in the back of Tom Pasquale's Expedition, tears cutting two trails down her well-powdered cheeks.

"And that Illinois driver's license has your photo right without the makeup, but I guess Swartzman goes with the belly and the hair?" He held the license up a bit and squinted. "Robert Osgood Bond. That's who the Illinois DMV says you are."

Torrez glanced over at Pasquale, who stood near the driver's side rear door of the Expedition, making LeeAnn Swartzman-Bond all the more distraught by impassively watching her unconvincing weeping performance.

"So, Mr. Bob Bond, tell me about the license plate," Torrez said.

"Look, it's all so simple. When we left home with the new car, it was a weekend. Nobody was open. I mean, what's a plate? A few bucks. Proof that we've paid the bureaucrats, right? Clay Bailey—him and his wife, Sally—they were gone to a wedding out in Bismarck. The truck was just sittin' in his barn there, so no big deal. I borrowed the plate for a little bit. They were going to stay on out there for a family reunion, and I figured we'd have the plate back before they knew it was gone."

"Stupidest thing I've ever heard," Torrez grunted. "Why didn't you take the plate off your own car...your old one?"

Swartzman shrugged deeply and thought for a minute. "'Cause when we traded in, the old plate stayed on the old car. Our Oldsmobile. It's at the dealer's."

"You could have taken this whole trip with a temp tag. And the dealer would have given you one of those."

"Well, yeah, we could have. But they're an attractive nuisance, if you know what I mean. They attract attention." He looked hopeful. "It's just a hang-up of mine, Sheriff. I never liked those paper permits taped in the back window." He tried to snuff his nose, the bleeding now all but stopped, on the shoulder of his shirt. "I mean, you know, it's a sign. Like 'Hey, look at me. I just got a new car!'"

"Hey, look at you," Torrez repeated. "And so..." He eyed the man for a long moment. "What did you think you were going to do with the pellet gun?"

"I..." He gave up and shrugged hopelessly.

"Yep. Not much thinkin' going on there. You're lucky I didn't just shoot your silly ass." He spun Swartzman-Bond around, opened the Fusion's back door, and guided the man inside. "Don't bleed all over the inside of the new car. Owner wouldn't like that much."

"But my wife..."

"She's fine." With both of the strange couple secure but separated, Torrez slammed the Fusion's door and glowered in mock-irritation at Pasquale.

"You find some of the strangest people, Thomas," he said. "And just as soon as we get another unit over here, we'll get him out of the car so he don't pass out." He paused. "You been keepin' your eyes open for Stewart?"

"Yes, sir." The Volvo sat untended, roasting in the sun.

Chapter Six

"It *is* a pellet gun," Tom Pasquale said. He had secured the weapon from the Fusion's center console and held it up, a large black revolver made to look like a Smith & Wesson. He deftly pulled open the piston lever that projected from the bottom of the grips. "No gas cylinder. It wasn't going to do him much good this way." From a distance, the gun looked remarkably realistic, and Pasquale looked at the sheriff with surprise. "Good call, sir. I wonder what he was planning to do with it? Use it as a hammer?"

Torrez shrugged. "Maybe he's gettin' tired of livin'."

"He thought about it, you know. I mean, *doing* something stupid with it. I was watching his face."

"Yep." Torrez snagged the keys off the roof of the car, walked around and unlocked the trunk, easing the lid up. He held onto it as he surveyed the contents, then tugged aside the corner of a homey-looking quilt, revealing three neat cardboard boxes, the lidded sort that originally had held ten reams of printer paper.

"Okay, then. Placin' bets?"

"Not with his mental equipment." The box lids were taped, and Torrez flicked open his razor knife and deftly slit the seal. With a finger on each end, he lifted the lid straight up.

"Huh."

For a moment, both men were silent. Some amorphous instrumental rendition of a decades-old Jefferson Airplane hit wafted out from the store.

"Who you got comin'?" Torrez asked.

"Taber is on the way, and dispatch was going to try and find Captain Adams. Estelle will be tied up at the hospital until Stacie shows up. Or CYF takes over."

"Good enough. I think Adams went fishing up in Chama, though."

As careful as if the cardboard box top were thin crystal, Torrez leaned it to one side, out of the way. The packets, sealed tightly in some sort of white, waxy paper, filled the box in neat rows, sixteen packets to a layer. Torrez tilted his head.

"Sixteen up, maybe four layers, so sixty-four bricks to a box, times three. That ain't bad."

He slipped his knife out, snapped the blade open, and used it to gently pry one of the packets loose. "Ain't no kilo."

"This is the economy, pocket-sized sample," Pasquale said.

"Of what?" Bob Torrez held out the little brick to his deputy, who accepted it and turned it this way and that. He held it close to his nose and inhaled deeply, looking puzzled. Nothing he had sampled or sniffed or chewed in his recent State Police seminar on illegal drugs shared this aroma.

"Don't look much like any joint *you* ever toked," the sheriff said.

Pasquale grinned. "Been too long, sir."

Sergeant Jackie Taber drove into the parking lot, taking the long way around the outside perimeter until she parked her black SUV behind Bob Torrez' old Chevy. She saw Pasquale lift a small white packet and hold it to his nose for a long, careful inhale, eyes closed like a wine-taster.

She took her time making sure dispatch understood where virtually the whole day shift was, got out and locked her unit, and then strolled along the side of Pasquale's SUV, looking inside at LeeAnn Swartzman-Bond. The young woman cowered.

In high school back in Detroit, Jackie Taber had been known as "Stump," a not-particularly-kind but dead-on accurate nickname prompted by her five-seven frame that carried one hundred eighty pounds—actually very little of it fat.

If anyone in the Sheriff's Department called her by her old nickname, it wasn't to her face. Retired from the Marines, Taber kept the brim of her Stetson the proper rake back from the bridge of her nose, and she folded her dark glasses and slid them into her pocket as she regarded first LeeAnn and then her husband in the Fusion. After a moment, she rounded the front of the old Expedition and reached out a hand to Tom Pasquale's right shoulder.

"So tell me." The lips moved, but if there was a voice, it hadn't yet amped up to a whisper.

"Bogus plate, no registration, Elvis costume, traveling under the alias of Swartzman but the driver's license says Bond. I got curious, but then we got caught up in the thing with Stacie Stewart leaving her kid and dog in the car. We nabbed these two as they came out of the store and got to the Fusion there."

"Nabbed." A smile hinted at the corners of Taber's mouth. "Well, you don't have much of a case, Thomas. Out of the whole list, only a bad Elvis impersonation is illegal." When his face went blank, she quickly added, "So what's that?"

Pasquale held out the opened packet to the sergeant. Even as she unwrapped it a little further, they heard a holler and then several thumps from inside the Fusion. Taber stepped around the car and ducked a little so she could glare at Swartzman, who, handcuffed securely, had been using his skull to drum on the window.

"Just relax, Elvis," Taber snapped, suddenly with plenty of threatening volume. She turned back to the sheriff. "What do you think, sir?"

Torrez had been head-down in the Fusion's trunk, probing corners, shuffling things around and lifting the corner of the mat. He straightened up.

"Alfalfa." The one-word pronouncement brought another smile to the sergeant's face. She rearranged the end of the plant "plug" with the tip of a pencil, examined it closely, sniffed it.

"Best not to taste it," Pasquale observed.

"Might be poison ivy?" She handed it back to the sheriff. "I think you're right, sir. But it's a pretty labor-intensive, expensive way to ship horse feed."

"So…" Pasquale said.

"So it's illegal to possess drugs, or possess with intent to distribute drugs, whether they're real or not. All kinds of trash gets passed off as the real thing."

"Maybe they're just usin' 'em for taste treats when they go to the horse track or something like that," Pasquale offered.

"Something like that," the sheriff said dryly. "Gives us an excuse to hold 'em for a little bit, anyway." Torrez placed the top back on the box. "Read 'em, then book 'em on possession and intent to distribute and auto theft," he said. "When you're talkin' to 'em, keep 'em separate and make sure the recorder works." He slammed the trunk lid down. "Call Stubby and have the car taken to impound. We might want to look at it again." He started to turn away. "Oh, and process the pellet gun into evidence, along with the horse feed. Are there personal possessions we need to lock up? What'd she have on her? Anything?"

"I…well, two small bags of groceries. They're in the backseat. And the two small suitcases in the trunk."

"You searched her?" Taber asked.

"No, ma'am. I thought that should best wait for you or the undersheriff. She's cuffed, but I didn't search her." That earned a sideways glance of disapproval from Sheriff Torrez, who certainly saw no point in being so politically correct, or at the very least, gender-careful.

"Then let's do that."

Sergeant Taber walked around to the passenger side of Pasquale's Expedition and opened the rear door, holding on to it with her right hand as she faced LeeAnn Swartzman-Bond. Pasquale looped around and positioned himself on Taber's left. "Step out of the vehicle, ma'am." Jackie stepped back half a pace to give the woman a small amount of room to maneuver, an awkward task with hands cuffed behind her back. Pasquale stood poised to assist, mindful that the tall step down to the ground gave many passengers trouble—whether inebriated or just plain clumsy.

LeeAnn leaned forward until her head was practically touching the security screen, and contorted her arms, leaning hard to the left. Before the deputies knew it was even there, the little chrome-plated automatic fired one round, incredibly loud within the confines of the SUV. The .25 caliber bullet struck Taber's heavy leather boot with a glancing blow, then dug into the hot, soft asphalt. The tiny gun promptly jammed, but Pasquale was already in motion. Actually closer to LeeAnn than his sergeant, Pasquale clamped his left hand around the woman's thin neck and forced her hard forward. With a viselike grip that locked the automatic's jammed slide open, he twisted the pistol out of her hand, hearing the little "pop" as her right index finger, still locked in the trigger guard, gave up a joint. LeeAnn screamed.

Pasquale handed the little gun to Torrez, who had leaped around the vehicle toward them at the sound of the gunshot. Then, with one hand on the woman's neck and the other clamped on the cuffs, the deputy eased her out of the Expedition.

"You broke my hand!" she wailed. "Howard, you can't let them…"

"Howard ain't goin' nowhere," Torrez said. "You okay, Sarge?"

Taber glanced down at her boot. The tiny bullet had raked an inch-long scuff along the leather just above the heavy black sole, hardly breaking the polish. "Nothing," she said.

Pasquale moved LeeAnn Swartzman-Bond until he could flatten her against the side of the truck. With the motion, she screamed again. Torrez, his phone already against his ear, lowered it for a moment and glowered at the small crowd of friendly shoppers who had gathered to watch the show.

"You all can leave now," he snapped. "It's all over." He turned his back and said to dispatch, "I need that ambulance back here at The Spree. Got a shopper with a broken finger." He didn't bother to await dispatcher Esperanza's response, but snapped the phone closed.

"Let me look." Taber lifted both of LeeAnn's hands a bit, prompting another scream.

"You broke it!"

"Looks like it." Sure enough, the second joint of LeeAnn's index finger had been modified so that the finger skewed off to the left. "We'll have you fixed up here in a minute, ma'am. Just stand still."

That was hard for the woman to do, wanting nothing more than to dance in painful circles, clutching her injured digit. Replacing Tom Pasquale's grip with her own, Taber pegged LeeAnn against the Expedition and did a quick search.

The pistol had nestled in a thin chamois holster at the small of the back under the tail of the woman's blouse, in the soft recess around her left kidney.

"I should have seen that when I put on the cuffs," Pasquale remarked.

"Yup," Torrez agreed. He watched as Taber continued her search from head to toe. "Well, well, well," the sergeant said, and once more the sound of hook and loop announced modifications. Keeping the tail of the blouse discreetly low, she peeled off the waist belt, and LeeAnn immediately shed twenty pounds of belly fat.

She managed a weak cry, tears now abundant.

"Is this yours?" Jackie ran a hand up the woman's neck and fingered a handful of long, black locks.

"No," LeeAnn moaned.

"How about it, then?" Jackie eased off the wig, leaving behind a natural head of cinnamon-colored hair cut short. "That looks better, anyway," the sergeant said, ruffling the top of LeeAnn's head as if she were a child. "Makes you look twenty years younger."

She glanced at Pasquale. "Don't do it until she's in the ambulance, but as soon as she's off this hot pavement, make sure the shoes come off. Clunky as they are, she could hide just about anything inside 'em." She pulled LeeAnn away from the vehicle. "Let's put her in my unit until the ambulance gets here. You

behave yourself," she said to LeeAnn, "and we'll put the cuffs
around front. Be easier for you. Maybe hurt less." She waited,
watching the woman snuffle. When she didn't answer, Jackie
added, "Are we going to wrestle again?"

"No." The voice was tiny, the lower lip dancing with pain.

"And when I loosen the cuffs, *don't* touch your finger. I know,
you're going to want to grab it with your other hand. You'll wish
you hadn't. Okay?" The sergeant's tone was soft, even sympathetic, and LeeAnn glanced at her gratefully.

"Yes."

Deftly, Jackie unlocked one side of the cuffs, and keeping
hold of the injured right hand, swung the left around to be re-
shackled in front of LeeAnn's now flat waist.

"Oh, it's sooooo broken," LeeAnn wailed.

"Yes, ma'am, it is. Things could be worse. The deputy could
have shot you."

That set off another cascade of tears. Her wail almost matched
that of the incoming ambulance.

"Take a picture of the bullet scar in the asphalt, and the
scuff on your boot," Sheriff Torrez reminded her. Pasquale had
anticipated that, and chalked a circle around the imperfection
in the hot asphalt.

"Bullet's still stuck in tar," he said. "I can see the heel of it."

"Then, there you go." Torrez nodded, then sighed. "That's
a lock." He turned in place, gazing around the parking lot as
Pasquale transferred Swartzman-Bond from the Fusion to the
Expedition. Torrez nodded across the parking lot toward the
now-empty blue Volvo. "So where's Skippy?"

"In Mexico by now," Pasquale offered.

The EMT unit idled in, the same two attendants who had
responded to the roasting child and pooch.

"You folks having just a real good time?" Mattie Finnegan
helped her assistant Burt Cosgrove roll the gurney out of the
back and snap its folding legs down. She beckoned at LeeAnn
Swartzman, the sheet-white face, tears, and grotesquely bent

finger sure signs of distress. The woman wavered on her feet, ready to collapse, Sergeant Taber providing support.

"Sit, you." Matty patted the gurney. "Before you fall down." As LeeAnn did so, Matty caught her right wrist, holding it firmly. LeeAnn whimpered.

"My goodness. Okay, let's stabilize this with an air splint," she said to Cosgrove. "Gentle air splint. Sheriff, I need the cuffs off."

"Nope."

"Nope," Matty grunted a fair imitation of the taciturn sheriff, not the least bit intimidated by his size or glower. "Look, turn the right one loose, and latch the left to the gurney, if you have to. That way, if she escapes, she'll be easy to find." She raised her voice an octave to imitate a mind-blown shopper. "*Look at the girl dragging that bed through the parking lot!*"

The sheriff nodded with irritation, and Jackie Taber unlocked the right side. She held onto it as the two EMTs arranged LeeAnn on the stretcher. As the patient was strapped down, Mattie patted her shoulder. "There now. You can faint all you want. And it's about two minutes to the ER. They'll fix you right up."

"You process Elvis," Torrez said to Pasquale, and to the sergeant added, "and you're going to stay with the woman?"

Jackie nodded.

Torrez started to turn away. "I'll give Stub Moore a call to come and get the Fusion."

"What about Stewart's wagon?" Pasquale asked.

"Ain't likely she's going to walk out the door. But we'll see." Torrez ambled back toward his truck, and Pasquale turned to Jackie.

"We'll see what?"

"He probably wants to wait and find out what the undersheriff has going at the hospital with Mr. Stewart and CYF."

"Well, Stewart could just come over and pick it up."

"Unless there's more going on than we think," Jackie said. "Let's get your catch booked in. Then we'll see." She rested a hand on Pasquale's left shoulder. "So what precipitated all this?"

"The license plate on their Fusion has a dent that doesn't make sense."

"Really."

"Like what always happens when you want to hitch up a trailer and overshoot the ball? The trailer hitch always smacks into the license plate."

Taber grinned. "Good catch, my friend. Good catch."

Chapter Seven

It took Todd Stewart five minutes to excuse himself from a mortgage meeting at Posadas State Bank and hustle out into the autumnal blast furnace to drive the two blocks to the Posadas General Hospital Emergency Room. His breakfast kept trying to rise in his throat, even though he told himself that clearly *someone* had made a mistake, and no matter how soothing the explanation and apology might be, the episode terrified him.

He walked to the ER's visitor doors head-down, cell phone glued to his ear. He paused as the doors slid open, but turned and surveyed the ER parking lot one more time before entering, searching for his wife's car. Two police units were parked nearby, and that caused his gut to clamp all the harder as he forced himself not to sprint for the ER doors.

From inside, Undersheriff Estelle Reyes-Guzman watched him. Maybe calm and cool were part of a banker's toolbox. She did not know Todd Stewart well, having met him only on occasion, usually just a casual greeting at the bank where Dennis Mears, twin brother of Sheriff's Department Lieutenant Tom Mears, was bank president.

Stewart was dressed for the heat, his trim, athletic frame in light blue seersucker jacket over light blue shirt and dark blue-and-red tie, with dark blue summer slacks. He took off his dark aviator glasses and looked up at the various signs directing visitors and patients this way or that. He might have chosen the

ER waiting room had Estelle not stepped out from the nurses' station to intercept him.

"Good morning, sir," she said. His handshake was clammy, and the undersheriff could smell the heat-stirred apprehension overpowering his cologne. He nodded, ignoring the two other officers who lingered in the ER office and waiting room.

"First of all, Ginger is just fine," the undersheriff said. "A little dehydrated, more than a little frightened, but officers responded before things got out of hand."

"What do you mean a little dehydrated?" Stewart snapped. "What's going on?" Estelle pushed the button on the waiting room inner door, and in a few seconds, one of the nurses pushed it open, allowing access to the non-surgical treatment rooms, the white curtains assuring privacy.

"She's in the last one," Estelle said. "Just for a little while to make sure she's all right."

"My God, what happened?" His gaze was riveted. "Where's Stace?"

Estelle could think of a dozen ways to answer that, none of them helpful. She settled for blunt. "We don't know, sir. I was hoping you could tell us that." She reached out for his elbow, dark eyes sympathetic. "But come see your daughter." She ushered him past the ER nurses' station, to one of the curtained cubbyholes.

The ER nurse, Marilyn Michaels, greeted Stewart with a bright smile. "What a sweetheart," she said. "She didn't like the IV one bit, but I mean, who does? She's *so* brave." The one-year-old looked lost in the sea of white bedding, pillow-bolstered in the pediatric crib. The crib sides were down, and a teenaged nurse's aide, whose name tag announced only "Tammy," stood by the head of the crib, arm resting on the pillow, fingers lightly stroking the child's forehead.

Ginger's little legs had been pumping, but she stopped when she saw her father. Estelle gave them several uninterrupted minutes together, and it didn't take that long before Todd Stewart had coaxed a giggle from the child. Even as he did that, Stewart glanced at his watch. Estelle shifted her position so that she could more clearly see the man's face. A doting, worried father, sure enough, but one on a schedule. He made no effort to pick up Ginger, perhaps apprehensive of the IV tubing and the swath of tape that held it in place near the cavity of her left elbow.

He straightened up, Ginger's tiny right hand glommed onto his left index finger.

"What…?" he started to say, then gently disengaged his hand. "Sheriff, is there somewhere we can talk?"

"We'll give you a few moments," the nurse said, and nodded at the aide, who followed her out of the exam room. The curtains didn't do much sound-dampening, though, and Estelle stepped close to the bed. As she did so, Ginger kicked again and burbled, then said a single word that could have been translated as "da-dee!" Estelle stroked the infant's silky left cheek, her swarthy fingers in sharp contrast with the baby-blond complexion.

Even though the other ER cubicles were empty, their curtains open, the undersheriff kept her voice low. LeeAnn Bond and her broken finger were still in the ER treatment room through the swinging doors, and when the orthopedist was finished with her, she'd enjoy the county's hospitality at the lockup along with her husband.

"Deputies were called to The Spree parking lot by a passing civilian who was concerned about the barking dog and a fretful infant, locked in a vehicle, sir. She had no way of knowing how long the child had been inside the car, and its windows were closed. So she did the right thing and called the SO."

Stewart's mouth moved as if he were trying to make words, but nothing came out.

"Actually, the sheriff himself responded," Estelle continued. "He was just a block away at the time of the call. The vehicle was your wife's blue Volvo, and it's still parked over at The Spree. With the ambient temperature today, being locked in the car with the windows up is a real danger to both child and pet."

"Well, God, yes." His deep blue eyes searched Estelle's face.

"Your wife was observed entering The Spree by one of our deputies, who happened to be in the parking lot at the time on other business. Just moments later, when the abandoned child complaint was called in and the sheriff responded, the deputy searched the store for Mrs. Stewart, and could find no sign of her, even with the cooperation and assistance of the store's staff. As it turns out, no one else remembered seeing her come or go. Of course, they're busy, and had no reason to notice."

"Abandoned child?" Stewart gasped. "I don't understand this. Ginger wasn't *abandoned*. Come on."

Estelle straightened up but allowed her right hand to remain on the pillow nearest the child's head. She had heard that familiar *Not in my family* hundreds of times before. "Did your wife have other errands today? Especially errands that she might walk to when she finished at The Spree? Maybe she was preoccupied with something?"

Todd Stewart shook his head in confusion. "No…well, I mean not that *I* recall."

"Do you know what she was planning to purchase?"

"No idea. I didn't even know that she was going there. Maybe she told me. I don't know." He settled in one of the small plastic chairs, elbows on his knees.

"Did the two of you have an argument this morning?"

He scoffed and straightened up. "Come on."

"That happens, Mr. Stewart. Was your wife upset about anything when you saw her last?"

"No, she wasn't upset. A little tired this morning, is all. She was at the volleyball game last night, and went out afterward with a couple of friends. I didn't want to go, so Ginger and I stayed home."

"Most likely she'll turn up here in a few minutes with a logical explanation for all this, but at the moment, we're concerned."

His pleasant the-customer's-always-right face hardened. "*You're* concerned? How do you think I feel about all this, Sheriff? I mean, it's just not possible. My God, how long was Ginger locked in that car?"

"Thankfully, probably just a few minutes. Fortunately, the civilian who made the first call used her best judgment. You can understand her concern, I'm sure. She did the right thing by not hesitating for an instant before calling the SO. When he arrived just moments later, the sheriff could see that the child was in some distress, and he made the decision to call the EMTs. In this weather…"

"You should have called me first."

And waited yet another ten or fifteen minutes? "Immediate medical attention for the child is our first concern, sir. Sheriff Torrez was not about to wait." The name was a wonderful defuser.

Stewart nodded quickly. "Of course. Of course. And what about little Rascal? The pup?"

"As a matter of convenience, he was dropped off at the Mesa View Animal Clinic. They know your puppy, and will be happy to keep him for you until it's convenient for you to pick him up." She offered a slight smile. "I didn't think it would be appropriate to just drop him off at the bank, sir."

The man looked vexed. "All this just because Stace takes a walk to have coffee with friends."

"No, sir." She waited a moment until she knew she had his attention, and he turned to look her way. "All this because an infant and puppy were left unattended in a closed car on what's working to be the hottest day of the year."

"Now, wait a minute. You make it sound like some big neglect case here. Stacie would *never*…" Stewart stopped. What a wife would *never* do was open to conjecture. What Stacie Stewart had *done* was now painfully evident.

He waved a hand helplessly, rose, and put a hand on each hip. "Look, you said that the deputy actually *saw* her go into The Spree?"

"That's correct. She saw him, as well. I'm told she waved a greeting at him."

"Which officer was that?"

"A civilian made the original 911 call, sir."

"But you said one of the deputies saw Stace go into the store. Which officer?"

Let's all grasp at straws, Estelle thought. "Actually, Sheriff Torrez responded first to the citizen's complaint of occupants closed in the vehicle."

"But you said someone actually *saw* Stace walk into the store," Stewart persisted doggedly. "That must have been before the sheriff arrived."

"That's correct."

"And who was that? I mean, who's working days right now? Is that Sergeant Taber?"

Estelle looked at Stewart carefully while she framed an answer. Stewart was looking for excuses, anything to shift blame somewhere else. "At this point, that witness information is part of an ongoing investigation, sir." Somehow, some way, the man would find a way to blame the deputy, or the sheriff, or even Miss Barber, the retired school teacher who had had the presence of mind to dial the police without a moment's hesitation. But in all likelihood, if charges were ever filed against Stacie Stewart, Deputy Thomas Pasquale's testimony would be central.

"Jesus H. Christ," Stewart muttered in a most unbankerly tone. "You're talking as if Stacie committed some big crime, for God's sakes."

"Sir, by the time the child was removed from the car, EMTs recorded her body temp at one hundred three degrees. The facts are simple, at least on the surface. Your wife parked her Volvo at The Spree, locked the doors with the windows up, and walked into the store, leaving behind Ginger and the puppy. The sun was baking directly through the rear and side windows. Some time afterward, a short time afterward, fortunately, a shopper noticed the child and the puppy in some distress, and immediately made the call. Sheriff Torrez responded, along with an EMT crew."

"Stacie knows better than to do any of that."

"Of course she does, sir. We don't know *why* she did it until we talk to her."

"Nobody just *forgets* that they have a child in the car."

"Unfortunately, it happens more frequently than we would like. Folks get distracted or preoccupied. Children and pets are left in unvented vehicles, kids are left behind at highway rest stops while the rest of the family drives away. Kids become a forgotten audience as their parents fight over some little frustration." She smiled gently at Stewart.

He drew a huge sigh. "Sheriff, we didn't fight, we didn't argue." He looked hard at Estelle. "When you find Stace, you'll let me know immediately? You'll keep me in the loop?"

"Of course, sir."

"Can I take Ginger home now?" The child jangled a large set of colorful plastic keys. Stewart smoothed his tie and bent down, nuzzling the child's forehead. The soft-toned bell that alerted the nursing staff to ER visitation chimed, and in a moment, Sheriff Robert Torrez held back the curtain.

"Hey," he said, and offered a huge paw to Stewart. "Looks like she's doin' just fine."

"We think so," Estelle said. "Mr. Stewart was just asking if he could take Ginger home now, and he needs to understand that decision is up to the medical staff here." She rested a hand lightly on Stewart's forearm. "There's a line of protocol now, sir. Just as we turned Ginger over to the EMT crew, *they* in turn delivered her to the hospital staff. I'm sure they'll let you take her the minute they're convinced her health is out of any danger. I would advise you that there has been a referral to Children, Youth and Families as well."

"Good God, what for?"

"It's standard procedure in these circumstances, sir. I'm sure Mrs. Benedict will be here shortly. You have someone at home who can care for Ginger today, or will you take time off from work, or what? She will ask you that."

"I'll take the rest of the day off, but here you're sounding as if Stacie isn't coming back."

"I wish I could give you an answer to that, sir."

"If somebody forced her into another car, the deputy would have seen it," the sheriff said bluntly. "What he saw was that she walked into the store. From there, we don't know."

Stewart's eyes searched first one face and then the other, as if trying to decide what tact to take—the sheriff's blunt, untempered assessment, or the undersheriff's calm understanding. "And now? We can't just sit around and wait."

"No, we won't do that." Estelle glanced at the wall clock. "Take some time to be with your daughter, then when you've had a chance to think your morning through, talk with Mrs. Benedict. On top of that, try and remember all the details of what was done, what was said in your household this morning. Any little thing." She handed him a business card. "I'll want some details from you. Stacie will probably have called by then, or gotten in touch with you. We can take it from there."

"You're not thinking of charging her or anything, are you? That's what it sounds like."

"That would be premature, sir. First, we need to *find* her. That's all that matters right now. Then we have to understand the circumstances. As I said, anything else would be premature, sir. In the meantime, we'll start the search process." She made an effort to sound more hopeful than she felt. "Just this one thing to get us started, sir. When did you last talk with your wife? Either in person or by phone. Be specific about the time."

"When she got home last night. Maybe eleven. And then this morning, at breakfast. I suppose, what, seven-thirty?"

"And the mood?"

"Just fine. See, Stacie just dotes on Ginger. Well, we both do. We were having fun at breakfast." He smiled, the proud dad. "See, Ginger just discovered that the puppy is a bottomless pit. She'd dribble some food off her high chair, and Rascal was right there to clean up. Ginger thought that was the funniest thing she'd ever seen. And her laugh. She has this big, bawdy laugh that just…well, it's impossible not to just melt, watching and listening to her. Anyway, Stace said that she and Ginger were going shopping down at the new store. That's right, she *did* tell me that. She said that she might meet one of her friends for lunch. Dana Gabaldon? Dana has a daughter, Adrianna, about

Ginger's age. Maybe a year older. Dana was at the game, too. Girls' night out sort of thing."

"Where do they like to eat when they do lunch?"

"At the Don Juan. As far as Stace is concerned, that's the only restaurant in town."

Estelle grinned. "There are folks who agree with her."

He nodded vigorously. "So, that's what I know." He avoided Sheriff Torrez' expressionless gaze and fished his cell phone from its small belt holster. "I'll call Dana."

Estelle held out a hand, covering his and the phone. "Actually, sir, let me have a chat with Ms. Gabaldon first. You need to spend some time with Ginger, make sure she's all right. I'll get back to you. And you have my card."

"You're going to be able to follow up on this today?" He looked off into the distance, beyond the painted wall of the ER, at a horizon that was suddenly more bleak. "My God, what am I going to do? I mean, she *has* to be okay and coming back, right?"

"We'll follow up on this right now, sir."

"You don't have to wait twenty-four hours or anything like that? For missing persons and things like that?"

"No. Was Ginger scheduled to be in daycare today?"

"Well, sure. Stace had to work. No, wait…she didn't, either. Friday is her day off. Jeez, listen to me. I don't know whether I'm coming or going with all this. She had Ginger all day. See, she and Dana had been thinking that Dana might take Ginger. It's tough for the Gabaldons to afford daycare, and by taking in Ginger, there'd be both some extra income and company for little Adrianna."

"But they hadn't started that yet?"

"No, she and Dana were thinking of starting next week, maybe. They were going to talk about that today."

She pushed the curtain to one side. Stewart didn't move. He looked down at the floor, shaking his head slowly. When he looked up at Estelle, his eyes were moist. "I just don't believe this," he murmured. "I don't know what the hell to do."

"Think hard about the last few days, the last few weeks. If anything that Stacie did or said jars your memory, don't hesitate to call me. Even little things can be important. And as we come up with questions, we'll be calling or visiting." She smiled encouragingly. "Take your time. Keep a cool head, sir."

Torrez nodded curtly at Stewart, then looked expectantly at his undersheriff. "Got to talk to you for a minute." He stepped back out of the way as one of the nurses entered. "Outside?"

Estelle followed the sheriff outside to the portico used by incoming ambulances. One of the units waited off to one side, ready to take LeeAnn Bond back to the county lockup.

Torrez lounged against one of the portico uprights. He didn't seem to mind whether he stood in the shade or not.

"Let's put everybody who ain't tied down on this," he said. "If we diddle around waitin' for the girl to show up, first thing you know, we'll find her dead in a ditch somewheres."

"It's hard to imagine that she was abducted, Bobby. Pasquale said that when he saw her going into the store, she waved at him, cheerful as can be. And if someone tried to grab her *inside* the store, there'd be all kinds of witnesses."

Torrez nodded. "She split." He said it as if it were a statement of fact. "Either that, or her husband knows *exactly* where she is, and ain't talkin'."

Chapter Eight

Before she had the chance to offer other possibilities, Bob Torrez added, "Clayton Bailey is dead." Estelle Reyes-Guzman looked up sharply at the sheriff. For a moment, the name didn't register, and clearly Torrez expected her to take the abrupt change in subject in stride. "The SO in Cathay said he was hit once in the back of the head. Don't know with what yet."

"The Illinois couple," Estelle supplied, and Torrez nodded. "When?"

"They think he's been dead a couple of days at least. And there ain't no wife, by the way, and they weren't at no family reunion out in North Dakota like Bond claimed. Bailey's been a widower for twenty years. A neighbor found him lyin' in the barn out behind his house. At the foot of an old stairway goin' up into one of the lofts. Somebody didn't look close, they might think he took a tumble, but the M.E. says no. Took a hit first."

"Bond, they think?"

Torrez shrugged. "Ain't going to be hard to figure out when Elvis left the building."

"They'll want him back."

"Yep."

"So was he surprised in the act of taking the license plate, and grabbed a handy two-by-four or some such?"

"He don't seem the type," Torrez said. "More of a talker. Seems to me like he'd try to charm the old man into lettin' him borrow the plate."

"He was type enough to make a grab for that BB gun you said was in the center console of the car."

"Yeah, well. Maybe him, but more likely the wife. She could do it." He made a wry face. "And the Cathay SO hadn't noticed that the plate was taken off the truck. Didn't notice it was missing."

"You're kidding."

Torrez shrugged again. "Anyway, it's *their* problem, not ours. My bet is that Bond is enough of a wuss to give the wife up just to save his own ass." He shrugged. "They'll let us know when they can spring a couple of guys free to extradite. I don't much feature spendin' our budget feedin' these two any longer than we have to. Or listening to 'em, either." Almost as an afterthought, he added, "We'll already end up payin' for a finger." He nodded toward the emergency room door. "So what are you plannin' now?"

"Stacie was supposed to have lunch with Dana Gabaldon. That's what Stewart said. On the way, I want to check with Posadas Electric and see what Stacie told them *yesterday*, if anything. See if she just walked away from there, too. Then I'll check with Dana."

"You think he knows anything he's not tellin' us?" Through the door, they could see Todd Stewart talking with Susan Benedict, the matronly representative from the county's Children, Youth and Families Department.

"I'm not sure. He's a hard guy to read. He's not exactly frantic, Bobby. At least not yet."

She opened her phone, scrolled through the directory, and then touched in the number for Dana and Eddie Gabaldon. Dana's friendly voice announced, "We can't come to the phone right now, but if..." Estelle hung up. "Not home. Or maybe outside."

"Eddie'd be over at the post office."

"Then that's what I'll do. I'll swing by the Stewarts' house in case she's out in the yard, and the Gabaldons', the post office, and then the Don Juan, and Posadas Electric. A quick loop to see if anything turns up."

"She ain't sitting around in her yard, that's for sure. Maybe she lied to her husband about meetin' somebody." He tipped his head to one side. "Or about *who* she's meetin'."

"She could have, Bobby. Or Todd could have lied to us."

Torrez nodded without much enthusiasm. "Good luck with that. In the meantime, we got enough charges to keep the Bonds off the street, but I'll talk to the DA. If the Cathay SO has any evidence that'll stick in a good murder case, they'll want to extradite sooner rather than later." He offered a rare smile. "We sure as hell don't want to hold things up, if they do."

◇◇◇

The Gabaldon home on North Twelfth Street, a modest concrete block ranch stuccoed to look like adobe, sat quietly under the punishing September sun. The single-car-garage door was closed, the driveway empty, all the house curtains closed. Having driven by the address a hundred times over the years, Estelle knew that the Gabaldons' car had been preempted from the garage by Eddie's collection of bikes, including a new tandem with a baby bob behind. She also knew that one of Eddie's fervent dreams was to beat fellow cyclist Tom Pasquale in a major mountain bike race. That would only happen if Tom lost a leg or a lung.

For a moment, the undersheriff parked several doors down and opened the computer. The Gabaldons had one registered vehicle, a silver 2013 Kia sedan. She jotted down the license plate number, then turned around and retraced her route, bumping over the steel bridge that crossed the arroyo just north of the intersection with Bustos. The Don Juan was handy, right on the corner of Twelfth and Bustos, and Estelle turned into the parking lot. No Kia.

She parked near the side of the building and got out. Inside, the Don Juan was a cool, dark cavern, with murals of the now-controversial Spanish explorer Don Juan de Oñate painted on three walls. A girl who looked so young that she should have been enrolled in middle school greeted the undersheriff with a tentative smile and raised eyebrows, but said not a word.

"Is JanaLynn on shift yet, Bonnie?"

"She's off today."

"Ah." Yet another of Sheriff Bobby Torrez' endless parade of cousins, JanaLynn knew every regular customer who frequented the Don Juan. Estelle took a step beyond the cash register and surveyed the restaurant. The early lunch crowd was sparse. "Do you know Dana Gabaldon?"

"I even babysit for her sometimes," Bonnie said brightly.

"Has she been in for lunch today?"

"I ain't seen her at all."

Estelle smiled at the girl. "You have the whole place to yourself, huh?"

Bonnie brightened. "Just me until right at noon." She glanced at the clock, still fifteen minutes shy of the lunch rush. "Then Claire comes in."

"Thank you."

"No problem."

But it is a problem, Estelle thought on her way back outside. For a moment she stood in the sun, letting it chase the remains of the Don Juan's frigid air conditioning, and then slid into her car, opening all four windows wide. The short drive a few blocks east on Bustos to Pershing filled the car with hot Southwest, a blanket of aromas that Estelle found more refreshing, mixed with the icy air pumped by the car's efficient air conditioning compressor.

Eddie Gabaldon's bike of the day was chained to the natural-gas meter on the side of the post office. He wouldn't have gone out to lunch, being the natural food fanatic that he is. The post office was empty of customers, and Estelle rapped a knuckle on the staff entrance off the end of the lobby.

"Eddie? It's Estelle Guzman."

"Just a second!" he shouted from somewhere in the back. In a moment the lock to the inner sanctum of the post office rattled and Eddie Gabaldon pushed the door open. "Hey, Mrs. Sheriff." He grinned widely, showing square, even teeth. Burly in build, Gabaldon hardly fit the image that Estelle conjured of professional bikers, those riders with thunder thighs topped by otherwise rail-thin bodies and hawk noses perfect for splitting the slipstream. Of course, neither did Tom Pasquale. But the deputy won races on the downhill sections, where his fearless lack of common sense ruled the race.

Eddie beckoned with a rubber-tipped finger, the little red thimble obviating the need to lick fingers for traction. "Come on in."

"I don't want to take your time, Eddie. Actually, I needed to talk with Dana for just a little bit, but she wasn't home."

"She took Adrianna down to Cruces to visit the mom." His heavy face scrunched up in resignation. "When *the mom* summons, you gotta go. I think she's going to stay overnight." He smiled indulgently. "Grandparents got to have their baby time, you know."

"Did she have company?"

"Who, Dana? Just the little monkey. Adrianna *loves* to ride in the car. Why? Which company are we talkin' about? Who are you lookin' for?"

"Actually, I wanted to chat with Stacie Stewart, Eddie. Todd said that she might be having lunch with Dana today."

"He be wrong." Eddie smiled. "Which, for a husband, isn't all that uncommon, you know. Did you call her?"

Estelle had tried Stacie Stewart's cell phone number a dozen times, earning the same brief, cheerful voicemail message each time. If it had chirped from the depths of the woman's purse, Stacie had proven immune to the "telephone imperative," that odd behavior that even prompted people to leap from the shower to answer, only to hear an ad warning that the warranty on their car was poised to expire.

"I haven't been able to reach her," Estelle said easily, and offered a smile. "But who knows? How's little Adrianna doing? I haven't seen her in a while."

"Wonderful. I'm afraid one of these mornings I'm going to wake up and find out that she's a teenager."

Estelle laughed. "That'll happen, Eddie."

He shook his head in bewilderment. "We got another one in the pod...did we tell you that?"

"How exciting!"

"Grandparents are nuts enough with one. Imagine with two, huh?"

"And due when?"

"Early spring. I don't know how you do it with those two of yours. They must keep you hopping!"

"They make life easier for me, actually. You'll see."

"Is the concert kid coming home for the big party?"

"We thought he was. But it turns out he has a recital at school that he can't miss, a bunch of paperwork, all kinds of things. He really *wants* to come, you know. Both he and Carlos are really close to their grandmother. And a hundredth birthday is a rare event. He hates to miss it, but..." she shrugged... "he has to do what he has to do."

"Wish your mom my best, all right?"

"I will do that."

"Do you want me to have Dana give you a call when she gets home?"

"Yes, please. And if you have the phone number for her folks, I'd appreciate that, too."

"And ditto Stacie, if I see her? I mean, usually I do, but not always."

Estelle smiled. "Sure. Why not."

With one more base to cover, Estelle drove back to the Sheriff's Department and woke up her computer, then called Todd Stewart. He answered on the first ring.

"What'd you find out?" he asked immediately.

"That Stacie did not have lunch with Dana, at least not at the Don Juan, sir. I'm told that Dana and her daughter went to Las Cruces to visit her mother. I'll be checking in with her in just a minute. What I need from you is Stacie's e-mail address."

"Her e-mail?"

"She isn't answering her cell phone, but who knows? We might get lucky. Some folks live with their e-mail."

"Well sure. I'm probably one of 'em, in my business." He rattled off the address. "What if she doesn't answer? I mean, what do we do in a case like this? I mean, if she doesn't come right back?"

"Then we try to find her."

His silence sounded miserable. Finally, voice diminished, he asked, "When these things happen…I mean…is there…?" that was as far as he could marshal his thoughts.

"Mr. Stewart, it isn't rare when someone decides to take a walk, for whatever reason, or whatever complicated flock of reasons. I know that sounds harsh, but you need to know that."

"Somebody might have…abducted her?"

"That's also a possibility. I personally think, given the circumstances, that an abduction is unlikely. The store was reasonably crowded, and the staff witnessed no altercation of any kind. Stacie is fit and strong. And she knew her child was outside in the locked car. Her being abducted just isn't likely."

"Then what *is* likely?"

"At this point, I wouldn't want to speculate, sir." It would be easy enough to tap into the small-town gossip vine, where some helpful soul might supply several possible answers to Stewart's question.

"She might have just left, you mean?"

"That is a possibility that we're exploring."

"But she left Ginger in the car."

"Yes, she did. But we don't know the *why*, Mr. Stewart. We know that the child and puppy were left in the car, that's right. But we don't know all of the circumstances."

The phone fell silent for a moment, and Estelle let the man think. "What should I do?"

"Stay home with Ginger. Stay near the phone. Keep your e-mail open. Be available to us." In the background Estelle heard a sudden burst of a child's laughter—Ginger's hearty roar of approval at something the puppy had done. She hadn't missed her mother yet.

Chapter Nine

Deputy Tom Pasquale leaned back in the chair, regarding the computer screen. Not a touch typist, and years before having paid more attention to the shapely neck of the young lady in the seat in front of him than to the high school English grammar syllabus, writing came as a chore for him. At the moment that Undersheriff Estelle Reyes-Guzman knocked on the cubicle door—the deputy's personal office was hardly more than that—Pasquale was stymied by the word "disguised." He deleted his last attempt and typed "dressed to look like," which may have been more exact in meaning, anyway. He looked up at the undersheriff.

"I may be here all week."

"The SO in Cathay will appreciate your efforts," Estelle said. "Sorry to interrupt, but I have a couple of questions for you."

"Sure." He pushed back from the keyboard, always pleased when he had the chance for more than a passing "hello" with the undersheriff.

Estelle entered the office and pulled the single steel folding chair out of the corner. "When you drove into the parking lot at The Spree, you came in from the north side?"

The deputy looked at the ceiling for a moment. "Yes."

"And you were driving toward the store, down the parking lot aisle that would be in front of where Stacie Stewart parked her Volvo. She was on your right." Her slender, expressive fingers drew the map in the air.

"Yes."

"When you first saw her, did you actually see her climb out of the car, or was she already starting to walk away from it?"

Pasquale hesitated. "I saw her when she was just leaving the car, about twenty-five yards away from me. I saw her slam the driver's door. She had a small purse slung over her shoulder, and she turned toward the store. She just walked behind all the other cars, staying out of the middle of the aisle."

"She was alone?"

"Yes."

"Did she notice you?"

"Yes, ma'am. She looked back at me and waved." Pasquale twiddled his fingers. "And then she continued on to the store, walkin' pretty quickly."

"You watched her all the way? You actually saw her go through the auto doors and enter the store?"

"Yes."

"There was no way she might have turned and walked along the storefront, where all the yard and garden inventory is on display?"

"No. I saw her go into the store."

"Did you see her for long enough that you could describe her mood?"

Knowing that his undersheriff appreciated precision without stinting on information that might turn out to be important, Pasquale thought carefully, framing his answer.

"Just busy. Not wastin' any time. Like she knew exactly what she was after." He shrugged. "Friendly enough when she saw me, but she didn't stop to chat. No big sexy smile for me."

"Would the sexy smile have been the norm?"

Pasquale ducked his head with embarrassment. "Well, no."

"No particular urgency, then? Did she seem preoccupied?"

Pasquale shrugged. "I don't know. Maybe, 'cause she wasn't wasting any time. She just kind of breezed by, you know?"

Estelle regarded the young deputy for a moment. "Give me your best estimate, Thomas. From the moment you saw her enter the store to when *you* went searching for her inside…how many minutes was that?"

He closed his eyes, replaying the mental tape. "Okay, she got out of the car, walked down the lot quickly and went in the store. That's a minute, or minute and a half. Then I cruised a little farther and saw the Fusion with the Illinois plate. I thought about that for a couple minutes, then called dispatch for the twenty-eight. Couple minutes there. The hit came back in another couple of minutes. I asked Mike to recheck for me. He did that, and then the sheriff called me on the phone. He was comin' in for the complaint about a kid locked in a car. Just a little while later, he rolls up, asks me where the complainant was, old Miss Barber, and I pointed her out. The sheriff drove over, and he and Miss Barber talked for just a little bit while he scoped out the situation. Then the sheriff went to pop the window, and at the same time told me to go inside and search for Stacie."

Estelle held up her hand. "At that point—from when you actually saw her enter the store until *you* entered after her—how many minutes do you suppose that was?"

Pasquale pulled a small notebook out of his pocket, found an empty page, and computed. He found an answer he agreed with and looked up at Estelle. "I'd guess between eight or nine minutes. Maybe as much as ten."

"So if she was taken, that's how long the abductors had to work. Grab her, keep her quiet, and exit the building—or for her to find a hiding spot where nobody would think to look. Nine or ten minutes."

"We looked everywhere, ma'am. Every storeroom, employees' lounge, bathroom, Dumpster, you name it. And Tilda had the whole store on camera, too. She was not there. No way."

"Are the cameras on DVD?"

"I didn't ask. God, if they are, we'll watch her walk right in, and see when she leaves."

"You need to give Tilda a call and see if the cameras are recorded. That's more important than the paperwork just now.

If she left the building by her own volition, that's the time window—nine minutes or maybe a little more."

"Let me call." He pushed back and reached for the phone.

Back in her own office, Estelle composed a carefully worded e-mail message to Stacie Stewart, saying nothing about Ginger or the puppy, but requesting a contact as soon as possible. She knew that the message was just a *delete* keystroke away from being a waste of time.

That finished, she opened her own notebook and found first the Summers' land line in Las Cruces, and Dana's cell phone. She hesitated, then dialed the Summers' residence. After seven rings, the answering machine kicked in. That in turn was interrupted by a man's abrupt, "Yeah-lo."

"Mr. Summers?"

"Speaking."

"Sir, this is Undersheriff Estelle Reyes-Guzman over in Posadas. May I speak with Dana, please?"

"Sure. She's out in the backyard at the pool. Just hang on a second."

Estelle did so, hearing the slam of a door and far off voices. A full two minutes later, Summers came back on the line. "She's gone out shopping or something. You want a call back? Is there some kind of problem?"

Two minutes to establish that she went shopping…or something? Estelle thought. "A call back would be good. Whenever it's convenient for her. No emergency."

"This is in regards to…?"

"If you'd have her call me, I'd appreciate it," Estelle said.

Summers hesitated, and then decided not to pursue the evasion. "Okay. Sure. I'm not sure when they're planning to be back."

"That's fine. Just whenever you see her next." She recited her contact number and then hung up, wondering if Mr. Summers, whom she had never met, had repeated her name to Dana—who would recognize it. She pictured the woman sitting beside the pool in a deck chair, perhaps sharing an intimate moment of conversation with her mother. If Dana Gabaldon was like a vast majority of young women, her cell phone was within arm's length.

"No dice," Tom Pasquale said. He had appeared in Estelle's office doorway, ghost-quiet until Estelle was off the phone. "They don't have recorders hooked up yet. Just a live feed. That's another thing on their 'to do' list."

"Everyone leaves a track, Thomas. Somewhere, somehow. We all keep looking until we find it."

◇◇◇

The new office of Posadas Electric Cooperative nestled just north of the hospital, and Art Acevedo's tiny yellow Smart Car was parked in the last slot at the north end, unthreatened by the flow of sharp-cornered utility trucks in and out. Estelle eased the Charger into the space beside the diminutive vehicle, recalling County Manager Leona Spears' comment about how cute the tiny Smart would look with a red and blue light rack mounted on top, and sheriff's stars on the doors. The sheriff had not been amused, largely because Leona had made the quip in public at a County Commission meeting—one of the rare meetings that the sheriff had bothered to attend. Estelle was fairly certain that Bobby Torrez hadn't realized that the county manager was kidding.

Art Acevedo was leaning on the receptionist's desk, pointing at something on the young woman's computer. He and Millie Wagoner looked up at the same time, and Acevedo beamed, his huge, round face looking far too much like a human emoticon. Straightening up, he extended a meaty paw, and even swung out his elbow as if preparing to crush her hand. But his grip was gentle.

"Sheriff, we got the air conditioning runnin' today, don't we?"

"Nice out there, nice in here." The office was typically frigid. "Do you have a few minutes?"

"You bet. Where's the big guy? We could all go to lunch together."

"Bobby is tied up with about half a dozen things. I wish we had the time." She followed Acevedo down the narrow hallway, past the gallery of huge photos showing Posadas Electric in operation. The gallery continued in the manager's office with various photos of Acevedo posing with governmental luminaries—including three of him schmoozing with former governors. A color photo enlarged to near-poster size and framed in heavy walnut hung behind Acevedo's desk. In the photo, Acevedo wore a hardhat and was shaking George W. Bush's hand. The president, smiling, was gesturing with his left hand at something off on the horizon.

"So, if I can't talk you into lunch, how about coffee? Tea? Cold beer?" Acevedo laughed pleasantly, and folded his hands on his desk blotter.

"Nothing, thanks."

"Well, that's easy. What's going on? You following up on that utility pole from last night?" Acevedo's face lost some of its good humor. "I heard the driver was flown out to Albuquerque. Banged-up pretty badly."

"I only read the report this morning, Art. But that's my understanding."

"Hard one. First he kills a deer, then goes off the lane and splits one of our poles." He grimaced. "All of that in a twenty-five zone on a gravel road."

"No twenty-five for that one. Deputy Bishop said it looked more like fifty or sixty."

"Christ. Well, they do it all the time, don't they? So what's on your plate this morning? Is one of ours in trouble?"

"Mr. Acevedo, has Stacie Stewart been in today?"

"I'm sure she is, somewheres. You want to speak with her?"

"If it's convenient."

He reached across to the phone complex and was about to push a button when he stopped abruptly. "No, wait...she doesn't come in on Fridays." His grin flashed. "You almost got me there." He glanced sideways at Estelle. "She works some amazing hours."

Estelle waved a hand as if Stacie Stewart's schedule was of little importance. "I'll catch her tomorrow. Thanks anyway."

"Monday will work," Acevedo corrected. Estelle rose, and Acevedo pushed away from his desk. "Come see us more often." His handshake was a repeat, and he kept his grip a little longer than necessary. "Have you been able to spend some time out at the project?"

"The Project," the nickname around town for Miles Waddell's *NightZone*, had consumed most of the county's resources for the past two years.

"More than enough."

"It seems like that's all we're doing." Acevedo shook his head in resignation. "It'll be a monster money-maker for us when it's all up and running. By Christmas, they're saying now."

"With luck."

"More like Christmas of next year, I'm thinking. If I see Ms. Stewart, you want me to have her call you?"

"Yes, please. When you saw her *yesterday,* did she happen to mention anything out of the ordinary to you? Trips out of town, or anything like that?"

"You know, I didn't see her much, 'cause I was out *there, "*and he nodded to the southwest, in the direction of the theme park. "But I saw her late in the day, gosh, not long before quittin' time."

"Did she say something like, 'See you Monday'?"

"That's exactly what she said. She asked if I was going to the big game, and I said I had to miss it. But, yeah…'*See you Monday.*' Why? What's going on?"

"We just need to talk. About daycare."

"Oh," Acevedo said, his expression showing complete understanding. "Well, I'll tell her you called."

"Thanks." Outside, she sat in the car for a moment. Did Dana Gabaldon know where her friend had gone? Did she know that Stacie's child, Ginger, had been locked in the car along with the excitable puppy? If that were the case, of course she would be reticent about talking with the law. The questions were worth spending two hours out of county. Estelle started the Charger, set the air conditioning for seventy-four degrees, and pulled out of the parking lot, heading south on Grande toward the interstate. In less than a block, dispatch had answered the phone.

"I'll be in Cruces for a little bit," Estelle said. "I should be back by four."

"Affirmative," Mike Esperanza said. "They got something going on at the school. They may be calling you in."

"Two hours, and I'll be back. The sheriff didn't say what it was?"

"That's negative."

Estelle had not driven two miles when the phone jarred her thoughts, and she thumbed the controls on the steering wheel.

"Guzman."

The sheriff's voice was amped a little beyond his usual whisper and he didn't mince words. "Needja back ASAP, Estelle. We got one down at the school."

"Accident of some sort?" Something going on? There *was* no school on this particular Friday. Bob Torrez didn't make contact with hopes of a meeting later in the week, or even later in the day. ASAP meant just that, regardless of what the *something* was. She braked hard and swung into the broad, jouncing center median.

"This ain't no accident," Torrez said, and that's as far as his explanation went. "How far out are you?"

"ETA five minutes."

"Make it three."

Chapter Ten

The gym annex had once upon a time been the middle school before being joined at the hip to the high school. Arranged roughly like a U inside the aging brick building, the old-fashioned, high-ceilinged classrooms ringed the gymnasium/auditorium. The building was three stories high, the first floor actually below ground level. At one point, the middle school had been earmarked for destruction, but escaped when plans for the bond issue to finance its replacement evaporated.

Sent to Posadas when she was sixteen to finish high school in an American system, Estelle remembered the middle school building well, especially the cafeteria, which occupied one end of the first floor. Public school nutrition had required only one or two lunches to make her homesick for Tres Santos and her adopted mother's spicy treats.

Behind the cafeteria were the locker rooms, boys' on one side of the building, girls' on the other. Back stairways led up to access the gymnasium/auditorium on the second floor.

As she swung the Charger into the school roundabout, she glanced at the dash clock. Not yet twelve-thirty. She whispered a relieved *thank you* at the absence of school buses. Even the faculty would be spared, unless someone had left the in-service meeting early, then drifted off to sleep while descending a flight of stairs.

Deputy Paul Escobar, one of the most recent hires, stood at the building's main entrance, behind a yellow crime-scene tape that tangled in a hedge at the corner of the building and then stretched out to the sidewalk, around the parking lot, and out of sight behind the high school. Estelle nosed the Charger up to the tape and switched it off. Response had been prompt. She saw several department vehicles, along with Medical Examiner Dr. Alan Perrone's red BMW. A small crowd had gathered across the lot, near the administration building.

"If you'd come right up the sidewalk," Escobar called to Estelle. A big, burly man who had taken to shaving his bullet skull, he carried about thirty pounds too much on his large frame, just enough to look sloppy under the otherwise neat, tailored lines of his uniform and Sam Brown belt. She reached the flight of steps leading to the main doors and stopped. An ambulance had already arrived, parked now with its lights winking and the two EMTs waiting inside.

Escobar moved a little bit to meet the undersheriff and extended an aluminum clipboard toward her. "I need you to sign in." She did so, forcing herself to take her time with the signature and time. As she handed the board back to him, he instructed, "The sheriff asks that you go through the doors and then stay right, going downstairs on the far *right* side of the staircase." He paused as if she might have misunderstood. "Then walk past the cafeteria and on down the far *right* side of the hallway, staying as close to the wall as you can. You'll see the yellow tape on the floor. Stay to the right of that, ma'am."

"Right," she repeated. He nodded soberly. "How many?"

"Just the one as far as I know, but I haven't been to the scene yet. Sheriff's not sayin' much, and he's not lettin' *nobody* extra inside except the lieutenant and the coroner and a couple of other guys."

Estelle groaned inwardly. That meant too many size-twelves clomping through the crime scene.

"I got the crowd contained over there by the fire hydrant," Escobar continued. "Even the EMTs have to wait." Estelle looked at the waiting officers and civilians. "Like I said, the sheriff ain't talkin'."

"And what else is new?" Estelle got an "oh-well" smile in return.

He tucked the clipboard under his arm and hitched up his uniform trousers. "Lemme know what you need."

"You're doing it, Paul."

The door was chained open, the brass latch already bagged. Inside, the foyer offered two immediate choices: upstairs to the classrooms on the second floor, or downstairs to the ground-floor cafeteria and beyond that, the locker rooms.

The stairs upward to the second- and third-floor classrooms were taped off, and she stepped far to the right to take the narrow aisle downstairs that the floor tape allowed. The yellow tape ran a foot away from the wall all the way down the hall, past the cafeteria on the right and, on the left, what had been the home ec and junior high shop rooms.

At the double locker room doors, the tape turned abruptly to the right. The right-hand door was propped open.

Inside, the spacious office shared by some of the physical education faculty now included a sole occupant. A thin, fine-boned and balding man sat sideways at a desk, his hands tightly clasped between his knees. He looked up, and Estelle recognized Barry Lavin, one of the school custodians. He'd been one of the custodians decades before, too.

Off to the right, past the lockers, she heard voices and footsteps approaching, and Lieutenant Tom Mears appeared, shepherding three others—State Police Sergeant Hector Dominguez along with Sheriff's Sergeant Todd Baker and Special Deputy Dick Jonas. Jonas waddled when he walked, and his body language said loud and clear that he enjoyed being in company with Dominguez and Baker, both veterans carrying command stripes.

"Sheriff wants us out of there until you have a look, ma'am." Mears kept his voice low, his back to Barry Lavin. He shook his head. "Pretty bad deal."

"Student?"

"No, ma'am. One of the faculty." Estelle frowned, and Lieutenant Mears added, "Looks to be Clint Scott. And you're going to need boots." He pointed at the locker room floor, where a sheet of water had advanced under one of the benches. "May I get them for you?"

Without taking her eyes off the water, Estelle handed the lieutenant her car keys. "In the trunk behind the evidence locker," she said. "Thank you, LT."

"You bet. Camera gear?"

She glanced at him. "Yes. The big black camera bag, also in the trunk."

"You got it."

The locker room included three rows of lockers, one on each side, and another down the middle. A long wooden bench split each aisle. Without conscious thought, her gaze found where locker 233 had been twenty years before—the door now missing, an empty gray space remaining. The nightmare of herself as a student in PE, struggling with the recalcitrant combination lock, still wasted brain space.

Rather than turning toward the likely source of water, the gang shower at the far end of the room, Estelle kept to the dry tile straight ahead. She took her time, examining each side of the locker room. Other than a pair of white socks wadded up on the bench and a couple of sprung locker doors that gaped open, the place looked worn but tidy.

Staying clear of the stream, she walked the length of the locker room, along the row of lockers and on the dry side of the wooden bench. Near the end of the bench lay a neatly folded pile of clothes, with socks stuffed inside a pair of running shoes. Estelle examined the pile without touching it—trousers, polo shirt, underwear, and a large white beach towel. "All right," she said softly, and turned away.

The shower room itself was just the way she remembered it, off to the right behind a step-up of ceramic tile. Water sheeted over the lip of the tile now in small surges—each time someone in the shower took a step and sent waves sloshing. She stopped and looked at the tiled sill. To overflow, the shower drain had to be plugged, and then enough water pumped in to fill the four-inch shower-floor pan up to the sill.

She moved to the shower room doorway. Inside, Sheriff Robert Torrez' voice was little more than a whisper as he engaged the medical examiner in conversation.

He looked up and saw his undersheriff. "I can get Linda comin', if you need her."

Estelle shook her head. "She shouldn't work this, Bobby."

"She's seen bodies before."

"I don't mean that. It's awkward, it's slippery, there are stairs coming and going…it's not worth the risk for her." But of course, if the sheriff so ordered, nine-months' pregnant Linda Real Pasquale would try her best to oblige. "She doesn't need to be here."

The sheriff made no comment, but watched Estelle as she stood to one side of the doorway, examining the shower from one side to the other. By habit, she ignored the corpse, the prominent landmark dead center in the twelve-by-twelve tiled room.

"Were Baker, Dominguez, and Jonas in there, as well?"

"Nope." And then the sheriff added, "Fats was doin' a ride-along with Baker. Otherwise he wouldn't be in the building at all."

"Okay." The shower room, like its twin on the other side of the building in the boys' locker room, included three nozzles on each of the three walls away from the silled entry. Coaches could run an entire team through in minutes. On the wall to her left, beside the center showerhead, a spray of blood arced up the wall, smeared in one spot four feet above the floor, as if someone had tried finger painting. The wall tile itself wasn't in the best of shape, but three spots showed what she thought could be fresh damage.

Coach Clint Scott lay nearly in the center of the shower room, buttocks squarely blocking the shower drain, arms flexed and fists clenched, his hands resting on his chest. He had collapsed flat on his back, feet toward the shower room entry. Estelle didn't need to ask if the victim was deceased.

Dr. Alan Perrone stood still, his hands in his pockets. He wore an old-fashioned pair of buckled galoshes with sterile booties pulled over them, his pants tucked neatly inside. The sheriff's rubber Wellingtons were similarly bootied.

Refusing to enter until she had secured the scene photograph-ically, Estelle stepped away from the shower room sill, watching the overflow of water running along the tile in a foot-wide river to the first locker-room drain. "Is someone hunting up a piece of screen for the shower drain?" Estelle asked.

"We'll get one."

"What do we have, Alan?" She moved once more to the doorway without stepping in, and Perrone stepped carefully toward her, until he was standing near the victim's feet.

"Just what we can see, Estelle, at least until we move him. It looks as if he's been shot four times. I was just telling the sheriff that it's going to be hell in this particular venue to establish just which shot came first, although we're making some good guesses. We need to drain this place. And who knows what surprises we'll find when we turn him over."

"In a little bit," Estelle said. "I don't want evidence washing away."

"Of course."

She scanned the room again. "Who found him?"

"The janitor. He's waiting in the office out front."

"All right. That's Mr. Lavin?"

Torrez nodded. "He ain't a very happy camper just now."

"I saw him sitting in the coaches' office when I came in. So Lavin just walked in here and there he was?"

"Yep."

The victim lay flat, his stature measured by the four-inch floor tiles. At six feet, four inches, he had towered over most folks with whom he was photographed, and Coach Clint Scott had been photographed often, loving the attention the media gave him. Estelle scanned the shower room again. There was no sign of struggle, no sign of fight or flight. No bar of soap sank or floated in the sea of water. No sodden towel had been tossed in a corner.

The man lay in four inches of water, blocking the drain, naked as he would be when taking a shower, hair plastered to his skull down to the waterline, where it then floated out in a brown halo.

"And you said that the shower was running when the victim was found?"

"That's what *he* says." The sheriff sounded dubious.

"And then? Lavin walked through here, right through the shower, around the body, and shut off the shower?"

"Nope. He says he went into the boiler room next door and shut off the main valves. He says he stopped at the shower entrance there, to one side, out of the water. Says he didn't step in, says he didn't track water around."

"Smart man. That shows an amazing presence of mind." Estelle looked back at the tiled locker room floor. Abundant prints marked the floor—a whole active volleyball team's worth, for starters. And then half a dozen cops. And somewhere in there, the killer.

In a moment, Tom Mears appeared at her elbow as she pulled on the blue latex gloves. He handed her the boots and set the camera bag on the end of one of the benches.

"We're going to need a piece of clean, new brass screen about eighteen inches square to cover the drain, LT. Flat, not all rolled up. Would you send someone to find that? Maybe give Jonas something to do."

She looked to the left, at the smear of blood on the wall between two of the showerheads, and then toward the center of the room where the corpse lay, the water around his body a garish deep pink aging to an amorphous brown. "Ay," she breathed and turned away. If Clint Scott craved privacy or dignity in death, he wasn't going to get it.

Sitting on the end of the bench, she shucked her shoes and pulled on the rubber boots, tucking her pant legs in, then slipped the sterile booties over the boots.

For a moment she regarded the contents of her camera bag before selecting a 24-70 mm zoom lens for her digital camera. With equipment in hand, she sat for another moment, regarding the locker room and the shower. She tried to sift through the cacophony of smells—the heavily chlorinated water now tinged with body wastes, the distinct aroma of burned gunpowder, and from the clothes that had been left on the bench, the strong odor of men's sports deodorant.

Retreating down the locker room, she shot a series of photos from as far away from the shower entrance as she could, and from both sides of the center locker row. Lieutenant Mears had placed an evidence tag on the bench near the folded clothes, and she recorded that collection from four directions.

At the shower, she stepped to the sill and shot a wide-angle view of the entire room, then zoomed in on the blood smear on the wall for a close-up. Again, she looked from it to the corpse, a good six feet from smear to drain.

Torrez and Perrone watched her work, without comment or impatience. They stood still, letting the water subside into a dull pane. She hated to disturb it. Moving slowly and making certain of each step in the four-inch-deep water, she crossed and stood near Clint Scott's feet. The coach had been a big, athletic man, sure enough, with broad shoulders, muscled chest, and flat belly. Approaching middle age, he'd kept his conditioning, his classical physique marred only by an old appendectomy scar and a more recent blemish above his right rotator cuff.

But now, surrounded by a pinkish-brown lake and collapsed in on himself, he looked more like a mannequin from a men's clothing store. He'd been at least that handsome, once upon a time.

Estelle documented the corpse from each side, then moved in for close-ups of each wound. She paused and looked over at Perrone. He stepped closer and squatted, careful to stay out of the water. "I'd start there," he said.

What appeared to be a heavy caliber bullet wound in the gut punctured three inches directly below the naval, dead center. The wound had bled profusely, soaking the crotch and thighs, indicating that the large arteries and veins of the groin had been lacerated open by the shot while the heart was still beating powerfully. Lots of pumping pressure there as quarts of blood gushed.

For certain, the groin gunshot all by itself would have been a fatal wound, giving Scott just a few seconds to stagger, doubled over in agony, toward the support of the wall two steps to his right—if he was facing the doorway when the shot was fired.

Estelle turned and looked at the doorway—six feet wide at the sill, a four-inch step. Had the killer stepped inside the shower room? Why bother? If Scott had been standing under the farthest shower, the one directly opposite the door, the shot would have been a scant ten feet. The blood smear, and what could have been a handprint, were off to the victim's right, half-way down the wall.

Had Scott recognized his assailant, and charged forward? Did he have time to do that? He might have thought about grabbing a towel, and might have made it to about the room's center when the first shot was fired. Estelle shook the image away. The natural tendency was to try and answer the "what happened" question before the survey of scene and the victim were completed.

"We need to ask Lavin which shower the victim was using." None of the showerheads were conveniently dripping.

"And then here," Perrone said softly. A second bullet appeared to have entered under the victim's left arm, forward of the armpit an inch or so, just visible past his biceps—likely if the assailant had fired even as Scott pitched toward the wall, groping for support, and in the process presenting his left side as a target opportunity. Without turning the victim over to search for an exit wound, there was no way to gauge where the bullet had rampaged, or what internal damage it had done. The wound near the arm was clearly a wound of entry, though—neat, almost round, about the size of a pencil eraser now with the elastic skin drawing in around the hole.

It could have happened that way, Estelle thought. "We'll call that number two."

And the damage continued. Another wound punctured the victim's right chest, just an inch or so to the right of the midline. If it had blown straight in, the slug would have missed his heart after punching through the heavy pectoral muscle, shattering ribs, and then likely macerating lung and liver. Or it could have angled to the victim's left, careening through the heart itself. She focused on the wound, noting the absence of powder flecks. The wound hadn't bled much, and she guessed that the gusher of even more vessels ripped apart had stayed within the vault of the chest cavity.

But if this was chronologically wound number three, the victim's blood pressure already would have been headed toward the basement. Maybe he was still standing, maybe on his way down. Any one of the three shots would have sent Scott sailing into a deep pit of shock and then unconsciousness, slammed to the floor of the shower, flat on his back.

Estelle squatted down, keeping her knees out of the water. She looked toward the far wall, where the shower might have been running. "If he started *there*, under the shower, and ended up *here,* he was out of the direct spray of the shower, even with it running." No one spoke. "So this is what we have. None of the four bullet wounds in the corpse are either under water, or in the spray. None of the entrance wounds, anyway."

She gazed at the blank look on the victim's face. No pain, no surprise, no anger. Just nothing. There was no doubt in her mind that he never felt the fourth wound, and she turned the camera on that. The shot had taken him in the center of his heart, and unlike the others, had been fired close enough that the corona of unburned powder granules marked the wound to the left of midline. The corona of powder stippling was circular, the size of a dinner plate. A single, tiny rivulet of blood—the sort of trail that might be produced by skin capillaries as the body's system pressure collapsed—oozed from the hole but did not cross the corona of powder residue.

Estelle stood to rest her knees, and glanced at the camera's battery icon displayed on the back. While she fished in her jacket pocket for another set of batteries, she said to Perrone, "Your thoughts?"

"Somebody wanted him *really* dead," Dr. Perrone observed. "I'm guessing that any one of the four shots would be fatal. I mean, this guy was quite the athlete, but this stopped him in his tracks. No fighting, no crouching in the corner, no trying for the doorway to escape, no defensive wounds." He glanced over at Torrez, who hadn't uttered a word. "Your shooter didn't want there to be any chance of his victim crawling away for help."

"No evidence that says he was given any chance at all," Estelle mused. "And to administer this last shot, the killer likely stood right over the victim. The corona is circular, not oval. Dead on. Maybe not for any of the other three, but for this one—he would have had to have stepped into the shower room. He would have stood right beside the victim. Or even straddled him."

"That's what I'm thinking," Perrone said. "That first shot, I'm guessing the one in the groin with all that blood, was certainly incapacitating—maybe even paralyzing if it broke the spine. Now, with someone hurt that bad? It takes a special sort of mindset to shoot again, and again. Seems that way to me. Cold, cold, cold."

Torrez pushed himself away from the wall, gloved hands still in his pockets. "Remember when Louise Smalley shot her husband out in their barn?"

Perrone peered at the sheriff over the top of his half glasses, puzzled at the reference to a decade-old crime. But then his face lit up. "I do, indeed."

"Louise shot until the gun was empty. *Sixteen* rounds in that nine millimeter of hers. Somewhere in that string, she managed to hit him once, and that did the job." He drilled a finger into his own left ear. "And the other fifteen went sailin' this way and that. She just kept goin' 'till the gun was empty. Bill Gastner had us measuring and searching all night until we found every one of those misses. 'Panic passion' he called it. She just kept jerkin' the trigger 'till the gun wouldn't fire any more. Some of the shots weren't even close—like *yards* away."

Torrez sidled closer to the corpse, little waves searching out from his boots. "Gotta wonder which shot was first, and I'm thinkin' same as you and Estelle. The groin shot threw blood all over. Even if the killer hadn't shot him again, he'd be dead in a

minute or two just from blood loss, floppin' around on the floor."
Torrez grimaced. "But it don't look like he flopped much. The
first shot, *bam,* he crumples and staggers away, makin' a mess
over on the wall. *Bam,* he spins around the way he came, and
starts to go down. Then *bam,* center mass puts him on his back."

"Look at the way his lower arms and hands have rictus, locked
upward as if he's trying to push something up and away," Perrone observed.

"That's right. And then the killer steps close and *bam,* the
fourth shot solid through the heart ends the story. Right then,
right there. Not much panic in *those* shots." Torrez made a
sound that could have been a chuckle. "This ain't no Mrs. Smalley runnin' in circles around the barn, chasin' after her drunk
husband through the cows and horses."

"That's grim." Perrone bent at the waist for a closer look.
"That's an interesting corona, and the only one. As you suggest,
it's as if the killer stood right over him for the last shot." He
looked up at Estelle. "Looked him right in the eye." He glanced
over his shoulder. "We going to get that screen?"

"Tom's on the way."

"Okay. I'm more than a little curious about what we'll find."
He straightened up. "Coach Scott has been teaching here a good
number of years, well-known and well-liked by a whole lot of
people. Big game last night…what, number sixty-five? And his
girls win another romp. Lots of press. And somebody pulls this
when the town is full of reporters. Big time mess. This is going
to a troublesome case before it's over."

"We'll keep it tight," Torrez said.

"Good luck with that." Perrone sounded skeptical.

"He started teaching just about the year I graduated," Estelle
offered. "Twenty-two years ago. I remember all the girl-talk
about him. Handsome, buff, single…*ay,* he was only four years
older than we were."

"Ah. Here we go." Perrone nodded toward the doorway. "So
you're putting him at what, forty-four or five? If this was his
first job out of college?"

Standing off to one side of the sill, Mears held out the square of screening. "This is what the hardware could come up with, Sheriff."

"Perfect." Estelle eased though the water and took the screen, bending the last of the rolled arc out of it until it would rest flat over the drain.

"And Mr. Lavin wants to know if he can go home yet. I told him not a chance."

"Not a chance is right. I need to talk with him. Ask him to be patient." She straightened up. "In your preliminary with him, find out who was the *last* person he saw leaving after the game last night. Maybe the assistant coach, Ms. Avila? Whoever it is, I'll want to talk with them. I saw Avila out in the parking lot. And find out if the game was filmed. If it was, I want the file… or disc—whatever they use."

"You got it. Oh," and Mears stopped short, "apropos of noth-ing…the SO in Cathay, Illinois is sending out two deputies to extradite the Bonds back home. Paperwork willing, they'll be here sometime next week."

"So much for their grand vacation," Estelle remarked.

She had squatted near the corpse, sleeves rolled up, the screen spread on the tile floor under four inches of water. "TOD here is going to be interesting," she said. "From after the game, when Scott was last seen, to just a few minutes ago, when he was found today by the custodian? That's a sixteen-hour window."

"The cold bath is going to complicate things a little," Perrone said. "But we'll see."

Estelle slid the screen closer to the body until she was satisfied that it would remain flat. "I think if you just slide his hips a foot or so up and over, we can do this. Don't roll him over yet. Just shift the body over far enough for me to slide the screen into place and make sure nothing slips by down the drain."

Sheriff Torrez straddled the body, a gloved hand on each hip. "Ready?"

"Yes."

Unable to work the way she was crouched, Estelle dropped to one knee. When she nodded, Torrez rocked the corpse up and away, giving her room to work. The victim's left buttock cheek was clearly imprinted with the pattern of the chrome drain cover. The screen slid into position, the powerful suction of the drain holding it in place. She stood up, ignoring her now soaked left leg. "Hold him up so I can catch that drain pattern on his butt," Estelle said. "I want the photo to include the victim, the screen, and the drain itself."

"Take your time." Torrez had braced his elbows on his knees, and watched impassively as she shot another series of photos.

"This is where I miss Linda."

"I hear ya," Torrez said affably. "Hell of a time to go on vacation."

Satisfied, she backed away. "Let him back down now." Torrez did so, and straightened up with a creak of backbone and leather. "You know, if the killer left here with the shower running…" she said after a moment.

"Lavin says it was still running when he arrived today," Torrez said. "He says that he walked in here just after noon, saw this mess, and called 911 right away. So the shower was runnin' since…could have even been yesterday a little bit after the game."

"And why would Scott use this one, anyway? There's a coaches' shower in their office." She shook her head. "This place wasn't full of steam, was it? Lavin will tell us for sure, but with the shower running hot for what, fifteen or twenty hours? It'd be pretty steamy ripe in here. The boiler would be working overtime. I didn't smell that when I came in."

"Hot, humid night, cold shower," Torrez offered with considerable skepticism. He shifted the body so it lay just to one side of the drain.

The water level in the shower took its time lowering, with an occasional gurgle from the drain. The screen remained clean. While she waited, Estelle shot more than a hundred digital photos of fragments as they became visible—and they were few and far between. Most were little chips of grout or tile, grouped below the wall that carried the blood smear. A deformed slug, its hollow point mushroomed deeply, lay six inches out from the wall.

"So we have one. Not enough flow to carry anything heavy to the drain," Estelle said. "Which means all the other bullet fragments are either still in the body or somewhere in this room. It's going to be hands and knees time, Bobby."

"Better'n scattered all through a barn."

Chapter Eleven

In deference to Estelle's first guess, the bullet tracks that had snuffed out Clint Scott's life were labeled one through four, beginning with the bloody groin shot and ending with the point blank round through the heart. Two of the wounds were through and through.

Number one had not exited, but showed huge bruising near the spine. Number two, the axillary wound, had entered on the left, then coursed across through the victim to plough a large, messy exit wound below his right arm at the back of his armpit. The third shot, dead on through the right chest, had not exited. "And even with a powerful handgun, that's not unusual," the physician said. "We'll find it during autopsy, probably snuggled up against the heavy spine of the shoulder blade, or maybe buried in a vertebra. No telling. But this…" He rested one hand on the victim's raised shoulder, pointing at the exit wound of the final heart shot.

"Unless what we think are obvious wound paths end up fooling us, I'm going to bet that this round blows straight through, just barely missing the spine, and then exits to smack into the floor tile." He touched a cracked, chipped portion of the tile a foot from the drain, still under an inch of water. "It hits here, still with some energy, ricochets up off the floor and enters the victim's upper back. In fact…" and he poked hard with two fingers at a spot near the wing of the shoulder blade, just beyond the wound carved by the ragged secondary entry of the ricochet.

"If you feel right there, I think that's number four *in situ.*" He drew patterns in the air. "Down, almost straight through, out, ricochet, back in again. It didn't penetrate very far after that."

He looked up at Bob Torrez who nodded, not appearing the least bit surprised.

"Essentially, the victim was thoroughly dead before number four. From the first three shots, his insides were just blown apart. The blood loss would have been huge, since his heart hadn't been altogether ruined yet. I mean, at this point, we don't know. Number two could have grazed the back of his heart on its way through. We won't know until autopsy. But after those first three shots, about all he could do, if he was conscious at all, was lie there and take it."

He relaxed his hold on the body and stood up with a middle-aged grunt, pushing a lock of blond hair back with his wrist. "When you find the gun, your ballistic tests will show how far away it was held for that final shot, but I'm guessing three or four feet, at the most." He pointed an index finger at the corpse and let his thumb drop. "Like that. Standing right beside him, and boom. Standing maybe on that side of the body, maybe this. I don't know, but it sure as hell spells *hate* to me."

The physician held out his hand to Estelle, who held the small evidence bag with the recovered bullet. "You know off the top what that is?"

She handed it without hesitation to Bob Torrez, who slipped a new acquisition from his pocket—half-glasses for close work. He peered at the slug, even as he had when they had found it near the base of the far wall. "I'm thinkin' either a .38 special or a .357 mag. Same bullet in either cartridge."

"Someone should have heard it," Estelle remarked.

"I'm kinda thinkin' .357, with all the damage. If it was just a .38, it was loaded hotter'n shit. Plus-P, probably. Somethin' like that." He looked at the bullet. "We got no shell casings ejected in here, so unless the killer picked up after himself, we're talkin' revolver. Ain't many autos that shoot either one. And you gotta wonder why just four rounds fired, in a weapon that holds five or six."

"He saved one or two for later," Perrone said with morgue humor. He held up both hands. "The victim has been lying in a nice deep pool of cold water, so TOD is going to be a little bit tricky. Lividity says this is where he fell and this is where he stayed."

Torrez nodded at Tom Mears, who had been standing in the shower doorway.

"I talked to the janitor for just a moment on the way in," Mears offered. "He said that when he was cleaning up after the game yesterday—last evening—he heard Scott call good night. So sometime between nine or so until Lavin found him this afternoon. That's our window."

Perrone nodded. "He's well into rigor, though. It wasn't as recent as even late this morning." He shrugged. "I'll tell you what I can after autopsy."

The physician reached out and shook hands first with Torrez and then Estelle, the clasp of rubber gloves making an unpleasant sucky sound. "Good luck with this. I don't envy you. I always thought Coach Scott was something of a primo don, but it's also my impression that he was well-liked. Worshipped by some of the kids, I'm sure. This is going to be hard. Maybe forty-four years old, but still vibrant. Still young enough to elicit some idol worship."

Lieutenant Mears stepped aside to let the physician pass. "Sheriff, Superintendent Archer is here and wants to see you."

"I bet he does," Torrez muttered, and Mears held up a finger. "And…"

"And what?"

"Coach Avila is here now, outside. And Frank Dayan is also here. Who do you want first?"

"Tell Frank to go home," Torrez snapped. "We ain't got nothin' for him."

"He won't leave like that, you know." The newspaper publisher could be counted on to complain, only half joking, that the Sheriff's Department had staged this event the day *after* the weekly *Posadas Register's* publication day, giving competing news organizations a week's head start on the scoop.

"With any luck, most everyone is still out at the mesa," Estelle said. "Miles was serving a fancy lunch. I'm surprised Frank chose to miss that."

Torrez glared at her as if she had notified the press. "What, he wants a picture of this on Page One?" The sheriff knew better than that, of course, but he'd never met a newspaper he would even wrap fish in, including the local *Posadas Register.* Estelle knew Torrez to be as adverse to publicity as Coach Clint Scott had cherished it.

"Tell Frank that I'll talk with him in a little bit," Estelle offered. "Make sure he stays outside the tape, though. Not a single footstep inside the school."

"Yes, ma'am. You want the superintendent first?"

"Just very briefly," Estelle said. "He has to know what we're up against here, and what *he's* going to be up against come school on Monday morning."

"You got it. We went through the clothes after we shot a bunch of pictures, by the way. Fiber by fiber. They appear to be the victim's. His wallet, ID, all that, still in place with about a hundred bucks in small bills, along with his car keys, a cell phone, and a pack of breath mints."

"Bag it all, Tom. Be especially careful with that phone. Messages or pictures, you never know what it's going to tell us."

"And you want his towel before Archer gets here?" He nodded at the bench where the white towel lay folded neatly by the clothing.

"A body bag will work better." She waited patiently until Mears appeared again, and they draped the corpse from head to toe under black vinyl. "Go ahead and send Archer back."

"It's going to be interesting to see how the rumor mill plays this one," Torrez said.

Chapter Twelve

Estelle left the shower to intercept Superintendent Glenn Archer back in the locker room. A gentle, warm-hearted man, he cherished his school. While no stranger to tragedy, this was the sort of brutal, senseless act that would haunt his dreams, and Estelle tried to think of a way to soften the blow. There was no way. Headlines all too often trumpeted this shooting tragedy or that, but Posadas had been mercifully spared over the years. Now the press would have a field day. Dr. Archer needed to be armed with blunt, unvarnished facts.

The superintendent walked down the row of lockers to meet Estelle and extended both hands as if greeting an old cherished friend…which was, in fact, the case. He had been principal of Posadas High School when the teenaged Estelle Reyes had arrived from Tres Santos, Mexico, for her final two years of high school. He remembered the current undersheriff of Posadas County as a shy, exquisitely beautiful youngster who had blossomed to graduate as salutatorian—whose heavy accent was polished in months until she became completely fluent, completely bilingual.

"This is awful," Archer said by way of greeting. "My God, I just spoke to Barry Lavin—this is terrible for him, walking in on something like this. What can you tell me?"

"Coach Scott was discovered shortly after noon by Mr. Lavin, sir. Coach was found dead in the girls' shower. He had been shot at least four times. When he collapsed, it appears that he fell on top of the drain, which accounts for the flooding."

"My God."

"My guess is that he was shot sometime late last night. That's Dr. Perrone's best preliminary guess. We have a time window from just after the game, when Barry Lavin last talked to the Coach Scott, until just after noon, when his body was found."

"My God."

She reached out and held his arm at the elbow. "Sir, we're going to need to talk with a number of people, and we'll start with Mr. Lavin. He's been very patient. Lieutenant Mears conducted a preliminary with him."

"Yes, absolutely. We'll do everything we can, certainly. My God. And think of his elderly parents…"

"If you would provide Coach Scott's contacts, we'd appreciate that."

"They're in Albuquerque, you know. His parents, I mean. Parents and two sisters, as I remember." He looked toward the shower. "Should I…?"

"It's not necessary, sir. The custodian already identified the victim, and of course, we all know him."

Archer didn't look relieved, but stood with both hands on the sides of his ruddy face as if fearful that his head might pop off his neck. "What happens now?"

"Sir, this building is absolutely off limits to students and personnel until we clear it. That may not come until early next week. It just depends."

"Oh, my. I think it would be best just to close school for a couple of days, come Monday, don't you?"

"That would work best on all accounts."

He leaned against a locker, his face gray. "No one saw anyone…?"

"We don't know that yet, sir."

"Of course. Of course." He looked back toward the coaches' offices, his head shaking slowly. "Is there anything you need?"

"Thank you, sir. We have the State Police Crime Lab unit on the way. They have some facilities that we lack. I have to confess that we're not hopeful that something magical will pop up to clear all this, but still. We'll take any assistance we can get."

"Should I…?" he hesitated, not able to frame the words of what he should do.

"It would be helpful if you would remain on campus and available. Everyone else is in Lordsburg today for the conference, and that's a big help, keeping the facility clear. But if you would stay? We may need keys to access various parts of the building that our master doesn't open, and we'll need employee information. If you'd be in your office for a while?"

"Certainly, certainly. As I said, I spoke just briefly with Mr. Lavin on my way in. He's most distraught. I'm wondering if he might need some medical attention."

"We'll see. The EMTs are just outside across the parking lot, if need be. We're going to need his cooperation, painful as that may be for him."

"I'm sure…no doubt of that."

"But for now, we're isolating him in the office."

"You don't think that he…?"

"At this early stage, we go one careful step at a time. And, sir…if we're not careful, this is going to turn into the worst kind of media circus. The press is in town in a big way, number one because of the game last night, and second because of the *NightZone* train deal. The most popular coach in the state found murdered the day after the game is going to dump lots of fuel on the fire."

She looked hard at the superintendent, forcing his attention. "The press will want to talk with you. For right now, I'm going to ask that you stick to the simplest script. Do *not* let yourself be drawn into a discussion of the crime scene, or the investigation. Sir, you *know* that somebody is going to ask you what you think. Could the killer have been a jilted lover, could it have been an angry fan of the visiting team? Could it have been robbery? Could it have been this or that? Please, sir. Just stonewall. Refer questions to me or to Sheriff Torrez. You might take a minute and compose a stock answer for the phone calls when they come. And they certainly will."

"Coach *Scott.*" Dr. Archer shook his head in disbelief. "Such a talented man. Such an asset to the school." He heaved a deep breath and straightened. "This is going to be hard, Estelle. His second grade class—*they* won't understand something this horrible. His team, his friends on the faculty…my God."

"Yes, sir. It would be helpful if you'd pull his personnel files for us."

"Certainly."

Her cell phone vibrated. The text message from Lieutenant Tom Mears was brief. "Coach Avila to the SO now. After we finish here, I'll start the process with her. We have the game DVD as well."

The superintendent thrust out both hands and folded Estelle's right hand in his. "You'll call me? For absolutely *anything?*"

"Count on that, sir. And sir, be careful of what you tell Frank Dayan. He's a local, he's a friend, and the tendency will be to discuss this tragedy prematurely. Stick to the same statement with him that you give the others."

"Frank?" Archer looked stunned, as if suddenly realizing that the school was going to be Page One news—and not celebratory cheering, either. The story would swell until even the national anchors would wallow in it.

"I was told he's waiting outside. At this point, we don't know any details."

"And nor do I." He grimaced, closed his eyes, and shook his head. "I should see the crime scene, I suppose. I don't want to, but I suppose I should. Someone from the school should."

"If that's what you wish, I'll escort you down there, but ask that you don't step in the water, or into the shower room itself, sir." Her tone took on an edge. "And *do not* discuss the crime scene with anyone else. I mean that literally, sir. Not with your secretary, not with Mrs. Archer, not with Frank, not with AP or UPI when they call. Not with any of the television or radio crews." She squeezed his arm. "We can't afford that sort of complication just now."

She hooked an arm through his and led him toward the shower, feeling the resistance in every step. A man now in his mid-sixties, he moved as if he were ninety. He reached out his free hand and grasped the side of the doorway when they reached the showers.

"Evenin', Glenn," Sheriff Torrez said as if they had casually met on the street corner for a chat. With surprising daintiness, Torrez reached down and peeled the body bag away just far enough to expose all four wounds.

"Oh, my God." Archer's voice was muffled behind his hand clasped over his mouth. "Who would…?" He shook his head, staring at the corpse for a long moment before his eyes wandered around the shower room. "All of this is just beyond my comprehension. Just unbelievable." He turned away, his head still shaking. "You know," he said to Estelle, "the school is such a closed community. And we try to keep it that way. We know the world is full of all kinds of horrors, but I think sometimes we embrace the old *NIMBY* so much that when something does happen, some awful thing like this…"

The torrent of words stopped as suddenly as it had begun. He ducked his head, jaw slack. Estelle thought for a moment that he was about to vomit. He shook his head helplessly again. "Thank God kids weren't in school. That they didn't see him like this."

He reached out a hand and took Estelle by the elbow. "I'll be in my office until you say otherwise." He tried to smile. "Any little thing you need, and no worries about the hour. I have a sofa. Just let the phone ring. Of course, who's going to sleep?" He started to turn away, then stopped.

"The last time I spoke with Mr. Scott…on Monday, I think. I mean I went to the game last night, too, but had to leave a few minutes early. The score was like twenty-five to two, and Coach Scott had every second- and third-string player off the bench to play. He gave the visitors every chance. But, anyway, last Monday, he was in his classroom, with those *tiny* second graders. Of course, they looked even smaller because Mr. Scott is such a big man. He was down on the floor, on his hands and knees, making a game out of some arithmetic concept. He had three of the kids hanging off him as if he were their private pony or something."

Archer tried to laugh. "He told me afterward that this was his last year for second grade. 'Too hard on the back,' he tells me." Archer shook his head slowly. "'Too hard on the back.' He's requested a transfer to high school. He has the certification, so why not? Work where you're happy. The elementary program will hate to see him go." Archer's face crumpled when he remembered that Clint Scott was not going to transfer anywhere.

Chapter Thirteen

Leaving the sheriff and Lieutenant Tom Mears to finish with the preliminary survey, including more blood and tissue samples from the swath on the wall and a complete survey of the locker room itself, Estelle found a fretting Barry Lavin in the coaches' office. He was no longer sitting, but paced nervously as if he'd been corralled inside an electric fence.

"Mr. Lavin, thanks for being so patient." She shook hands with him and found his grip cold and clammy.

"Probably don't have much choice, right?" His grim smile showed teeth that ended with the first pre-molars. "I told the lieutenant everything I know, so…"

Estelle sat down in a swivel chair, pulling it out from behind the desk, and waved Lavin toward a heavy wooden chair. Surveying the three teachers' desks, all relics from half a century ago, she asked, "So which of these is Coach Scott's?"

"His office is on the other side of the building. Outside the boys' lockers. Him and Head Coach Harvey and Coach Avila. Coach *Emilio* Avila, I mean. When he's got work to do in here for volleyball, he uses Coach Marilee's desk on this side. That way, nobody needs to go huntin' for him." Lavin pointed at the desk beside Estelle. "Emilio's better half. Marilee is, I mean." Pulling out a hideously dirty handkerchief, he blew his nose loudly, then regarded the cloth distantly, as if he really didn't see it. "Never seen *nothing* like this." He shook his head, clearly not referring to the hanky.

Estelle withdrew her notebook. "So tell me what happened from the final game buzzer onward."

He ran a hand through thinning hair. "Well, like I told the lieutenant, we deal with the mess. We start up in the gym, push the bleachers in, run the big floor mop and bag up all the crap. Volleyball ain't too bad. Nowhere near the draw of basketball. With a small crowd, it don't take long."

"You say 'we.'"

"Oh. I mean *me*."

"How long does it take to finish the gym?"

"Not so long. Push the bleachers in, wheel the net supports back out of the way, roll the net...then run the chem mop. Maybe half an hour."

"Then?"

"By then the kids are finished down in the locker room. Visitors are over on the boys' side, our gals over here. I can hear 'em." He rolled his eyes. "I mean our kids. Whoopin' and hollerin'. They are the *noisiest* flock of chicks you ever heard. I can *hear* 'em in the locker, in the showers..." He hesitated, then continued, "When they run screechin' down the hall to outside. And then the cars drivin' away. I'm out by the front doors then." He grinned. "Tryin' to keep some peace in the parkin' lot. And I gotta say good night, you know. I've known these kids since they were..." and he held a hand three feet off the floor. "When I drove the activity bus, you know. You see 'em all day, every day, over the years. You get to know 'em."

"I would imagine so."

He looked at her sideways, slyly. "I know your two, Sheriff. That younger one, he's a pistol. Asked me a couple weeks ago if he could run the floor waxer." He laughed a brief cough. "I can see it, the orbital standin' still and old Carlos whippin' around, hangin' on to the handles for dear life."

"You said no, I hope."

He smiled as if to say, "silly question," but instead said, "I don't think there's a single thing on this earth that he *isn't* interested in."

Estelle felt the acute pang of knowing that when she returned home, she would have to find a way to explain Coach Scott's death to her son, who had enjoyed immensely his second grade year with Clint Scott just three years before.

"So the spectators leave, then the team leaves."

"Yup, except for a few parents waitin' out in the parkin' lot for the slow ones."

"Then?"

"Then Coach Marilee follows the last girls out. Always does. She don't leave until they're all gone."

"Did she speak to you?"

"Said good night. I told her to enjoy the day off. Don't think she thought that was funny. That teachers' workshop thing, you know. I saw her out in the parking lot a bit ago, so I guess she didn't attend over in Lordsburg." He shrugged.

"And then? After the last one is gone?"

He regarded his hands carefully, brows furrowed. "Then I go back in and polish the hall floor. Got some little stinker who likes to kick black marks along the floor tile. Can't let that stay, so I polished the hall. Done with that, put the polisher away, and checked the doors. The doors to the locker room are closed and locked, and I holler 'good night' to Coach Scott, 'cause I can see the light is on in the office. He hollers back for me to have a good weekend."

"He stayed behind when you left?"

"Yeah." Lavin hesitated. "That ain't unusual. He's got to call the game in to the newspapers…with this winnin' streak the Jags got goin', there's some interest in this little old backwater place." He leaned forward, resting his elbows on his knees. "You know, those were the last words I ever heard him say. 'Have a good weekend.'"

"And you're sure it was his voice you heard?"

Lavin looked puzzled. "Of course, I'm sure."

"So as far as you're concerned, the building is locked up, and all is quiet when you leave. And Coach Scott is hard at work in this office."

"That's right. And he ain't one to ignore the newspapers or TV, that's for sure."

"Everything locked. Even the back door."

"Especially that one, 'cause the locks don't work like they should. That's why we have the chain around the push bars. That latch is worn, and it's just as apt to stick open as closed."

"I remember those when I was here a hundred years ago."

Lavin smiled. "Ain't been *that* long, Sheriff. Now, *I* was here a hundred years ago, and I remember when this scared little Mexican kid started here." His eyes crinkled, and Estelle purposely avoided the urge to reminisce.

"So," and she pointed first at the doors outside the office, "locked, locked up in back, and locked out front."

"Yup."

"And the doors on the other side of the building?"

"Locked. I checked 'em soon as the last of the spectators and visiting team left."

Estelle regarded him thoughtfully, and he met her gaze, his eyebrows finally lifting as if to say, "So? Now what?"

"When I walked down the hall a few minutes ago, I could look up the back team stairway and see the back doors." The "team" stairway, identical to the one just inside the front foyer, allowed teams, or physical education classes, to run directly from the locker room up to the gymnasium, bypassing all the classrooms.

"Yes, ma'am."

"The chain is not locked now."

He looked as if she'd slapped him. "'Course it is." He rose from his chair.

"Show me."

Chapter Fourteen

They left the coaches' office and once in the hallway turned right, up the stairs. The outside doors were closed, the hand bar closed, but the chain hung loose, the large padlock open.

"Please don't touch," Estelle said quickly as Lavin reached out toward the lock.

Lavin backed up a step, and stabbed a finger at the offending door. "This door was *locked*. I know it was."

She peered through the door's wire-mesh glass. A sidewalk circled the building, and ten feet out from the sidewalk, a chain-link fence skirted the parking lots.

"I open it in the morning, when school is underway, and lock it up at night. Fire marshals would have a cow if they knew it was chained up during school hours with this place full of kids. Can't do that, 'cause if it's chained, you can't get in, you can't get out. First thing in the morning—maybe about seven—I open it. Last thing in the day, I lock it."

"Last night, after the game, after everyone has gone, you checked this door?"

"I did."

"Rattled the chain, checked the lock?"

He looked uncomfortable. "Nope. I *looked*. I mean it's pretty obvious if that big old lock is undone, doncha think?"

"I would think so."

"Besides, the chain wasn't hangin' down like that. It was snugged up proper."

"Mr. Lavin, I hope you're impressed with how important this is," Estelle said gently. "Someone either stayed behind in this building after everyone else had left—someone *besides* Coach Scott—or someone entered, perhaps through this door. Maybe they were invited. Maybe not. But if it's at all related to the homicide, we have to know with complete certainty."

He squared his shoulders a little, adding an inch to his five-foot-seven. "Look, Sheriff, I know when I got to cover my ass and when I don't." He pointed with authority, stabbing the air, indicting the door and its sagging chain and lock. "That door was locked secure Wednesday night. I know it was, 'cause I opened it first thing on Thursday morning. I locked it Thursday night after the game, after everybody left. Period. End of story."

"Who has keys other than you?"

"There's a set on the keyboard in the principal's office. Central office, for sure. Coach Harvey's got one, bein' head coach for football and track." He paused. "And Coach Scott has one."

"Would he have any reason to unlock this at the end of the day…once you'd made sure it was secure?"

"Can't think of one." He shot a sidelong glance at Estelle. "You're sayin' that he let someone in?"

"I'm not suggesting anything, Mr. Lavin." She pulled the small phone off her belt and touched the autodial for Tom Mears. "Lieutenant, I'm on the landing by the back door. Have you finished the print survey out here?"

"Yes, ma'am."

"When you checked back here, was the door open at that time? What was the position of the chain and lock?"

"It was hanging loose, Estelle. I photographed the whole deal, tried for some prints, especially off the push bar, but there were so many people around, the prints aren't going to mean anything. I have one or two from the brass lock, just partials. Unless there's something else you found," Mears replied.

"The back door. It was apparently unlocked sometime *after* the game."

"We processed inside and out."

"What a mess. With the game, there's going to be herds of people in and out. We're not going to be able to separate anything out."

"Well, it's worth a try," Mears said. "By the way, you know that photo of the tagger art that's circulating from this morning? From the *NightZone* railcar?"

"I have a copy."

"Right. They got almost the same thing on the back wall of the school. Go out that back door and you'll see it on the wall. They didn't finish, but got a good start on it. It's high enough up that they would have had to have used a ladder."

Estelle fell silent, digesting that. "I haven't been out there yet. I'll look now. You took photos of the graffiti?"

"Yep. I mentioned it to the sheriff, but he wasn't too excited about it. Did you have a chance to read Bishop's report on that MVA last night? The one with the Garcia kid?"

"I saw that."

"A ladder he had stowed in the truck bed went through the back window when he smacked into the utility pole. Bishop found two spray paint cans rolling around in the truck bed, and a backpack with several more in the cab. I told Bishop to follow up on it and talk with the kid whenever he can. He's in sad shape, though."

"Bishop should do that sooner rather than later," Estelle said.

"You got it. I told the sheriff about the back door being open."

"An easy invite."

"Yup. By the way, I left the area to meet with Coach Avila and her husband down here at the office. You'll want to talk with her. And there's a video you need to see."

"Of the game?"

"A little more than that, considering the circumstances."

"I'll be just a few minutes more. Thanks, LT."

She beckoned Lavin. "The lieutenant says that you have problems with graffiti." Using her elbow, she pushed the left side of the double doors open. The shade was cool behind the building. She held the door for the custodian. "Stop here on the concrete, sir."

"Now and again we get the taggers, but we clean it up right away." Lavin saw the partial art panel, spread across the difficult surface of the brick. "Well, shit." He stepped back and regarded the work, his face beet red. The spray painted rendition was complex, even though obviously unfinished, a genuinely artistic mix of rich colors, predominantly yellow, green, and black, with high lights of blue, red, and purple. The tagger had managed to finish only one corner, with a few outlining strokes promising much more.

"This is something new, then?"

"Yeah, it's new. I check out here all the time. Kids like to smoke out here, you know. Makes a goddamn mess. It wasn't here earlier in the week, I know that. Most of the time, they like to hit the back walls of the two portables that face the parking lot. Smoother and easier to paint, I guess. "

"How about last night?"

"Couldn't tell you. I didn't step out here last night."

"This looks like it would take a small fortune in spray paint by the time it's finished," she said. By reaching upward, she could touch the bottom border of the rhomboid design. The paint was fresh, but dry. She broke the skin of a tiny rivulet of over-run, and the color was still tacky. *An easy match,* she thought. Sergeant Howard Bishop was a methodical man, and he would have collected the paint cans from the wrecked truck from the night before.

"Gettin' this off the brick is going to be a son of a bitch." Lavin's head wobbled from side to side. "They think that's all we got to do, is clean up after 'em."

"This is a good spot to choose," Estelle said, more to herself than Lavin. "Odds are good they wouldn't be seen working at night, but it's up high enough that people driving by would see it come daylight. They didn't have a chance to finish. A long way to go, in fact."

"I ain't no art connoisseur." Lavin punctuated the word with considerable venom.

Estelle palmed her phone again, this time reaching Bob Torrez. "Yep."

"Bobby, if you have a minute, can you come out back?"

"Yep. I'm lockin' this place down, anyway. EMTs took the body, but the SPs won't be able to come for a while. I think we got it covered. Interesting tracks, but ain't much else to go on." The sheriff didn't elaborate, but Estelle knew that he would, at the appropriate time.

As she waited for him, she moved away from the wall, all the way back to the chain-link fence. The sun on the fence was so warm she could smell the hot steel. Lavin remained on the concrete step in the shade of the school, watching the under-sheriff's every move.

When she happened to glance his way, he shook his head. "I ain't sayin' to ignore it," he said, "but it seems like you got bigger problems inside. A good man dead, I wouldn't think you'd care much about some penny ante vandalism. That's more our problem than yours."

"I agree," Estelle replied. "Except for the timing." She rubbed her hands together. "Everything points to the tagger—or *taggers*— being here last night. You have loud gunshots *inside*, in the quiet of the night. Somebody *outside* might have heard something, even with the shots muffled by the building. This paint isn't cured, which means the tagger was here recently. Maybe last night after the game." She studied Lavin for a moment, and he looked away. "And didn't finish. Something interrupted his work."

"Hadn't thought that way." He looked up at the graffiti with fresh interest. "You gotta wonder. They carryin' their own ladder around now?"

"That may be exactly what they're doing."

"Well, that's up there a ways." He snorted. "Next thing you know, they'll be drivin' around in a bucket truck like the power company so they can reach the high spots. What a god-damn…" Lavin chopped off the curse as the sheriff appeared in the doorway, opening the door with his elbow against the upper corner of one of the glass panes.

"Huh." Torrez regarded the graffiti. "Mears told me about this. Sometime since when?"

"The paint is still tacky in some of the thick runs," Estelle said. "With the dry, hot weather, it had to have been recently. I'm thinking maybe even last night. They wouldn't work during the daytime. I'm curious about why they didn't finish."

Torrez watched Estelle as she took several photos, including a series of the two deep scuff marks where the ladder's legs had dug into the gravel.

"After the game, maybe. They'd run the risk of being seen any earlier. Sometime during the night. And there's a possibility that they saw or heard something. Maybe heard what was going on inside."

Torrez looked dubious. "One thing we ain't got time to do is chase taggers all over town." He let his breath out in an exasperated hiss.

"You saw Bishop's report on the MVA last night?"

"The Garcia kid? Yeah." She saw the flash of connection cross his handsome face. "Well, shit."

"Bishop will check the contents of the truck. But so far, we have a ladder, and we have spray paint cans. And the timing fits."

Torrez glowered at the wall, eyes narrowed. "That little rat." He turned and nodded at Estelle. "Did you talk to Waddell in the past few minutes?"

"No. Did everything go all right with the train ride this morning?"

"I guess. I ain't heard otherwise. But he's got one of these up top." Torrez nodded at the graffiti. "Right on the face of the big dish."

Estelle stared at the sheriff in astonishment, and he shrugged. "That's what he says. I was thinkin' of takin' a run out that way after a bit. I don't really give a shit about what some tagger's been up to, but the drive will give me some time to think."

"It's not like that dish is just sitting out in the middle of the prairie unguarded, Bobby. That's serious trespass. They cleared the chain-link and all?"

"Yep. That ain't a big deal for some little squirrel."

Estelle stood still for a moment, gazing at the graffiti. "Maybe they'll be back here tonight to finish," she mused.

"Not with all the cops around," Torrez grunted. "And not if it was the Garcia kid. He's beat up pretty bad. If he's the tagger here, he ain't going to paint *anything* for a long time." He turned his back on Lavin and lowered his voice even more. "We're gonna do another sweep in the shower when things dry out, but what we got now is the one slug that hit the wall, and a few chips of tile that cracked off. Nothin' else until Perrone is finished with the autopsy. Nothin'."

He stretched up to his full height. "Remember, like you ain't got enough to do, we got us a mom that's gone missing on top of everything else. Where are you headed now?"

Estelle hooked her hand through Torrez' elbow and walked him to the corner of the building, out of Lavin's earshot. "When I'm finished with Lavin, I need to talk with Coach Avila. And LT says that I need to look at the game video. I don't know what he's found."

"Some bad guy sittin' in the bleachers, givin' Scott the evil eye?"

"Who knows, Bobby. I'll tell you one thing…we don't need Coach Scott's last moments going viral on the Internet."

"Who shot the video? Don't one of the kids usually run the game camera?"

"There you go. My point, exactly. The contents of that camera chip could already be spread around the world via Twitter, Facebook, YouTube, you name it. Maybe we'll be lucky and catch it before that happens. That means talking to the camera kid to make sure he hasn't burned a copy."

Torrez shook his head slowly, frowning at Estelle. "Tell him that if you see anything from the game tape showin' up on the Internet, we're going to put his sorry ass in jail." He glanced back toward the doorway. "I keep bein' reminded that Frank Dayan is outside. You want to talk to him on your way?"

"I'll make it a point." Estelle was surprised that the sheriff had given any thought at all to the editor's presence. "And I'll make sure that I touch bases with Leona as well. I'm surprised she's not standing at the front door right now, pounding on the glass."

"She does that, and *her* sorry ass will end up in jail," he harrumphed, but he softened it with the faintest of grins. "Maybe she's learned a few things over the years."

"Maybe." But surely, Estelle thought, County Manager Leona Spears would not be denied basic information that *she* could feed to the hungry press. "Give me a few minutes with Lavin to finish up."

Torrez held out a hand to stop her as she started to turn. "We looked hard down in the locker room. Lavin ain't cleaned the locker room yet, like he usually does right after a game. He was fixin' to do it today. We got footprints on the tiles, all over the place, most likely from the girls."

The sheriff locked his fingers through the chain-link fence and rocked it gently in frustration. "The killer didn't step in the water that was runnin' when he fired that last shot, and then he didn't track it over the dry tile floor in the locker room. We ain't going to get that lucky. We looked everywhere that the overflow wouldn't have flushed away. Scott didn't step out of the shower to greet his visitor, or to grab a towel and cover up. I'm thinkin' that whoever shot him just did it before Scott had any chance at all. He might have been able to take a couple of steps—about from the shower to the center floor drain—before the first shot was fired. And that was it."

"It looks that way."

"What I'm sayin' is that there didn't look to be no conversation goin' on before the shots. No threats, no negotiations, no nothin'."

"And that's unusual. Shooters usually have to work up the courage to pull the trigger."

"Yep." He glanced over at Lavin. "I got some things I got to do, so when you're finished, lock up with a sheriff's seal. Ain't no doubt that we're going to be spending more time back in here. Perrone said he'd push the autopsy as fast as he could. Tox is going to take forever, but I'm thinkin' that's not going to tell us much. Not this time. We might get some help from the State Police, but it ain't going to be before tomorrow."

Chapter Fifteen

The custodian had his back to them, gazing out into space, studiously avoiding the appearance of eavesdropping. As Estelle approached, he glanced at his watch. She opened the outer door for him and beckoned.

"You want everything locked up now?" he asked.

"Do what you usually do." She watched as he made a great show of snugging the interior chain tight, snapping the hefty lock in place.

"Ain't nobody comin' in now," he said. "You folks going to need a key?"

"If we don't already have one, we'll borrow one from Dr. Archer." She steered him gently toward the stairs. "Tell me what you did today, when you found the body. What time was that?"

"Look, you don't need to tell Dr. Archer this. I took the morning off. Well, that ain't true. I decided I was gonna take the *day* off. But then I come in right around lunchtime, maybe. The *front* door. I was feelin' a little guilty that I hadn't cleaned the showers and locker room, see. Each time they're used, we disinfect 'em. Squeegee down the tiles, spray the floor. It don't take long, and I was going to do that so they wouldn't sit dirty over the weekend, both sides. Boys' and girls'."

They walked down the stairs and stopped in front of the locker room doors. "These doors were locked when you came in today?"

"Yes. But unless you shoot the pin to lock 'em *open*, they always lock by themselves. Never had trouble with 'em."

"Then…"

He pulled the right-hand door open, away from the rubber stop on the floor. "I went in, and right away, I could hear the shower running." He held out a hand as if leading the way to the locker room, but remained rooted in place. "I walk in, and I see water's overflowing out onto the main locker room floor, the river headed right to the floor drain, and I think, *What the hell?* And I go to see, stayin' clear of the water overflow, and there's coach lyin' in the middle of the shower room floor, naked as a jaybird, right over the drain, water just like Niagara Falls comin' out over the threshold. It looks like he's floatin' in the Red Sea or something. And it don't take no rocket scientist to see that he's got to be dead. I mean, *dead.*"

"Did you enter the shower room?"

"Not me. Not this kid. I know better'n that. I mean, I knew there wasn't a damn thing I could do for him."

"But the shower was still full on?"

He nodded vigorously. "But I'm not about to go sloppin' through four inches of water to turn it off. I know better. So I just go into the boiler room and shut things down."

"Just the one showerhead?"

"Well, sure. Just the one. Hell of a lot of water, though. Them are those old-fashioned institutional showerheads with a hell of a flow. Damn near knock you down."

"And you didn't step into the shower room, maybe walk around the body? To turn off the water."

"Nope." He nodded vehemently. "I already told you I didn't. I *know* better than that, see. Just turn it off in the boiler room."

"When you left on Thursday night, when you last spoke with Coach Scott, would you have been able to hear the showers if they had been running?"

"'Course. They weren't. And I could tell from his voice that he was just workin' in the office. I could hear him talkin' on the phone."

"Show me where you turn the showers off."

"Right in through here." Across the locker room foyer, across from the coaches' offices, Lavin opened a plain, gray steel door with a No Admittance sign. The hardware all looked decades old but spotless, and he bent down near the far wall. He touched a large bright-blue valve. "This right here? All it does is control cold water to the showers and the bathrooms. That's why it's painted blue. On, off. That's all. Just cold."

He dropped his hand down to another valve six inches below, this one red. "This one controls the hot water. It's regulated at one-eighteen degrees. That's kinda low, but we don't want kids scalded. You can see that they're both off now. You want 'em turned on?"

"In a minute. Who has access to all this besides you?"

"Just the boys in maintenance. Them and me, we got the only keys to this door."

She looked back through the door toward the office. "I'm puzzled why Coach Scott would have used the main shower room. Don't they have a single shower in the coaches' office?"

Lavin stared at the floor. "Well, that's our fault, Sheriff. See, there's a leak somewhere with that little unit. It's leakin' down behind the wall someplace. We're going to have to tear a section of wall out, and…well, we just ain't got to it yet."

"So he doesn't walk around to the other side of the building to use the facilities in the boys' locker room? Over where his own office is?"

"Well, I guess he *could*. But sure as hell, this time he didn't. Maybe he likes the smell of perfume or something."

The last comment surprised Estelle, and she looked hard at Lavin.

He added quickly, "I mean, a lot of 'em, kids and coaches both, don't shower here at all. Lots of kids would rather go home a little stinky and use their own bath, you know what I mean?"

"Exactly." Estelle remember her own aversion to the gang showers.

"So you saw the body, went and turned off the water, and called 911."

"Yep. That's exactly what I done."

"You didn't check the body for signs of life, *then* call for help?"

"Nope. I ain't touchin' *nothin'*. I've been a hunter all my life, been in the service. I know what the hell bullet holes look like." He rubbed his own chest as if chasing away sympathetic pains. "And I know what *dead* looks like. Somebody did the coach in proper. CPR wasn't going to help." He sucked in a hard breath and pointed at the water control valves. "Unless you guys have messed with 'em back at the showerhead, if I turn on those two valves, away we go. The shower's going to be on, still. Just the way he left it."

Movement behind her drew Lavin's attention, and Estelle turned to see the sheriff standing quietly in the boiler room doorway.

"We're wrapped," he said. "State's going to send down a two-man team in the morning if they can." He nodded in question at the valves.

"Mr. Lavin, in just a minute or two, I'm asking you to put the main control valves where they normally would be," Estelle said.

"No problem."

"I want photos of the spray pattern," Estelle said to Torrez. "We need to know how far out the spray goes onto the shower room floor. Mr. Lavin, will you wait here, please?"

"Sure. I got all day. All night, too, if you need it."

She patted his arm at the sarcasm. "I know. We're going to be upsetting a lot of people with this investigation. But I'm sure you understand how important this all is."

As the two officers returned through the locker room, they heard the loud hiss of the shower.

"Two possibilities," Estelle said to Torrez. "And either one is going to shed some light."

With camera in hand, she stopped at the shower entrance. The showerhead directly across the shower room launched its large stream with gusto.

Chapter Sixteen

Traces of fingerprint powder marked the chrome handles, and with a gloved finger, Estelle turned the cold water control by touching the very tip of the handle. It rotated closed easily from the full open position, and the flow dripped to a stop. "Cold on, hot off," she mused.

Torrez, who had not stepped into the room, said, "Hot, stuffy evening, got to be double-stuffy in here after the team's done. Cold shower might feel good."

"Scott was using number five, right here in the middle of the back wall." Estelle looked toward the sheriff, who stood with one boot up on the threshold. "Suppose the shooter appeared where you're standing now. Coach is at the farthest point from the door, but natural enough. The spray reaches out halfway to the drain." She turned the cold water on again, marked where it sprayed the floor tiles, and turned it off. She waited for the final drip to stop, then stood directly under the showerhead, where the main body of spray would be.

"So he's standing here. The killer appears in the doorway. What would the normal person taking a shower do when company suddenly appears?"

"Gotta wonder why he wouldn't turn his back to the door and then maybe turn off the water," Torrez replied. "Try to figure out how he was going to get to his towel, out there on the bench. Unless he's some sort of exhibitionist."

"That would be the expected thing."

"Unless he expected his visitor to join him." Torrez grimaced down at the floor and shook his head. "Somethin' goin' on here we don't understand, Estelle."

"You think?"

"Yeah. I think." He didn't laugh at the frustrated amusement in Estelle's voice. "In the first place, the coaches got their own shower in the office up front. Same on the other side. Why would Scott parade all the way down here to the girls' gang shower?"

"That's an interesting choice of words, Bobby."

"What?"

"Why would he *parade* down here. His clothes were folded neatly out on the bench, so we could assume he undressed right there. For one thing, Lavin tells me that the coaches' shower back in the office is out of commission just now. So it's either this one or walk around the building, through the cafeteria and all that, over to the boys' side. And on top of that, is *he* the one who made sure the back door was open and inviting?"

She surveyed the shower room, the aroma of the heavily chlorinated water just starting to overshadow the other smells, and then glanced at her watch. "Before we turn him loose, let's talk with Mr. Lavin again, Bobby."

"What are you thinkin'?"

She shook her head quickly. "My mind is scrambled. Maybe with the two of us…" She didn't add that, even though tact wasn't his strong suit, the sheriff's intimidating presence might shake some small memory loose from the custodian. "And when we've done about all we can do here, I need to know what Coach Avila has to say."

Barry Lavin was sitting in the coaches' office, chair leaned far back against the wall, his scuffed brown work shoes propped on the edge of Coach Avila's desk. At the sight of Estelle and the sheriff, he snapped his feet off the desk and leaned forward in the chair, hands clasped tight over his belly as if he'd eaten something that didn't agree.

"We appreciate your cooperation, Mr. Lavin. We're just about finished up here, but this building will be sealed and off-limits for the weekend, at least. The State Police Crime Lab is on the way to give us a hand." Estelle sat in one of the wooden chairs, but Torrez stood in the center of the doorway, one shoulder against the jamb.

"We're puzzled." Estelle leaned toward Lavin, elbows on her knees. "I need your help with something. The hot water in the shower was off, just the cold on. That's not so unusual, the weather being what it is. Do you have any idea how many gallons a minute those showerheads run?"

"You mean like full on?"

"Yes."

"Don't know. They're no water-savers, that's for sure. Old-fashioned, but we've never had no problems with 'em. They get cleaned regularly, that's one reason."

"What's your best guess?"

Lavin pushed out his lower lip in thought. "Three gallons a minute, maybe. Take a five-gallon bucket and count would be the easiest way."

Estelle frowned and sat back in her chair. "That still wouldn't tell us anything. I mean, let's say that once the drain was plugged it might take two hours to fill the shower room with four inches, until it overflowed over the sill." She shrugged. "That doesn't get us anywhere. You talked to Coach Scott for the last time at what time?"

"Be right at ten o'clock last night, when I was leavin'."

"*Ten* o'clock. And you found him just after noon today."

"Just about."

"All right. That's a window of fourteen hours. The water fills the shower room, and overflows down to the next drain in the locker room. All that could have happened by midnight. And then it just runs all night, and all the next morning. We don't know." She took a deep breath. "This is what puzzles me, Mr. Lavin. You personally chained and locked the back door at the end of the day yesterday. After the game, after everyone *except* Coach Scott had left."

"That's what I did."

"So it follows that unless there was someone else with a key to the padlock in the building, Coach Scott would have been the one to unlock the back door." When Lavin remained silent, Estelle asked, "Was Coach Scott meeting somebody here after-hours?"

Lavin didn't answer, but Estelle saw his fingers tighten. Following suit, his lips compressed into a thin line of disapproval as his face struggled with emotions.

When it became clear that Lavin wasn't about to answer, she said, "Who was he meeting?"

The custodian's face jerked as if he'd been slapped, and he refused to meet her gaze.

"Look, it ain't my place to get in the middle of all this and I ain't going to do it." His back straightened a little with resolve. "I do my job best I can, and what else goes on just ain't my business."

Estelle let the silence hang for a moment, then said, "Mr. Lavin, let me make this as clear to you as I can." Her voice was scarcely more than a whisper. "Someone murdered Clint Scott in cold blood. The killer didn't just jump him outside a bar and beat the crap out of him so he could rob him. Or stick a knife between his ribs. That's not what happened, sir. Someone came into *your* school, after-hours, when Scott was here alone. That door up on the landing tells me that either the killer was *invited* in, or he just took advantage of the open door. When it's chained and locked, it's not possible to open it, short of using a wrecking ball. And the door wasn't accidentally left unlocked earlier. You said it was locked. And you'd know. You don't make mistakes like that."

She paused when Lavin looked up, taking her gaze full-on. He said nothing. She continued, "I think that the killer was invited in. Maybe Scott opened the door and left it open for just that reason. That makes sense to me. And your reaction to my questions tells me that you know more than you're saying."

It was Robert Torrez who broke the ensuing silence. He hooked over a chair and sat close enough to Lavin that the custodian shifted uncomfortably. "Look, this is the way it's gonna play, Bud," Torrez said. "You can either talk to us, right now, or you can answer to a Grand Jury. That's the route we're going to have to go. Other than the killer himself, *you* were the last one to see Scott alive. *You* discovered the body. *You* had time to make whatever arrangements you wanted." He stopped and regarded Lavin impassively. "This ain't something that's just going to go away, Bud. You need to talk to us. Tell us the way it was."

"This whole thing…" Lavin began uncertainly. "The whole thing *isn't* my affair."

"Yeah, it is," Torrez snapped unsympathetically. "Your school, your turf. You know what goes on."

Lavin looked off at the far wall as if reading the events calendar that hung there. His head shook slowly, more of a nervous oscillation than a 'no.' "I don't think I should be sayin' any more."

"That's what the killer counts on, Bud." The sheriff leaned back in his chair. "He counts on you keepin' your mouth shut. He figures you're too gutless to speak up. And that makes you an accessory." Lavin's jaw dropped open and he blew two or three quick breaths. Torrez read the incredulity, the panic, and pressed it. "An accessory to murder. By not tellin' us what you know, you're aiding and abetting—you're covering for him. So, do the right thing."

Estelle reached out and rested a hand lightly on Lavin's knee. "You said that this wasn't your affair, Mr. Lavin. I understand that, and I understand your apprehension. But if not yours, whose is it?" Her open hand became a fist, and she gently thumped his kneecap. "Who came through that door, found Coach Scott, and then executed him? Because that's surely what happened. There are no signs of struggle, not even a dropped bar of soap. He didn't even have time to turn off the water or grab a towel."

The silence that followed was heavy, but both Estelle and Bobby Torrez let it hang there uninterrupted.

"All those years," Lavin said finally, "I was sitting here thinkin' it through. All those years Coach Scott has been coaching the volleyball, and track before that. All that, and goin' on five championships, sixty-five games now without dumpin' one. And that ain't all he's done. You know how many scholarships he's pulled down for the kids?" His face scrunched up. "It isn't fair. It just isn't."

"It happened for a reason, Mr. Lavin. And that's what we need to know."

Lavin drew a long, shuddering sigh. "You could be diggin' a ton of dirt, Sheriff."

"That's a possibility."

"Yeah. A ton. And it is *not* up to me to take the first shovel."

Estelle stared at him until he finally lifted his eyes and met her gaze. "Mr. Lavin," she said, "let me tell you what seems like one obvious way this all could have gone down. Coach Scott had something going on the side here. A lot of tongues in the community are going to be wagging in that direction. But look… he was single, good-looking, successful—what's the big surprise? Sure enough, maybe he was planning to meet someone here. There's nothing wrong with that, when you come right down to it. Unless he was meeting a favorite student. Maybe somebody underage."

She paused when Lavin's eyes flinched, but he didn't rise to the bait. "And then it all went wrong, somehow. Whoever showed up *wasn't* the person he expected. But I have to wonder. When the killer appeared in the shower doorway, was Scott surprised to see him?"

"Not *him*," Lavin said, then looked as if he wished he hadn't.

Chapter Seventeen

The custodian pressed his lips tightly together and crossed his arms over his chest, fortified against any further probing questions.

"It's not going to do no good," Sheriff Torrez said calmly. "This ain't going to go away."

Lavin glanced toward the door, as if contemplating escape. After a long moment, he closed his eyes and seemed to be working hard at controlling his breathing. "Look," he said, "I won't...I can't...I don't know." He stopped faltering and shook his head. "This is *not* the sort of thing I'm gonna do. Just not gonna do it."

"How's obstruction of justice sound to you?" Torrez' face was expressionless, and Estelle could see Barry Lavin drawing into himself.

"Just one thing, Mr. Lavin," Estelle said. "Give us just one thing."

"I don't know what you mean by that."

"I don't know who you're protecting, sir. If it's Coach Scott, he's beyond your help now. If you're worried about smearing his reputation, the quicker we can clean up this mess, the better. If you know who came in here last night, and you're protecting the killer, that's a huge mistake. There's every possibility that he'll strike again. If Coach was expecting a *woman* to show up—and you implied that was the case—is that whom you're protecting?"

Lavin looked at his watch. "Look, I'm not *protecting* nobody. That's what I'm sayin'. All this?" and he waved a hand helplessly around his head. "It's not any of my affair. Talk to Coach Avila, if you want. She knows as much as I do. Maybe more."

His face paled when he realized what he'd said.

"And what do *you* know?" Estelle persisted quietly.

Lavin shook his head, determined. "You talk to her, all right? If she says—" He stopped suddenly, then added lamely, "Well, talk to her."

"So you have a number where we can reach you at any time, sir?"

"'Course." He pulled a slender cell phone from his left breast pocket and held it up for inspection. "Always with me. You never know."

"Indeed, you don't."

As she jotted down the number, Torrez leaned over and in a perfect stage whisper said, "Might be easier just to take him into custody on an obstruction charge. That way, ain't no question about where he is."

Lavin's knuckles clenched white around his phone. "No cause to do that," he said. "Jesus, how the hell does something like this happen? Upsets everybody's life."

"Especially Scott's," the sheriff murmured.

"Sir, we'll escort you out the front door. The building will be locked and stay that way until we clear it. There will be a sheriff's seal, chain, and lock on each door. There will be an officer posted, twenty-four/seven. We *will* prosecute anyone who tampers with the seals."

Lavin relaxed a little. "When are you going to open the place up, then? I got a lot of work to do around here."

"Your work will have to wait." She offered him a brittle smile and extended a business card to him. "If you decide to remember something that we need to know, call me. Anytime. And as we sift through this, we'll need to talk with you again."

She escorted Barry Lavin out of the office and up the hall toward the front of the building, staying on the narrow walkway indicated by the yellow tape. He didn't utter a word as she pulled the outside door closed behind him.

Despite the security for the crime scene, Estelle held no illusions that a significant clue would surface, that the invited State Police investigators—if they arrived at all—would have an "*Ah ha!*" moment. So far, it appeared that the killer had been careful but unhesitant, perhaps just dumb-lucky. If he—or she, as Lavin had hinted—had exchanged even a half dozen words with the victim, Estelle would be surprised.

This assault had been no talkfest. Scott hadn't even had the time to turn off the shower, which he surely would have done to be able to carry on what would pass for a normal conversation. That would have been his first move. But he hadn't done that. He might have taken a step or two forward, but the shower behind him had remained full-on. And then hours of cold water had rinsed away most of what little evidence there might have been.

Even the shooting itself puzzled her. Each of the four shots was a direct center-mass hit, including what was probably the second round as the victim convulsively spun sideways. In the heat of emotions, that was a difficult shot—made after a quick recovery from the recoil of the first. Or dumb-lucky.

True, the range was short, but Estelle had seen people miss from three feet, so distraught or excited or enraged they had no real idea where the muzzle pointed—the "Mrs. Smalley in the barn" syndrome she remembered. This shooter was no Mrs. Smalley. *Calculating* was the first word that came to mind. And that first shot to the groin? Was that intentional?

Lavin had suggested a woman might have visited in the quiet of the night, but somehow that did not fit Estelle's impression of the crime. Certainly a woman *could* have pulled the trigger. Powerful handguns were not just the province of men. In his own abbreviated way, the custodian had never said that the shooter was a woman. He had implied only that perhaps Coach Scott had been *expecting* a woman. It hadn't played out that way.

Chapter Eighteen

Marilee Avila's head was down on her folded arms, using the corner of Lieutenant Tom Mears' desk as a pillow. A wastebasket was drawn close to her feet. Mears himself was next door in the small conference room, stoking the coffeepot for another round—a recipe for a long, tough session.

Estelle watched Avila for a moment. The coach wasn't sobbing, and she wasn't dead. Her back moved slightly with each breath. Maybe sound asleep? *Who could blame her?* Estelle thought. She stepped away from the office and slipped into the conference room.

The lieutenant turned at the sound of the door closing. "Well, good afternoon." Mears sounded way too cheerful. He glanced at the clock as if to make sure as the second hand swept past four-thirty. The day had evaporated. The lieutenant pointed at one of the pump carafes. "That's plain hot water, if you're looking for tea."

"Thanks. I saw Emilio Avila sitting out in the foyer. What time did he come in?"

"His wife called him from the school parking lot, I think. He was waiting here when we arrived. He's had a long wait, but I didn't want him in on the interview yet."

"Absolutely not. What's Marilee been able to tell us?"

Mears puffed his cheeks. "Well, no bombshells, unfortunately." He leaned a hip against the counter and watched the pot, arms folded across his chest. "At least not from her. After a game, it's her habit to leave after all the kids have gone home. She makes sure that everyone has a ride, blah, blah, blah. She leaves all the record-keeping, the stats, all the news contacts to Coach Scott, and he does those chores right after each game." Mears shrugged. "She says that's what he did last night, and he told her he was expecting a long session of it, too—all the interviews. Lots of interest when you're a winner."

"But there's something else? You said you'd watched part of the video."

"I watched some of it. I skipped here and there, and happened on one little section that you need to see." He turned and regarded Estelle. "I know how much you appreciate coincidences."

"What are you saying?"

"There's a little section of the film that shows Coach Scott keeping company with Stacie Stewart and Dana Gabaldon." He watched the expression on Estelle's face as her black eyebrows pulled together in the center. "It might be more accurate to say they were keeping company with *him.*"

"I want to see that first."

Mears nodded thoughtfully toward the TV/DVD unit on the counter. "I surveyed a bit here and there, then marked it at the spot. By the way, what did you think of Lavin?"

"I think he's a scared man, LT."

"He's been in the military, had some experience over in Bosnia. He would know firearms."

"Yes, he would. And despite the country bumpkin persona he likes to project, he's quick. His reaction *not* to enter the shower, but just to turn off the water at its source—that's resourceful thinking. But beyond that, I don't know." She nodded at the television. "I'm ready."

The screen came to life, and Mears turned the volume down. The camera operator had used a tripod, and clearly knew how to keep the camera steady through a variety of shots.

"Now, most of the time, the cameraman pays attention to the game. But right here..." And then the camera's eye drifted to the stands to catch Coach Scott explaining something to newspaper publisher Frank Dayan, his hands as active as a fighter pilot's explaining a complex combat maneuver to another pilot.

"A good personality shot," Mears said. "The way he zooms in on the faces so that they fill the frame?"

Just down the row, right at courtside, were two men with a gigantic television camera carrying the Channel 9 logo—serious hardware that Estelle was sure the high school cameraman would love to possess. The student camera started to roam again, looking for interesting faces.

"Stop," Estelle said quickly. Mears froze the frame. "Back up just a bit."

Scott and Dayan once more engaged in conversation, and they weren't alone.

Seated behind Scott and to his left was a startlingly attractive woman whose blond hair was teased into a windblown look. Beside her was another woman, the camera catching only the side of her smooth face. "Stop there." Even as the camera froze, it caught the blonde as she leaned forward a bit, resting one elbow in a companionable gesture on Scott's left shoulder—just for an instant, a few words exchanged, Scott laughing about something the woman said. She then turned to her companion and the conversation continued even as the camera swept past them.

"Again," Estelle said.

"That's Stacie Stewart," Mears said. He zoomed the frozen frame slightly, capturing Stacie with elbow touching Clint Scott. "And Dana Gabaldon."

"Again."

The lieutenant obliged.

"Did you find any other bits that include her?"

"Not in a quick survey. We're going to have to watch the whole tape, from the beginning."

"We need to. Back up a few feet. When we show this part to Coach Avila, I want to catch her off guard. I want to see her reaction. If you'd back up to the last shot of the game itself? Before the camera swings to take in the coach and his fans?"

Estelle rose, and it was exhilaration that boosted her pulse. "And then, you'll work on this? Maybe use Tom Pasquale when he comes on shift tomorrow morning. The day shift is driving him antsy, especially since he's been caught up in depositions and missed rolling on *this* call. He'll appreciate watching the game tape."

Mears laughed. "He's *always* antsy. That bit with the couple from Illinois helped cool his adrenalin a little. He and Jackie can team up to watch this."

"Who do you have watching Scott's place?"

"Jonas volunteered. Dispatch checks in with him about every fifteen minutes."

"Wakes him up every fifteen, you mean." Estelle smiled. Dick Jonas was having difficulty meeting the physical requirements for the department, but was trying. An intelligent young man in every other respect, his obesity had been a roadblock, his weight ruining his knees and hips. Sheriff Torrez' response to an employment application had simply been, "No," looking disgusted as he said it.

Estelle had been a little more tactful, giving Jonas a target goal of two hundred pounds for his six-foot height. That meant shedding more than a hundred pounds, and Jonas was determined. Shed the weight, and they would review his application—that was the deal. Even so, Sheriff Torrez had made sure that Jonas didn't stay in the crime scene. He'd been escorted out by the lieutenant—although maybe Jonas hadn't interpreted it that way.

But in an understaffed, strapped county like Posadas, even an unschooled special deputy could serve a purpose out of the limelight, and keeping watch over a residence, under constant contact with dispatch, was one of those tasks.

"Does Coach want anything?"

Mears shook his head. "She's trying her best not to throw up."

"*Ay.* Facing the kids next week is going to be a challenge for her. "

Chapter Nineteen

This time, when Estelle walked into Mears' office, Coach Marilee Avila looked up with bloodshot, wet eyes. She clutched a wadded tissue and dabbed away the tears as she stood up. A small, compact person, she was obviously in misery. Her gut contracted in spasms as she clutched the edge of the desk for support.

Estelle felt an initial wave of sympathy for the woman, but circumstances were too tangled to let those emotions rule the day.

"Sheriff, what's going to happen?" She lurched a step forward and clasped Estelle's hand with both of hers. Estelle ushered her back down into the chair before she fell into it.

"Earlier today, you came to the school. About the time all the emergency personnel arrived?" The undersheriff kept her tone quiet, even sympathetic. "How did you find out about Coach Scott's death?"

"I was telling Tom—the lieutenant—that I live only a block and a half from the school, over in that neighborhood behind the old pharmacy off South Pershing? My God, the lights and sirens. Naturally my first thought was for one of the kids, you know. Lots of our senior athletes drive, and…" She stopped and dabbed at her eyes as the tears started again. "There's kind of a hedge along that little arroyo there, and I could see middle school and all the activity. So I knew…"

"You weren't with the rest of the folks in Lordsburg at the in-service?"

Avila tried for a game smile. "Guilty as charged. You tell me what standardized testing has to do with teaching phys ed, and then maybe…"

"So you were home, saw the commotion, and drove over?"

"I *ran* over. But the deputy wouldn't let anyone into the building except the cops. I saw Ginny Trimble, and she said that she heard that something had happened inside. She didn't know any more than I did."

"And Ginny is…?"

"She's a senior starter on the team. One of our stars."

"Where does *she* live?"

"Down the way a little. On MacArthur, I think."

"What brought her back to the school?"

"I don't know."

Estelle pulled the small notebook from her hip pocket. "Did you see any other students? Besides Ginny?"

Avila shook her head. "And now that I think about it, Ginny said that she was on her way over to study with Michelle. Michelle Sena? One of our other seniors on the team. She and her mom live over on Tenth, just across Bustos, north of the school. That's probably how Ginny happened by."

"Study on a Friday with no school, after an exhausting Thursday night, with a weekend coming up? *That's* dedicated."

"These kids are, Sheriff. They know very clearly what they have going here."

"You left the school after the game on Thursday night about when?"

"I suppose about nine. Maybe nine-thirty at the latest."

"Short game."

"Oh, my." A trace of a smile broke through. "If the JV game hadn't been first, we'd have been out of there by seven o'clock. *Almost* a shutout. I felt kind of bad for the Colts. They tried hard, too." Marilee Avila clearly preferred becoming lost in reminiscences about the game.

"Did Coach Scott have any arguments this past week that you recall?"

"Arguments how?"

"Just that. Arguments. Serious differences of opinion." Estelle paused. "Something serious enough that someone would want to settle it with a gun."

Avila blanched. "My God, no. You're kidding. Coach was one of our most popular faculty. The second-graders adore him."

"A second-grader didn't shoot him, Coach."

Avila flinched. "Our players respect him deeply, Sheriff. Like I said, they all understand what sort of momentum they have going here." She grimaced. "Or *had* going." Her shoulders slumped. "You know, Coach Scott spent *hours* working out strategy. Yeah, I know. Strategy in *volleyball?* But listen, *that's* what the team had. You know, a lot of high school coaches, especially in the less popular sports, aren't experts. I mean, they coach because the school can't afford to hire a bigger, specialized staff. So they hire a new science or social studies teacher, and the first question is, 'What can you coach?' And most young teachers appreciate the coaching increment they get, even if it isn't a fair trade for the hours."

She heaved a huge sigh. "In some schools, volleyball is truly a minor sport. It's not uncommon for the players and coach to show up and just bat the ball around, hoping the other team will make a mistake first. They never progress beyond the "set, set, spike" mentality. Coach Scott taught our girls to *look* for the advantage. Always heads up. Always looking. Never caught flat-footed. Find a weak spot in the other team and pound 'em there."

"He wanted aggressive players."

"Absolutely. Constant pressure. Nobody relaxes, not even when the score shoots out of control like it did last night." She leaned forward, face intense. "Look, Coach studied the game, Sheriff. He watched the game videos. He even *scouted,* if you can imagine that. He wanted to see volleyball move up the ranking of important sports."

"A dedicated man," Estelle said quietly. "So who was he seeing?"

Marilee Avila jerked as if she'd been struck. "Seeing?"

"Thursday night, after the game. He was working late in his office. It appears that he opened the back door so whoever it was could gain access."

Avila stared at the undersheriff in disbelief. She tried to start a sentence a couple of times, then gave up and rose to her feet. She turned toward the door, then uttered a long, shuddering sob and changed course slightly, stopping with her forehead leaned against the doorjamb.

"Coach Avila, this is obviously painful for you. But please… help us with this tragedy. We have a witness who is suggesting to us that a woman might have been involved with Coach Scott's death." She paused, watching Avila's body go so tense that her shoulder muscles bulged under her powder-blue polo shirt. After a moment, Avila turned away from the door and collapsed back in the chair.

"Why would anyone *shoot* him? That's what you said happened."

"We're still investigating every angle of this, Coach. But right now, yes. We believe that Coach Scott was shot four times. We'll have some definitive answers after the autopsy."

Avila bit her lip and made an odd little peeping sound of anguish.

"Someone wanted him dead. There was no sign of discussion, no negotiation, no self-defense."

"In the office?"

"No. In the shower." Avila's hand drifted up and covered her mouth. Her gaze riveted Estelle, searching.

"They forced him into the *shower*?"

"We don't think so. It appears that he was *using* the team shower. His clothing was folded neatly on the locker room bench." Estelle shifted in the chair. "And Coach, what I'm telling you is in absolute confidence." *Not likely,* Estelle thought. Coaches Marilee and Emilio Avila would spend a sleepless night discussing the murder.

Estelle regarded the woman for a long moment. What did Marilee Avila know that Barry Lavin was himself privy to?

"How long have you been involved with the program, Coach?"

"Me?" She frowned. "I started coaching in 2007. So nine years."

"Volleyball from the beginning?"

She nodded. "And golf for a couple of years. But that didn't work out." She smiled at Estelle's raised eyebrow. "Our local golf course is not good enough for competitive play. Other schools won't put up with the rattlesnakes, tumbleweeds, and cactus. So it's impossible to host matches. But that's okay. The interest wasn't there, either."

"Scott had been coaching before that?"

"Oh, yes."

"They never gave you the head coach position. Wouldn't that be expected with an all girls' team?"

"Coach Scott already had a lock on the spot, Sheriff. But we work well together. I covered the areas where…where it might matter. When we travel, I take care of all the team logistics—when we stay in a motel, I organize who rooms with who, that sort of thing."

"And supervise the locker room."

"Of course."

"Is there ever a time, routinely, when Coach Scott might have been alone with the girls? With the team?"

"Absolutely not." Avila snapped out the answer, the umbrage flushing her face. "You watch the game videos. He sat in the first row of bleachers, usually, just like the team did, but almost always down court a ways, always on the visitors' side of the net. He liked to sit with Frank Dayan, from the newspaper. *I* was the one pacing the floor, or caught up in head-to-head talk with one of the players. Coach liked to watch from a little distance to see if his game strategy was working. To see if the opponents were rattled."

"Tell me about his personal life."

"I can't do that."

"Can't or won't?" Estelle saw the young woman's cheek muscles flex.

"Look, Coach Scott's personal life was none of my business."
Her lips compressed for a moment, then she took a deep breath
and let it out slowly.

"But at one time…" Estelle guessed, correctly reading the
young woman's body language.

"At one time—" and she stopped abruptly. Her head flopped
back until she was staring at the ceiling tiles. "All right, yes. We
dated. For a few months, *years* ago. Before I was married. We
ended it by mutual consent." She snapped the words off as if
they were made of thin, brittle glass.

"Why was that?"

Avila frowned. "Why was what?"

"Why did the relationship end?"

"Mutual consent. We'll let it go at that."

"You have a family now."

"Emilio and I were married eight years ago." She smiled
for the first time. "And, yes—Emilio Junior is seven, Maria is
five, and Belinda is three." Her smile widened. "Maria started
Kindergarten this year. Em is in Mrs. Annuncio's second grade.
Belinda goes to Little Bear Day Care."

"During volleyball season, you had occasion to interact with
Coach Scott on a daily basis. Who was he seeing most recently?"

Again, Avila fell silent, answering with just a quick shake of
the head. With fingers none too steady, she fished a little tin of
lip balm from her pocket.

"Would you like some coffee? Anything at all?"

"I'd like to go home with my husband and forget that this
ever happened." She wiped her eyes with the wadded tissue.
"But that's not going to happen, is it?"

"No."

"A lot of people are going to be hurt by all this." She looked
up and met Estelle's gaze.

"Most likely. It's a small town, in all respects."

"That's not something I want to be a part of."

"I understand that." *And Barry Lavin said essentially the same
thing.* "But if *everyone* ducks, then a killer walks free."

Marilee Avila turned and lowered her head, hiding her face in her arms. Estelle waited patiently, letting the young woman struggle. After a couple of minutes, Avila pushed herself upright, and took time to blow her nose and dab each eye. "I need to tell you why I broke up with Clint, all those years ago. I mean *really* why."

"All right."

"It's really pretty simple. I just came to *dislike* him." She gazed at Estelle as if somehow the undersheriff might not understand her, or even believe her. "I mean, you'd think—what's not to like? He's...he was...about the most handsome thing on two legs in a town that isn't known for its abundant social opportunities. You know what I mean? But he was absolutely, one hundred percent, involved with himself. Sure, he liked the little kids, but sometimes I think he liked them *because* of the good press that he won by teaching them. He loved to see his picture in the paper, and nothing better than a classroom shot with the six-foot, four-inch Clint interacting with the cute little kiddos. They came about to his knees."

"That's understandable, I suppose."

"Oh, sure it's understandable. And he was a good, conscientious teacher, too. It wasn't just show." She closed her eyes and tilted her head back again.

"So, as you said...what's not to like?"

Avila's laugh was just a husky whisper. "As a coach, there was a streak of genius there, too. A really, really wide streak. I mean, he *really* knew sports. He understood them. Made a science of them. He could encourage his athletes to do the most amazing things, to make the most amazing *effort*, you know? He's put together an enormous scrapbook of the volleyball team's record the past six or seven years. The one he did is back in the coaches' office. On the shelf behind my desk. The biggest—that humungous black one—that's all volleyball. It's an amazing collection. I look through it from time to time. Can you estimate the number of times his picture has been in a newspaper?"

"Many."

"Yes. Many. And there's nothing wrong with that, either. It's no secret why he makes sure Frank Dayan has the choice seat, the choice quotes. Look, the more photos, the deeper the hero worship runs. And that's a powerful force, Sheriff."

And sometimes heroes get killed, Estelle thought.

"But when it comes to homelife, Sheriff, it's so one-dimensional. I would never have expected that. But *dull.* At least to me. He could spend an entire evening analyzing a game video. He'd take one player at a time, and trace her movements. List the strengths and weaknesses. Learn what to work on during the week."

"The school got its money's worth."

"Oh," and her laugh was strained, "I'll say."

"I've seen bits of last night's game video, Coach, but I'd like to watch some parts again with you. Maybe you can talk me through it. Volleyball isn't my game. Will you take a few moments to do that?"

Marilee Avila rose with an effort. "Of course." Her enthusiasm was underwhelming. "The lieutenant has the DVD."

They moved to the conference room, where Mears knelt in front of the laptop, taking notes on the settings.

"Showtime?"

"Yes." Estelle turned to Marilee as the coach settled into one of the conference chairs. "Who filmed for you last night?"

"Jim Kelly films all the games, Sheriff. He's a senior this year, and we'll sure miss him next season. Back in the day, we didn't even film volleyball, but we don't miss a game now. Part of the reason is that Jimbo and Martha are like this," and she linked two fingers.

"Martha?"

"Martha Grier. You'll see her in the film. *Statuesque* might be a good word for her. She's just shy of six feet, but I swear she could slam dunk a basketball. She doesn't jump. She *soars.*"

The game coverage caught the action filmed from the top row of the bleachers, and Kelly was obviously a practiced hand. His transitions were smooth, and he clearly understood the game. He had a narrative flair, Estelle noticed, making use of the camera's capabilities for quick zooms. Each server dominated the frame at the instant of ball contact, and then the camera tracked the ball without jerks or miscues. As long as it was in play, the ball never left the screen.

Between actions, Kelly focused on individual teammate expressions, or once in a while caught an interesting spectator moment. If a player pumped a fist in exaltation, the camera zoomed in to catch the portrait in solo frame. If a girl walked with head down, hands on hips, in frustration at the rare missed shot, she received her few seconds of solo video time. The coaches also were featured with rich personality shots—moments of tense apprehension, moments of confab with players, moments of irritation with the line officials. If Kelly was infatuated with Martha Grier, he kept his *amour* under control. She appeared in the action when it was logical that she do so.

"In all my glory," Coach Avila said when her own face filled the screen. Kelly had left his perch high in the bleachers to move the camera down courtside. Coach Avila was nose-to-nose with one of the players, the conversation intense.

And then the camera's eye drifted to the stands to catch Coach Scott explaining something to newspaper publisher Frank Dayan, the scene Estelle had watched several times. This time, she turned just enough that she could study Coach Avila's face. A slight narrowing of the eyes would have been caught by a poker pro. Without being prompted, Mears froze the tape.

"Coach, is this the first and only game that Ms. Stewart attended?"

After a slight pause, Avila said, "Ah, no. She's a regular. I think she played when she was in high school."

"Does she always sit with Coach Scott?"

"No. Usually in the same general section of the stands, I guess. But what…intimate like this? I guess I hadn't noticed. But I *did* notice last night."

"Did the two women leave the game together? Dana Gabaldon and Stacie?"

"I can't tell you that." She tried to smiled. "When I'm in my game mode, that's about all I notice."

"They stayed for the whole game, though?"

"No. In fact I did see that they were gone well before the end. I didn't actually see them leave. I mean, I had other things to pay attention to. I guess Mr. Dayan was getting an interview with Coach Scott, because he stayed until the bitter end. The Channel Nine crew did too."

Estelle watched as Coach Clint Scott rose from the bleachers, sure enough a large man, one who moved with grace and assurance. He stood beside Avila for a moment, she petite beside him, and then he beckoned several benched players over. Estelle watched as he forced eye contact with each athlete, head bent forward, hands in front of his face drawing pictures in the air. As he finished, he gestured with the power fist in the traditional "go team" exhortation. Then, hands thrust in his pockets, he ambled back to his seat, a quip bringing a smile to newspaperman Frank Dayan's face.

"Fast forward and see if there's coverage that shows the moment Stacie leaves."

But cameraman Jim Kelly had missed that opportunity. A sweep of the stands showed the two women in place, hands high over their heads clapping in unison with the crowd. A few minutes and a few points later, a fleeting shot recorded them already gone.

Estelle turned back to Marilee Avila as Mears zipped the images back to Coach Scott attended by the two young women. "Was Scott having an affair with Stacie Stewart?"

Avila stared at the screen, now frozen with Stacie Stewart's elbow resting on Scott's shoulder. She slowly shook her head. "I honestly...I mean I *honestly* do not know, Sheriff." She shrugged helplessly. "I mean, you know how rumors work."

"I wish that I did."

"No, really. Sure, we *hear* things. She was gone from Posadas for a long time, working somewhere over in Texas, I think. And then she's back, and marries Mr. Stewart, over at the bank. I've never seen *him* at a game, but what does that mean?"

"She could have been having an affair with Coach Scott, then."

Avila held out both hands toward the frozen image. "What you see is what you see. Make of it what you want. I know they appear to be casual friends in that game disc. That's all."

Many scenarios jammed their way into Estelle's mind. Stacie had left the game either after the final shot, or during the final seconds. The scoring outcome was never in doubt, so it made sense to leave before the rush. The crowd, perhaps two hundred people, *was* immense by volleyball standards.

Later, leaving husband, baby, and puppy dog at home, did she come back to the locker room? And there the void. What was certain was that Stacie Stewart had inexplicably vanished the next day, leaving daughter and puppy in a sweltering Volvo...just a short time before Barry Lavin discovered Clint Scott's body.

Without explanation to Coach Avila, Estelle rose abruptly and left the small conference room. She headed for the hallway, taking a detour to the side exit. Once outside, she breathed in the heat of late afternoon deeply, and shut her eyes, letting the peace and quiet of the public safety building's modest interior courtyard settle her nerves and slow her pulse.

Deputy Tom Pasquale had reported that when Stacie Stewart saw him in The Spree parking lot, she had "twiddled" her fingers at him in recognition. The deputy didn't recall that the young woman had actually *smiled* at him. Maybe by then, she had nothing to smile about.

"Estelle?"

She turned to see Mears holding the door open. He stepped out into the courtyard and let the door close behind him.

"Three things, LT," Estelle said. "Three things that might talk to us about motive...before any more time passes. Number one, we need a search of Scott's house. Top to bottom. I wish I could say what I'm looking for, but I can't. And ditto Stacie Stewart's effects. Todd Stewart isn't going to like us rummaging through his wife's possessions, and he might not let you do it without a warrant, but then he has no choice. Can I leave you with both of those?"

"Sure. You said three things."

"Dana Gabaldon. I haven't been able to connect on the phone. Let's try it in person. I have to know what she has to say."

Chapter Twenty

Even as she passed The Spree, Estelle saw the wink of emergency lights ahead on Grande, just on the town side of the interstate off-ramp of the interstate, directly across from the Posadas Inn. As she neared, she first saw Sergeant Taber's blocky form walking back toward the passenger side of her department Expedition, both the officer and her vehicle incredibly bulky compared to the lithe Corvette that the deputy had stopped.

Out of reflex, Estelle glanced at the dash clock—5:22 p.m. Where the day had gone, the undersheriff wasn't sure, but she *was* sure that Sergeant Taber was taking on an extra shift, back-to-back.

The Corvette's highly polished maroon paint winked under the sun. The car sat so low it was hard to imagine how the driver slipped it on—sleek as an evening gown. As Estelle cruised by, the Corvette's driver had raised the power window, and with the tinted glass and chancy light, it was impossible to tell if it held one occupant or two.

Jackie Taber raised two fingers in salute as Estelle drove by, and seconds later, the undersheriff's phone awoke, the sergeant's voice amplified by the car's sound system.

"You heading out for a while?"

"Just a quick run to Cruces to find Dana Gabaldon. Nice catch you have there."

"Pretty nifty. She rolled the stop sign just as I cruised by. I'm not sure now that I shouldn't have just let her go. I mean, it's not like there aren't other things to keep me busy right now."

"Speaking of which," Estelle said, "I have a favor to ask. LT has the game footage, and I'd like you and Pasquale to watch it, start to finish. Stacie Stewart is one of the stars in one short section, but we need to know what else there might be of interest."

"You got it. I sense pizza time."

"Tom and Linda might appreciate that. Give Linda a hug for me. Bobby and LT are going to talk the judge out of a warrant to go through Stacie's papers. And they've got Scott's house covered. I'm headed to talk with Dana, so if you'd find time to survey the game film…"

"You bet. I'll get on it as soon as I finish up with these kids here. I'll give 'em one of my special stern warnings. Won't take a minute."

"The slippery slope can start with a rolled stop sign," Estelle quipped.

Taber let out an odd little laugh. "The driver just turned eighteen years old, with what appears to be a valid Kansas license. The car is registered in her name, with a valid temp tag in the window, registered to a Miss Angela Trevino out of Ridgeway, Kansas. And she's the happy driver, although both she and her passenger are nervous as cats just now. Does the name ring any bells?"

"No." Estelle had braked hard under the interstate overpass to access the eastbound ramp, and now the Charger accelerated hard up toward the interstate. "Who is she?"

"She says that she's a student at Leister Conservatory in Missouri. There's no student parking permit affixed to the corner of that fancy new windshield, but a little place like Leister might not have student parking, anyway. So *that* jibes. And, I might add, Miss Angela is a really, really beautiful young lady."

Estelle's foot had lifted off the gas at mention of Leister, and she let the Charger drift over to the right-hand shoulder of the interstate as she fought to force her heart back into place.

"What are you telling me, Jackie?"

"Her escort is a fifteen-year-old student at the same school." Sergeant Jackie Taber rarely had difficulty being blunt, but she clearly hesitated this time. "Your son is with her, Estelle."

The Charger had been rolling slowly along the shoulder, and now jarred as she slammed on the brakes. Sergeant Jackie Taber let the silence ride as Estelle tried to fumble the right words. The undersheriff remained speechless.

"Francisco says that they drove over for your mother's birthday celebration tomorrow night, and he also said something about a church service Sunday morning?"

The church service was one of Teresa's requests, a simple mass of thanksgiving at the Iglesia de Tres Santos, the little mission in the tiny Mexican village just south of the border where Teresa Reyes had lived for seventy-five years. The "birthday celebration" was, at Teresa's demand, just a quiet family dinner.

"They're headed for Twelfth Street right now. Do you want to talk with them before I turn 'em loose?"

"Of course…I mean no, I don't. I'll…Jackie, you're not joking with me…?" Estelle knew that was silly the moment she said it.

"Nooooo."

"It's my *son* in the car?" That sounded dumb, too, but Estelle could think of nothing else.

"Francisco Guzman, age fifteen, with a school ID card that shows his home address as 112 South Twelfth Street, Posadas, New Mexico."

"*Ay.* Look…I…no. I don't know what I want to do. I need to talk to my husband before I say all the wrong things." *Por Dios,* Estelle thought. *This is impossible.*

"You going on to Cruces, then?"

"I really need to, Jackie. I mean, with what you're telling me, right now it's the last thing I want to do, but I *have* to. But… *ay,* ignorance was bliss."

Taber's chuckle was low and quiet. "You want me to impound the car, put Miss Trevino in one of the women's detention cells, and send this Francisco character back to Leister on the next bus out of town?"

Estelle's groan was closer to a whimper. "Are you one hundred percent sure that it's Francisco?" *What a stupid question,* she almost added. Sometimes it seemed easier to face ten armed felons than a single, willful child.

"I can't imagine that there are two Franciscos in the world, my dear. He greeted me by name in his usual polite fashion. I think I blushed. He's a doll."

"How can Leister...?" Estelle stopped. The academy's stiff behavioral policies surely didn't allow underage students to roam around the countryside with teenaged girls, unchaperoned in powerful sports cars. "Jackie, I don't know what to do. For now, just make sure they make it safely to the house. That'll give me some time."

"I figure if they drove all the way from Kansas, they can manage a few more blocks. Your mom's going to be thrilled, though, huh?"

"Yes, she is." Estelle let it go at that, still unable to reconcile the conflicting emotions. A big, heartfelt hug first, and then kick Francisco's butt down the road for about a mile. And the girl? This Angela Trevino? What, *who* was she? A fellow musician, obviously. Estelle knew she could hardly expect her fifteen-year-old son to live in a cloister until he reached thirty-five. But at *fifteen,* driving across the country with an eighteen-year-old more-than-companion, in an eye-catching sports car with all the temptations of speed and...

She shook her head violently, trying to clear the images. "And I'm serious about the escort all the way to Twelfth Street, Jackie." The calm side of her brain scoffed. What, the kids, just successful at driving from Kansas, were not going to be able to make it across the small village without incident?

"Lights and siren all the way." Taber's droll humor read the undersheriff's mental anguish just right.

"Please, no. But I'll be back as quickly as I can." She thrust the Charger in gear and pulled onto the interstate, not even noticing that the powerful car scorched burnouts for impressive yardage. In another moment, she had Leister Conservatory on the phone.

The operator had a soothing contralto when she asked how the call might be directed, but Estelle was in no mood to be soothed.

"Dean Baylor's office, please. Or his cell phone."

"Just one moment."

The moment was only seconds, but felt as if it had lasted an hour. At last, the dean's secretary, Lucy Delfino, came on the line, sounding a little out of breath.

"Ms. Delfino, this is Undersheriff Estelle Reyes-Guzman over in Posadas, New Mexico."

Before she could continue, Delfino chirped with delight. "And how are *you*? My gosh, I haven't seen you since Chelwood Commons! If you'd called five minutes later, I would have missed you! We're all in kind of an uproar at the moment. We were just on our way to dinner, and then on to a student recital. It's just a lovely evening. I hope your day is going well?"

Estelle almost burst out laughing. *I won't mind so much when he's fifty-two and she's fifty-five. But fifteen and eighteen?* Instead, she took a deep breath. She had no desire to discuss previous concert venues, even though the Chelwood Commons concert off Chicago's Lakeshore Drive had been a marvelous, cherished experience. And her day *hadn't* been up there on the perfect-day charts. Her fingers clutched the steering wheel so hard they left dents in the leather. "Ms. Delfino, I need to speak with Dean Baylor."

"Now, Dean Baylor is on leave for health matters, Sheriff. We're expecting him back in March or April, if all goes well. But Dr. Gunnar Peterson has taken over as acting-dean, and he's in his office right now. That's what I meant when I said we were in an uproar." Lucy lowered her voice to a conspiratorial whisper. "At least I think he's in his office. This is his second day on the job, so he's working late. We all are. Would you care to speak with him?"

"I would. And please forward my best wishes to Dean Baylor."

"I will do that. Just one moment."

The voice that came on the line was brisk, carrying a heavy Scandinavian accent. Peterson ended each phrase with a curious upward rush, as if preparing the conductor's baton for the following, decisive downstroke.

"Yes? This is Dr. Peterson. And how may I help you today?"

"Doctor, this is Undersheriff Estelle Reyes-Guzman from Posadas, New Mexico. My son is one of your students. Francisco Guzman? He's one of the senior…"

"Francisco!" Peterson blurted. "My word, yes. Young Master Guzman. I had the honor of teaching Francisco in advanced theory last semester. My word, what a talent. What a *scholar*. And what an honor to talk with you. It's sheriff, is it?"

"Undersheriff, yes. And thank you. I'm curious if you know where Francisco is at the moment."

"Of course we do. And by the way, his recital last week? It was magnificent. He and another student—Miss Angela Trevino? I will tell you this…I have never seen two, ah, two *souls* who can join in musical flight the way those two have."

It's the "souls joined" that concerns me, she wanted to say. *One surprise after another.* "I'm thrilled to hear that, Dr. Peterson. That's in part why I'd like to talk with him. With Francisco."

"Yes. Well, of course. Let me ask Ms. Delfino about the young man's schedule."

"And of course he's not there," Estelle said aloud, but apparently Dr. Peterson had already shifted the phone away from his ear.

In a moment, his lilting voice came back on the line. "Mr. and Mrs. Trevino, those would be Angela's parents, came to school and picked up their daughter, and, it seems, your son, for a very special family observance. It seems that both Angela and her maternal great-grandmother celebrate their birthday anniversaries on the same date."

None of which puts the two kids shooting a stop sign at an interstate exit ramp in New Mexico, driving a fresh-off-the-showroom-floor Corvette, Estelle thought.

"I have to add, Sheriff Guzman, that we had something of an upheaval here with Dean Baylor's unexpected illness. I'm not sure we would have interfered with genuine family plans of this nature in any case, but I understand your concern. Now, this might put your mind at ease somewhat. Dr. Trevino, that is Angela's mother, is provost at Castleton State, near their home in Emporia. There was to be a brief recital arranged at Castleton just this past Wednesday night, and I confess it was a somewhat private affair—it's not on our usual conservatory calendar of events, so it was not posted in the conservatory newsletter. Provost Trevino arranged the whole thing, but just for the family and friends. Small and intimate, she told us."

"I'm delighted." Estelle's tone suggested that she was anything but. She computed hours. A Wednesday night recital…and now here they were, late Friday afternoon, almost evening. From Castleton, Kansas. The 'Vette hadn't been loafing at fifty-five, and Francisco had no driver's license. That didn't concern Estelle so much as where the kids might have spent Wednesday and Thursday nights. Maybe they cruised straight through, chaste in their deep bucket seats.

"It's been a hectic summer schedule for the students, and sometimes a little time away from such concentrated studies can pay huge dividends. I'm sure Francisco mentioned the *two* recitals? So special."

"I'm sure." She braked hard, waiting for a moving van to negotiate its way around a sagging pickup loaded with bales of hay and pulling a stock trailer loaded with at least four saddled horses, their muzzles savoring the air rushing past. The moment the moving van was safely back in lane, she pushed the Charger hard. "And no, he didn't mention them."

"Well, the one for Miss Trevino's great-grandmother, and then this next weekend for Francisco's own grandmother's one hundredth?"

"Of course."

"Because neither was, or is, a school function, travel arrangements were made by Provost Trevino."

"They certainly were." Estelle's jaw muscles ached. "Dr. Peterson, thank you. I'll get back to you." She switched off before he had a chance to reply.

Her own thoughts swirled, and she forced herself to relax, even letting the speed drift back to a sedate ninety.

"My son has his own life," she said aloud, then shook her head and replied, "Not at age fifteen, he doesn't." For the rest of the drive to Las Cruces, she debated with herself, trying to imagine what her husband would say, what *Oso* would think. Of all the scenarios she had imagined as a parent, this was not on the list. Her fingers drifted to the auto-dial several times. Dr. Francis Guzman's calm serenity was but an electronic connection away. Still, she hesitated. If he was working, cell phone interruptions, especially of this nature, were anathema. If he was home, the fancy Corvette would be now parked at the curb in front of their Twelfth Street home, and he'd be greeting the road-weary kids, enjoying the surprise.

Nothing in the past years had prepared her for something like this, she reflected. She had long marveled at her supremely gifted son's deep common sense and obviously firm foundation, traits that made his astounding musical gifts all the more endearing. He was not a primo don, not a neurotic, drug-spaced basket case whose only exception came at the keyboard. He was, most of the time, thoughtful and considerate. The year before, he'd refused to fuss during a concert in Mazatlán, Mexico, even when it became apparent that some threat might exist for his personal safety—even when he had found himself surrounded by protective *federales*.

His world was family and music; increasingly over the past few years as his concert venues multiplied, she was not always sure of the order of the two. That he had elected to make the trip for his grandmother's birthday pleased Estelle deeply. Doubly so that he had included someone else's special relative in the effort. The *how* of the trip was another matter that she would have to reconcile...that and not being included in the advance planning so that everyone could enjoy the twinges of anticipation.

"Just how far can titanium apron strings stretch?" she finally asked aloud, and laughed helplessly. The car was not full of helpful spirits ready to offer reply. The obvious trouble was that after more than two decades with the Sheriff's Department, she'd seen more than her share of crushed and mangled cars, with lives inside snuffed in an instant.

It was a year to be treasured when no high school student wrapped himself around a tree or dove his car into the abandoned reservoir up on the mesa...or, as had young Efrin Garcia the night before, crashed his truck into a utility pole after slaughtering a deer.

She'd seen ruinous teenaged love affairs; she'd witnessed myriad family disputes that fractured relatives apart. In a small, rural community described as "boring" by some, drugs reared their ugly heads all too often. The many shades of the nightmare were impossible to reconcile.

Estelle imagined the maroon Corvette gliding through the night. Didn't Provost Trevino, Angela Trevino's mother, remember how quickly, how effortlessly, a teenager could drift off to sleep? And she had *approved* this trip? A push of that damn right-hand foot pedal could rocket the 'Vette to nearly two hundred miles an hour. *What was she thinking?*

Chapter Twenty-one

Dana Gabaldon's parents, the Summers, lived in a new development west of the river, their brick fascia house on one of the cul-de-sacs nestled at the base of the first river bench. Dana's Kia was parked in the driveway, sharing the space with a Day Cruiser stern-drive boat, expensive enough to pay for a couple of Kias.

Estelle took a moment to talk her nerves down as she wrote the routine trip comments in her log, concentrating on that entry and the purpose of her dash southeast. If Dana Gabaldon knew anything about Coach Clint Scott's murder, that would be evident now. If she had heard nothing, that could be useful now, as well.

She glanced up and saw that Dana Summers Gabaldon had stepped outside and now walked slowly along the winding flagstones through the cactus garden. Her hands were jammed in her back pockets, and she walked with head bowed, like someone who was keeping a watchful eye for snakes. She made no effort to hide her early pregnancy with child number two, but her turquoise blouse was loose and comfortable. Once blond, Dana's auburn hair now showed bronze highlights.

The undersheriff closed her log and got out of the car. "Good evening, Dana."

The young woman tried to smile, but had a hard time making it stick.

"I'm so sorry," she said, not exactly the greeting Estelle had expected. *I didn't do it!* would have surprised the undersheriff less. Or a quick hide in the back bedroom. Or a parent to cover for her.

"For what, Dana?"

"For evading you when you called earlier." She turned and looked back toward the house for a moment, then pulled her right hand from her hip pocket and held it out toward Estelle. "Hi." She managed to crowd considerable relief into that one syllable, and her grip was strong. "I'm sorry to make you drive down here." Her hazel eyes held Estelle's.

"I really wanted to talk with you, Dana. So meeting you here is a good thing."

"Yes, ma'am." She nodded and stepped over to the car, turning so she could rest her rump against the back fender. She slipped her arms across the top of her belly.

"Let's find a quiet spot," Estelle said. "Can I buy you an iced tea or something?"

Dana pushed off. "Please come inside, Sheriff. Mom and Dad went out to the airport." She smiled tightly. "He's working on his sailplane this evening. We'll have peace and quiet. And Adrianna is down for the count."

"Perfect," Estelle agreed. "When's the baby due?"

Dana held the storm door for her. "Early March. We're trying to decide whether to take a sonogram or not. Maybe it's better to be surprised."

Well, maybe. "Eddie must be thrilled either way." At the post office, Dana's husband had seemed excited, in his own quiet way.

"In orbit," Dana replied. She gestured toward the living room, where the seventy degrees felt like winter. Without asking, she slipped into the kitchen, ran ice from the fridge ice maker, and filled the glass from the sun-tea pitcher. Enclosing the glass in a red-checked napkin, she handed it to Estelle. "Wherever is comfortable for you."

Estelle settled at the end of a long, curving sofa set. "Dana, we're concerned about Stacie Stewart."

Dana didn't reply, but movements to prepare her own iced

tea were deliberate, even thoughtful. She returned to the living room and sat a cushion away.

With her right index finger, she traced the rim of her glass, forehead furrowed.

"We found her daughter and the family's puppy locked in Stacie's Volvo station wagon in the parking lot of The Spree earlier today." *Or was that yesterday?* Estelle thought. The hours blended into an impossible potpourri.

No gasp of astonishment or incredulity greeted that, and Estelle continued, "A citizen was prompt in calling 911, fortunately. Sheriff Torrez responded and removed the child and puppy from the car. Both are fine, both are back with…" Estelle had been about to say *their family*. "Both are back with Todd."

Dana nodded, a single, slow bob of the head.

"You don't seem surprised."

Dana took a deep breath. "May I tell you what happened?" She tried for a smile. "The whole sorry escapade?"

"Please."

"Thursday night, Stacie and I went to the volleyball game— that was my idea, but Stacie was just a little excited, too. She used to play, you know. After the game, I got home about nine or so, and I was surprised when later that evening, Stacie called and asked me if I'd do her a favor. I mean, it was almost eleven when she called, and that's way late for us." She smiled. "I was up *eating,* which seems to be my favorite hobby just now. Otherwise I might not have heard my cell."

"What did she want?"

"She asked if I'd pick her up at The Spree right at eleven the next day. Today, that is. She asked if I'd park at the end of the store, over by the employees' door. She'd see me there. And that's what I did."

"So at eleven Thursday night…yesterday…she was already planning to go into the store, leaving her child and pet behind in the car. Why wouldn't she just walk across the parking lot from her car to yours when she saw you enter the parking lot, Dana? Why plan to go into the store first?"

"I don't know. Now, today when I stopped by the store, there were already cops there in the parking lot, so maybe…I don't know. But see, she wouldn't have known about that the night before. She wouldn't have known that they would be there. I mean, when I got to the lot to pick her up, I could see one of your department units parked right by the front of the store, along the sidewalk."

"And then?"

"She came out the side door, got in the car, and asked if I'd take her down to the Posadas Inn. That's just a couple of blocks south, and I was sort of surprised that she didn't just walk. But I mean, no biggie."

"What was her mood?"

"I'm not much of a psychologist."

"But nervous? Angry? Withdrawn?"

"Withdrawn is a good choice. *Distant.*" Dana nodded. "Distant. Usually, Stace is on the huggy side, you know? And kinda flighty. But she seemed determined this time. Serious and determined."

"What did she tell you?"

"Nothing. She asked if I'd go right back to the store after I dropped her off and pick up Ginger and Rascal, that little Jack Russell they bought. Cute as a button, but oh, my God…"

"Had she mentioned anything about your taking the child and the puppy when she called the night before? About making a break, maybe? That she might be thinking of leaving home for a while?"

"No." Dana tried to take a sip of the tea, wrinkled her face in anguish, and set the glass down on the table. "She never said anything about it."

"What about at the game?"

"Not then, either."

"At the game, she appeared relaxed? Everything was all right in her world?"

"Well, that's always hard to tell, Sheriff. But I think so. Nothing out of the ordinary that I noticed."

"So—as she asked, you dropped her off and then returned to the store to pick up Ginger and the puppy."

"Well, that's what I was *supposed* to do. She gave me a set of keys for the Volvo, and I asked her what I was supposed to do with the car, then. She asked if I'd park it back in their driveway." She shrugged. "I mean, I was okay with that. It's just a couple of blocks. But it seemed odd, even a little frightening to me. I mean, what was she thinking?" Dana sighed. "And she wouldn't say. I mean, I said, 'Isn't there something I can do to help?' And she'd say, 'Just for a few days, Dana.' And I didn't mind *that,* 'cause see, we had been talking about me babysitting Ginger."

She reached out and placed her sweating glass on a coaster. "It's all so strange. I mean, if she was so intent on leaving town or something, or having some rendezvous with a tall, dark-haired stranger at the motel, why not just leave the kids in the house? Or ask me to come to the house for a little bit? I mean, what's with the car left in the parking lot of a store? That's really bizarre thinking."

Estelle didn't answer, but to her, Stacie Stewart's convoluted plan was consistent with a mind trying to cope with a life that perhaps *she* didn't understand. Nothing could be simple or straightforward. Or had she witnessed something the night before that had thoroughly spooked her? And yet, Estelle thought, Stacie had made no effort to avoid being seen by Deputy Tom Pasquale. If she was running then, she was a good actress, showing no panic.

Dana put her elbows on her knees and leaned forward to rest her chin on her hands. "I mean, if she wanted to leave her family, why not just take Ginger and the dog to the bank, drop 'em on Todd's desk, and say, 'I'm outta here'? Or leave 'em at home and give Todd a warning call. I mean, *why?*"

"Was that what you thought? That she might be meeting someone at the motel?"

"Well, the thought crossed my mind. I mean, that's the cliché, isn't it?"

"Do you think that's what she was planning? To leave her family?"

"She wouldn't say. But now that I've given it some thought, she really *has* been up and down in the past few weeks." Dana frowned. "She's preoccupied with *something*. I don't know what." She smiled painfully. "Life has been sort of a roller coaster for Stacie, if you know what I mean. Not always easy."

"You sat with her during the game. Did she talk with anyone else during that time?"

"Sure. She knows a lot of people. And she and I sat right behind Coach Scott and Frank Dayan. It was fun hearing them talk. And I have to say…" She paused. "She's never talked to me about it, but I *know* that she has a crush on him. I mean, you can see it. And it's not a new thing, either."

"No girl talk?"

Dana made a face. "Sure, some."

"After the game last night, do you know if she went home right away?"

"I don't know that."

"Could she have gone back to the school?"

Dana looked puzzled. "Of course she *could* have. I mean…" She stopped. "She told me…" She stopped again. "Have you talked with Coach Scott?"

"No."

"That might be a place to start. You know, the two of them have been sort of on-again, off-again?" She smiled, but with no humor. "Small-town romance sort of thing. She lived in Lubbock for almost ten years, and you'd think that would have cooled things down. But as soon as she came back here, boom. There she and Clint are, having their little affair again. Then the baby came, and she told me that she was going to break it off with Clint for good. But then again…"

"Then again what?"

"Well, she'd talked about her homelife now and then. She can't *stand* that puppy, you know. That was Todd's choice, and maybe good for Ginger, although I think that right now Ginger is really too young. The pup is spoiled, he's nippy...but Todd thinks he's wonderful. Of course, he's at the bank all day, and doesn't have to take care of the little squirt. If I take Ginger in for daycare, they'll have to find a place for him. So there you go..." She shrugged and then paused.

Estelle waited patiently.

"She and Todd have never matched very well," Dana said finally. "I mean, we make our choices, don't we? Not that Eddie is the world's most exciting person, but Todd Stewart always struck me as dull, dull, dull. And maybe that's the attraction with Coach Scott, I suppose. Impossibly handsome, exciting—" She stopped quickly. "Well, I *guess* he might be exciting if you like talking about sports, huh? I mean, he's the guy for whom the term *one-track mind* was invented."

"You two talked about that a lot, then."

"No, not a lot."

"Stacie was looking for a way out, you think? Of that relationship with Scott?"

Dana mused about that for a moment. "I think so. Well no..." She held up a hand. "I *know* she was. At least that's what she claimed."

"I watched the game file. Stacie seemed comfortable with Scott. There was a clear shot of you all sitting in the bleachers, and at one point, Stacie props an elbow on Scott's shoulder, from behind."

"I remember that. I didn't know the little rat with the camera was spying on us." She smiled. "That's Stacie, though. She's a toucher, Sheriff. If she talks with you, she has to touch at the same time. So the arm on coach's shoulder? I didn't give it a thought. I suppose it made for a nice picture. That kid—Jim Kelly, I think it is—he does such a good job with the filming. And of course, he's in love with Martha Grier, so he's motivated. I'm surprised the whole video isn't a portrait of her." She frowned then. "Small towns are just wonderful, aren't they?" She looked across at Estelle. "I keep wondering what will happen when Todd

Stewart notices that as Ginger grows up, she starts to show some tallness genes that banker dad can't account for."

"You think so?"

Dana took her time answering. "I have no right to say that. So what do newspaper reporters say at a time like this? 'Off the record.' That's what it is. I can *think* it, though."

"And Todd doesn't have a clue?"

"I seriously doubt it. "

"Stacie had given no hint to you that she was thinking of actually leaving Posadas?"

"None. I'd like to slap her a good one, right upside the head. This whole thing stretches the 'What are friends for' adage just a bit much."

"Where did she go, did she say?"

Dana shook her head. "She wouldn't tell me. She said that if she did, I'd tell somebody else, so it was better if I didn't know." She looked up at Estelle. "Well, duh. Yeah, I would. I'm worried about her, Sheriff. I really am."

Dana looked up at the ceiling. "I've thought about it for the past few hours, and I'm thinking now that she wanted to leave *everything* behind. I suppose that everybody thinks about that, one time or another." She shrugged. "Just like that. Everything. You could do that with a bottle of pills, or by just walking away. All she had with her was her handbag."

"What was the deal at The Spree? How were you planning to handle that? "

"Oh, my God. That. I figured, hey, swing in, find the car, get Ginger and the little furry terror, and go from there. I was going to keep 'em until Todd came home from work...or maybe call him and ask him what the heck was going on with him and Stacie. But then I pulled into the lot, and there's cop cars, and an ambulance, and the doors of the Volvo open...I even saw old Miss Barber overseeing the operation."

She looked at Estelle, her face pained. "I should have stopped. I know. I should have. But I didn't. For one thing, the sheriff was right in the middle of it, and I have to tell you, Bob Torrez scares me to death. I know it's just his manner, Estelle, but my knees get weak just thinking that I might have to talk with him."

And you still might, Estelle thought. "You're not alone there, Dana. So you just drove on by."

"Yes, ma'am. I just drove by, and I know I shouldn't have. If I had seen your car there, I might have stopped." She held her shoulders up, then sighed. "But probably not. I drove down here today, just so I wouldn't have to be alone, with Eddie at work and all. And then Mom asked me to stay over, so I will. Her radar mind thinks something is wrong, so we'll talk later tonight, when Dad goes to bed. And you know, thinking back on it, I decided that what was going on between Todd and Stacie was none of my business. And that's what Mom will say, too. Kid and dog are safe, so…the easy route out of it."

"I'll ask you this again, Dana…do you think Stacie was going to the inn to meet someone?"

"I have no idea, Sheriff. Really, I don't. If I knew, I think I'd tell you."

"You *think* you would." Estelle smiled.

"Yeah…I think. My brain's a mess with all this." Dana shook her head. "I don't know. I've never seen Stace like that. Just switched off, you know? And up 'til now, everything seemed so serene, so…even *happy*, you know? At least content, if not ha-ha happy."

"Someone was going to pick her up at the inn, maybe. Or she could have been catching the one-a-day bus."

"Maybe. I don't know. She wouldn't tell me. No long good-byes, either. She darn-near slammed the door in my face. And off she went, as if she had an appointment. Must have, I guess. She didn't want to talk to me. And usually she really engages my little Adrianna, you know? But nothing. She asked if I'd pick up Ginger and the dog…that's what she called the puppy…the *dog*."

"Did you actually see her enter the inn? She went inside?"

"I didn't wait. I headed back toward the store parking lot. It was hot, and I was worried about Ginger, left in the car. You don't just leave kids or pets to roast like that." Dana picked up her glass again, but with no interest in its contents. "Could she be charged with something? Stacie, I mean?"

"Well, I'm not the district attorney," Estelle started to say. "But…"

"But you're undersheriff. You know the law. And you've seen this sort of thing happen before…and worse, probably."

"Yes. Because Stacie made arrangements to have the child— and the dog—picked up, we're not looking at child abandonment here, Dana. Less-than-perfect judgment, maybe. When you picked up Stacie, you didn't know right away that she'd left her child and pet in the car. Why she didn't direct you right *then* to the Volvo is a mystery to me, but she didn't. Sometimes people make up their minds, and don't want to be reminded of what they're leaving behind. She didn't want to hear one last 'Mommy!' wail from Ginger to break her resolve. We just don't know."

"But she could be charged."

"Yes. Child endangerment, perhaps. We'll see. That's not important now. Ginger is safe. What's important is finding Stacie. We need to make sure *she's* safe, too. We don't know her frame of mind, other than what we can assume from your description of events."

"Does this sort of thing point toward…?" and her face screwed up in anguish. "Toward suicide, maybe?"

"I can't answer that. But her life right now is a mess, Dana. The best thing we can do is find her and talk with her. I don't care if she hightails it to Peru. We'll find her."

Dana looked squarely at Estelle. "That's not really the job of the Sheriff's Department, though, is it? I mean, if no big, awful law has been broken, that's a lot of resources spent just to talk with a mom who maybe had a breakdown of some kind."

"If it were that simple," Estelle said, "but tragically, it's not. Not this time."

"Meaning what?" Dana's voice was small, apprehensive.

"Dana, I drove down here because I wanted you to hear this from me first." She set her iced tea glass carefully on the end table, and shifted position on the couch so she could face Dana directly. "Dana, Coach Scott was murdered sometime late last night. He was discovered by one of the school's custodians. He had been using the team shower in the girls' locker room. Someone made their way into the school, and shot him."

Dana's jaw hung slack as all the color drained from her face. Her right hand fluttered almost to her mouth, then quivered in mid-air. "What?" she whispered.

Estelle repeated herself, and Dana's head shook back and forth as if fending off the words. "You can't mean that."

"I'm afraid that I do, Dana."

As if her spine had lost all its means of support, she sagged back against the sofa cushions. "Someone *shot* him?"

"Yes."

"And he's dead?"

"Yes."

The girl executed a slow-motion roll to one side, feet drawing up, until she lay in a fetal position, her face hard against the cushions just inches from Estelle's knee. She held that position for only a moment, then pushed herself upright.

"You can't..." she started to say, then changed course. "You think *Stacie* could do something like that? Is that why you came down?"

"I don't know what she could do, Dana. All I know is that you two were among the last people to see the victim alive."

"But because you saw the two of us sitting with Coach Scott, you started thinking that she *might* be involved somehow?"

"We go with what we have, Dana. It's urgent that I talk with Stacie."

"Was there...was there evidence left at the scene that points to her?"

"At this time, we're still sifting through what we have, Dana."

"But you said Coach was *shot*. Stacie doesn't even own a gun." She frowned. "I don't know. Maybe Todd does. But..."

Estelle watched the inner struggles play across the young woman's face. The undersheriff stood up and fished a business card out of her breast pocket. "If you think of *anything* else, don't hesitate to call me. Twenty-four/seven. I know you'll have questions, but right now, I've told you all I can." She held out a hand and took Dana's, holding it for a long moment. "And thanks for talking with me today. I really appreciate it."

"This is all so horrible. It makes me sick. I mean, all those poor kids at school." She looked up at Estelle. "But Ginger is okay? I mean, for sure?"

"For sure. She's with daddy." Estelle nodded. "And the *dog*."

Chapter Twenty-two

On the one hand, Estelle had a hard time imagining Stacie Stewart holding a large handgun steady enough to pump four bullets into a former boyfriend, especially with the last round a careful *coup de grace* at point-blank range. Certainly, jilted—or *jilting*—lovers had murdered before, with guns, kitchen knives, baseball bats, poisons, toasters, or automobiles.

But balancing that doubt was Stacie Stewart's curious behavior. It was hard to imagine a mother simply leaving an adoring family, from all reports taking nothing along but a conservative purse. No suitcase of clothes thrown hastily together the way distraught women did in movies. Who was Stacie Stewart meeting at the Posadas Inn? And from there, bound for where? Mexico? Texas? Montana?

If she had caught the one bus that stopped in Posadas each day, she could have ridden to El Paso, Albuquerque, Denver, or a dozen other destinations. She could have made a connection at any of the airports. She had had all afternoon to do so while authorities flogged around in the shower, photographing bullet holes.

Dana was right. As long as Stacie wasn't involved in the murder, any other law violated would go down as a slap on the wrist, if that. Expending all-too-scarce department resources to satisfy a charge of endangerment of a child—especially since the child was essentially uninjured—was chasing a misdemeanor.

That could be stretched to include felony abuse, in a case where the abandonment actually resulted in harm to the child.

Stacie, no matter how her unstable mental condition had been shaken up, had made arrangements with Dana to pick up the child and puppy. Dana was on her way back to The Spree parking lot when she was spooked. The undersheriff could easily imagine the district attorney stifling a broad yawn and dismissing the whole episode…unless the young woman could be tied to Clint Scott's horrific murder.

Estelle tried to relax in the driver's seat, letting the cruise control keep a smooth eighty-five in the passing lane of the interstate. If one of the deputies hadn't done so already, she would get a recent photo of Stacie Stewart from Todd, and see if anyone at the Posadas Inn could shed light. After all, Stacie might not have even gone inside that motel—Dana had been too flustered to notice or remember. But the closer she drove to Posadas, the more difficult it was to concentrate on the case.

From brand new black asphalt so smooth that it lulled, her car flashed through a section where the tar strips, temporary stopgap measures to hold the road together, beat a steady rhythm under the tires. As the *Posadas, 12 miles* sign approached, she thought of the hours and hours the two teenagers had spent in their high-powered sports car, flogging it toward this tiny village.

However the mileage was sliced, roughly a thousand miles separated Edgarton, Missouri, from Posadas, New Mexico. Edgarton, the quiet, picturesque town that was home to Leister Academy, was truly in the middle of nowhere, a good description for Posadas as well. Add to that some more miles—long miles—to Miss Trevino's home in Castleton, Kansas. Sixteen hours at eighty miles an hour? No one did that, not even in the thundering Corvette. It had to be fueled, and just one stop blew the average. The kids had to eat, although a big bag of Cheetos and six-pack of Coke could take a teenager a long way. Estelle grimaced. And on the interstate, state cops with finely tuned radar abounded. Touch even eighty-five, and they'd check the kids out, especially for the love of stopping a hot rod.

In a few more moments, she took the Posadas exit, amusing herself by pulling the Charger to a solid halt at the stop sign at the bottom of the ramp. The dash clock flashed 8:02 p.m., and she turned onto Grande northbound. The village, so small that a mile hike would take a pedestrian anywhere in town, was quiet for a Friday night, although The Spree's parking lot hosted a fair crowd, shoppers reveling in the twenty-four/seven schedule the new store boasted.

The village's seven bars and saloons would have ramped up as well. The huge crews working out at *NightZone* had bolstered the county's economy in a spectacular fashion, and they would have come into town for a little noisy R and R.

For the first time since the closing of Consolidated Mining decades ago, there were moments when business actually bustled…enough that County Manager Leona Spears chortled over the increased tax revenues.

All of that vanished from Estelle's mind as she turned south on Twelfth Street. A block ahead, haloed by the light on the other side of the street and catching the last glints from the setting sun, the low, lean profile of a maroon Corvette crouched at the curb in front of the Guzman residence. The hood was up, the rear hatch open, and the yawning passenger door faced the sidewalk. As she pulled up behind the rocket, a small head appeared to one side of the headrest, and in a moment Carlos shrugged out of the car, a huge grin on his face.

"Mamá, Francisco and a friend are here!" he shouted as she stepped onto the sidewalk. He stroked a hand along the swell of the back fender. "Isn't this amazing? It's hers!"

She reached out and tousled the thatch of black hair, then folded him into a hug. "Some surprise, huh? You're going to spend the whole night out here, guarding it?"

"Oh, *caramba.*" His eyes twinkled. "You think she'll let me take it for a spin?"

"Oh, absolutely, *hijo.*" The image of the eleven-year-old trying to see over the steering wheel and then the swoop-fendered hood, or even reaching the pedals, forced a smile.

"They're inside. They were talking with Grandmamá, but she's about to go to bed. It's neat you were able to come home for a little while." He patted the car once more, loathe to leave it. "You think it's faster than The Beast?" He looked from the Corvette to his now-displaced love, Estelle's department Charger.

"*Sin duda, hijo.* But radar's faster yet." She kept her hand on his square shoulder as they walked to the house, an unpretentious brick ranch-style, nestling now in deep shade from the five elms that over the years had drunk enough water to float an aircraft carrier. Her husband's SUV was not in the driveway, just her own personal Taurus. With a feeling of warm relief, Estelle saw that Addy Sedillos' Nissan pickup was parked ahead of the Corvette. Carlos Guzman's nickname for Addy, "The Family Coordinator," was apt. Carlos might no longer require "sitting," but the one-hundred-year-old Teresa Reyes did, and that, combined with Dr. Guzman's frenetic schedule and Estelle's own, kept Adorina "Addy" Sedillos busy.

"Did Papá happen to call?"

Carlos shook his head soberly. "He was home for a little bit earlier, before Francisco and Angie got here, but Dr. Guzman called about ten minutes ago to report that he'll be locked in consult with Dr. Perrone for a bit longer." He grinned at his own droll delivery, then turned serious. "Some nasty autopsy thing that Dr. Perrone wanted to finish ASAP."

"We'll talk about that," Estelle said. "But right now, is there any food left in the house?"

"Sure. Lots, Mamá. Oh, and Addy said that *Maestro* and I were probably going to stay over at Padrino's for the next couple of nights. Is that okay? Padrino has something going on out at the mesa, so he might not be home right away."

"Surprise, surprise," Estelle chuckled. *That's one worry down,* she thought, thanks to the quick thinking *nana.* "Then we might manage a normal dinner. Fashionably late, but I'll take what I can get."

"We might, Mamá, if you're home for a while."

She looked at him affectionately. "For a few minutes, I promise."

"We'll throw something together, then." His sunny countenance darkened again and his shoulders slumped. "We heard about Coach Scott. Gilly next door told me. Is that really true?"

"I afraid it is, *hijo.*"

"I guess both you and Papá are involved with that." He nodded as if that covered it all, then added, "Mr. Dayan has called for you several times."

"I don't doubt it." She had seen the newspaperman's number, now a list of calls, on her caller ID. That he would have also tried her land line was expected, and no doubt the inbox of her e-mail was cluttered. Estelle wondered if by now there was a single person in Posadas who hadn't heard some version of Scott's death.

"This is a tough one?" Carlos asked.

She wrapped an arm around his square shoulders. "Oh, *sí.* This is a tough one, in many, many ways, *hijo.*"

Chapter Twenty-three

Carlos opened the storm door for her. Addy Sedillos stood at the mouth of the hallway, leaning forward, an arm on each corner as she listened to a voice coming from the depths of the house.

"Not that long," she called in reply just as Estelle stepped inside the house. "And your mom's home, so don't dawdle!" With a wide grin, she pushed herself upright. "How's this for a surprise?" she said, and stepped quickly to Estelle to envelope her in a hug. "Did you know these folks were coming?"

"Surprise, surprise," Estelle responded again dryly. In the living room, her mother was sitting in her one and only rocker, her aluminum walker near at hand. Two days shy of the century mark, Teresa still refused the convenience of a wheelchair, preferring to inch along, even though bent considerably out of the vertical. Sitting on the fireplace hearth beside Estelle's mother, her left hand clasped firmly by both of Teresa's, was Angela Trevino.

Estelle had no need to guess, since Carlos, always the master of what might become an uncomfortable situation, said brightly, "Mamá, this is Angela Trevino from Leister Academy, one of Francisco's classmates. Angie, this is my mother, Estelle Reyes-Guzman, undersheriff of Posadas County." He spoke with perfect aplomb, without a trace of puff or posture.

Angie already, Estelle thought.

The girl rose to her feet the moment she saw Estelle, her smile brilliant but a bit restrained. Her grip when she shook hands was firm and lingering. "Mrs. Guzman, this is a pleasure. You know, I missed meeting you at Chelwood Commons. I've heard so much about you from Francisco, and I have to say…" She paused, a hint of blush touching her olive cheeks. "His descriptions of you were glowing, but they didn't do you justice."

Estelle's first choice of under what conditions to meet her elder son's first "girl friend" did not include packing utilities. She had shed her light suit jacket for the drive home from Cruces, and at the moment, her vest, badge, gun, cuffs, mace, and small handheld radio offered not the warm, cozy image that she might have otherwise chosen. Angela didn't seem to mind, nor did she seem in the least intimidated.

"Well, I'm too tired, dirty, and grumpy to be *glowing*, but you caught us all by surprise, Miss Trevino." She couldn't help noticing the strength of the girl's grip—anything but dainty. "Welcome to whirlwind central."

"Mamá, how was your day?" Estelle stepped close, bent, and hugged the tiny woman, struck once again by how frail she had become.

"Out the window, I see this fancy car drive up…who do you suppose gets out?" Teresa pointed a bent index finger in the girl's direction. "And the grandson." She paused, dark eyes regarding first Angela, then Estelle. "Who's to think?"

"Francisco wanted to surprise you, Mrs. Reyes," Angie said.

"Well, he succeeded," Estelle added with a bit more acid than she would have liked. She regarded the tan hard case that rested on the floor under the protection of the piano, the rectangular case about right for a tenor saxophone or in this instance, one of those flat, high-tec electronic cellos. "That fits in the car?"

"Just. With a little careful finagling. It's a good thing that it's not a traditional cello, or we'd have to tie it on the roof somehow." Angie laughed. "Francisco thought he was going to have to hold it in his lap, but there's no room for that. The car is gorgeous, but it's not the most practical thing."

"I can see that. Let me shed about ten pounds, then we can relax. How about a few minutes out on the back patio? It's a perfect evening. And did the butler offer you something to drink?"

"I did," Carlos said instantly. "Iced tea, hot tea, iced coffee, hot coffee. Diet Coke. Regular Coke." He closed his eyes, ticking the items off on his fingers as he rocked back and forth. "Fudge. *Empanadas.* Cheese."

He took a breath, and Angela laughed, a delightfully throaty chuckle. "Nothing just now, but thanks. We've been snacking nonstop since we left Kansas. Addy said something about Carlos making his signature dish…green chile lasagna? I need to work on some empty space." She rested a hand on her flat stomach.

"Well, *I* need an iced tea, please, *hijo.*" Estelle extended her arm toward the back door just as Francisco padded down the hall, barefoot, his summer outfit consisting only of a pair of white shorts.

"Hey, Ma!" he said, eschewing the *mamá* that had worked for the first fifteen years of his life. Finally breaking the hug, Estelle held him at arm's length, one hand clamped on each bare shoulder, the muscles like rock. He smelled of a fresh shower, his hair a finger-combed tangle.

"*Por Dios,* look at you. You've put on some weight, *hijo.* At least they're feeding you between concerts."

"Oh, a little. Plus I've discovered soccer, and I'm in a training program that tries to make us fit." He grinned. "The side benefit is that it makes it easier to sit on a piano bench for hours without falling face-first into the keys. Beethoven takes no prisoners, you know."

"I've come to appreciate that. Soccer, now?"

He shrugged. "It's just intramural, but it's fun."

"Well, the fighting trim suits you, *hijo.*" *The little boy is gone,* she thought. *Too fast.* "Angela and I are going to sit out back for a little bit. Now that we all know how beautiful you are, go put on some clothes and join us." He made an impatient face. "We have a lot to talk about," she added.

Carlos met her at the sliding door, and extended the glass of iced tea toward her. She took it, and bent a little toward him, the other hand affectionate on the back of his head. "Give us a few minutes, okay, *hijo*?"

"Sure," he said, understanding perfectly. "Did you want me to see if Padrino is home yet? We're having lasagna with key lime for dessert, and he kinda likes that."

"*Kinda* likes? By all means. You may have to try his cell phone, though. Let it ring about a hundred times."

She held the back door for Angela. "Padrino is Bill Gastner, a legend in these parts. He's the boys' godfather."

"Many, many miles were spent recounting Sheriff Gastner's history," Angela said. "I feel as if I've known him for years. There is apparently a short list of people whom Francisco thinks very highly of, besides his immediate family. I think Bill Gastner is probably number one on that list. I look forward to meeting him."

Francisco reappeared, this time wearing an ebony polo shirt with the *Steinway* logo in gold over the left breast pocket, making a dramatic contrast with the white shorts. He slid the door shut and then ducked under the table's umbrella.

"So," Estelle said, "this is a delightful surprise. I wish we could have enjoyed a little *anticipation* of it as well." She leaned forward, the creak of leather reminding her that, despite her intentions, she had forgotten to shed those ten pounds of hardware. Francisco looked uncomfortable, but chose not to respond.

Her words punctuated by the rip of hook and loop fasteners as she pulled out of the vest, she asked, "How did this trip come to be?"

Francisco held out both hands on the table, cupped together in the "this is how it is" gesture. "Angie's great-grandmother celebrated her one-hundredth birthday earlier in the week, up at their home in Ridgeway. And it was Angie's eighteenth birthday as well. Her folks drove down to Leister to pick her up so she could take part in the celebration. They invited me along, since Angie and I had worked on a piece of music for both of them…well, for all three. Angie and her great, and *mi abuela*." He shrugged as if to say, "That's it. It seemed like the logical thing to zip on over here and perform the piece for Teresa, too."

"Ah." *Every decision you make now*, she thought. *Every one, made on your own without someone leaning over your shoulder, telling you what to do...* She felt left behind, since this young man had obviously been marching to his own drummer for longer than she cared to admit.

Estelle turned, elbows on the chair arms and her hands knotted together under her chin. "So...your parents picked you and my son up at the academy, and drove you back to Ridgeway, Kansas. And there you found the Corvette parked in your driveway, a big yellow bow on top?"

"Pink." The girl stretched out her arms just far enough to rest both hands on top of Francisco's right arm. "My dad's extravagant idea of a birthday present for me." She adjusted her position slightly. "You would have to meet my dad to understand. He's petrified that I'll turn forty, and suddenly discover that the only serious relationship I will ever have is with my cello. So he buys me a boy magnet."

The tone of her voice hinted to Estelle that Angie would have been just as delighted with a fresh tablet of music manuscript paper.

"I can't imagine that happening." Estelle glanced at Francisco. "The turning forty part without company, I mean. You two met when?"

"This past spring," he said. "We both were taking one of the enrichment classes they encourage at Leister. This one was instrument repair."

"A hands-on, how-to class," Angela added. "A fun break. And a challenge, to do things right. I did a good job on one of Mateo Atencio's flutes." She smiled brightly, and Estelle remembered the tall, elegant, handsome teen flutist who had accompanied Francisco to Posadas for a home concert. "When I finished, the school didn't even have to redo it."

"It's the sort of class for people who decide to teach, like in a public school?" Francisco interjected. "Like when little Buzzy's cornet gets run over by a bus? There isn't always an instrument repair facility in town."

"So that's where you two met."

"Well," Francisco said, "we didn't *meet* there, but circumstances brought us closer together." He leaned forward. "She's been accepted to Julliard, by the way." He rested his hand on top of hers.

"Just 'by the way'? Angie, congratulations."

"The car is going to sit at home while she's in New York."

Wonderful. "When do you go?"

"Next fall," Angie whispered. "I'll finish this year at Leister, and then New York. I am excited and terrified."

"I would think so." Estelle sipped her tea. "So the two of you decided to attend your great-grandmother's birthday anniversary at your home in Kansas—your birthday and hers. And then you decided to drive out here from Kansas for Grandmamá's one-hundredth."

"Yep." Francisco sounded as if the decision was the world's most natural.

"And your parents were all right with that?" She regarded the girl thoughtfully. Angela Trevino was startlingly beautiful, as Sergeant Jackie Taber had reported, but she was no emaciated fashion model…too much muscle through the shoulders for that. Her fingers were long and strong, her hands actually quite large. Hers was the body of an Olympic slalom skier or champion swimmer, lots of power combined with confident grace.

"After many, many admonitions," Angie said. "My folks are fans of Francisco's, and after a little discussion, they decided it would be a good adventure for us. 'Away from those stuffy old classrooms,' my father said."

"And your mom?"

"She was all right with it when she heard that the only way we could do it was to drive straight through. It's the motel part that worried her."

Estelle laughed as another element of worry lifted. "She has a point, you know. That Corvette must act a little bit like a chastity belt."

"Ma, you're embarrassing me," Francisco protested.

"You'll deal with it," she replied, and added to Angie, "I look forward to meeting your mom and dad."

"Mom wasn't just red-hot on the idea of all the driving on the interstates, but she came around. And I have to tell you," and she leaned toward Estelle, "after about the first five hundred miles, *I* wasn't so red-hot for the idea anymore either."

"And you did the trip nonstop?"

"Just quick pit stops, Ma." Francisco said. "Food, gas. Food, gas. Food, gas."

"And the *only* time we got stopped was by your Sergeant Taber, right here in Posadas. No ticket, just a warning for rolling a stop sign. She was very nice, by the way. No nonsense, but very nice."

"She can be." Estelle glanced at her watch. "So…you're here for how long? How long do we have in order to figure out what to do with you?"

Francisco looked puzzled. "What day is this?"

"This be Friday," Estelle replied.

The boy looked relieved. "Okay. We have to be back at Leister on Tuesday night. I'm supposed to be playing demos for a History of Music lecture on Wednesday, so, yeah…any time on Tuesday works for me. Angie has a meeting with the dean on Thursday morning, so she's got some extra hours. It's lookin' like we need to leave Sunday sometime."

"Mamá asked that we take her to a short mass Sunday morning in Tres Santos. Do you remember Father Anselmo?"

"Sure."

"He's saying a special mass just for her. It would be wonderful if you'd be able to accompany us to that."

"Perfect. I've been to Tres Santos, what…once, that I remember?"

"It will mean a lot to her if you go, I'm sure."

"Do they have a piano?"

Estelle smiled. "No piano. Father Anselmo brings his electronic keyboard."

Francisco beamed. "That'll work!"

"The mission was always a study in simplicity," Estelle said to Angie. "And after it burned in 1980, they've made do with even less. When they rebuilt, they chose expediency—a small frame structure with wooden benches. An altar was donated from Janos. As mother is fond of saying, 'It's the faith that's important, not the building.'"

"You could take your cello," he said to Angie, whose only response was a raised eyebrow. "Something simple and short, like Mozart's *Laudate Dominum*. That would be special."

"You think?" Angie didn't sound wild with enthusiasm.

"Yes, I do. I have the music somewhere in one of my old piano books from years ago."

How many years is "years ago" when one is still only fifteen? Estelle mused silently.

"I always thought that piece was the definition of 'elegant,'" Francisco added.

"I'll play it for your grandmother tomorrow, maybe. If she would like…" She nodded thoughtfully.

The patio door slid open, and Dr. Francis Guzman filled the opening. Burly and well over six feet tall, he had long ago earned the affectionate nickname *Oso*, or "Bear" from Estelle. Neither Francisco nor Carlos had inherited his brawn, instead favoring their mother's lean, chiseled look. His beard, trimmed short, broke into a wide smile.

"Wow," he said, and let that suffice. With a quick step, he crossed to Estelle and enveloped her in a crushing hug, then straightened up, still holding her hand. "This is quite the surprise." He stepped around the table and Francisco disappeared in the folds of another ferocious hug. "We're going to have to start calling you Rocky." He stepped back a bit and encircled Francisco's upper right arm with both hands. He glanced over at Estelle. "Remember when this used to be a little twig?" He released the boy and held up an index finger as he thumped the flat of Francisco's chest with the other hand. "Don't go away. I have to meet…" He looked expectantly at Angie, who had risen and circled the small table. She held out a hand.

"I'm Angela Trevino. I'm also a student at Leister." The last word was partially muffled as Dr. Guzman used the proffered handshake as a handy way to pull the girl into another mammoth hug.

"Wow," he said again as he released the girl and found an empty chair between his wife and son. "So…" He shook his head and turned, about to sit down as the door slid open, this time for Carlos, who carried another glass of iced tea. The boy leaned over and placed it carefully on the table, then turned just in time to be snatched up by his father. Carlos, at nearly eleven, was not a wisp of a child, but Francis stepped away from the chair, grabbed the boy around the waist and spun him away from the table, flipping him upside down with a ferocious growl so it appeared as if he were preparing to pile-drive the youngster's head into the flagstones. Carlos screeched. After a moment, Francis lowered him until his hands could touch the stones, then let him collapse back to earth.

"Not long before I can't do that anymore," he huffed to Estelle as he fell back into his chair.

"Did you see the 'Vette outside, Papá?" Carlos straightened his clothes and sat Buddha-style on the flagstone step leading into the dining room.

"I thought maybe that was something your mother confiscated after a traffic stop."

"I wish it was confiscated," Carlos said. "They came all the way from Kansas!"

"They would have to," Francis said reasonably, and Carlos made a face, having heard the joke dozens of times.

"If they didn't come all the way, they wouldn't be here," Carlos finished for his father. "Angie said I could drive it!"

"Absolutely. For your sixty-fifth birthday, *hijo.*" Francis clasped his hands over his stomach and regarded Angie. "So— break the news gently, now. The two of you drove, that's obvious. What's in Kansas?" He tipped his head a little sideways, regarding his elder son critically while Francisco explained the round-robin route that he and Angie had taken, first with her parents and then heading west solo in the birthday-machine.

"A spur-of-the-moment impulse," the doctor mused when the tale concluded.

"Well, sort of. We—I mean Angie and I—talked about it for quite a while, after her folks drove us to Kansas, and then sprang the surprise car on her. See," he said, sounding like a talented car salesman, "*Before* they gave her the car, we hadn't figured out a way to get home for just a weekend. I guess we could have taken a bus or something. Fly into Albuquerque or Cruces, maybe. But there's a lot of hassle with that, no matter how we did it. Somebody had to pick us up at the airport, take us back...all that."

"How many hours?"

"The drive? I guess somewhere around twenty. We listened to a lot of music, and did a lot of other work. The car makes a good think-chamber sort of place. A lot of the time, I was working on the piano-cello duet for Grandmamá. I should say *we* were working on it. We finished the rough-out about the time we stopped in Lubbock for gas."

The physician frowned at his tea glass, then shifted it to spread the little puddle of condensation across the plastic tablecloth's pattern. "I'd be a liar if I said that two teens driving cross-country nonstop in a flashy sports car didn't concern me just a little bit."

"We were careful, Papá. And Angie's a good driver. And the cruise control is a great gadget for avoiding speeding tickets."

"But all the while, we didn't know anything about this trip, or where you might be."

"We checked in regularly with my folks," Angie offered. "And I have to admit that I forgot to do that once in a while. If I missed a deadline, my phone let me know. When we stopped for fuel, I would call."

He smiled. "Maybe you'll teach my son how to use a phone."

"I'm always apprehensive that I might interrupt something," Francisco tried.

Francis leaned forward, turning his head so that he could look toward the kitchen. "You know that box that sits with the land line? The answering machine?"

"Yes, Papá."

"We'd like to be able to look forward to your visits. To know you're coming."

"Yes, sir."

Francis turned back to Angie and regarded her for a long moment as if he were pondering what drug to prescribe. "It must be difficult for you."

"Sir?"

"The balance. Balancing who you both are—what you're both becoming—with the normal, run-of-the-mill world and its business. My first inclination is to wrap you both in a safe cocoon until you hit the world concert stage as adults." He flashed a grin. "But, Angie, I guess your birthday says that you're already there, aren't you? Whether we like it or not." Neither youngster spoke, and the physician added, "I'm not sure that I would balance the very real *risks* of a trip like this against what you could stand to lose with one mishap."

"And you and Mamá do that every day when you walk out the front door," Francisco said gently, sounding far more mature than the fifteen-year-old he was.

"Well, your mother does." Francis smiled again at them both. "But…here you are. And somehow, you guys have to get back to school, which means a return trip, and again I'd be lying if I didn't admit that that worries me a little." He pulled his shoulders up in a slow shrug. He turned to look at Estelle. "Maybe we can ship them back via UPS."

"I'll take care of the car!" Carlos chirped.

"Yeah, you will." Francis stretched out and rested his fist on top of the boy's head. "First things first, though. Is Bill on his way over?" He looked at his watch and grimaced.

"He said he wouldn't miss it," Carlos informed them. "He said he was just about on his way, Papá."

"Perfect. The late night meeting of Insomniacs Anonymous." Francis leaned forward, chin on hand, and watched Estelle's phone spin a slow, lazy circle on the table where she had placed it earlier. "You want to turn that off?" He grinned, but it was an expression of resignation. He looked at the little window where the incoming calls were displayed. "Especially from him."

"*Ay,*" Estelle whispered.

Chapter Twenty-four

"I'm really sorry to be calling so late, Estelle."

"No, you're not, Frank." Estelle stepped inside and closed the patio door behind her. She kept her tone light, even playful.

"Well, see, I was desperate. I have an Associated Press feed deadline coming up, and I feel like I'm running barefoot down a gravel road trying to catch a fire engine."

"Nice image, sir. I'd like a photo of that. What can I do for you?"

"Look, Estelle, this is a horrible thing. Just horrible. For a good man, for the community, for any reason we can think of. What can you give me about Coach Scott's murder? Anything at all yet? I mean, other than 'the investigation is continuing'?"

"That would be accurate, along with those other favorites like 'We're exploring new leads but have made no arrests.' You're going to have to be patient with us, Frank."

"Patience, the AP doesn't have. And what new leads? I tried to talk with our favorite sheriff." He hesitated. "That didn't go at all well, for the ten seconds that our conversation lasted. Is it true the school is locked down?"

"Empty and locked, Frank. 'Lockdown' implies something else that is not accurate in this instance…like kids inside, under possible threat. That's not the case here."

"Okay. I'm not sure I see the difference, but we'll go with 'closed.' Archer tells me no school Monday. Or maybe on into Tuesday."

"That's my understanding. Whatever it takes."

"So…what can you give me?"

"Are you doing a special edition?" The regular issue of the *Posadas Register* would be released Thursday, which meant Frank Dayan and his tiny staff had plenty of time.

"No, I hadn't planned on that."

"Then by later in the week, the whole complexion of this case may have changed, Frank."

"Well, I have my AP feeds all the time. This one is a big deal, Estelle."

"I understand that. It was for Coach Scott, as well."

Dayan made an odd little humming sound, as if he couldn't decide how to respond to Estelle's comment. Finally, he said, "Dr. Archer said that it was brutal, but he wouldn't comment beyond that."

"He's correct. But then again, I can't remember a murder that *wasn't* brutal, Frank. That's the nature of the beast with which we're dealing."

Silence followed that.

Finally the newspaper publisher said, "Something like this rocks the community."

"I would imagine so. And I don't mean to be snide, but it seems to me that's the way the media usually describes something like this. 'Rampant rumor' may be more accurate, but people don't like to see that in the headline."

This time he uttered a resigned chuckle. "You're a hard person to quote. Although maybe I disagree. 'Rampant rumor' might look good in a headline."

"The Sheriff's Department is not releasing any details of the murder at this time," Estelle said. "It's premature, and we have too many loose ends."

"Thanks. At least you admit that it's a murder."

"Most certainly it is that. You may quote me on that, Frank."

"So what's the Las Cruces connection?"

"I beg your pardon?"

"I understand that you took a fast trip to Las Cruces this evening. I was assuming it was somehow related to the case."

"Assumptions," Estelle said cryptically. "Just out of curiosity, who told you that I went to Cruces?"

"Ah…I don't want to get anybody in trouble, Sheriff. I think I heard it on the scanner. Just a mention. I knew you weren't going there for back-to-school shopping. What was the deal?"

"Frank…please. It's too early to spread all our cards out on the table."

"No persons of interest?"

"You know I can't tell you that."

He exhaled loudly. "So, if not that…is there anything you can tell me about the Bonds' case?"

For a moment Estelle drew a blank. She had given no thought to the odd couple from Illinois who currently enjoyed the county lockup. "Ah, the Bonds. They are awaiting arrangements for extradition back to Illinois."

"Local charges pending?"

"I'm not sure what the district attorney has decided."

"But I'm hearing there was an assault on one of the officers."

"In the course of the apprehension, a small caliber weapon was discharged. One shot. I don't know if it was accidental or intentional. The bullet grazed one of the officer's boots and was recovered from the asphalt of the parking lot. And if you print that she was shot in the foot, I'm going skin you alive and short-circuit your AP leads, Frank."

That brought a laugh. "So they were armed."

"Indeed, they were."

"Both?"

"One had an uncharged CO_2 pistol, but anything that can be confused with a weapon *becomes* a weapon. The woman was in possession of the .25 caliber automatic. The gun discharged once and then jammed."

"Wow. Strange folks. What were they planning?"

"I couldn't tell you."

"Were they in possession of any drugs? Contraband? Stuff like that?"

"About sixty pounds of alfalfa. Wrapped in tidy little packages."

"You're joking."

"It's too late in the evening for that, Frank. I'll ask Lieutenant Mears to make the bundle available to you for a photo, if you'd like."

"You bet, I'd like. What was the hay for?"

"An excellent question. No comment from the Bonds."

"For sale as fake narcotics?"

"That's one possibility."

"I understand that Tom Pasquale made the original arrest. In the parking lot of The Spree."

"He made first contact, yes."

"What tipped him off?"

"A routine computer check turned a switched license plate."

With the excitement of a little kid, Frank Dayan changed direction. "And both dispatch and the EMS response log show an abandoned child case, too. Just about the same time. A child left in a car, or something like that?"

"Your sources are efficient, Frank."

"Well, it's been a busy day. Night. Whatever the hell it is right now."

"Did you have a good train ride this morning?" The question seemed an effective way of switching Frank away from what she knew would come if she didn't—questions about Stacie and Todd Stewart.

"Oh, fantastic. Have you had a chance to take that ride?"

"No."

"Well, you should. You know, it's my opinion that in a short time, folks are going to become believers. Miles Waddell really has something going with that project of his."

"He'll appreciate hearing that, Frank. Or seeing it in print. Most of the time, he's the butt-end of ignorant rumors."

"I've sifted a few of those myself. 'Our mesa-top missile base.' Things like that. By the by, I'm heading up to the mesa again later tomorrow. Any chance of seeing you up there?"

"Probably not. My plate is full at the moment."

"I just wondered how the investigation of the graffiti vandalism is going. I was going to see what photos I can get."

Estelle sighed. "That's what the taggers want, all right. Some good Page One publicity, Frank."

"You're thinking it's a bad idea?"

"Yes, I am. But you're the newspaper guy. It's your call. Whoever the taggers are, what they want is for people to see their work. I hate to see them encouraged, Frank. But, like I said, it's your call."

"Well, I'll check it out. I don't understand how they got up on the big dish in the first place."

"I don't follow?"

"They painted a panel up on the rim of the big dish. Up on top. Can you imagine? They must have used sky hooks. Nobody saw them get past the security fence, and nobody saw them up there."

"I'm sure Miles was delighted."

"Oh, you know how he is—Mr. Mellow."

Estelle looked at her watch. "Anything else, Frank? I really need to go."

"Just thanks for talking to me."

"You're welcome. Any time."

"You don't mean that, and you know it."

"Well, *almost* any time. Good night, Frank."

Chapter Twenty-five

She punched off the phone, and startled as a pair of muscular arms encircled her shoulders from behind.

"We could be featured in *Successful Parenting* magazine," Francis whispered in her ear. "Keep the kids up until all hours and feed them rich lasagna to fuel their dreams."

"Well, as Bill Gastner is fond of saying, 'Events conspire.'" She turned and snuggled against her husband. "What was your day like?"

"Now that's another long story. And I think Alan Perrone is going to be contacting you about the autopsy, when you both have the chance."

"Anything unusual?"

"As far as I'm concerned, the whole thing was unusual. Bobby managed to stop by for a few minutes. He thinks the gun involved was a thirty-eight, not a three-fifty-seven. Two of the rounds didn't go through and through. The two that did weren't hugely explosive in exit, like we'd expect from a magnum. Still," he shrugged, "it was obvious to me that the last shot was meant to make very sure. Scott was essentially gone when that last shot was fired through the heart."

"Did anything change Bobby's mind about the trajectory of the shots?"

"I don't think so. No stippling with the first three, so the shooter had to have been some distance away. At least eight feet or so."

"No surprises, then."

"No." He stretched hugely. "Long day, and I'm still pooped from last night." He drew her back into another hug. "You already know about that from the patrol log, I'm sure. The kid tangled with a deer, then lost it and sent his truck into a utility pole. What a mess. Bishop said for sure he was speeding, which he'd have to be to inflict that much damage. And no seat belt, so among other things, he suffered a ruptured spleen when he smashed into the rim of the steering wheel. That, along with a broken left elbow, cuts and bruises, head laceration with a possible concussion. Really nasty."

"Over near where he lives?"

"That's the ironic part," Francis said. "He *walks* home from the wreck, if you can imagine that. Only a hundred yards or so, but still. By the time he got to his front door, he would have been just about crawling. I'm surprised he made it."

"*Ay.* Who made the ambulance call?"

"I'm told that it was his mother. She was home, thank goodness for that."

"What did he tell the deputy?"

"I'm not sure he said much. By the time I saw him in the ER, he was right on the verge. We pumped some blood into him, and he's lucky. The medevac was over in Cruces, and got here in a hurry."

"So he's at UNMH now?"

Francis nodded. "Tough little bugger, for sure."

"Efrin. He's Art Garcia's little brother, I think. *That's* been a couple of years."

"That?"

"This guy here would know." She nodded at the shiny Dodge SUV that had glided up to the curb. Bill Gastner took his time getting out, and when he closed the door behind him, he stood for a few moments, looking up at the sky. At one time a big, burly fellow, Gastner had shed considerable weight. Still he was nothing approaching svelte, but at least not carrying the sort of poundage that crippled knees and hips.

He walked around the SUV, just the trace of a gimp marking his progress. He carried a cane that could be folded out into a minimal canvas seat—a "photographer's stool," he called it.

"You guys keep this up, and you'll join us denizens of the night." Gastner stepped carefully up onto the sidewalk, then ambled toward them. "Kids go to bed, after all?"

"No. They're lying in wait inside. A special night, I guess. That's my excuse."

He pointed the cane toward the Corvette. "Is this their ride?"

"Yes. Non-stop from Kansas."

"Ah, the energy of youth." Gastner's imitation of W.C. Fields was spot-on. "How's the grand lady?"

Estelle laughed. "*She's* the only smart one. She went to bed a bit ago."

Gastner walked halfway to the front stoop and stopped again. "My radio about burned itself out today."

"It's been busy."

The old man ran a hand across the short gray stubble that topped his round skull. "Frank Dayan's going to have a stroke, I think. *And* Leona Spears tried to corral me. *And* Arnie Gray, for God's sakes. It's been a while since a county commission chairman tried to nose his way into your business. I don't know what they think *I* can tell 'em. Or *would* tell 'em, I should say." He stepped into a bear hug with Estelle, then turned loose and shook hands with Francis. "You look as if you've been up 'round the clock yourself, Doctor."

"A very, very interesting day," Francis replied.

"I just had a conversation with Frank," Estelle said. "Leona hasn't called me, which is a surprise." The county manager, an accomplished gadfly, liked to talk with Estelle, who would listen to her, as opposed to trying to pry information from Bob Torrez, who wouldn't.

"You know, just a nasty time." Gastner followed that with a resigned shake of the head. "Any ideas who Coach Scott crossed?"

"Only the vaguest of notions. Slim possibilities."

"At least you know it wasn't simple robbery. I wouldn't think a shower would be the place for that." He dug the tip of his cane into the sod, flipped the canvas seat open, and gently lowered himself. "Ah, that's the ticket." He folded his arms across his still-ample stomach, balanced with his feet spread wide. "You know, a little bit full of himself, that guy," Gastner said. "I got to know him years ago when he was one of the assistant football coaches. Surprised the hell out of me when he jumped to volleyball." The former sheriff's passion for Posadas Jaguars football was no secret. "A little more center-stage, maybe. Hell of a record he's amassed, though."

A small form appeared, gazing through the screen door. "Padrino is here, and the lasagna is cool enough to cut," Carlos announced in a loud stage whisper.

"The words I long to hear." Gastner rose from his stool, folded it, and followed Estelle and Francis inside. Both boys earned hugs, and then Gastner stopped and stood stock still, hands on his hips, regarding Francisco's traveling companion.

"Padrino, this is Angela Trevino, from school," Francisco said.

Gastner reached out and took Angela's hand thoughtfully. "What a pleasure, Angela Trevino from school. And you play what, other than this young man's heartstrings?"

Angela ducked her head in amused embarrassment at Gastner's blunt assessment, but then offered a radiant smile. "The cello, sir."

"She's headed for Julliard," Francisco added.

Gastner turned his head and cocked an eyebrow at the fifteen-year-old. "And you haven't decided yet whether that's a good thing or not." He paused. "Unless you're going along."

"Most likely not, Padrino."

"Most likely not." Gastner was clearly amused at Francisco's precise manner of speech. "Well, time will tell. So you two vagrants *drove* down here from," and he waved a hand eastward, "somewhere over there. Long haul."

"Yes, sir."

"And you're off again when?"

"Sometime Sunday, we think."

"Well, even a short visit is better than none at all." He pointed an index finger at both boys, one of whom was delivering the dish of lasagna to the table. "You two are staying at my *casa,* right?" He looked at Estelle. "Right?"

"That would be perfect, if you'll have them," she said.

"Well, you have a key, so make yourselves at home. And you know where the food is, or bring what you like." He leaned forward and inhaled deeply. "On the off-chance that there might be any leftovers from *this.*" He circled Addy's waist with one arm as she set a large glass bowl of Caesar salad on the table, along with a large loaf of garlic bread. "We should do this more often," he added.

For the next half-hour, conversation played light, with Gastner a seemingly inexhaustible source of questions for Francisco and Angela, but he skillfully included Carlos as well. At one point, his fork laden with lasagna, he leaned over close to the small boy, who had made it a point of securing the chair on Padrino's immediate right, and said in a gruff stage whisper, "Do you have *any* idea just how good this is, kiddo?"

Carlos nodded vigorously. "Thank you."

"You're entirely welcome. The question is, did Adorina lend her talents to it, or is it a solo performance?"

"Carlos made it all by his lonesome," Addy said from the kitchen. "You're lucky there aren't chocolate chips in it."

Dessert was another of the little boy's trademarks, a key lime pie's crisp, cold flavor helped to mellow the aftereffects of the lasagna's green chile. Finally, as dishes were being cleared to the kitchen by the younger generation, Estelle leaned close to Gastner. "Do you remember anything about Coach Scott that might shed any light?"

Gastner grimaced. "Are you kidding? I don't even remember getting up this morning." He shook his head. "No, as far as I'm concerned, he was just another face in the parade of coaches who come and go. Except he never left, for some reason. He found whatever he was after right here in lowly old Posadas." He sipped his coffee thoughtfully. "Maybe a classic example of a big fish in a small pond." He set the cup down carefully. "You know, I never actually spoke to him. Face-to-face, I mean. One-on-one. Never had the occasion."

He lowered his voice another notch. "Somebody just walked into the school after-hours and found him alone?"

"Yes. It appears that way. He was in the shower."

"Good God. So what's the direction so far?"

"We're concerned...*I'm* concerned, that Stacie Stewart might be somehow involved." His grizzled eyebrows shot up at that, but he waited as Francisco approached.

"We're going out to the patio for a bit," the boy said, and Estelle watched as her older son escorted Angie Trevino, a hand light on her elbow, out through the sliding doors. The boy was mindful to close the door behind him, rather than leave the screen gaping, giving his parents and Padrino privacy. Carlos clanked and banged in the kitchen, and Addy leaned on the counter.

"Shall I buzz over to Mr. G's place and get the rooms ready?"

"By all means," Gastner said. "Use the two adult bunk beds in Buddy's room. The bedding is in that closet. Lock up all my valuables, put a padlock on the fridge, and chain the pitbull. And warn the neighbors."

"That would be wonderful, Addy," Estelle added. "Thanks so much." She pulled the girl into a hug.

"Are you headed out again tonight?" Gastner asked.

"I need some sleep," Estelle said. "I'm starting to go in circles."

He watched Addy head out the front door, face thoughtful. "So what's with this Stacie Stewart thing?"

"She's disappeared, Padrino. She went to The Spree, left her baby in the car along with a puppy, and that was the last we saw of her. Tommy Pasquale watched her go inside the store, and that's it. We haven't seen her since. Todd is trying his best to cope, but he doesn't know which way to turn."

"Huh."

"This is what bothers me, Padrino. LT and I watched the volleyball game video from the night before. There she is, sitting immediately *behind* Coach Scott, buddy-buddy with her elbow resting on his shoulder. And then sometime shortly after the game, he's murdered and the next day, she splits town. Hubby has no idea where she went. *That's* what worries me."

"I can't see hubby working up the gumption to go on a shooting rampage."

"Nor I…unless he's up for an Academy Award acting job. When I saw him earlier at the hospital where the EMTs took the baby, *that's* what his mind was on—not murder. And by then, Scott was dead."

Gastner pursed his lips. "So what happens tomorrow?"

"We need to go through Scott's house and see what we turn up. I need to go through Stacie's things, which Todd is not going to like."

"Not that that matters."

"No, but…Then we hit up Scott's colleagues to see what we can turn."

"Sex, drugs, money, or power…that's what makes the world go 'round. Any or all."

"There was no apparent physical fight, so no forensic trail there. And there's no sign that the killer and Scott stood in the shower, having a spirited conversation before the shots were fired. I mean, he didn't even have time to turn off the water. It's a puzzle. As I recall, the kind of case you liked the best."

Gastner smiled. "That was back when I could remember from one minute to the next where the puzzle pieces went when I found a new one. You have a hell of a team, Sweetheart. Use every one of 'em." He leaned back and peered toward the kitchen. After a moment he was able to gain Carlos' attention. "Seconds on key lime? Carlos, how about that?" He held his fingers an inch or so apart. "Just a little savory piece, sort of a shot for the road?"

"Coffee with it?" the boy asked.

"Of course. Thank you." He turned back to Estelle and her husband. She was resting her head on Francis' shoulder, eyes heavy. "I'll scarf down the pie, and then get out of here." He cocked an eyebrow at the physician. "What keeps you busy these days?"

"Same old, same old," Francis said. "Right at the moment, it's babies on the way, elderly folks breaking various body parts, and the occasional teenager trying to defy gravity."

Gastner laughed. "Why do I not miss all of that?"

"Francis said they were working on Efrin Garcia last night in the ER," Estelle said. "He's about eighteen or a little older… Art's younger brother? You would remember Art Garcia, I think. He had a passionate love affair with trying to manufacture his own meth. Not especially successful, either."

"Oh, indeed, I do remember the lad. Art's father skipped to Mexico, leaving wife and kids behind. We thought he was probably the brewer behind the meth. It would have been better if he'd taken Art with him. But that was a while ago—I wasn't even sheriff then. But Efrin? How'd he get into trouble? Miles was wondering why he wasn't working today up on the mesa. He mentioned it to me when we were over in the theater on the tour. I think he wanted to show the kid off to the press. I mean, that's *quite* the mural he's got going."

"Sir?" Estelle pushed herself upright, leaving a hand firmly on her husband's shoulder.

"The kid is an amazing artist, if we're talking about the same Efrin Garcia. He's working on a huge mural that will circle the planetarium theater from one end of the curved screen all the way around the audience to the other end. What I saw was a section he just finished that features the Horsehead Nebula. *Most* impressive work, I gotta tell you. But Miles was a little concerned because the kid has about a hundred feet to go in order to finish up, and he decides to take a day off. But he's pretty quick with his airbrushes."

"He won't be finishing up any time soon," Francis said. "If he's very lucky, he'll live."

"What the hell happened?"

"Way too fast on one of our excellent county byways. First it's a deer, then he loses it and clips a utility pole. No seat belt, and he was tossed out. We shipped him off to UNMH. He might make it. We managed to stabilize him for a little bit." Francis grimaced. "Bad deal."

"Well, shit. Does Miles know?"

"We didn't know he worked for Miles, Bill. And he was in no condition for conversation."

"And now he's up in Albuquerque?"

Francis nodded. "Medevac transported him last night."

Gastner relaxed back in his chair, regarding the empty pie plate almost wistfully. "I was glad to see him hooked up with Waddell's project. There's lots of opportunity there for a talented artist. Kid gets in on the ground floor of a project like this, and there's no limit for him."

Estelle stared at Gastner for a moment, then rose suddenly and left the room. She returned in a moment with a photograph. "Did you get one of these earlier?"

"I did. Nice shot. They found that this morning on one of the railcars. There's another one on the dish itself, if you can figure that one out. Waddell was going to have a chat with Efrin later today."

"So he thinks Efrin did this?"

"We *know* he did. Well, let me amend that. *I* know he did. That's the first thing I told Miles, but he's one of those nice guys who would rather deny the possibility that somebody has crossed him. But he'll come around. You take that photo up to the theater and compare it with Efrin's mural and decide for yourself." He traced around the photo of the graffiti with his finger. "Same brilliant colors, same heavy use of deep space blacks. Same washes of really clean shades of gray. That's what drew my eye. Same clarity of design. I mean, I don't care much for modern art, and I sure as hell don't care much for gang graffiti, but this is a cut above, right? The kid is an airbrush artist."

Estelle remained silent.

"So you heard about the dish being defaced?"

"Both Bobby and Frank mentioned it."

"Yeah...I was thinking of breaking Frank's camera arm so he wouldn't get a photo of it, but right now the design is so high up, I don't think he can. Too far away. They had the dish parked like this," and he cut his hand sideways through the air, indicating a horizontal attitude, "while they worked on something or other. It's been that way for several days. And then they were doing something with the azimuth hardware this morning and tipped the dish almost all the way upright, as if it was listening to something just over on the horizon." He hand-chopped the air in a vertical line. "So there's the big dish facing out for the whole world to see, and what do you suppose is painted high up on the rim?"

He shrugged and added, "Were it not for my new job with Waddell, I would never have seen it." He held up two fingers, one to each eye. "But the crew sure as hell did."

"Your new job?"

"Of vast importance, too. Waddell wanted my input and advice about where to locate the new benches. See," and he drew a circle on the table, "this is the dish and the fence around it. Miles wants places for tourists to stop, rest, and gawk when they take a break from hiking the access trails. He's got a really nice, really ugly, and really insecure chain-link around the dish itself right now, and outside of that, he's marked about eight places where he's planning to put benches around the circumference of the site when the new arty fence is built. So, I go up there and sit and ruminate at different times of the day, making sure we don't install permanent benches that put the person staring right into the sun or some dumb thing." He shrugged again. "I'm good at sitting and ruminating."

"So you think Efrin Garcia painted the dish as well as the railcar."

"I do. And the only time the kid could have done it without sliding off into space was when the dish was parked, lying on its back. Even then, he'd have to be like one of those damn geckos that can cling to window glass. Go take a look. Take the photo of the railcar with you. Same use of color. Some design elements that are derivative." He chuckled. "Don't I sound like some goddamn art critic, though?"

"How would he get up there?"

"Piece of cake. Remember, Efrin is only eighteen or so. Monkey in human clothing. There are access ladderways all over. When the dish is parked the way it was, all the walkways line up. All a kid has to do is a pull-up to reach the first one, and up he goes, one stairway after another. The hatch out to the dish surface is secured with a couple thumb screws." He smiled. "At the moment, it is, anyway." He chuckled again. "Miles is going to change the fence, but that's always been in the works. Day by day, though, he's getting a bit less trusting. That in itself is an interesting evolution to watch."

Estelle frowned. "How'd Efrin avoid all the security to climb up there in the first place? All the workers?"

"Well," Gastner said dismissively, "dark night, dark T-shirt, dark pants...no problem."

"And because he works on the mesa, it would be no problem to *be* there at night. He wouldn't have the problem of getting through security down at the gate."

"Perhaps so. Have you talked with him?"

"No," Estelle said. "Bobby made sure that everyone saw a copy of the railcar photo, but I didn't give it much thought. I was busy with other things."

"Efrin's not talking at the moment," Dr. Guzman offered.

"How long was he without medical attention after his crash?"

"That's hard to say. Not too long, actually. I think that's why he's still alive." He rubbed his side. "Lots of blood loss from the lacerated spleen. Perrone said he got six more units in Albuquerque, in addition to the four we pumped into him. When he was brought to the ER, his pulse was rock bottom."

"Well, he'll keep." Gastner watched Estelle's face as she regarded the tablecloth with more concentration than it deserved. "What?"

"Are you up for going for a ride, *Padrino?*"

"What, you mean right now?" He glanced at his wristwatch. Dr. Guzman groaned, and Estelle clamped both hands on the doctor's forearm.

"I have to do this while I'm thinking about it," she said. "It won't take long."

Chapter Twenty-six

Gastner's new SUV was comfortable enough, and Estelle raked the passenger seat up to make it less so. Just being chauffeured was a refreshing change, even though by not taking the Charger, she was leaving her "office" behind.

She reached down and turned on the Sheriff's Department radio. Even though the seventy-seven-year-old Gastner was long retired, both the department and he understood that he was a valuable resource for such an understaffed county. A radio was a cheap price to pay for an extra set of eyes and ears.

"Oh, sure," Gastner quipped as she did so. "Sometimes I really do remember to turn that damn thing on. Where to?"

"I want to drive by the middle school again. As long as we're talking graffiti, I want to show you what we have there, around by the back door of the middle school. In fact, why don't you go by way of Pershing? We have Esperanza sitting the place until about two, and then he and Jonas will switch. Jonas is covering Scott's. If we don't give the folks some sleep time, the whole department will be a bunch of zombies."

"She said, doing a fair enough imitation herself." In a moment, Gastner pointed ahead. "The light's out." Sure enough, the back of the old middle school loomed dark, not haloed like the rest of the school grounds. He let the SUV idle quietly into the parking lot. Up ahead, nestled into the shadows by the new gymnasium, Deputy Esperanza had parked the older department Crown Vic.

"You want to let him know we're here?"

"No," Estelle said. "Let him figure out what to do."

They parked in the corner of the lot, the back of the school just yards away, across a swath of gravel. Before she had the chance to nag Gastner about the insecure, tricky footing, he was pulling himself out of the car, cane-seat in hand. She joined him, slipping her arm through his. "Consider it companionable," she smiled.

"That's a nice way to put it."

The light over the door was dark, as was the big sodium vapor light a few yards away. Estelle focused the beam of her flashlight upward, illuminating the parking lot fixture. "Somebody's good with an air rifle," she said.

"Even those are going high-tech these days," Gastner said. "I used to think my Daisy Red Rider was the cat's meow."

Both of their flashlights illuminated the graffiti. "The same, no?"

"I'd say so. Sure. What little of it he managed to finish."

She stepped closer, and reached up with the light to touch the lower right corner of the design. "Those two parallel marks look like they were scraped across the design. I could imagine a ladder doing that if it skidded out from under him." She slipped the small digital camera out of her pocket, and it fired up with a jingle that sounded loud in the quiet night. In a moment, she handed it to Gastner. "Maybe you can see the damage more clearly here. I took these when Barry Lavin gave me the tour earlier this afternoon."

He examined the photo displayed on the small camera's view screen, and then held it up to compare with the wall. "My trifocals aren't made for this."

She reached over and touched the screen. "He only finished about a third of the design, and then quit for some reason."

"Huh. Maybe he ran out of paint. Maybe somebody caught him at it." He rested his hands on his hips. "So…tell me why we're wasting so much time with just another panel of gang art?"

"The obvious reason is that it's within two heartbeats of a homicide scene, Padrino."

"Well, sure enough. But so are a lot of other things."

"There's just too much happening all at once for some of the threads not to be tied together. Scott at the ball game, making friendly with Stacie Stewart. Then she disappears the day after the murder? I don't like that. Now we have gang graffiti that crops up right on the back wall outside the murder scene." She shoved her hands in her pockets. "Did Efrin Garcia do this? And the train? And the dish topside?"

"Well, I think he did," Gastner said. "But I've been wrong before."

She nodded at the wall. "Okay, say he did, Padrino. This panel isn't finished. What interrupted him? Something did, and he goes speeding off home, and piles his truck into a utility pole. All of that is why I'm spinning in circles just now, trying to find a path to follow."

"It'll be interesting to ask Mike if anyone drove by. I assume he's keeping a list." The Crown Vic had not moved from its position. As an unschooled rookie, Esperanza's instructions were to use the radio, not to confront. He had either recognized Gastner's vehicle, which was unlikely, or hadn't noticed their arrival.

Back in the SUV, Gastner turned to Estelle. "You want to talk to Esperanza now?"

"I do. But don't pull up beside his car. Maybe just stop out in the bus lane."

When he did so, Estelle slipped out of the SUV, closing the door gently. She took a path that brought her under the elms beside the gym wall, toward the rear of the Crown Vic. The deputy's window was open, his elbow resting on the sill. He didn't startle when Estelle materialized by his arm. His head was against the headrest, mouth open, sleeping the deep slumber of youth.

For a long moment, the undersheriff stood quietly, then reached past his arm and deftly unclipped the heavy sheriff's badge from his uniform shirt. Minding her footing, she stepped away and returned to Gastner's SUV. He grinned when he saw what she held in her hand.

"I did that once."

"I know you did. To a young Todd Baker, if I remember correctly."

"You do."

As Gastner drove out the back entrance to the parking lot, she slipped the small cell phone out of its belt holster and auto-dialed the Sheriff's Office. Ernie Wheeler answered on the first ring, sounding alert.

"Ernie, how often have you been checking Esperanza's status?"

"Every fifteen," Wheeler replied.

"Do it every five for a while. He's having a little trouble staying alert. Each time you call, have him change location around the school grounds. Keep him in motion. And Bishop is on tonight, right? Have him swing by Esperanza's location now and then for a little conversation."

"You got it. Are you ten-eight?"

"Ah, no. Bill Gastner and I are just cruising, checking some things. I think we'll probably head up to the mesa for a few minutes."

"All right. Stay in touch. The sheriff is out tonight, too. Said he couldn't sleep."

"I can understand that." She switched off and smiled at Gastner. "Ernie the Mother Hen."

"You're serious about going out there? A few minutes ago, you could hardly keep your eyes open."

"I'm awake now. And I want to see the dish."

"With it lying on its back staring straight up at the sky, you won't be able to see the graffiti."

"Then we'll wake somebody up and have them stand it on its ear for us. All this gives me time to think, Padrino. And I have an old friend who used to cruise the county in the wee hours, instead of lying awake in bed, staring at the ceiling."

"He still does."

Southbound on New Mexico 56, they encountered only a solitary SUV, Sheriff's Department emblems on the doors, light bar on top blossoming briefly as Deputy Alan Bishop flashed past them, headed toward town—and no doubt a conversation with Mike Esperanza, whose frantic embarrassment would serve to chase away the drowsiness. The veteran Bishop, well into his second tenure with the department after leaving Posadas County for a stint in Oregon, wouldn't make Esperanza's experience any easier.

Just west of Victor Sanchez's Broken Spur Saloon, County Road 14 headed north from the state highway, and out of long habit, Gastner buzzed down all four windows and opened the sunroof. He let the SUV drift slower and slower, driving on the truck-pounded rock-hard lanes of the gravel road to keep the crunching of tires to a minimum. With plenty of celestial light, he reached forward and turned off the headlights, the dash panel going dark, save for a few idiot lights.

"Back in the day, I would have jerked the wires on those damn lights," Gastner said. "You wouldn't think a simple 'everything off' switch would be so difficult."

The great dome of stars, slashed through one side by the wash of the Milky Way, reached right down to the horizon, without a single porch light out on the prairie to mar the display. Miles Waddell's mesa loomed ahead, just a black shape against the starry sky. By careful design, none of the development was visible from any public highway.

"I miss the Torrances," Gastner said, glancing at Estelle. He pointed ahead to where the rancher's double-wide mobile home had rested at the base of a rock jumble below the *NightZone* mesa. "Had some good coffee and pie there a time or two."

"A couple hundred times, would be more like it." She reached across and squeezed his forearm affectionately.

"Yep. All gone now, and Miles added those acres to the pot." He sighed. "A good thing, I suppose. Now, with Prescotts selling out to him, too, he's got room to stretch out to the east. Did you know that Christina Prescott is working topside for him now?"

"I didn't know, but I'm not surprised. She's a jewel."

"Victor will miss her down at the saloon, but this gives her something a little more interesting. Her parents' ranch never produced much. Other than a couple nice kids, maybe." Gastner shrugged philosophically. "Of course, Guy Prescott might have been a more successful rancher if he had spent the time and money on his place that went to the Broken Spur Saloon."

"Christina is working the restaurant?"

"She *is* the restaurant…everything but the kitchen itself. She is the boss, and a damn good choice, too. Waddell has some fancy Italian chef from Florida onboard starting next week. Guess who's going to work hard as the official taster?"

He grinned and slowed the SUV another notch, then pulled far to the left across the gravel road until his tires touched the left shoulder. One of the newer department Expeditions glided up beside them and stopped, Estelle's elbow on the sill almost able to touch Sheriff Robert Torrez'.

"Hey," Torrez said, "what's goin' on out here now?"

"I want to see the vandalism of the dish. Try for some photos."

"Huh."

"Bill is sure the work is Efrin Garcia's."

"Yep."

"The docs think he's in pretty tough shape."

Torrez gazed ahead at the prairie, jaw working. "Perrone mentioned that. The little rat will make it, all right, tough as he is. He ain't the one to worry about, anyways. Art's around now. Mears saw him a day or two ago, cruisin' around in his mother's Lincoln. I drove out to their trailer, but missed 'em." The sheriff tapped the steering wheel. "Wouldn't be surprised if he headed south. Ain't nothin' for him here."

"You talked to their mother?" Her *Lincoln* hardly painted an accurate picture. The old barge was a fifty-dollar car, on the good days when it actually ran.

"Nope. If Efrin's up in Albuquerque, that's where she is, too." He turned to look at Estelle. "Stewart is going to want to talk to you again, as soon as you can."

"I want a warrant from Judge Hobart to go through her effects."

Torrez shook his head. "Hobart ain't going to give you that. Leavin' the kid in the car for a few minutes don't add up to felony abuse. Not unless she's tied into something a whole lot worse. Skippin' town ain't going to do it."

"Did you happen to stop by the office and watch any of the game film that the LT has?"

"Nope."

"She and Scott were close, Bobby. There's something there."

"Like some affair or something?"

"Yes."

"You think maybe Stewart found out about it?"

"They weren't very subtle, that's for sure. Any number of the town's blabbermouths would have seen them. And they'd talk. But I don't see Todd Stewart grabbing a gun and killing the man."

"It's happened before."

"Yes. But I can't see it that way this time. Not the way this was done."

Torrez' shoulders hunched in a sigh. "Yeah, well. Maybe you'll be able to talk Hobart into the paperwork. I wouldn't bet on it, though."

"You're headed topside?"

Torrez grimaced. "I don't think so. Wasn't plannin' on it. I think now that I'm pointed in this direction that I'll just head on north, then cut back to town past the airport." He pulled the SUV into gear but held it against the brake. "Your son doin' okay?"

"Yes, they are."

"I'm talkin' about the one with the girlfriend and the hot car." The crow's-feet at the corners of his eyes deepened.

"Yes, he is. A surprise visit. They'll head back Sunday."

"In the 'Vette?"

"Yes."

"Tell 'em to be careful."

Estelle patted the windowsill. "As you'll discover in about fourteen years, Bobby, telling teenagers *anything* can be an adventure."

Torrez actually managed a pained smile and quickly changed the subject. Little Gabe Torrez wasn't walking yet, but the time would come.

"Bill, you doin' all right?"

"Reasonably so, yes."

Torrez let the Expedition ease forward. "You two stay out of trouble."

He didn't wait for a response, and Gastner didn't move his own vehicle until the sheriff's dust had settled. For a few moments, the SUV's bulk was silhouetted against the wash of stars, then it disappeared over a rise.

"He's sounding so *sheriff*-like," Gastner remarked.

Chapter Twenty-seven

At the security gate at the base of the mesa road, Gastner swiped a card through the reader and waved a salute at Lou Haus, the gatekeeper who appeared in the doorway, clipboard in hand. Short, impressively round with bulky shoulders, Haus could have been a pro wrestler.

"Is Miles topside?" Gastner asked.

"Yes, sir." Haus glanced at the wall clock behind him. "Should be, anyway."

He stepped to Gastner's door and peered in at Estelle. "Nice evening, Sheriff." He flashed a grin full of perfect false teeth.

"It is that. I have a question for you, sir."

"Shoot."

"Efrin Garcia works topside. When's the last time he checked through you?"

"Efrin? He's that artist kid, right? He's staying in one of those contractors' trailers out behind the restaurant complex. He goes into town once in a while." He held the clipboard at an angle so the light played across it as he ruffled pages. "He came down, let's see. Thursday, it says here. That would be during Ignacio's swing shift. Right at four forty-five in the afternoon." Haus scanned the other pages. "Hasn't come back up yet, though. Not unless he slipped through without checkin' in."

"Does that happen often?"

Haus huffed a little. "Not on my shift, it doesn't." He cocked his head. "He's staying in C-3, if you're looking for him. But

I don't think he's topside, though. One of the guys said that he heard the kid took a fall of some kind and ended up in the hospital. I heard that, but I don't know if it's true. We hear all kinds of things, you know."

"I bet you do," Gastner said. "We're going to scoot up and have a talk with Miles, and then visit the big dish. They got a crew up there?"

"You bet. They're workin' on that thing twenty-four/seven. Electricians been thick as flies. I heard they got power to it now… so they can move it some."

"This, I gotta see," Gastner said eagerly, as if he hadn't seen the huge radio telescope half a hundred times already.

"You got the gold pass, Mr. G." Haus reached out and patted the gold emblem affixed to the inside corner of the SUV's windshield. "Any time, anywhere, day or night."

Gastner gave him a brief salute and pulled the car into gear. The gate closed promptly behind them.

"Mr. G?" Estelle grinned.

"Big stuff," Gastner replied. "It doesn't warm me up the way Padrino does, though. But I *do* have a gold pass." Around the first curve, he slowed abruptly, giving way to a herd of seven nervous mule deer that skipped off the pavement. "The train and tram are a hell of a lot safer than this road, especially at night." His headlights illuminated the bright white and yellow pavement markings, all in the European fashion to avoid the clutter of road signs.

"When did they first notice the graffiti on the dish face?"

Gastner made a tipping motion with his hand. "They were testing something about the elevation mechanism. One of the electricians noticed it."

"They haven't messed with it yet, I hope."

"I don't believe so. They're waiting for us. Amend that. They're waiting for you or Bobby. But it's a *fait accompli* to figure out who did it. It fits the identical pattern used on the train, and now the school. A very busy little monkey. And by the way, are you going up to interview him, assuming he survives the night?"

"Yes. I'm going to see if Jim Bergin will fly me up to Albuquerque in the morning. He can have me there in two hours at the most. And then two back. I can be home by noon."

"And then? Suppose Efrin admits to the graffiti. Then what?"

"He was at the school, would have had to have been, shortly before or after Clint Scott was killed. He may have seen something. Heard something. Any little thing. I think Efrin the tagger was interrupted." She held up both hands as if clutching a softball. "There's just too much going on in too small a space. Somebody knows something."

"You're thinking the killer saw Efrin—we're assuming now that the boy is for sure the tagger—and scared him off?"

"Maybe. That's the best straw I've got at this point."

They rounded the final curve, the macadam so smooth that driving on it was like riding in an air car. The road divided, and then narrowed to a single lane that wound across the mesa-top. The edges of the road were marked with double lines that glowed bright blue in the glare of the headlights.

"Have you been here since they finished the roadway?" Estelle shook her head. "I don't know if Miles is right or not in this, but folks who tour the big dish site are going to use company golf cart type thingies. No car traffic. Cars with parasols, and the whole works. Max speed about eight miles an hour."

"Swank. Company drivers?"

"Yep. And this road on top? It's all one-way, even with the contractors still on site. I'm not sure they like it, especially since the trip back to the restaurant and lodge is along the south edge of the mesa. And that edge is why Miles is requiring company drivers for the carts when things open to the public. I've done the loop, and it's phenomenal." He grinned at Estelle. "Gold pass, you know."

The dish loomed ahead, dwarfing the various vehicles parked near its base. It was tipped nearly vertical, and if the taggers had thought that their artwork would dominate the dish, they'd gotten it all wrong. The panel of graffiti was a flyspeck, a small nuisance, high up on the rim.

Gastner parked beside a white Dodge dually pickup with NZ plates. Miles Waddell saw them, and excused himself from the group with whom he'd been talking. He carried a rolled up set of plans, letting it ride on his shoulder as he walked.

"He's got you working these damn odd hours now," Waddell said as he tucked the rolled plans under his arm and shook hands with Estelle, both of his enveloping hers. "And what a mess *this* day has been, from one end to another." He flashed a smile. "Good PR, though. Lots of exposure." He turned to face the dish, neck craned. "You know, I don't have anything to do with this part of the project, but they tell me things are moving right along for them. Lots of computer issues, all that kind of stuff. But the dish looks good, doesn't it?" He put his hands on his hips approvingly, as if watching a favorite child play. "Best darn billboard that I have. I get goose bumps every time I stand under it. I mean, just look at that. Sixty meters across that thing."

He turned back to them and his expression lost its bonhomie. "I heard about the homicide downtown, at the school? Damnedest thing. I just don't get it. And now you have to waste your time with this crap. You know, Bobby was up earlier, looked at the graffiti and just shrugged."

"I hope that's what I can do," Estelle said.

"We're damn lucky we didn't find a body lying under the dish. Kids have no sense of mortality. Come on, let me show you." He didn't mention Efrin Garcia's name in connection with the tagging.

He strode past the workmen, who regarded Gastner and Estelle with interest.

"Gentlemen," Gastner said affably. "Didn't Miles warn you about midnight tours?" That earned tentative smiles.

"We need hardhats," Waddell prompted, and led them into a small equipment room, an entryway into what must have been one of the main control rooms in the base of the dish. It was difficult to tell exactly, since the room looked as if a madman had stored a mile or two of computer cable there, with every flat surface covered.

"Ah, Arnie," he added as a tall, gangly man with wisps of carrot-colored hair entered behind them. "Folks, this is Arnie Sewell, the stud duck for the mechanics of this project. Arnie, you know Bill already. This is Undersheriff Estelle Reyes-Guzman, who has my personal warrant to visit anything on this mesa any time that she wants. They're interested in our new art up top."

"Ah." Sewell's face carried no expression. "The paint isn't much of an issue for us, but the little son of a bitch stepped in a couple of places he shouldn't have. What exactly did you want to do, Officer?"

"If it's possible, I'd like a photo that shows detail," Estelle said.

"That's a tough call, unless you have a damn good telephoto lens? If we stow the dish so you can access through the hatch," and he held his hand palm-up, "taking a photo of anything all the way across on the rim is going to be a challenge. If you have a decent telephoto, we can stand it up all the way, and you'll be able to focus in on the vandalism while you stand on the ground down in front. That's what I'd suggest. Standing on the dish itself is possible, but..." He paused and shook his head dubiously. "There are some problems with that."

"That's what I need, though," Estelle said. "I need to know how he got up there in the first place."

Sewell puffed out his cheeks. "That part's easy." He looked down at Estelle's stout leather shoes as he handed them bright yellow hard hats. "What kind of soles?"

She cocked a foot up, showing the finely ridged crepe.

"That'll do nicely." He drew out a small phone, tapped a key, and waited for a moment. "Rick, we need the dish parked for visitors topside." He nodded at her. "Let's wait outside. More fun that way." He grinned.

Even as they stepped out, motion was obvious—slow, majestic, just a giant moving shadow against the heavens. "Look, I need to finish up what I was doing," Waddell said, and he shook hands with Sewell. "If you need me, holler. Bill and Estelle, when you're done here, stop by the theater. I'll be over there. More show and tell."

As Waddell walked off, Sewell said, "So…how did he get up on the dish? I have to admit, that's not hard. For one thing, a lot of this system is automatic. It really has to be, since we're talking *really* fine adjustments when control aims the dish. That's the work of the computer links. To make it simple, when the operator wants to find some coordinate set, he types the coordinates into the computers and they do the rest."

"I would think some of our winds would be a problem," Estelle observed.

"Oh, that's right. They can be." He rocked his hand back and forth. "Wind touches thirty-five knots, and the system automatically calls for the dish to stow. That's a pretty big sail we've got up there. When we ask it to park, all the walkways line up so you don't step into thin air."

"That would be nice. Where would the kid have to access the walkways?"

Sewell beckoned, and they walked around the base, side-stepping hardware. With no more than a steady hum, the giant dish blanked out the sky, continuing to tilt so that it lay on its back, a dark shadow nearly two hundred feet in diameter. Sewell drew out a flashlight. "Here is the best place." He illuminated the girders above them. "The normal access to the first ladderway is inside the core…just down where we were a bit ago with Miles. But the kid didn't get in there. He could have gone right up these girders here. It's not much of a climb to the first ladderway. The lowest one."

"And all the ladderways would have lined up then?"

"Yes. Open pathway." His hand drew a zigzag. "When it's parked."

"We think this might have happened this week sometime," Estelle said. "When did you first discover the vandalism?"

"Could be. The dish has been parked for the past couple of weeks. So anytime in that window. We saw it—actually one of the men working fence saw it—when we rotated up. That would have been yesterday morning." The shadow moving across the sky paused. "You want to go up?"

"I do."

He pulled his phone out again. "Can we have all the lights, Rick?"

A circuit snapped somewhere deep in the bowels of the structure, and the walkways were bathed in light. "Every time we turn on the lights, our landlord flinches," Sewell laughed. "They're hooded, and automatically dim, but still. Most of the time when we're in actual operation, they're all switched off." He laughed. "The dish doesn't care. It's listening, not looking. But *Miles* cares."

"I'll watch from here," Gastner said as Estelle followed Sewell up the narrow ladderway. "Been there, done that."

Seven ladderways later, with just enough breeze to accentuate the height of their perch, Sewell stopped. Just above them, the vast white underbelly of the dish now rested horizontal with the ground, so huge that in no direction could they see the rim. Up another short passageway, this one enclosed inside a center core that was surprisingly spacious, Sewell nodded at the hatch in front of them. The fit of metal to metal was flawless, with two large knurled thumbscrews the only indication that they'd reached the hatch.

"These dogs are routinely torqued down just about finger-tight…snug but not enough to misshape the panel, although the door is actually pretty heavy. Our little vandal would have had to know that all this was here, and that he could access it."

"No locks?"

"No." He spun out the retaining screws and let them hang from short tethers of light-gauge stainless steel cable. The panel hinged silently straight up and then out to one side, the complex hinge mechanism itself a thing of engineering beauty. "If the hatch wasn't actually attached to the framework of the dish, it would be only a matter of time before somebody slipped with it, and the thing would go sliding down the dish face like a toboggan."

Estelle could feel the change of air as the core room opened to the void. "Let's see what we have." Sewell reached over, moved a switch guard, and snapped the toggle up. Instantly, the dish was bathed in light from a dozen directions. He moved to one side. "Step up waist-high to the rim. You'll get a view."

In every direction, the sea of white stretched away from the hatch. When viewed from the ground, the actual superstructure that supported the dish suggested that the dish's curve created a deep bowl, but that wasn't the case. The dish was actually surprisingly shallow, perhaps twenty feet deep from belly to rim. The night air whispered, and Estelle found that both hands automatically clenched the rim of the hatch until her knuckles turned white.

The graffiti was a panel approximately six feet long and three feet high, a little postage stamp against the flawless background.

"What do you think?"

"I think the kid was nuts," Estelle said. "This would be quite the challenge. Not the walking out there so much, but carrying his bag of spray paint cans along, and then working on a slope?"

"And that's what appeals, I suppose. My theory is that the little bugger didn't realize how big the dish actually is…how big he'd have to make his mark before it really showed up." Sewell laughed. "And we'll just paint over the thing anyway. No big deal. But it'd be interesting to know how fast his pulse was when he climbed out through this hatch."

"About like mine," Estelle whispered. "But we're at the bottom of the bowl, so there's nowhere to fall." Supported by its complex of three large box beams, the radio telescope's apex rose above the dish. Estelle noticed the ladderway that actually led up one of the supports to the central basket-like apex. "I'm surprised he didn't go up there."

"Lots of safety gear required for that climb," Sewell said. "Not that he would care about that. But there's no panel up there, either. Let's ease it some." He turned away from the ladder and palmed the radio. He conferred for a moment, and Estelle worked at loosening her grip on the rim of the hatch. A slight jolt, and then she had the disconcerting feeling that the heavens were sliding by, so slowly she couldn't be sure of motion. But sure enough, the giant dish tilted, the rim dropping against the backdrop of stars. In a moment she could look straight across from the hatch toward the graffiti across a valley of white.

"It's easy footing," Sewell said. "In dry weather like this, it's not slippery in the least, and you have good shoes." He thumped the grab handle that he had hinged out of its recess. "Hold on here until you have your bearings. Then we'll just walk kind of a great circle over to the graffiti. And we'll stick to the seams between panels. There's more support that way."

Estelle made sure the camera was secure in her pocket, and watched the ease with which Sewell stepped up and out onto the dish's surface…as if he were a foot above the ground, rather than one hundred-twenty feet up. He held out his hand. "With the dish like this, there isn't much suggestion of height," he said, accurately reading her concern. "About the only view is straight up at the stars…especially if we'd turn off all the damn lights."

He kept a light hand on her elbow as she stepped out through the trap door. "Basically I need a shot of the graffiti panel that fills the frame. There's enough light here that I won't need the flash. What's important to me are the exact design shapes and colors. They're as characteristic as a signature."

"Okay." He regarded the little camera. "Just follow me."

As if walking across high on the slope of a valley, they crossed the expanse. Estelle stepped gingerly, following a pace behind Sewell, stepping on the seams as if the surface were thin and fragile. There was nothing to suggest that it was, though, and in a moment she relaxed. She imagined Efrin Garcia trudging across on his way to work, lugging a knapsack like a school kid, spray cans clanking.

They stood immediately below the graffiti, and Estelle could see the faint scuff marks of the tagger's shoes.

As she prepared her camera, Sewell remarked, "Don't ask me to translate this stuff. Just designs, I guess."

"The stylized 'P' and 'F' are representative." Estelle drew close to the design. "And the colors."

"You have an idea who did this?"

"Yes," Estelle said, and let it go at that. She couldn't imagine that Sewell hadn't heard about Efrin Garcia's escapade. She spent the next twenty minutes photographing the design, and the camera's images were spectacular, with even lighting and no shadows. Efrin would be proud.

Chapter Twenty-eight

The curve of the planetarium theater's giant screen reminded Estelle of the dish surface she had just left behind, gleaming, almost flawless white, impossible to view the whole at a glance. At the border of the screen, the walls of the theater appeared to fade into the night sky, an inky black from floor to the crown of the planetarium's domed ceiling.

"The neat thing is," Miles Waddell explained, "this is designed as a three-way purpose kind of facility. We have this wide screen for traditional viewing…hell, we could sit here and watch *Star Trek* reruns off cable if we wanted to. But the three-hundred-sixty-inch reflector telescopes just to the west of this building have either single feed or coordinated feed to here, so the audience can sit back and have a view of Saturn's rings that'll knock their socks off. Or a super nova somewhere. Or what the Martians are building right now."

He grinned and turned in a circle, head back and arms raised as if directing the *Hallelujah Chorus*. "Or all three at once. Then, we can use the entire ceiling as just about the neatest skyscape planetarium projection you ever saw. The programs are endless. That housing over there?" He pointed both hands at the mound in the center of the room. "That's where the projector lives." He grimaced. "It's not *there* yet, but it's coming. It's coming from Switzerland, in fact. When all is up and running, there will be a show every hour, on the hour. No tickets required. Just slip in the dark alley entrance at any time. Glow worms on the floor keep you from breaking your neck."

"I hate to interrupt, Miles, but…" The man's excitement was contagious. She walked across the silent carpeting to the far wall, where the giant mural of the universe spread across the bottom fifteen feet of wall space, capped by the black ceiling. So perfectly done was the fit and finish that the mural appeared to be a free-standing wall suspended against the depth of deep space.

Drawing near to the mural, she stretched out a hand. "This wasn't done with spray cans of enamel from the hardware store."

"Oh, Christ, no," Waddell said. "I hired this kid, Efrin Garcia? You know him, I'm sure. You should see the rig he uses. Three different sizes of airbrushes, the neatest little compressor you ever saw, all kinds of replaceable nozzles and stuff? Wow. You got to wonder how he affords it…on my dollar, I suspect. See how perfect these lines are?" He touched the subtle outline around Jupiter's great red spot. "That's all airbrush. And look at this." He strode up the side aisle a dozen feet, stopping near the tower of scaffolding. "This is the space dust and unknowable crap in the Horsehead Nebula, the cosmic *stuff*. The shading that he accomplished just blows me away."

"The dust and unknowable crap," Gastner repeated with a grin. "Your astronomy background is bleeding through with all this technical jargon, Miles."

"Yeah, I know. But Efrin is doing such a *great* job." He turned and pointed toward the rear of the theater. "It'll reach all the way to the back of the theater." His eyes closed, and he stepped sideways to the first row of seats, falling into one of the padded, reclining rests. "So tell me. What the hell happened? He didn't come to work today, and one of the guys tells me that he crashed his truck into a damn line pole near his house. Is that true?"

"Yes."

"Oh, Christ. You can see the work we have ahead of us. I don't even want to *think* about him getting into trouble, or hurt. You know," he continued before Estelle had a chance to slip a word in, "what amazes me is that he's a *local* talent. I didn't have to hire some famous *artiste* from Chicago or someplace like that. This is home brew, and let me tell you…" He nodded at the wall. "He's as good as they come. He's going to be all right?"

"Maybe." Estelle sat down beside Waddell. "His injuries are life-threatening, Miles. A badly lacerated spleen. Broken ribs. Smashed left elbow. Bruises from head to toe. One ear nearly ripped off his head." She turned on her camera, found the remarkable portrait of the dish graffiti and held it out to Waddell. "He did this, didn't he?"

The rancher turned the camera so that it was pointing at the mural, comparing images. "You can see that he did. I mean, crude as this one is, done with just the damn spray cans…it's his work. The colors, the design. The guys found it, and told me about it. You know," and he pounded his fist against his own thigh, "this is about like shitting in his own nest. I mean, when he's up here working, I can see the pride he takes. I can see that it *means* something to him to be working here. So he turns around and tags my goddamn railcar? And then squirrels up the dish and shoots his mark *there?* What, he thinks we're not going to find out? He wants to throw all this away? What's with these damn kids, anyway?"

Again before Estelle could continue, he added, "You know, I'm not going to let him do that. I'm not. We're going to work this thing through, and he's going to understand what he has going for himself here, and by God, he's going to finish this wonderful thing and go on to bigger and better." He swept a hand the length of the mural. "He's going to carry this theme all through the park before we're finished."

Estelle handed him the camera, previewing the photo of the defaced *NightZone* passenger car. "And you're sure this is his work as well."

Waddell hardly glanced at the design. "'Course it is. Nobody handles airbrush work like that kid. No one I've ever seen."

She reached across and thumbed the left view button. In a moment, the photo of the middle school wall slid into view. "And this. At the middle school."

Waddell nodded. "I mean, we can't be absolutely sure, I suppose, but yes. I'd bet on that. Either him or some copycat."

"We're guessing now that he was interrupted before he could finish. I don't see any other reason for him *not* to finish the design once he's started."

Waddell handed the camera back and then sat with his head supported in both hands, as if he had a sinus headache. "I'll deal with him when he comes back. We'll have him clean and repaint the car. I don't know about the damage to the dish."

"Mr. Sewell said they'd likely just paint over it."

"Probably. And he's hurt badly?"

"He's listed as critical. Lots of blood loss, and then the surgery. It's a tough road."

"Christ. That's going to put him out of action for weeks."

"And that's if he's very lucky."

"Shit," Waddell muttered. He gazed over at the artwork on the wall. "I mean, it's incredible, isn't it?" He took a deep breath. "What do you think happened? He got crosswise with some other gang member, or what? Is that what this is all about?"

"We don't know, Miles. We haven't seen any significant gang activity in this town for a good long time. Now, all of a sudden."

He turned his head just enough to be able to look sideways at the undersheriff. "Related somehow? His being at the school and the murder? I mean, that's why you're up here in the middle of the night, right? You're not chasing taggers."

"We don't know the relationships. But it's too close in both time and location to be ignored. Efrin is certainly a person of interest at the moment. He may have seen or heard something. That's why we need to talk with him. That's crucial."

He studied her for a moment. "So…cut to the chase. What can I do to help?"

"If you hear anything, let me know. You know how the rumor and gossip vine works."

"Do I ever."

"Anything you hear that you think might link the Garcia

boy with Coach Scott's murder. Was someone else helping Efrin with this mural?"

"Solo all the way. We had a crew in here setting up the scaffolding for him, but other than that, he didn't want anyone else interfering."

"What's he using as a source for the space images? I mean, I've seen lots of professional images of Jupiter. *That's* not just something from a boy's imagination."

"Maybe you've seen that big fancy coffee table book that they put out of the Hubbell images? Amazing stuff, right? We'll be selling them in the gift shop. I gave him one to use. He really took to it. The only directions I gave him was that I wanted *science,* not science fiction."

"Did Efrin ever talk about the school? I'm wondering why he would target there, except maybe because of all the publicity they've been getting lately."

"Well, sure. The big spread on the volleyball team? Gotta jump in there and put his mark on that, too." He shook his head in disgust. "He told me that he was the first one in his family to graduate high school. He was proud of that, and proud of this commission." Waddell stretched out his legs, sliding down in the seat, hands clasped over his belly. "I don't think he's ever managed a bank account in his life." He shook his head in wonder. "I told him, look…I'm willing to pay you well, but in return, you have to work with me to guarantee both your future and mine."

Again he turned and regarded the mural project. "I told him that this wasn't the sort of thing I wanted to start, and then have to hire some commercial hack halfway through the project because Efrin couldn't finish it."

"You've been very generous, sir."

"Well, yeah. But see, it pays me in return." He grunted a painful laugh. "And now, look at us. Halfway done, and the kid is in the hospital. Christ."

"And he agreed with you? About the bank account?"

"He did. Eagerly, he agreed. We set him up an account at Posadas State, and I do direct deposit with him. I don't just hand him a wad of money at the end of the week. It goes in the bank, and he's got to think a little before he takes it out. You haven't been able to talk with the boy yet?"

"Not yet. He was out of it by the time they brought him to the ER, bleeding profusely from the head, coughing up blood—and it went downhill from there. They transported him to Albuquerque as soon as they could. If there's any chance he can talk, I need to run up today."

Waddell glanced at his watch, and then grimaced at Gastner, who had remained seated in one of the plush theater chairs throughout the conversation. His eyelids drooped, but he jerked alert when he realized he was the focus of attention. "All your bad habits," Waddell chided. "Going on midnight, and most normal folks would be home blowing Zs."

"We all learn the art of sleeping with our eyes open, and an attentive expression on our faces," Gastner said.

"I've noticed that about my crews," Waddell laughed. "Now, let me help, all right? You need to go to Albuquerque? Let me help you get there and back without wasting time. My contractor has his X at the Posadas Airport. It's at your disposal."

"The X?"

"A Cessna Citation Ten. What a rocket."

"I didn't know you flew, Miles."

"I don't. My head honcho contractor does, though. He's offered the plane and crew any number of times, and I've used them now and then to coordinate stuff that doesn't work well over the phone. That big dish? That cost about five trips to California, on top of a thousand phone calls and teleconferences." He shrugged. "With what I'm paying for this job, big deal, right? So, you want Albuquerque? That'll take an hour or less each way. Just say when."

He raised his eyebrows expectantly. "You can tell Grand Dame Leona Spears that there will be no charge to the county. Consider it my personal thanks for all you do."

Estelle closed her eyes for a moment, visualizing the staff roster for the approaching day shift.

As if sensing her hesitation, Waddell added, "I get the impression that this is no time to be turning down a favor. Let me help."

"Can we leave here at eight this morning?"

"Done." Waddell pushed out of his chair with his typical frenetic energy. "Only one catch…I want to go along. If the kid is conscious, I want to talk with him."

Estelle turned to Gastner, but he was already shaking his head. "No thanks, Sweetheart. So much I have to do, plus I have an appointment for lunch I can't miss."

"An appointment with a green chile burrito?"

He grinned and said to Waddell, "She knows me too well."

Chapter Twenty-nine

"What's the matter?" Gastner said. He held the ignition key in place but didn't turn it. Instead, he frowned at Estelle, who was gazing out the windshield at nothing.

"One more thing," she said.

"This is the best time, while the world is quiet and dark."

"Efrin Garcia. The ambulance picked him up at his home when his mother called 911. By the time he made his way home after crashing into the pole, he was coughing blood. She didn't waste a second, and she did the right thing. EMTs said that his blood pressure was close to nil by the time he arrived at the hospital."

"So let me get this straight. He hits the pole, gets thrown from the truck, and still drags himself a couple hundred yards home, then collapses?"

"That's what I'm told. Complete with a ruptured spleen and some bad fractures."

"Ouch."

"Now, his brother Arthur has been seen around town. The sheriff knows their old car, and apparently Arthur is using that from time to time. But he didn't show up at the local hospital—Efrin's mother rode in the ambulance from their home, then she flew with him on the medevac to Albuquerque, but Arthur didn't. That's odd, don't you think? That he doesn't show his face?"

"But he wasn't in the truck with Efrin."

"Well, maybe he's out carousing and doesn't even know that his baby brother bought the farm. I mean, there's normal folks who think, and then there's Arthur Garcia, who isn't the sharpest tool in the box. Ask Jamie Herrald, his parole officer. That's who he's reporting to."

"He's just another square in the checkerboard, sir. I'd like to talk with Arthur, too. See what he has to say for himself. If we keep turning over rocks, eventually we might get lucky and hit the right one."

"What's he going to tell you?"

"I have no idea. Suppose he was with Efrin when he was working on tagging the middle school. I mean, that's possible. Help hold the ladder. Pass up paint cans? Maybe the tagging was Arthur's idea in the first place. But regardless, there's the possibility one or both of the brothers saw something at the middle school."

"Maybe, maybe. They live over on Fifth Street, as I recall."

"All the way at the south end."

He nodded and started the SUV. "We'll swing by there on the way back into town." At the bottom of the hill, night shift Security Officer Juan Ignacio stepped out to meet them, in no hurry to raise the gate. He ducked his head and smiled at Gastner, then tipped his cap in salute to Estelle.

"Long day?"

"You bet. Juan, when was the last time Art Garcia was up topside?"

"Art?"

"You know him, Juan. Efrin's older brother."

"Yeah, I mean I *know* him. But no…I haven't seen him since…" and he looked uncomfortable. "Gosh, a long time. He doesn't come out here much."

Gastner's eyes locked on the security guard's face, his jaw thrust out pugnaciously. "'Much' means he comes out once in a while. When was the last time?"

Ignacio looked down at the clipboard, as if trying to decide if the list was high security. "I didn't see him cleared to go *up,*"

Ignacio said. He ruffled pages. "He came in with his brother on Tuesday, it says here. My guess is that he was helping Efrin work on the mural at the theater. They were putting up a scaffold and everything."

"What time did he leave?"

Ignacio turned his Maglite for a better view of the pages. "Says here that both him and Efrin left around seven p.m."

"Long day."

"You guys should know. That's the normal way now," Ignacio nodded. "There's a big push to have this place one hundred percent by Christmas. I think they'll make it."

"When was the last time you saw Efrin come through?"

"I usually don't. See, I go on shift at midnight, so if he went through earlier than that..." He splayed the pages again. "Haus has him comin' down Wednesday night at eleven thirty-five. And then Cooper signed him in again on Thursday morning at ten after eight." He looked up first at Gastner, then at Estelle. "So he's in and out all the time."

"Thanks, Juan," Gastner said. As Estelle's passenger-side window spooled up, he added, "I arrested both Juan Ignacio and Art Garcia one night when they were both in elementary school. I think they were third-graders, maybe fourth. They were trying to hot-wire a pickup truck parked over near Grundy's on Bustos." He laughed at the memory. "They saw me coming eastbound and ducked down so I wouldn't see 'em. Boy genius Arthur had his foot sticking out the door, and he forgot to pull it in. Two fourth-graders heading for the big-time."

"I remember that," Estelle said.

"At that point, they both should have been recalled as defective. Would've saved us a lot of trouble later on."

"Ignacio turned out all right."

"Yep. Maybe. That's one of my continuing worries, Sweetheart. Miles Waddell is about the most generous human being I've ever met. He's that odd and wonderful combination of being personally driven, but at the same time he really cares about the people in his world. I hate to see him taken advantage of."

"He's pretty acute that way."

"He can be. He *can* be. But like Juan back there, what do you want to bet that the boy is on the phone with Arthur right now, telling him that we're curious? Would we be surprised?"

"I wouldn't bet against that," Estelle said. "But if we swing by Garcia's house, we might get lucky."

Half an hour later, Gastner slowed the SUV to a crawl as they turned south on Fifth Street, a street that was paved as far as the country club, and then jolted into dirt as it crossed a deep arroyo. He turned off the headlights and lowered all four windows. Surging out of the arroyo, the gravel lane skirted a grove of brush and stunted elms, then swept into a tight curve. The tracks were obvious.

"He lost it here." Gastner stopped the truck and picked up his flashlight. "And there's Bambi." The deflated carcass of the smashed deer lay against a spray of cacti.

Across the road, another fifty yards ahead, the utility pole canted to one side, spears of wood splinters jutting. Tire tracks cut through the vegetation.

"They towed the truck to the house?"

"That would be the logical thing to do. It's just on a bit."

"Don't start expecting logic," Gastner scoffed. He let the SUV idle down the lane, and slowed when they reached a driveway off to the left, heading toward a veteran mobile home.

"Her car isn't here," Estelle whispered as they turned into the narrow, rutted driveway. Abundant tire tracks hinted at where the huge, low-slung barge of a sedan would park when it was home, squatted near a cactus bed, nosed up against what had once been a camper trailer. Now, the trailer provided a place for a discarded mattress to lean against.

"*House and Garden*," Gastner growled. "That's Efrin's truck." The battered Nissan was parked within two steps of the front door, where the contract tow truck operator, Stub Moore, had dropped it off. The truck was a good two feet shorter than it had been before taking on deer and pole. The left side of the grill was crushed inward, the semicircular imprint of the utility pole bent in to drive the radiator into the engine block.

Estelle slid out of the SUV, flashlight in hand.

Half of an extension ladder rested in the bed of the truck, and the back window was shattered. Pieces of the glass still clung to the window molding, itself partially pulled loose from the cab.

"*Ay,*" she whispered, and she could feel Gastner's presence as he stepped up close behind her.

"Somebody bled like a stuck pig." He played the light beam around the inside of the cab. The keys hung from the ignition, and what looked like blood had splattered over the seat, on the steering wheel, the dashboard, even on the headliner.

Kernels of busted glass littered the truck bed as well. Estelle brought her flashlight close. The ladder had been shoved into the truck with its plastic feet rearward, out beyond the battered tailgate. "There's dried blood on the ladder itself." She drew back and looked around at Gastner, then reached out and almost touched the raw aluminum ends of the ladder rails. "Right here at the tip?"

"I'll buy that. Who'd it cut, if Efrin went sailing out the door?" He reached out and rocked the sprung door. Its frame was nearly bent double.

Stepping to the door of the trailer, she rapped on the thin aluminum of the doorjamb. No one stirred. She rapped again, then reached out and tried the knob. The door was locked. Turning in a slow circle, she surveyed the dark neighborhood. Through runty trees, she could see a light in the distance, a single bulb over one of the golf course's storage sheds. Farther down the lane, an older adobe home was dark, with no porch light.

"We need a crew out here, sir. We don't know what happened."

"Agreed. Who's working graveyard now?"

"Bishop is on by himself tonight." She had phone in hand, and when he answered, Bob Torrez sounded as if he sat just around the corner.

"Yep?"

"Bobby, we're over here at the Garcias' on Fifth. Efrin's truck is here, but his mother's car isn't. Bill and I are looking at the truck—broken back window, lots of glass and blood around the interior. There's a ladder in the back, with broken glass in the truck bed and what looks like blood on the ladder itself."

"Okay."

"We can't just let it go. None of that jibes with Efrin being pitched out of the truck when it hit the pole."

Silence greeted that, and then Torrez said, "I'll be over in a couple of minutes," and disconnected.

"Now is when you wish you had your car," Gastner observed. "But I'm pretty well stocked."

"You are?" She couldn't help smiling at the old man.

"Well, you know," he said offhandedly. "Sometimes, it's handy to have an evidence bag or two. A little this, a little that. I even have a couple blood boxes."

"That will cover it. Right now, all I want is some of the glass fragments, and some of the dried blood. And some pictures." She pulled the tiny camera from its belt holster. "And some idea of what happened here. I'd like that." For a moment she stood quietly, gazing at the truck. "Bishop didn't see any reason not to have the truck just towed the few yards up the road to here. He said it didn't make any sense to take it to a wrecking yard, or to the sheriff's impound." She shook her head doubtfully. "Maybe, maybe not." She nodded at the bed of the truck. "Let's start there."

After a series of general, all-inclusive photos of the area, the truck, and its contents, she had Gastner hold the two flashlights so she could try close-ups of the ladder ends while avoiding use of the flash. A tiny fragment wedged in the junction of the top rung and the left rail winked a reflection in one of the resulting photos.

"Glass," Estelle said.

"Maybe so." Gastner remained noncommittal.

Headlight beams touched the unmowed verge as the white county Expedition stopped out on the road. The sheriff got out and strolled over toward them.

"House open?" Torrez asked by way of greeting.

"No, it's locked. No sign of Arthur yet."

Torrez shrugged and turned in place as if inventorying the neighborhood. "What did Francis say about Efrin. Any guesses?"

"He thinks the young man's injuries were consistent with a truck wreck." She pointed at the distorted steering wheel. "That nailed him, for sure. The broken elbow too. He wasn't wearing a seat belt, and he got tossed around hard."

"And mom is up in Albuquerque with him now."

"Yes."

"And Arthur ain't."

"No sign of him."

Torrez looked across at Gastner. "How are you doin'?"

"It's a gorgeous night to be out and about," Gastner said. "I'm the official flashlight-holder."

Torrez actually laughed. "I always knew you were good for something."

"Damn right."

"Then let's do it."

Dried blood samples, looking like microscopically thin brown wafers, lifted easily from the Nissan's plastic seat cover, using a single-edged razor blade. The tiny samples were placed in a series of thin, plastic specimen boxes.

"Right side of the driver," Torrez observed. "He bled heavy. That don't make sense."

"And right side is where the severe ear laceration was, Efrin's right ear and scalp." Estelle agreed.

"How's that gonna work?" Torrez turned in a circle, gazing off into the night. "Truck hits the pole, he goes out the door." He bent down, aiming his flashlight at the mangled doorframe. "If he twisted around, maybe." He examined the door for another full minute. "No blood, no tissue on the doorframe itself. If this is where the right side of his head got caught, you'd think there'd be something."

The three of them stood away from the truck, and Estelle pointed at the back window.

"Something smashes through the back window and hits him.

That's the way most of the glass went. Even up on the dash, around the vents."

"Yep."

"The ladder, you're saying?" Gastner asked.

"I think so. It hit so hard that a fragment of glass caught in the aluminum."

"How's that going to work?" the sheriff asked again. "Hold this." He handed his flashlight to Gastner. "If this is ridin' in the back, one end down against the cab, the other up on the tailgate, what's it gonna do when the truck hits the pole?" He lifted the ladder sharply. "It's gonna pitch right on over the roof. Or swing wild sideways. It ain't going to bust through the window and punch all the way through to the dashboard."

"Maybe when the truck bounced over the deer," Gastner offered.

"Maybe," Torrez said. "And then it keeps on bouncin' on down the road until it hits the pole?" He raised an eyebrow skeptically and exhaled loudly. "Look, you headin' to the city in a little bit this morning?"

"Waddell offered the contractor's jet, and I took him up on it," Estelle said. "We leave at eight, and I'll be back by noon. Bobby, I *have* to have some time with Efrin. To talk with him. There's all this," and she held up the collection of evidence bags, "and there's evidence he might have been at school, maybe in time to hear or see something that tells us more about Scott's murder."

"Okay." He reached out with a toe and thumped the back tire of the little truck. "If the kid dies, we're going to wish we had all this in evidence."

"Absolutely."

"Then let's get Stub back out here and get it towed in. Ladder and all. And make sure everybody keeps an eye out for numb nuts. If he's still drivin' his mother's car, he ain't goin' far, and he won't be hard to find. Pasquale seems to have a good nose for findin' things." He looked at his watch. "That'll work. I'll get Stubby out of bed. And make sure we bag the rail ends of that ladder."

"We'll wait until the tow gets here."

"Nah. Go on ahead. I'll stay in the area. But lemme know what you find out in Albuquerque. ASAP."

Chapter Thirty

Her house was quiet and dark when Bill Gastner dropped her off shortly before two a.m. Despite Francis being on-call for the emergency room rotation, Estelle had hoped that his SUV would be parked in the driveway. It wasn't, and her wistful dream of being able to snuggle against *Oso* for three hours of sleep winked out.

Light illuminated the stained-glass panels beside the front door, nice touches created by younger son Carlos during one of his many experiments in the arts. She keyed the door and swung it open to see Angie Trevino seated at the dining room table, several sheets of music in front of her. The girl offered a brilliant smile.

"What a day for you," she said softly, voice husky. "I was just having some green tea. May I make you some?" She rose from the table, placing her pencil just so, beside her cup. The light cotton bathrobe was cinched tight, accentuating her lithe but sturdy figure.

"Absolutely wonderful." The last thing Estelle wanted at the moment was to be conversed awake, but her curiosity won out. "What time did Dr. Francis leave?" They had agreed years before *not* to interrupt each other's work except in dire emergencies, so avoided something as simple as a phone call just to chat, or even a text message to be read at leisure.

"I think it was about midnight," Angie said. "I heard him leave, and then couldn't get back to sleep, so I decided to finish some work. I hope that's all right."

"Of course it's all right. It's *welcome.*" She noticed the dark circles under Angie's eyes, but resisted the temptation to glance in the hallway mirror to see how her own compared. "What's the work?"

"The cello part for your mom's birthday mass. I wasn't happy with what I had written…well, with my transcription of what *Mozart* wrote, and thought I'd spend some time with it."

"My mother will be so pleased."

"She is a dear. By the way, Carlos mentioned that the acoustics in the church in Tres Santos aren't very good, so I was making some adjustments for that." She paused at the sink, teapot in hand. "You know, he is a remarkable little boy. There's a rendering of the church's interior there on the table that he drew for me. Basically the church is just a box, so that's not so bad. He says it will be like playing in a large garage."

Estelle laughed. "My son studies these things, and he doesn't make suggestions lightly."

"That's what Francisco said. What a pair those two are." She looked up at Estelle. "You and your husband are very fortunate." Angie sounded eighteen going on forty.

"Thank you. We think we have a couple of keepers."

Angie watched the pot as the gas flames caressed the bottom. "I hope you're not angry with me for this road trip."

"Apprehensive, maybe. Not angry. Francisco acts so mature sometimes, it's easy to forget he's only fifteen. And there are times when that includes the judgment of a fifteen-year-old." The young woman looked down at the counter, and Estelle added, "It's hard to cut apron strings, Angie. This whole experience with the academy has been something of an ordeal for us. For Francis and me."

"Sometimes…" she glanced at Estelle, "my dad is afraid that the only thing I'll ever hug is the cello." She shook her head and sighed. "He's a funny guy, my dad. He really believes that there is absolutely nothing on this planet that a check in the right amount won't cure. You know—and I think this is funny, but it's pure Dad—without telling us, he went to some auction in

New York and bought the most amazing cello for me. I mean, the Gignone is *amazing*. Some critics say it's better than a Guarneri. And you know what? It'll turn out to be an amazing investment, too, if you wanted to think of it that way. Dad is well aware of that aspect of it, but he also thinks that since the cello is so fantastic, I wouldn't have to practice so much! How's that for logic?"

"It'll make its own music."

"Exactly. For a man so smart, he can be really dumb sometimes."

Estelle thought of the early hours alert for a flight crew to prep the jet parked at Posadas Municipal—Mr. Trevino would appreciate Miles Waddell's checkbook approach to challenges.

"There are lots of situations where money is what starts the ball rolling, sometimes good, sometimes not so." Estelle said. "What does your dad do, actually?"

"He sells breeding interests. Doesn't that sound exciting? This bull, that bull—this stud, that stud—he makes sure that they stand for the highest prices. And he's *very* good at what he does. He's sort of a realtor for livestock services. An agent, he prefers to call it." She smiled brightly. "And on top of that, he's a financial investor. A very, very successful one."

"And your mom—she's provost at the college."

"Yes. A more unlikely couple you'll never find. He dotes on me, she makes sure the barbed-wire fence around me stays in good repair. I guess that's her version of the apron strings idea, right?" She held up both hands, balancing. "He thinks I practice too much, she thinks I don't practice enough." She grinned. "Mom is the one who had trouble with my turning eighteen."

"Third cupboard." Estelle directed. She found it pleasant to be waited on, and sat at the center island while Angie found the cups, the bulk-tea spoon, and the canister of tea.

"And how much *do* you practice each day?"

"Well, that depends on your definition of practice, I suppose. I'm involved somehow with things musical most of the time, in one way or another. But actually sitting with the cello, working specifically on some aspect of performance? I suppose five or six hours a day. More, if I can find it."

She turned and looked at the counter clock. "I haven't played since we arrived, and I didn't play in the car. So that's something of a record for downtime. But almost the whole trip, Francisco and I were thinking, working, talking music. It's not something that just starts up when we pick up an instrument."

"Of course not." She studied Angie as the girl relaxed at the kitchen counter. The long, heavy eyelashes that seemed to stroke the air with each blink were natural, the skin of her face so smooth as to invite a caress. And the eyes...lavender in this light, an unusually dark shade that would shift and morph. Estelle wondered, if she were to ask her son, how Francisco would describe his girlfriend's eyes, for surely he would have become lost in them a time or two.

Estelle lifted the tea holder out of the water, letting it drip for a moment. "You and Francisco have spent time with each other since...?"

"We met last year after one of our recitals. I mean, from a distance before that, but the recital in Little Rock was our first sorta date, I guess."

"A sorta date?"

Angie smiled, just a tinge of blush touching her cheeks. "Leister is pretty strict in that regard." She blushed a little brighter. "Well...that sounds silly, doesn't it? I mean, here we are, right?"

"Here you are."

"But Leister thinks we're at my house in Kansas. We didn't ask them if we could do this trip. We just did it."

"One of those 'easier to ask forgiveness than permission' moments."

"That's exactly right," Angie said in her careful, thoughtful way. She glanced down as Estelle shifted a bit on the kitchen stool, her suit jacket swinging out to reveal the holstered handgun, badge, and cuffs.

"You know, yesterday afternoon, when we first came into

town? That was the first time in my entire life that I've talked with a police officer. Sergeant Taber seems like a really nice person."

"She is. We're fortunate to have Jackie on staff. She could work anywhere in the world. But here she is."

"Francisco said that she was shot two years ago? That Mr. Gastner saved her life?"

With her knuckle, Estelle reached up and knocked a couple times on her own vest. "It was one of those moments during a traffic stop when everything goes to hell in a heartbeat. The charge of birdshot hit her square in the chest." She tugged a bit at the top of her vest. "There's a ceramic insert there, so she wasn't hurt. But the blow knocked her down. Bill Gastner happened to respond as civilian backup, and became involved."

Angie grimaced. "The man died, Francisco said."

"Yes, he did."

Shaking her head slowly, Angie refilled Estelle's cup. "How awful that must be."

"More so if Officer Taber had been hurt. The man made a choice. He fired once at Jackie, then turned the shotgun toward Padrino. That was it. The lawsuit afterward took up too much of our time, but turned out all right."

"How could they *sue?*"

"Oh, that's the last refuge, Angie. It wouldn't have mattered if the guy had managed to shoot three or four *more* people. When he gets hurt, the family sues. Go figure."

"But they didn't win…"

"No."

"Wow." Angie shook her head in wonder. "How long have you known him?"

"Padrino? Since I was a little kid in Tres Santos, Mexico. He and my Great-uncle Reuben were friends. And then I started work for the department when I was twenty-one, when Padrino was undersheriff." She stopped abruptly and sipped the tea, eyes fast on Angie Trevino. "I'm supposed to be interrogating *you.*"

"But I'm boring," Angie said. "I've been playing the cello since I was six. And if you ask my dad, that's *all* I've been doing.

He pictures me old, gray, wrinkled, sitting in a rocking chair, clutching my Gignone as my only company."

"It all depends on what you do between now and that rocking chair, Angie. I'd say that you're off to a dramatic start. You and my son both. You both have an incredible amount to share with the world. That's the responsibility with talent like yours."

Angie looked down at her cup pensively. "Hmm," she murmured. Estelle let the moment grow without interruption. Finally the violet eyes lifted and locked on Estelle's. "Do you ever regret the directions you've taken over the years?"

"Not for a heartbeat."

The young woman smiled. "That's what I want...to be sure, and then to be content with the way things work out."

"And the great thing is that there's no way to be sure until after the fact," Estelle said. "That's what keeps us up at night." She yawned hugely. "*Por dios,* I have to curl up for a little while. I have a flight at eight, so it's a short night." She stood up, nodding at the sheet music. "Good luck with that, Angie. I have to find a way to stop the world so I can step off and find time to hear it on Sunday." She started to walk past the girl, but paused. She stroked the back of her hand down the girl's cheek, looking down at her as if trying to X-ray every cell. "I'm glad you're here, Angie. And I'm going to ask that you be thoughtful with my son. And that he be thoughtful with you. And I mean that in the deepest sense of the word."

As she left the kitchen, she saw Angie pour another cup of tea and settle once again at the table. In the bedroom, Estelle took two minutes to shed her heavy belt and its accoutrements, then stripped down to her underwear, enjoying the huge relief of shedding the weight of belt and vest. The sheets were cool and fragrant, and for several minutes she lay on her back, her left arm over her eyes, blocking out the faint ray of light from around the bedroom door. In a moment, she groaned.

"Shut off, brain," she whispered, and reached to the nightstand for her phone. The wireless Internet connection was always slow, and she waited for it to boot, running light fingers over the tiny touch-screen. Her first attempts garnered nothing except to understand what the name *Gignone* meant to string players. Another moment or two of persistence took her to the website of an exclusive violin dealer/auctioneer in New York, and under "recent notable sales," found a brief report of the most recent purchase of a Pietro Gignone cello. The instrument had somehow avoided the penchant for instrumental nicknames, but had sold in auction for 1.9 million dollars. The buyer was listed as Derwood Trevino of the United States.

Chapter Thirty-one

Estelle tried to relax in the Cessna's plush seat, already knowing that she wouldn't be able to doze while in flight. After her
husband had returned home, just moments before three a.m.,
she had managed two hours of rest as his strong fingers dug the
kinks out of weary muscles. She'd finally drifted off, but when
the alarm intruded, her eyelids felt as if heavy bags were attached.
On board the corporate jet, she rested her head against the seat
back. She willed each set of muscles to welcome the brand new
sun that flooded through the jet's small windows.

Waddell had requested "wheels up" at eight, and sure enough,
the two Rolls Royce engines began the spool-up at seven-fifty.
Miles Waddell had been busy with paperwork, not trying to
engage Estelle in conversation, but he put the folders aside as
the engines lit. "We'll be off in a couple of minutes. Coffee?
Tea? Soda?" He looked around the surprisingly spacious cabin,
designed for work around an oval table. "Hell of a rig, huh?"

"Spectacular." Estelle tried to sound cheerful, but accepted
flying only as a necessary expediency. "And nothing, thanks."
Her phone vibrated and she fished it out of her pocket.

"Good morning."

"Hey," Sheriff Torrez said. "You in the air yet?"

"About to be."

"Okay. Keep me posted. Taber and Pasquale are headed over
to Stewart's place this morning. We'll see what they turn. Todd

Stewart says he'll cooperate. Me and Mears are hittin' Scott's in just a couple of minutes. Gayle put out an APD on Garcia."

Gayle Sedillos Torrez, the sheriff's wife and the department's office manager, had taken time off with the arrival of baby Gabe. Now, she found time to occasionally visit the office, where she accomplished more in an hour than most would in a day.

"See if the coach kept a datebook, Bobby."

Torrez fell silent for a moment, then said, "He'd be one to keep score, wouldn't he?" He grunted in what could have been frustration. "We don't know what rock Arthur Garcia is holed up under. Maybe he found a way up to the city."

"We'll see about that in just a few minutes." She felt the aircraft start to drift forward. "We're taxiing now. An hour up, an hour there, another one back. I'll be home by eleven. We'll touch bases then."

She hung up, and tried to relax as the fancy rocket sled turned to line up with the east-west runway. Miles Waddell sat facing her, a wide grin lighting his features.

"I get such a kick out of this bird," he said. "Great way to see New Mexico."

Before she had time to frame an answer, the massive acceleration forced her back into the seat. The climb-out to the west was so steep that Cat Mesa, the massive bulwark north of the village, became little more than a modest lump as it disappeared well below and behind them. The day was perfectly clear, and the view, with the X-Cessna's sharply swept wings, unobstructed. In what seemed like only a couple of minutes, she caught sight of the wink of Elephant Butte under the glare of the rising sun.

The cabin leveled a bit from its initial impossible angle, but the climb continued as if the Cessna wanted to stick its slick nose out into the black of space.

Somewhere south of Socorro, the ferocious ascent relaxed a little, and Waddell lifted one side of his ear phones. "You can listen to the cockpit chatter on these, if you want," he offered. "We're starting our descent to Albuquerque in about eight minutes."

Estelle looked at her watch, then looked again. Down below, the Rio Grande ribboned south, the verdant farmland boundary just a narrow hint of prosperity against the harsh New Mexico landscape. Far to the east, she caught a glimpse of enormous crop circles, watered by the overhead irrigators.

Waddell leaned forward so he didn't have to raise his voice. "The kid is in a bad way, the docs tell me."

Estelle turned away from the window. "It's frustrating, Miles. At the moment, he's the one person who might be able to tell us what happened."

"Might."

"That's right. We have no single path that we know we should be following. It's like a maze. Lots of things that shouldn't be, but none of them pointing us in an obvious direction."

"You don't actually suspect Efrin Garcia of playing a part in the shooting, do you?"

"No. Right now, I think that he's a case of being a young man in the wrong place at the wrong time. I'm interested in what he might have seen or heard. We know now that he was in the area, but we're not sure exactly *when* he was there. There's always a chance that he saw something that could help us…but I don't hold my breath on that, either. If he saw the killer, if he somehow witnessed the crime…then he's lucky he's not dead as well."

The whine of the jets didn't change, but the nose relaxed downward a few degrees, and they flashed north, the ribbon of the interstate far below.

"Mr. Waddell, we'll be touching down in about six minutes." The pilot's voice on the intercom was gracious. "You have a ride waiting for you at the Goodman-Banks hangar just southwest of the terminal. We'll be standing by for the return flight whenever you're ready." The "Fasten Seat-Belts" message board chimed just as the engines retarded a bit more and they started a gentle swing to the west.

"A fellow could get used to this," Waddell said, and pushed his seat-back vertical. They had time for a brief view of the western side of the city, including the landfill, the racetrack, and a scattering of developments before they crossed the river and the interstate and their tires scorched tracks on the runway. Braking hard, they turned off at one of the several intersections and taxied rapidly for what seemed like miles before slowing for a hard turn toward a private hangar.

The hangar doors gaped. The pilot slowed the jet's taxi to a crawl, and Estelle felt the nose wheel trundle over the door's bottom track. The engines spooled down to silence, and she saw that a white crew-cab pickup truck waited off to one side inside the open hangar, just far enough inside to be out of the sun.

Waddell reached out and handed a card to Estelle. "I know you have one of these, but just in case. When your business is finished, away we'll go. You won't have to wait on us." He rose from his seat and watched as the pilot made his way to the door release.

The Cessna was nosed halfway inside the hangar, the engines and tail assembly brilliant in the morning sun. As Estelle stepped out into the cool shade of the hangar, she felt the gentle bump as the tow bar was attached to the nose gear. The pilot touched her elbow as she made the final step down to the hangar's polished concrete floor. His name tag labeled him as PD Ackerman.

"That was a very smooth landing," she said. "Thank you."

He grinned. "I learned to fly in a Luscombe before the military got a hold of me." He left it to Estelle's imagination to figure out what a Luscombe might be, but she had seen a Luscombe 8 that Posadas manager Jim Bergin had owned—a tiny two-seater with high wing and manners that encouraged a gentle touch on the controls. Ackerman nodded across the hangar toward the parked pickup truck. A trim young woman waited by the front fender. "Marion will take you wherever you need to go, ma'am. When you're ready to return, just tell her. We'll be ready to roll the minute you arrive back here."

He escorted her across the gaping hangar as if she somehow might get lost in the intervening hundred feet.

"Marion, this is Posadas Undersheriff Estelle Reyes-Guzman," Ackerman said. "We're on a round-robin without much downtime." Marion's grip was firm and professional. Just as the doors of the white Ford F-250 sported Goodman-Banks logos, so did her pressed white shirt and the ball cap that tried to keep her thick blond hair in some sort of order. Her ponytail reached nearly to her slender waist.

"Marion Banks," she said. "It's a pleasure to meet you, Sheriff. Did you have a good flight?"

"Just a little pokey."

Marion blinked, and then beamed. "It *is* amazing, isn't it?" She glanced at her watch. "But not bad. Not too pokey." She reached out and opened the truck door. "I understand we're headed to UNMH?"

"Yes, please." Estelle looked back toward the plane. Rather than accompanying them, Miles Waddell was striding toward the back of the hangar, where a series of doors lead to offices and lounges. As she slid into the pickup, Waddell turned, grinned at her, and touched the brim of his Stetson. Estelle reflected that the rancher, now rancher/developer, was losing no time in getting used to this lifestyle. She wondered if he would enjoy meeting Derwood Trevino, Angie Trevino's father with the quick and deep wallet. Miles might not be impressed, but Derwood? Certainly.

"I appreciate you doing this," Estelle said as the girl guided the truck out of the hangar and headed for the frontage road at the posted speed limit plus twenty.

"Anything to get out of the office," she said. "And I'm standing in for my dad. He wanted to meet you, but he couldn't spring himself loose. So you have me."

"And your dad is…?"

"I'm sorry. I thought maybe you had met him. Paul Banks? He's half of the Goodman-Banks team."

"And I'm delighted. How long have you worked for the firm?"

"My second week." She smiled again. "I've been away at Caterpillar in Peoria for a while, trying to learn all there is to know about the parameters of digital wear indicators." She raised an eyebrow at Estelle as she maneuvered deftly through traffic. "Sounds exciting, huh?"

"Anything can be exciting in the right circumstances."

"Well, one way to make money is not to spend it needlessly," the girl said. "If you have an app on your computer that tells you that the drive links on your D-9 are close to failing, it makes a lot more sense to fix it while it's ambulatory than have it sit crippled in the field."

"An ambulatory D-9. I like that. So your background is in engineering, then."

"BS, MS, Purdue."

Estelle laughed. "You're overqualified as a chauffeur, but I appreciate it. I assume you've met Mr. Waddell?"

"Oh, several times." She beamed. "What a character. You know, as soon as he heard about this project, my dad told Bayard Goodman that we had to win the bid, whatever it took. I think it was building the narrow gauge out from the village to the facility that intrigued my dad the most. That and Mr. Waddell's insistence that every step of the way...every step, we tip-toe. He didn't want the land ripped up any more than necessary. And you know, it's funny. We're a big company, but for this one? We're almost not big enough. We've had to search out some specialists."

She turned the truck deftly into the driveway of the hospital, a place where there was no apparent easy parking. "You've been here before?"

Estelle nodded. "Too many times."

"Oh, no. Not as a patient, I hope."

"Both sides of the bed."

"Ah...I'm sorry. Then you know where you're going. I'll wait for you in the front lounge after I find a place in the shade to park." She fished out a business card. "That's my cell. Just buzz me when you're ready to leave. Or if something unexpected comes up and you need a ride somewhere else."

"Marion, thank you. This is wonderful. I won't take long. I really need to get back to Posadas."

"Great. Me too. I'm flying back with you folks. I look forward to hearing your take on this whole thing. This project of Mr. Waddell's."

Chapter Thirty-two

The university hospital was rush-hour busy, but Estelle chalked it up to her own culture shock. Five people in Posadas constituted a traffic jam. Here, everyone appeared to be going *somewhere* altogether too fast, and at the same time urgently talking with *someone* on a handheld gadget.

A girl tagged as Melanie at one of the information desks looked hard at Estelle's belt hardware and then asked to see her credentials. Seeing that this visitor wasn't with APD, Melanie took her time reading the ID and commission card, then handed them back without comment. She pulled a small map over, and like a desk clerk at a motel telling a patron where to find the room, penciled the route through the various rabbit warrens. This time she smiled as she handed the map to Estelle. "Have a good day."

"You bet." In due course, the undersheriff reached bed 3-C in the intensive care unit. Other than various beepings from a fleet of monitors, the place was spooky quiet, with people talking in hushed tones.

A woman whom Estelle took to be a senior nurse, gray hair wound into an old-fashioned bun, stocky and efficient in her movements, was adjusting a drainage tube that issued from Efrin Garcia's thin, bruised chest just below a long incision, the stitches like miniature railroad cross ties wrapping around the ribs on his left side. Adelle Sturges, RN, straightened up with a satisfied, "There." She turned to see Estelle standing by the foot of the bed.

"Hello, whoever *you* are." She gave Estelle a quick up and down survey. "Give me a minute to fix his dressings." She tended to the task, and in a moment Efrin lay quiet, freshly bandaged, intubated and sheeted, hooked to at least half a dozen machines that all agreed: the boy was alive.

Estelle extended her hand. "I'm Undersheriff Estelle Reyes-Guzman from Posadas County. I really need a few minutes with Efrin, if that's going to be possible." Ms. Sturges' handshake was perfunctory but firm.

"Oh, my sweetie is doing just *fine.*" The nurse grabbed a handful of sheeted toes and waggled them from side to side affectionately. If Efrin was doing fine, he didn't summon up the energy to agree, or open his eyes, or cause a little twitch in the monitor feeds. He looked very much like an overly thin, beaten kid who hadn't decided whether or not to step through death's door.

Estelle picked up the chart from the end rail of the bed. Nurse Sturges didn't appear to think much of that. Her mouth went prim and tight, one hand now protectively on Efrin's forehead.

"Elbow, spleen, various contusions and abrasions. One twelve-point-seven-centimeter laceration behind the right ear, possibility of a mild concussion." Estelle glanced up after reciting the chart and surveyed the wreckage. Sure enough, bandages covered the right side of Efrin's head, his ear hardly a bump under all the mummy wrappings. His left arm was cocked awkwardly in its fiberglass cocoon.

"What's the surgical schedule on the elbow?"

"I think you should talk with Dr. Chabra on that," the nurse said. And then, as if embarrassed to be stonewalling, she added, "I know they haven't done any surgery on it yet, because of the issue with his spleen."

"He's off transfusions now?"

"As of earlier this morning. But my goodness, what a time he had."

Estelle read the notes that reported, in their typical multisyllabic style, that a fractured rib had lacerated the spleen.

"A lucky young man," she said, and slid the chart back in the keeper. Advancing up the bed, she put a hand on Efrin's right knee, leaning close until her face was only inches from the boy's. "Efrin, are you with us yet? Can you understand me?"

His shallow breathing hiccoughed.

"You're going to be okay." She hesitated, choosing her words carefully, aiming at what the boy would want to hear, not couched in threats. "No one is going to get even close to your mural while you're here, Efrin. Mr. Waddell is so proud of what you've done. He showed it to us last night."

His black eyebrows twitched a little.

"He wishes you well, and wants to stop by to see you a little later. Maybe that's silly, huh, Efrin? Maybe after all this, the last thing you care anything about is some unfinished mural up on the mesa. But we all want to see it finished, Efrin. We want to see *you* finish it. And then we want to see you go on to even bigger projects."

His lips moved, and he lifted his right arm ever so slowly, carrying the array of tubes with it. He turned his head slightly and reached across to itch the corner of his left eye. His lips moved again as his hand relaxed onto the sheets.

She watched his eyes, and saw that they appeared to focus.

He groaned and flexed one knee. "What happened at the school, Efrin?" Estelle's mouth was no more than two inches from Efrin's bandaged right ear. "We know you weren't able to finish the panel." When there was no response, she added, "Tell me what happened that night. Tell me how it happened."

"He pushed the ladder." Efrin Garcia's voice was surprisingly strong, then regressed into scarcely a whisper, as if someone had turned down a rheostat. "He came out and saw me and yelled at us." He hiccoughed again. "I fell, I broke my arm. I got..." he pulled a long, shuddering breath. "all tangled up in the ladder."

"You said, 'yelled at us.' Who was with you, Efrin?"

With no indication that the boy had heard her, Estelle leaned closer, reaching around his head to caress his cheek, to keep his head from lolling away from her. "Who was with you, Efrin?"

Still no response.

"He drifts in and out," the nurse said.

Efrin's eyebrows furrowed again. "He never liked me 'cause of my…" That was as far as he got before his eyes first refused to focus, then closed as he drifted off.

Even as Estelle straightened up, Efrin jerked, and his eyes opened briefly. "She saw what happened," he rasped. His mouth lolled, and his eyes remained open just enough to expose the bottom arch of color of his irises. He drifted away from the unfinished thought. *She* witnessed? Who was *she?*

"Has he had any visitors?"

"Just his mom," the nurse said. "She flew in with him, and has been here the whole tour. All yesterday, all last night. I talked her into going down to the ICU lounge just a bit ago for a nap."

Ms. Sturges sighed and patted Efrin's left ankle as she surveyed the monitors. "Rest is what *he* needs, at this point. The lounge is just down the corridor to the right if you want to visit with her." She frowned hard at Estelle. "And the same applies to you, Sheriff. You look beat."

Estelle smiled at the mothering. "Time for all that," she said.

◇◇◇

Eustacia Garcia had appropriated the entire yellow couch, her shoes neatly stowed on the floor at one end and a hospital-issue blanket pulled up to her shoulders. Estelle felt a wash of sympathy when the woman turned slightly to look at her. Despite being up all Thursday night, followed by a long, sleepless day on Friday, then a second restless night, she was finding rest elusive.

"Mrs. Garcia, do you remember me?" For years, the woman had worked at Trombley's Pharmacy, and when that business had closed, Eustacia Garcia had moved one door south on Grande to Posadas Home Builder's Supply, selling nuts and bolts instead of pills and potions. A husband hadn't been in her life for a dozen years.

Her face screwed up with the effort of swinging her body from prone to sitting, and she mashed the blanket in one corner of the couch, then held out a limp hand. She allowed her fingers to be pressed, but offered nothing in return. She looked at the badge holder on Estelle's belt as if surprised to find out that the Posadas County Sheriff's Department might take an interest in her son.

Black eyes in a round face—that would be the description that Estelle would find most apt for Eustacia Garcia—regarded the undersheriff wearily. "Did you see my son?" Her face was unlined, but puffy.

"Yes, I did." Estelle sat on the couch beside Mrs. Garcia. "He will recuperate just fine."

"They had to take out his *spleen*."

"I understand that. That's a serious thing. But he's young and strong."

"Yes. And now," Eustacia Garcia's voice sounded far away, "they have to operate on his elbow."

"That's what I understand."

"We don't have that kind of money."

"That's not something to worry about just now, Mrs. Garcia. What's important is that he heals up strong and true."

"Such a time he's had. Just so terrible." She looked up at Estelle. "You know his work?"

Both kinds, Estelle thought. "Yes. Mr. Waddell showed us the mural at the new facility on the mesa."

Eustacia's eyes brightened. "I haven't seen that yet. But from what Efrin says, it must be something. That's all he talks about now."

"You need to go out and see it." The image of the old, beaten Lincoln negotiating the narrow access road didn't inspire confidence. "The easiest way now is the train, Mrs. Garcia. Mr. Waddell will be most happy to provide you with a pass."

Her round face crinkled. "Oh, I don't want to bother them."

"It isn't a bother showing such work. Mr. Waddell is extremely proud of what Efrin does."

"I would like to meet him one day. He's been so good to my son."

Estelle smiled gently. "Be sure to do that." The smile faded. "Mrs. Garcia, I wanted to talk to you about Efrin's *other* artwork. His tagging. The graffiti." She opened the leather folder and withdrew the series of photos.

"Oh, that," Eustacia said, and waved a hand in dismissal. "You know these boys." *You know these boys,* Estelle thought. A little graffiti here and there, maybe a cross-country trip with a girlfriend in her powerful car…*maybe we don't know these boys.*

"The night he was hurt, before he wrecked the truck, he was in the process of spraying this one." Estelle held out the photo of the school location. "This is on the back wall of the school. He was using a ladder, and barely got started spraying when he fell."

"Ay."

"Who was with him when this happened?"

Eustacia shook her head as if the whole affair was incomprehensible to her. "No…I mean I don't know. Efrin, he comes and goes on his own, you know. With his brother now, they come and go."

"Was his brother with him when he did these, you mean?"

She shook her head as if the comings and goings of her children were a complete mystery. "I don't know."

"Arthur didn't come up here with you, did he?"

"No," and her expression said, *why would he do that?* She shook her head. "I rode in the ambulance, with my son. And then we flew." Her eyes widened. "I never want to do *that* again."

"Was Arthur with Efrin last night?" Estelle shook her head to clear the cobwebs. "I mean *Thursday* night. When Efrin was hurt?"

"No. I don't think so. Well, maybe he was. I wasn't paying attention." She nodded. "Efrin came home, all beat up. I heard him out in the yard. I went to look, and he was on his hands and knees, he was so bad. He couldn't even walk. And the *blood. Por Dios,* the blood." She turned her head and rested a hand on her own right ear. "So much blood. He tells me that he hit a deer and then crashed into that electric pole just down the road. And then he starts to throw up, right there in the yard. I was so scared."

She looked up at Estelle, her head oscillating back and forth at the memory. "So I called the ambulance. Efrin, he's choking and crying and he can't move. He's like lying on the ground, on his right side, all curled up. I can't touch him. And then I see his elbow. *That's* all crooked, you know?"

"Arthur wasn't there?"

"No. I say, 'Where's your brother?' 'Cause he has my car, you know. But Efrin, he can't answer me. So I just stay with him until the ambulance comes."

"You did the right thing, Mrs. Garcia. Later, when you were at the emergency room with Efrin, did Arthur come by? Did he follow in the car?"

"No. I mean, I don't think so. I haven't seen him." She shook her head again. "All this *blood.* I didn't know what happened." She wrung her hands. "So they took him to the emergency room. Your husband was there, too. And Dr. Perrone. And before you know it, here we are. All the way up here."

"Is Arthur coming to pick you up? Has he been able to reach you on the phone?"

Eustacia looked puzzled. "I haven't even thought about it. Maybe he will. I know he was thinking of taking the bus over to Tucson, to see his father." *Whether his brother lives or dies...a little vacation time.*

"Has he talked to Mr. Herrald about that?"

"I...with who?"

"Mr. Herrald. Jamie Herrald. His parole officer."

Eustacia hesitated. "Oh. That's right. I was going to ask him that, but he acts like it's none of my business. And maybe it's not." She shrugged. "He's twenty-three now. He comes and goes..." She raised a hand and waved ineffectually.

Estelle carefully slipped the photos back into the folder. "And during the trip north in the ambulance...you never asked Efrin exactly what happened?"

"He couldn't speak. He was what do you call it?"

"Sedated?"

"Yes. I held his hand the whole way. That's the best I could do."

"And you're here for him now. You're right. That's the best thing, Mrs. Garcia. He's sleeping now, and so should you. Did they offer to find a motel room for you? Efrin will be here several days, I'm sure, before they can transport him back to Posadas."

The woman patted the couch. "Oh, this is fine."

"No, it *isn't* fine. The hospital will provide better for you," Estelle insisted. "I'll talk with them about it."

Leaving the lounge, Estelle scouted until she found a lounge where she could use her phone, and Sheriff Bobby Torrez answered on the second ring.

"Yep."

"Arthur Garcia," Estelle said without preamble. "We need to talk with him. If he's not in town, his mother said that he might be heading out to Tucson to visit his father. I think that he was with Efrin at the school."

"Okay." *Mr. Excitement.*

"I need to know everything there is to know about him. What his parole officer says, where he's working, when he got home, where he's going to live, all that."

"Well, you wait a couple of days, and old Arthur will screw up somehow. Then he'll be back in the slammer, and you'll have all the time to talk to him that you need. He's a worthless piece of shit."

"We can't wait a couple of days, Bobby. And you were absolutely right to impound Efrin's pick-up. At this point, I don't know exactly what happened with it, but something's not right. Mom doesn't have a clue, and Efrin is lapsing in and out of consciousness and can't tell me much. He started to say that someone came out and caught him on the ladder. Maybe he got pushed, maybe not. He says that he fell and got tangled up with the ladder. Went down hard."

"You going to keep after him?"

"Yes. Just before he passed out, Efrin said that 'she saw' what was going on. Now, who is the *she?* We have to know that, Bobby." She took a deep breath. "If we take Efrin's word at face value, we have three people to account for. He talks about 'us' being there, about a 'he' who sees him on the ladder, and a 'she' who sees the whole thing."

A long silence followed before Torrez said, "Okay. Look, Pasquale may have found where Stacie Stewart is headed, by the way."

By the way? Estelle leaned back against the wall. "But he hasn't heard from her? Hasn't spoken to her?"

"Nope. But he thinks she's headed for New York. And that's just a maybe. Pasquale found out that she's got an older sister there. Stewart confirmed that she and the sister are close."

"New York, as in the city?"

Torrez hesitated, his command of geography a little sketchy with any place east of Tucumcari.

"Somewheres up there. Pasquale's going to look into it. If she caught a jet out of El Paso or something, she could be there by now. Maybe we'll get lucky."

"I want to know if she saw Coach Scott after the game. If they went out together. Anything at all. Tell Tommy that's important."

"Yep. He's on it." It sounded as if Torrez stifled a yawn. "Nothin' out of the ordinary at Scott's place, though. He wasn't hidin' any great secrets that would make a difference. No handy scrapbook of victims or nothin' like that."

"Anything new at the school?"

"Nope. But that back window of the truck didn't bust when he hit the deer or the electric pole, either one. We found a couple of the spray paint cans down along the fence. Chrome yellow and white. And some busted automotive glass."

"That shattered back window of the truck...that's not going to happen by pitching spray paint cans at it, Bobby. We're looking at the ladder for that."

"Perrone helped us do a quick and dirty blood type before we send stuff off to the lab. Consistent with Efrin's. It's startin' to look like he's the only one bleedin' out there."

"Well, that's something. By the way, Waddell's outfit will fly me home direct, as soon as I'm finished here. Flight time up was forty-two minutes."

"Find out what you need." Torrez switched off without further comment.

Chapter Thirty-three

Estelle made her way back to Efrin's room, and was surprised to see him with his good arm wrapped around behind his neck, helping to hold his bandaged head off the pillow. He appeared to be watching a physician make adjustments to the plumbing issuing from his lower chest. "It's going to hurt for a good while, yes indeed," the doctor said. "But the fewer painkillers we load up on you, the better it'll be."

He turned and saw Estelle. She stepped into the room and held out a hand. His name tag said *S.C. Chabra, M.D.,* and when she introduced herself, he beamed a broad smile, impossibly white teeth even brighter against the smooth, dusky complexion. A spray of gray at each temple prevented him from looking sixteen years old.

"Ah, let it be so." His smile widened. "Soneil Chabra, and the world is a small place. Tell me you are related to Dr. Guzman? At the Posadas clinic?"

"My husband."

"Ah, of course. Well," and his head-to-toe appraisal of the undersheriff was frank, "he is a most lucky man. I talked to him this morning about our mutual friend here." He regarded Efrin kindly. "One good thing that is not wasted on the young is recuperation, you know. He will heal rapidly. I suspect that we will move him out of intensive care by tomorrow evening. But I am thinking that he will need to remain with us for several days. Especially since the reconstructive surgery on the elbow is scheduled only for Monday morning. Other issues must stabilize before that."

He turned back to Estelle and rested a hand low on his own ribs on the left side. "Unfortunately, damage was such that a splenectomy was necessitated. Two broken ribs, and a fragment lacerated the spleen, that coupled with significant bruising. Such a time. At first," and he shrugged, "we thought that laparoscopic surgery might be possible. I'm sure you are familiar with that process?"

"Yes."

"Unfortunately, in this case, with so much tissue damage, bleeding, and transfusing, and such, we thought it best to do a standard open splenectomy. Particularly to look for other hemorrhaging. And of course, to stabilize the bone fragments."

"I need to talk with him," Estelle said. Despite the obvious discomfort, Efrin's eyes were wide open and wary, not helplessly comatose as she'd seen a few minutes ago.

"Most certainly, you may do that." Chabra looked at his watch. "He has been out of anesthesia now for some twenty hours. At the moment, even though he is lightly sedated, he is sorting through a good deal of pain, between the lacerations to the head, the fractures of the elbow, and the surgery. He has ample reason to hurt, you see. But perhaps talking with you may take his mind off the discomfort." He reached out and waggled Efrin's sheeted foot. "And Mrs. Guzman, it is a pleasure to meet you. My regards to both you and your husband." He shook her hand again, then beckoned to Nurse Sturges.

Estelle moved to the side of the bed and gazed down at Efrin Garcia, a skinny, wary, hurting little twerp. "You've decided to be awake for a while," she said.

"I ain't never hurt like this before," he murmured, and let his head slump back on the pillow. He drew his uninjured arm down slowly from behind his head as if every joint in it had decided to visit the pain centers out of sympathy. "My freakin' elbow. And it feels like they tried to cut me in half."

"They just about did. And you're going to hurt, but a little less each day." She regarded him with sympathy. "So tell me."

"What?" A little bit of umbrage, a little insolence already, less than two days after the surgery. She smiled as she fished a tiny micro-recorder out of her blouse pocket and placed it on the sheet covering the right side of Efrin's skinny chest. Efrin eyed it with suspicion.

"So tell me, Efrin Garcia, what happened? We know you hit a deer and crashed into a pole. But what's the rest?"

"I need a lawyer."

"Do you? I think you've been watching too much television, *hijo*. What have you done wrong, other than spraying a little paint in a few places where it shouldn't be? You're going to tell me that I should see the other guy?"

He frowned, and Estelle watched him without comment. Finally, he said, "I had a good job goin' with Mr. Waddell, too." He sounded genuinely sorry for himself.

"Yes, you did. And still do, *hijo*. He's eager for you to finish the theater mural."

"You saw it?"

"I did. It's amazing work. You must be proud. I know Mr. Waddell is."

"And that's what he said?"

Estelle nodded. "So, you tagged the train car." She shrugged. "You tagged the radio telescope dish, too, and then you went to the school, to do some more art. What? The *NightZone* mural isn't enough for you? You're thinking about throwing that all away?"

Efrin closed his eyes with a grimace as if even his eyelids hurt. For a few seconds it appeared as if he was fading out.

"Hey." Estelle nudged the boy gently on the right shoulder. "Now's the time to be tough, *hijo*. Someone interrupted you when you were tagging the school. Tell me. Was Arthur with you?"

That question prompted another long moment of silence, but his frown deepened. "Look, he don't have *nothin'* to do with any of this. He just got out, and he can't run no risks like this."

"But he was with you?" Efrin didn't answer. "Sheriff Torrez will talk with him, and if we find out you're lying to protect him, then Sheriff Torrez will want to talk with *you*, Efrin. And you think you hurt now? The sheriff isn't much for sympathy."

"I know he ain't."

"Well, then. Some simple answers. Arthur was with you? That's just a yes or no."

"Yeah." Another long pause. "He was. But he was just helpin' me. Steadyin' the ladder and holdin' the light."

"What time was this?"

Efrin covered his eyes, then his hand slid down as his index finger picking at the edge of the bandage over his ear. "After the game. Way after. Everybody had gone home. And the place was dark, man. Somebody had busted the lamp over the back door of the school, and the parkin' lot light wasn't lit either. I was workin' by flashlight."

"Around ten o'clock, maybe?"

"About then." He took a long, slow breath, and jerked as a lance of pain shot through him. "I think I'm dyin' here."

"Not likely, *hijo*. But a clear conscience will help you heal faster." She leaned closer. "And if you *are* dying, a clear conscience will help you get where you want to go. So tell me what happened."

"We got jumped, that's all."

"How did it happen? Jumped by who?"

He took another long, careful breath, almost as if experimenting to find out where the pain lurked, and stopped abruptly. A look of stunned surprise shot across his face.

"So don't be doing that if it hurts," Estelle said. "Tell me what happened. You said somebody jumped you, and I need to know who that was."

"I got me a good start on the design—I mean, I know where I'm goin' with it and stuff, and Arthur, I hear him say, 'So who's the chick?'" Efrin stopped, waiting for breath. "I turned a little, but didn't see nobody, but Arthur, he says that and then all of a sudden the back door of the school busts open, and there's Coach Scott. Ain't no chick, man. He's one scary dude, man."

"So Coach Scott caught you in the act."

"Yeah. He stands there by the door, hands on his hips like he owns the place."

"Did *he* push the ladder?"

"He tells us to get out, and Arthur, he gets all charged up. All huffy, you know? Like he's going to *argue* with this guy?" Efrin looked as if he wanted to laugh, but settled for a whimper and grimace. "Shit." He closed his eyes and waited for the assault to pass. "Scott came on like he was going to grab the ladder, and Art took a swing at him. Well, *that* didn't help things. The ladder gets pushed…I don't know, maybe he didn't mean to. But it skids on the smooth brick and there I go. I ain't never had anything that hurt so bad. My arm's all crooked and stuff."

"What happened then?"

"And then Art, *he* decides to be Mr. Hero. He's got this stupid pistol and he pulls it on Scott."

"He had a gun with him?"

"Yeah. I don't think it was loaded or anything like that. But he was pretty proud of it. I mean, he showed it to me once. It didn't have no clip, and he was lookin' to buy one somewheres."

"So out comes the gun."

"Yeah. Maybe he thought it was going to scare Mr. Scott. Well, that ain't what happened."

"What did?"

Efrin covered his eyes with his good arm. "Arthur, he ain't too fast, you know what I mean? And he's not in such good shape now. Scott was takin' a step or two toward me, 'cause I'm still down on the ground, cryin' like a little kid. Art sticks the gun in Scott's face, and next thing I know, I see it go flyin'. Scott knocked it right out of Art's hand. I try to get up, and Scott gets the gun and he says, 'you two thugs get off school property,' or something like that."

After a long, careful breath, Efrin added, "I got to my knees and then stumbled toward the truck. I hear Art yell, 'You got to give me back my gun,' or somethin' like that. I hear Scott say,

'Yeah, right. It'll be waiting for you down at the Sheriff's Office.' I heard him say that."

"Scott was going to turn the gun in to us?" Estelle's pulse jumped. Out of prison, on parole, and a firearms charge. If the gun was turned in to authorities, Art was toast, and he would know it.

"I guess. I had the truck started, and I hear him shout, 'Don't forget your damn ladder!' And wham! My back window blows and something smacks me right in the head. He's got that ladder right through the window, blowin' glass everywhere. I didn't even know if it hit me, but then I'm…bleedin' all over."

"And where's Art all this time?"

"I don't know. He ain't going to take on Coach Scott, that's for sure."

"Art had driven himself that night?"

"Yeah. He had my mom's car. He had it parked over in the back of the lot, where it's real dark?"

"But you didn't see him leave that night?"

"I didn't see *nothin'*. I was hurtin' so bad I don't know *what* I was doin'. I made it a ways away from the school, and almost got home. Then this deer jumps out on the road, and I'm goin' too fast, and I hit it. And the truck spins in the gravel."

"Art wasn't following you home?"

Efrin shook his head. "I hit that pole and finished the job, that's for sure. That's what they tell me. I was lyin' there, eatin' dirt and grass, and started to crawl home. I think my ma found me."

"You're sure it was Clint Scott?"

"Sure it was him. I know him good enough. I mean, I was in his class back in second grade and all." He closed his eyes and tried to smile, the bandage tape pulling the corner of his mouth. "Almost flunked second grade. How bad is that?" Efrin took another slow breath to see if the pain was still there. It was.

"Then what?"

"Mother Mary, this hurts." He tried to shift position. "Don't they got something for the hurt?" he managed.

Estelle glanced at the tubes and suspended bags and gadgets. "They have you on morphine drip already, Efrin. You're going to have to tough it out." She touched his left shoulder. "I just have a couple more questions for you. Then you can sleep it away."

For a minute, it appeared that Efrin had faded out, but then he whispered, "There ain't nothin' else."

"A little bit ago, you said something about *she*. That a girl, or woman, someone, showed up at the scene. What did you mean by that?"

"That's what Arthur said. I didn't see nobody."

Estelle reached out, picked up the recorder and looked at it, but left it running. "Efrin, you never saw Arthur, or talked to him after you left the school?"

"No, ma'am. I know I got home somehow, and that was it. I passed out, that's for sure. I remember hearing my mother screaming at me, but anything else? I don't remember. Not any of this shit." He lifted his left arm an inch, and almost managed a rueful smile. "I never wanted to do no drugs, Sheriff. But if you got a pocketful of 'em right now…"

"They'll give you all you need, Efrin."

"I think they like seein' me hurt."

"They like seeing you *responsive, hijo*. If that requires a little pain, so be it. You're doing a good job for somebody so broken up. I'm proud of you."

Efrin gazed at her for a long moment, then closed his eyes.

"So tell me," Estelle said. "Why the tagging? You thought that your employer was going to welcome your painting the side of his train? The dish? You thought the school needed a touch-up?"

"We was just playin' around. Art didn't think they'd be able to figure out who did it, but hell, *I* knew. I mean, they *know* my work."

"Ah. That's the trouble with having so much talent, *hijo*. You can't hide it. Where did that design come from?"

"I seen it in a magazine. Arthur told me what it represented, but I don't remember. Just neat graphics."

"But *nothing* like your mural, Efrin. That's world-class."

"Yeah, well." She heard a faint note of pride.

"Why those locations? Is there some particular reason why you chose them?"

"They was in the papers. The newspaper? All the stories lately. That big write-up in the Sunday paper about the train? And the mesa project with the telescope and stuff? That's been hot in the papers, even on TV. That and the volleyball team. They're all hot shit right now. Like that big spread in the local paper last week, and then again in the Albuquerque paper? All that publicity. That's good shit, man."

"So you just decided to grab some coverage for yourself? Is that what Art wanted?"

"Somethin' like that." He tried another smile.

"Who is Art trying to impress with all this?"

"I don't know, man." He shook his head. "I just don't know. I know that it meant a lot to him, so I did it. That's all."

"What Big Brother wants," Estelle said softly.

"Well, he's had a hard time," Efrin said. "Is all this going to get Coach Scott in trouble? Are you going to arrest him for what he done to me?"

"You think I should, *hijo?* It sounds to me like all he did was bump the ladder. That and take Art's gun away from him."

Efrin fell silent for a moment. "If I die, maybe."

"You're not going to die, my friend. You may feel like it right now, but that'll pass, day by day."

"Did you guys get the gun? I know that Art said he paid pretty good for it."

"We'll see about that."

Efrin closed his eyes. "I can't pay for all this."

"Not to worry."

"Does Coach Scott know I'm here? I mean, is he going to show up?"

"Not likely. What about Arthur, though? Where would your brother go if he didn't want to wait around home, or if he doesn't come up here?"

"He's got friends in Socorro, Cruces, Albuquerque…you name it."

"Good gang friends?"

Efrin made a face. "He ain't in no gang. My brother, he made a mistake or two when he was younger. You know all about that. But he ain't touched the stuff since they sent him up a couple of years ago. He's straight now. We were going to see if I could get him a job out at the park, too."

Estelle leaned close and whispered, "So you painted Mr. Waddell's train, you crawled up in the dish and vandalized that… that's all good thinking, Efrin. I'm sure Mr. Waddell is impressed. Those are all great ways to help somebody apply for work." She straightened up and stepped away from the bed, pocketing the recorder. "And Coach Scott is dead, *hijo.*"

Efrin cringed so hard that the pain made him gasp. He turned several shades paler. "What?"

"Somebody shot him to death inside the school, just minutes after you left. He's dead."

"But he…"

"He's dead, Efrin."

He reacted as if the words were hammers. When he could finally speak, his voice was small and distant. "You mean someone just went into the school and shot him? They broke in and did that?"

"They didn't have to break in. The back door was open. Besides the killer, you and your brother probably were the last ones to see him alive."

Efrin didn't respond. His right hand drifted across his chest to rest gently on the bandages from his surgery, but he picked it up again immediately and covered his eyes.

"I need a more accurate time, Efrin. What time did you go there?"

"I don't wear no watch."

"Did you go up on the mesa first?"

"That was the night before. That's when we did that. And then when Arthur heard they was going to run the train, he wanted one on that. So we did that down at the yard, before we went over to watch the end of the game."

"So the school tagging was just later in the night, then. After the game."

"Yeah."

"What time? I want you to think about this."

"Maybe half past nine, maybe ten."

"And just before that, you two were at the game. That's what you're saying?"

"We went to the game to watch the chicks play."

"And then after the game, you went to work tagging the school. How long did you work before Coach Scott came out?"

"Ten minutes, maybe. Maybe less."

Estelle consulted her notebook. "The hospital in Posadas checked you in at ten twenty-three."

"If you say so."

"And your brother?"

Efrin's cheeks flushed, and he glared at Estelle. "Look, my brother don't have nothin' to do with *none* of this. He just held the ladder for me. He passed paint cans up to me. When we got attacked, he ran…just like I did. That guy…he's big and he's scary. But we didn't have nothin' to do with no shooting."

"And he didn't really *attack* you, did he?"

"Well, I fell. That's his fault."

"Where did Arthur go after you were taken to the hospital?"

Efrin tried to shift in the bed, a whimper escaping through clenched teeth. "I don't know where he went."

"Does Arthur own any other guns, Efrin?"

"I don't know."

"You don't sound convincing when you lie, *hijo.* "

"Well, yeah, okay…maybe he does, but…"

"But what? He had them before he went to prison?"

"Yeah. Long before that."

"How long is long? He's only twenty-three now. He was sentenced to three years on a felony drug charge, and served sixteen months. When did he acquire this gun that you say Coach Scott confiscated?"

"I don't know. He traded a friend out of it, I think." The boy glanced sideways at Estelle, loathe to open *that* door.

"When was this?"

Nurse Sturges appeared from the hallway and frowned at Estelle.

"Just a few minutes," Estelle said.

"Not any longer than that," Sturges admonished. "And there's another gentleman here who wants a few words with Efrin." She left, shutting the door behind her.

"Is that gonna be Torrez?"

"No. Mr. Waddell said he wanted to visit you for a bit. When was this that Art traded for the gun?"

"He was going to give it to me for my birthday. But he didn't have no clip for it."

"How nice of him. What were you supposed to do with it?"

"Just shoot it out on the mesa. You know. Just mess around."

"Which birthday, *hijo*?"

"When I turned eighteen."

"So, recently."

"I guess."

"And *did* he give it to you for your birthday?"

Efrin's right hand beat a little tattoo on the bedding to counter the pain. "No. My mom told him to get it out of the house. She didn't want it around."

"Smart lady. What kind of gun was it?"

"Just some cheap foreign thing. I don't know. And I don't know what the stink was all about. He just liked to carry it 'cause he liked the looks of it."

"So…no birthday present for you."

He closed his eyes. "That's okay. He bought me an old ATV instead. We'll get it running one of these days."

"Your brother's good to you, *hijo*."

"Yeah, he is."

"Would your mom know where Arthur is right now?"

That earned the smallest of shrugs. "I don't think…maybe. Probably home, watchin' television. Or hangin' out."

"With?"

"Just the guys."

"How about a couple of names? Who does he run with?"

"I don't know. Him and Iggy, a lot."

"Iggy?"

"Mauricio Ignacio. We grew up together. My mom don't like him much. He's always gettin' into trouble with the cops. Ask that Pasquale guy."

"You mean Deputy Tom Pasquale?"

"Yeah. He likes to bust Iggy for anything he can. But I heard that he's gonna get a job up on the mesa, too. His big brother works the gate nights."

For a long moment, Estelle stood quietly, regarding the young man. "What?" he asked finally.

I think Mr. Waddell is going to have to tighten up his hiring practices, Estelle thought, but she kept the opinion to herself. She reached out and patted Efrin's right knee. "I think Mr. Waddell wants to visit for just a minute, *hijo*. You do what you want, but this would be a *really* good time not to act like a jerk." Efrin's one visible eyebrow lifted in surprise. "If you want your job back, if you want the chance to finish that wonderful mural, then play it right." She nudged him again. "Apologizing wouldn't hurt." She watched him mull that for a moment. "That would be a good place to start. And then, for the next few days, you do exactly what the doctors tell you, *hijo*. We'll be talking again."

"Am I going to have to talk with the sheriff?"

"More than likely." Whether Bob Torrez' reputation was deserved or not, there were times when it was a useful tool.

He grimaced. "You'll make sure my mom gets home okay?"

"Yes." She gave his knee a final pat. "It would be nice if you'd think about your mom *before* you do stupid things, *hijo*."

Chapter Thirty-four

"Where you at?" Sheriff Robert Torrez sounded completely unperturbed.

"Right now? We're just leaving Socorro behind." Estelle leaned over and looked down through the several layers of haze and smoke. "It looks like a pretty good forest fire over by Mount Withington."

That didn't earn so much as a grunt of interest from Torrez. "Look, Arthur Garcia showed up. How long before you're wheels down?"

Showed up? Estelle turned and gestured to Marion Banks. "ETA?"

The young woman held up a finger and made her way forward. In a moment, she returned. "Did you see that nasty fire over to the west of us?"

"I've been watching it. How far out are we?"

"The pilot says sixteen minutes."

Estelle returned to the phone. "I heard her," Torrez said. "Look, when you land, come direct to the mesa ASAP. Over at the new theater. You know where that is?"

"Yes. But Garcia showed up *there?*"

"Yup. Bring Waddell with you." He hesitated. "We're just going to wait this one out."

"What's going on, Bobby?"

"Garcia is makin' some interesting demands. See you in a few minutes." He broke the connection. Estelle sat for a moment in silence, thoughts racing. She redialed, and was more than a little surprised when the sheriff answered.

"What?"

"What do you mean, he's making demands, Bobby? He's armed or something?"

"Yup."

"Armed with what?"

"He's got one of them cheapo imported revolvers, and one of those little semi-auto nine-millimeter assault pistols with the big-ass magazine."

Por Dios. "And what's he doing?"

"Just a minute." The phone cut off, and Estelle stared out the window, willing the miles away. The jet suddenly didn't seem so fast, the great expanse of the San Augustin plains taking their time to inch past. A tiny course correction brought the isolated mountain town of Reserve into view.

Torrez came back on the line. "Look, Mears and Taber are in there talkin' to him. Gastner is there as well. I'm about twenty minutes out."

"They're the best."

"Yeah, but he's got Christina Prescott, and he's got that gun to her head."

Estelle groaned with frustration. The young man was clearly talented in at least one thing—making an already bad situation far, far worse.

"Does he have a phone?"

"Don't think so."

"Tell Mears to get one for him, then have Garcia call me direct."

"Be a minute."

"And, Bobby—Efrin says that the night he was hurt, Art had a gun with him. Some kind of pistol without a magazine. Efrin says that when Coach Scott came outside to confront them, the ladder went down somehow, and then Art pulled the gun on Scott."

"Well, shit. That's ain't too bright."

"True, in this case. Efrin says that Coach Scott took the gun away from Art, and told him that he was going to turn it in at the Sheriff's Department. He never had the chance, obviously. It makes sense to me that Art would have tried to stop him from doing that."

"You're sayin' he came back to the school with another gun."

"One with all its parts."

"That's what it looks like."

"So how long 'til you're on the ground?"

"I'll get back to you."

She twisted in her seat and saw that Waddell was deep in a briefcase full of paperwork, oblivious to the outside world. He could stay that way, she thought, at least until the tires screeched on the Posadas Municipal Airport pavement.

Marion Banks caught her eye, and one pretty eyebrow lifted. "Is everything all right?"

"No." Estelle softened the cryptic answer with a weary smile. "The sooner we're on the ground, the better."

Marion held up a finger. "Let me." She rose and moved forward, leaning close to the pilot's left shoulder. Their conversation was brief, punctuated by a series of nods from both pilot and co-pilot. Marion returned to her seat. "He's calling Posadas to let them know that we're driving straight in, and we'll be fast taxiing in to the FBO. That's about the best we can do."

"Good enough." *Maybe.*

Her phone vibrated. "Guzman."

Jackie Taber's silky voice was soothing. "The sheriff filled you in a little?"

"A little. What is going on, Jackie?"

"LT is handing off the phone right now to Mr. Garcia. The kid's a space-case, so it might get interesting. He's holding a gun, and he looks comfortable with it."

"Tell LT not to provoke him in any way."

"He's clear about that. He's just leaving the phone on a seat next to Garcia and retreating. That's what the kid wants. Now he's saying he wants to talk to you and nobody else. All he has to do is press the auto-dial and you're on."

"I got it. Thanks, Jackie." She clicked off and waited, the phone poised.

After what seemed like enough seconds to fly halfway across the neighboring state of Arizona, her phone vibrated.

"Guzman."

"You talked to my brother." The voice was tight.

"Yes."

"He's going to die, ain't he?"

"No. He's had one surgery to remove his spleen, and he's doing all right in post-op. He has surgery coming up on his left elbow later tomorrow or Monday morning. He'll be fine when it's all over."

"You ain't lyin'?"

"No. Why would I lie about something like that, Arthur? Come on. Your mother is with him, and you should be too."

"I got to talk to him."

"Give the phone to Lieutenant Mears. I'll give him the numbers. But first, you need to let Christina go. She can't help you."

"Yeah, she can. She ain't goin' nowhere until this is all over."

"What is it that you want, Arthur?"

"I want to talk with my brother."

"Done deal."

"And I want to talk with Mr. Waddell."

"He's here with me. We'll be at the airport in just a few minutes. But he's not going to go into that room as long as you're threatening Christina with a gun."

"I lose the gun, you won't talk with me. They'll just shoot me."

Probably true, Estelle thought. Fortunately for Arthur Garcia, Sheriff Robert Torrez was still en route. That bought Arthur a few minutes, anyway.

"So why all this nonsense, Arthur? We know that you helped your brother do some extra artwork up on the mesa. And on the train. And at school. Busy as you guys were, that's all just a petty misdemeanor. It doesn't warrant any of this." She paused as the nose of the jet lowered a degree or two. "Is that revolver that you're holding the same revolver that killed Coach Scott?"

"You better know it is," Arthur said quickly, and Estelle caught the surge of sorry pride in his voice. "My brother ratted me out?"

The undersheriff almost laughed. "Way too many gangster movies, Arthur. No, your brother said you had nothing to do with his accident. He had no idea what happened later at the school. But you went back to the school later, didn't you, Arthur? Scott had threatened to turn in one of your guns to the cops. The one he took from you. When you went there, Scott was still there."

"Yeah, he was. I caught him in the shower, man."

"Brave of you."

"Hey, that guy's psycho. I was just going to tell him that he had to give the gun back. Something like that was going to screw up my parole. He had no cause to do that."

"Even when you stuck the thing in his face and threatened him?"

"It don't work."

"But he didn't know that."

"No. But I was going to tell him that he had to pay for whatever my brother needed, 'cause he was the one who knocked into the ladder. And then he knocks *me* down, and then he throws that ladder like some big spear into the back of the truck. I saw it go right through the back window. He didn't have cause to do that."

"So you accosted him in the shower."

"He saw me and started to come for me. He was comin' right at me, right out of the shower. I had to do something."

"Four times something."

"Yeah, well. I don't know about that. I just shot until he went down, man. It was self-defense, the way I see it."

"So don't make it worse. Christina is no threat to you. She needs to be out of there. You hurt her, and you're dead, my friend. Just like that."

"I talk to my brother and Waddell, and I'll let her go. You tell Torrez that."

"We'll set all that up when I get down," Estelle said. "Play it smart. Just a few more minutes. Let me talk with Christina."

"You don't need that."

"Yes, I do. Just hand her the phone. It's no risk to you."

"You tell the cops to stay out of this room."

"They will."

A pause, a shuffle, and then a husky voice said, "This is Christina."

"Are you all right?"

"Just scared."

"Okay, you have every reason to be, but just wait it out, all right? Garcia isn't going to hurt you, and my officers aren't going to charge in and force a confrontation. They're content to wait it out. Everybody gets out of this safely, Christina. No heroics."

"I understand," Christina said calmly.

She pictured the girl, hardy ranch stock used to wrangling fractious horses, building fences, clearing storm-clogged culverts—even sweet-talking local drunks at the Broken Spur Saloon into peaceful submission. Christina Prescott was more than capable of making Arthur Garcia's day more memorable than he ever bargained for. But he hadn't hesitated in killing Coach Scott, and now, as a felon facing a murder and weapons charge? He would never again see the light of freedom, and he was smart enough to know it.

"Christina, I know you could probably break Art Garcia into little pieces. But please. He has a gun, and he's used it before. Just be patient. All right?"

"Yes."

"Smart girl. I'll be back to you in just a minute." She broke the connection and redialed Jackie Taber. "Leave Mears' phone with Garcia for now," Estelle said. "He just admitted to killing Scott. He claims that he went to see Scott to get a gun back. Apparently Art was carrying it all the while they were roaming around the county painting things. Unloaded, but who knows that. Scott confiscated it after a confrontation at the school, and was going to turn it into us. Arthur went back to school, caught Scott in the shower. He says he shot when Scott charged him."

"Dictate terms at gunpoint," Jackie said. "Well, okay. That always works. But it's as good a line as any, I suppose. Right now the issue is one very frightened Christina Prescott who's got a nutcase holding a gun to her head."

"We play it slow and easy," Estelle said. "Nobody gets hurt."

"Absolutely."

"Thanks. We'll be on the ground in a couple of minutes. We're just north of Cat Mesa now. I'll bring Miles out with me."

"Sounds good. Himself just arrived. He's talking with LT."

"Ask him to be patient, Jackie."

The sergeant laughed softly. "You bet. We can always ask."

Chapter Thirty-five

The jet screamed a fast approach over Cat Mesa, dropping like a graceful rock to swing east and approach the west end of runway nine-zero. Nose high, the Cessna cleared the boundary fence and touched down on the numbers, braking hard.

As the sleek jet sighed to a stop by the fuel island, Estelle rose and beckoned to Miles Waddell. He listened carefully, eyes riveted on hers, as she explained what she knew.

"And they're in the theater?"

"Yes."

He shook his head in distress. "I've only met the brother once, I think, a couple of weeks ago. I wasn't impressed. Why Efrin idolizes him, I couldn't guess."

"Strange chemistry," Estelle said. "Right now, I'd like you to follow me up there in your own vehicle. I'll go on ahead and talk with Bobby."

"Okay." He reached out a hand toward Marion Banks. "You're all set?"

"Oh, sure," she said. "One of the company trucks is parked in the hangar. I'll take that up the hill."

Estelle shook hands with the girl gratefully. "Thanks so much. You can't imagine what this means to us."

The Charger was an oven. But after the frigid air conditioning of the executive jet, even the hot air off the airport's tarmac felt good through the open windows. Turning west on the old state highway, she punched on the embedded phone.

"Hey," Bob Torrez said as he connected.

"I'm just leaving the airport. Is he still holding Christina?"

"Yup. He's got that revolver dug into her skull with the hammer cocked. Even if I had a clear shot, I wouldn't take it."

Estelle's heart hammered. "Listen, Waddell is coming right behind me. I don't know what Garcia wants from him, but I'm not sending him into that room, Bobby. So everyone just sits still until I get there."

Southbound from State 17, the county road was pounded hard after two years of heavy construction traffic, and the overpowered sedan was able to make good time. Only two oncoming belly-dump haulers took to the ditch to give her room, and she arrived at the *NightZone* entrance with fingers aching from clamping the steering wheel.

Bruce Cooper, the young man at the gate, opened it without being prompted, and under other conditions, Estelle might have enjoyed the dramatic, glass-smooth drive up the macadam access road to the mesa-top. As she rounded the first curve, she caught sight of Miles Waddell's hulking diesel pickup behind her, just turning into the park entrance.

"Where are you at?" The sheriff's quiet voice bloomed out of the car's stereo.

"Just coming out on top. Miles is a half-mile behind me."

"Okay."

What was *okay*? Estelle wondered. Ignoring the arrows on the roadway, she took the narrow road against traffic, cutting off a large section of loop.

In a moment, she entered the circle drive that fronted the restaurant, theater, and planetarium complex, and it looked as if the first soiree for the facility was a police convention. Estelle swung in hard to clear the curb and the front bumper of Torrez' Expedition.

The sheriff appeared at the bank of six doorways.

"Nothing's changed," he said. "He'll talk to Jackie, and she's settled him down some, but he ain't lettin' go of the gun."

"How's Christina?"

"Hangin' in there. She's a tough gal."

The clatter of a diesel pickup announced the developer's arrival. "Miles can come into the common foyer, but that's as close as he goes," Estelle said. "So let me find out what this creep has to say for himself."

The right-hand side of the double doors to the theater/planetarium opened on silky hinges, and forty yards away Estelle saw Christina Prescott sitting in the farthest chair in the first row. Directly behind her, the gun resting against her skull, sat Arthur Garcia. Estelle stopped and let the door close softly behind her. She held out both hands, spread wide.

"Arthur, were you able to call your brother?" He looked like a fat version of his younger brother—same inky black hair, thick on his wide skull, too much fat on his face for his dark, expressive eyes to do justice. He jerked the gun against Christina's skull, and she winced.

"I tried to. They said he was asleep. They're just jerkin' my chains." He tried for a tough-guy sneer.

"Hang on." Estelle pulled out her own phone, holding it up so he could see that it wasn't a weapon of any sort. She scrolled down a list and touched auto-dial. As she did so, she asked, "Christina, are you all right?"

"Yes."

Estelle nodded and spoke into the phone, her eyes fixed on Arthur Garcia. Sure enough, the revolver's hammer was cocked, and Arthur's fat index finger was in the trigger guard. Estelle held the phone in her left hand, her right resting on the butt of her own automatic. Because she had already made her final decision, her mind was calm and clear.

A hospital staffer came on the line. "This is Undersheriff Estelle Reyes-Guzman. I need to speak with Nurse Sturges." She waited for a couple of heartbeats. "I don't care what she's doing. Get her on this phone. This is a police emergency." She frowned hard and then relaxed. Lowering it away from her face, she said to Garcia, "They'll find her. Just be patient."

"Get rid of that gun you're carryin'."

"No. I'm not going to harm you, Arthur. And you're not going to harm Christina." She said it so matter-of-factly that Garcia appeared flustered.

"Ah, Nurse Sturges? This is Undersheriff Guzman. We met not long ago in Efrin Garcia's room. It's imperative that we get Efrin on the phone."

She listened for a moment. "Sure. Do that, please." Estelle had been walking toward the narrow elevated stage below the screen, moving obliquely away from Garcia. She watched him, and saw that his hand was steady. And why not? What sort of challenge was this, after blasting four rounds through a naked man, defenseless in a shower?

"Efrin? Can you hear me clearly? All right, I want you to listen very carefully. Your brother Arthur is here with me. We're in the theater with your mural. Will you talk with him? He needs to know that you're going to be all right. Hold on."

She bent down, laid the phone on the polished oak of the stage, and shot it across toward Garcia. It stopped six feet from him.

"Put your hands up on your head," Garcia said. "I mean it. Do it now."

Estelle did so, and was surprised at the agility of the heavyset young man. He kept the revolver pointed at Christina, an easy shot.

"Christina, just hold still," Estelle said, and then thought, *Cheap gun, we hope it has a hard trigger.*

Arthur grasped the phone. "*Hermano?*" He immediately crossed back to the protection of his hostage.

Apparently Efrin Garcia had a lot to say, because his brother stood head down, frowning at the floor.

"You shouldn't a' ratted me out," he said finally, and glared at Estelle as if she were in charge of what his brother said, lying two hundred and fifty miles north in the Albuquerque hospital. "Yeah, well now there's nothing I can do. They got me here. They ain't going to let me walk away."

He listened for another minute, and it seemed to Estelle that his posture relaxed just a bit.

"Yeah. I'm going to do that. No. I don't want to talk to her now." He lowered the phone. "I gotta talk to Waddell. He's outside, ain't he?"

"I won't bring him in here as long as you're holding the gun on Christina." Estelle, hands still on her head, walked across to the first row of seats, and sat down ten spaces from Christina. "There. You have me now. Let her go."

"You'll bring Waddell in if I do that?"

"No. Not as long as you have that gun. Nobody comes into this room. Let Christina go, and you can talk with him on the phone. He's not coming in here." She heard a faint knock from the back of the hall, a small, singular sound that the perfect acoustics delivered clearly. She knew what it was. It would be inconceivable for Robert Torrez, he of the single-minded hostage negotiating technique, to stand patiently out in the foyer, waiting for something to happen. He would think in terms of contingencies. Was he now in one of the three projection booths? Or snuggled up against the mid-floor planetarium projector? From any of those vantage points, his shot would be clear and easy.

"Okay. She can go," Arthur Garcia said, as if he'd come to the same conclusion as Estelle.

"Just a minute." She pointed at the phone. "Slide that over to me."

He did so. One burly arm hugged Christina close. Estelle cleared the phone and appeared to select another number, the hall remained silent of ringtones. She knew where the sheriff was, and she knew that he could hear her without the alert of the phone.

"Bobby, let this one go. He's going to let Christina out, and I need for him to talk to Waddell." She wasn't sure if the sheriff had heard her, or was ignoring her, or was already gently squeezing the trigger on his .308. She immediately pushed the auto-dial, and out in the foyer, Miles Waddell answered instantly.

"Mr. Waddell, Arthur needs to talk with you for a minute. And Christina is coming out. Just stand near the first set of doors."

"I need to come in there?" Waddell asked.

"Absolutely not. You stay out in the foyer. Arthur will be on the phone." She held it out toward Arthur, and he pushed Christina away with the muzzle of the revolver. Holding the gun now on Estelle, he slid into a seat two paces down from her.

"Waddell?"

"He's out in the foyer. That's as close as he's going to get."

Garcia reached for the phone.

"I'm on the line," Waddell said. "She's done you a favor, my friend. Now it's your turn to do something smart."

"Hey, man, look…my brother wouldn't a' done any of that taggin' if I hadn't talked him into it." Arthur turned and gazed at the partial space mural.

"I don't care about the vandalism," Miles said. "That's not what all this is about, is it?"

"If I give myself up peaceful, you got to let him finish this mural."

"I *got* to?"

"Yeah. I mean, he needs to. You don't know how proud he is of all this, man."

"That's the only reason you came up here?"

"Yeah. That's it. Look, Efrin didn't have nothin' to do with that coach gettin' himself killed down at school. Efrin didn't even know I went back to settle things up. I had to get my gun back, man. And then Coach charged me like that, and there wasn't nothing I could do."

"You could have turned and run," Waddell said. "How far is a naked man going to get, pursuing you through the neighborhood?"

"Yeah," Arthur said bitterly. "That's going to happen." He snuffled and dragged a finger across his nose. "Look, man, I ain't got nothin' left now. That guy messed with my brother, and I settled things. I screwed this up so there's no comin' back. I know all that. But Efrin—he's different. He's going to be a famous artist someday. You gotta let him have that chance."

"He already *is* famous, my friend," Waddell said. "Look... I'll cut *you* a deal. You give that gun to the undersheriff. You can trust her. You do that, and you'll come out of there in one piece. If we find out you're not lying to us...that your brother had absolutely nothing to do with Mr. Scott's murder...then maybe we'll have something to talk about. That's the deal. "

Garcia lowered the phone. "You heard him?"

Estelle nodded. "It's recorded, Arthur."

He nodded and lowered the revolver, then reached out to place it in her lap like a little kid sharing a favorite toy. The ends of the revolver's cylinder were clearly visible, and she could see that the gun was not loaded. "Okay," Arthur Garcia said. "If that's what I got to do." He slid out of the seat to his knees, bowed his head, and laced his fingers together on top of his skull. Only when Estelle snapped the cuffs on his wrists, bringing his hands down behind his back, did the little red dot of light that had hovered on his skull wink out.

Chapter Thirty-six

District Attorney Dan Schroeder took the gamble. A defense attorney might argue that Art Garcia, chubby and uncoordinated and not much of a fighter, had to defend himself against the tough and quick-thinking Clint Scott, whether the coach was naked or not. The four carefully placed shots told a different story, and that's the version that made sense to the district attorney. There had been no risk for the assailant. The young man had returned to the school, had sought out Scott, and then basically executed him in the shower. That pointed to a first-degree murder charge. Arthur Garcia would never have to pay rent again.

Arthur, perhaps with the notion of avoiding lethal injection—which New Mexico was usually loath to administer anyway—turned into a fund of information. The idea for the graffiti design he had appropriated from a passing BNSF freight train whose boxcars were rolling billboards for spray art. And it made sense to him that his tagging kudos would benefit from spraying targets that had recently garnered lots of publicity—Waddell's locomotive, impressive venue of Waddell's telescope, and even the gym where the Posadas Jaguarettes had scored yet another romp and stomp, much-ballyhooed victory.

The only catch, he told them, was that he didn't have an artistic bone in his body. That's what younger brothers were for.

One thing Arthur Garcia did not know—and Estelle quizzed him relentlessly. The "chick" he had seen approaching as they worked on the school wall was nothing but a shadow to him. She could have been four feet or six feet tall. She might have been blond, or brunette or bald. He maintained that the approaching figure was a woman because of the sashay of her hips. "Men don't walk like that," he insisted.

The vague description of what might have turned into an important material witness did not coalesce. Had the woman been fearful for her safety? If so, why choose to walk around *behind* a darkened school building so late at night? And when she saw taggers working so diligently on the wall, she had vanished like a puff of smoke.

Had she witnessed Coach Scott's confrontation with the two young men? Did their raised voices scare her off? Did she see one of them draw a pistol? If so, she had not lingered. The Garcias had not seen her again—not that they had had leisure time to look. And she hadn't called police.

Sheriff Robert Torrez sat down in one of the cushioned chairs in Estelle's office, crossed one leg over the other and regarded his undersheriff.

"This is the issue." Estelle patted the pile of depositions that was growing on her desk. "The back door was unlocked when Clint Scott burst out and confronted the two Garcia boys. They didn't hear the rattling of a chain, or the turn of a lock. Bam! The door flies open, and there he is. He must have heard the boys talking, or the thunk of the ladder on the wall…something. He gets up, takes the stairs two or three at a time, and looks out that little side window in the foyer. He sees their flashlights. He bursts out and confronts them."

"Yep."

"So why was the door *already* open? Why was the coach so primed that he heard what had to be comparatively faint noises coming from outside? When he went up to check, was he expecting to see someone else, and blew his stack when he saw what was going on?"

"I'd guess."

"He was waiting for someone."

"Coulda been. And it coulda been the *chick*, right?"

"That would explain a lot. It would explain why she was there in the first place, going around to the back door. It explains why he made sure that those heavy doors were *open*. Maybe even a pebble on the threshold to catch the door. He was waiting for her. So what she sees as an altercation, maybe even one involving a gun, does she stay? No. She flees the scene."

The sheriff regarded Estelle with amusement, a rare expression for him.

"Coach Avila said that she saw one of the girls on the team walking back toward the school the next day—Ginny Trimble? She said she was attracted by all the cops converging at the scene. But there's no evidence that says *she* was at the school after the game."

"You already asked Todd Stewart about what time his wife got home after the game?"

"I did. Stacie Stewart told her husband that she went out for a bit with Dana Gabaldon. Dana says that she didn't. Maybe she was headed to talk with Scott, and spooked when she saw the taggers, and then the fight."

Torrez sighed mightily. "It don't matter a whole lot, anyways. Garcia confessed, and he ain't protecting nobody. If Stewart witnessed anything, that's just a little loose end to tighten up."

Estelle smiled. "Yes."

Chapter Thirty-seven

"Posadas County…I'm going to have to find a map."

"West of Deming, east of Lordsburg," Estelle said. "About fifty miles west of Las Cruces."

"Oh, now wait a minute. I was with a detachment at Fort Bliss for a while back in the eighties. We'd go over to Tucson once in a while."

"Then you drove right through the heart of Posadas County, ma'am."

Pinnacle County Sheriff Sharon Naylor laughed abruptly. "How about that. And you're the undersheriff out there."

"I am." Estelle reached out and adjusted the computer screen so she could see Sheriff Sharon Naylor's portrait more clearly. The eastern sheriff appeared trim and formal in her dress uniform with its five shoulder stars. Her portrait dominated a classy web page, laden with colorful photos of the New York State Finger Lakes country.

"Hold on a minute. I'm pulling you up. Got to know who I'm talking to before we get down to business here." A pause, and then Naylor said, "My goodness."

"Ma'am?"

"That's a charming photo of you, Estelle Reyes-Guzman. And the big buff hunk on the other side of the page is your sheriff. Mr. Robert Torrez. Is he a good man to work for?"

"The best, ma'am."

"Can't be. I'm the best. What's your husband do? You're hyphenated, so I assume you're married."

"He's a physician, ma'am."

"Well, good deal. Mine operates one of the major marinas down on the lake. So…you didn't select our department out of thin air for a chat this lovely evening. And you're lucky to catch me on a Saturday. I just stopped by the office to check a few things, and then was going to head home for dinner. That's how busy I am just now. Much more of this and I'd guess that crime is going out of fashion."

"I don't think there's a ghost of a chance, ma'am."

She chuckled dryly. "So what can I do for you?"

"I have a brochure here for Pinnacle Estates Winery. Outside of Casaroga?"

"Nice place. I'm not a wine drinker, but I'm told it's pretty good stuff. They've won all kinds of awards."

"The brochure lists the owners as Clifford and Elise Gordon?"

"Sure. Nice couple. They've worked their butts off renovating an old stone house and barn. Hell of a nice spot."

"We have reason to believe that a woman from Posadas named Stacie Willis Stewart is Elise Gordon's younger sister."

"That could be. I don't know Mrs. Gordon that well. I mean, I would recognize her in the grocery store, of course. What have we got going on?"

Estelle spread out the brochure that had been found among Stacie Stewart's papers. The photo of the Gordons, taken as the couple leaned smiling against one of the mechanical grape harvesters, showed husband and wife, he broad of shoulder with a shoulder-length mane of brown hair pulled back in a ponytail, and Elise Gordon stamped from the same mold as her sister, Stacie Stewart—pretty, blond, curvaceous. Her blue jeans and waist-tied blue denim shirt appeared molded in place.

"She may be a material witness to a homicide, Sheriff." She quickly recapped the murder of Clint Scott, the subsequent arrest of Arthur Garcia, and the concurrent disappearance of Stacie Stewart after abandoning child and dog.

"And she would be involved in this shooting how?" Naylor asked.

"I don't think she was. At first, she was a suspect simply because of circumstances. Odds are good that at one time or another, she had had an affair with the victim. Now we think she just left it all…her husband—*and* her boyfriend. *And* her two-year-old daughter."

"What's he do? The husband?"

"He's a banker, ma'am."

"Huh. Well, wife leaving husband has happened before. What makes you think she witnessed the shower murder, if that's what you're saying?"

"Actually, I don't think that she did. We know that earlier in the evening, she attended a volleyball game at the school. She sat with the victim, and appeared to be pretty chummy with him. Later, sometime after that game, I think she witnessed the victim beating up the two young men who were caught in the process of painting graffiti on the outside wall of the school. I would be interested to know about that."

"Why would she have been there?"

"I think she was coming to meet with Coach Scott—the victim. Maybe to make her break with him final, maybe to rekindle, maybe…who knows why."

"What, she was going to take a shower with him?"

"The only one who can tell us that is Stacie Stewart, ma'am."

"But you have the shooter?"

"We do. We have an uncoerced confession, we have the murder weapon and matching ballistics. We know that one of the two brothers who was confronted by Coach Scott returned to the school later that night—probably less than an hour later—and then killed Scott." She briefly recounted the issue with the confiscated gun.

"You're kidding," Naylor said. "How did that turn out? Did he take his gun back?"

"No. One of the deputies found it stashed in one of the coach's filing cabinets."

"Duh."

"What can I say."

"So this guy *shoots* the coach, and then doesn't recover the confiscated gun."

"It appears that way. He might not have been able to find it. He might have panicked. Maybe he thought someone would have heard the gunshots."

"And the little brother?"

"He's up in intensive care in Albuquerque right now. Broken elbow, broken ribs, ruptured spleen that had to be removed."

"The other brother—the shooter—he wasn't hurt?"

"No. Nothing more severe than a scrape or bruise, if that. He was no match for the victim."

"So, two young men…why didn't the coach just do the smart thing and call the cops?"

"He can't answer that," Estelle said.

"And ain't that the way it always is, though? Testosterone for brains." She laughed dryly.

"Likely so, ma'am."

"So the one mental giant goes home, or out to his car or wherever, and fetches the old equalizer," Naylor mused. "The way courts work today, you'll be lucky to win a murder-two out of this one. Look, I'm sure I have half a million questions, but let's cut to the chase. What can I do for you?"

"We've tried calling the winery, with no luck. I don't know if their phone is out of service, or it's after-hours, or what. And there's no listing for the Gordons' personal number."

"Or they see your area code on caller ID and don't want to have anything to do with you," Naylor chuckled.

"Sheriff, anything pending against Mrs. Stewart will end up as no more than a petty misdemeanor. No one is going to pay extradition costs for that. We simply want to talk with her. Lots of unanswered questions remain. We need to know what she did, why she did it, what she saw that night. Whether they win it or not, there's going to be a first-degree murder charge against the brother in this killing, unless there turns out to be some kind of extenuating circumstances—and she might help us uncover those."

"Tell you what, Undersheriff. It's a gorgeous evening here, and I have never actually visited Pinnacle Estates. You have a recent photo of Mrs. Stewart handy?"

"Of course."

"Good. Fax that to me right now, and I'll take myself a tour. See if she's there. There's a nice little restaurant at the winery, and they won't be closing early on a Saturday night. I know my husband wants to eat there, anyway. You're certain that this young lady left your town Friday at noon?"

"Yes." Estelle rearranged her notes. "She took the bus to El Paso, and she hit that connection just right. Then the flight to Rochester, New York, with one stop in Chicago. The flight landed on time in Rochester at ten-fifteen your time Saturday morning."

"Makin' tracks. Well, we'll just see. Fax me that photo, and I'll get back to you ASAP. Keep your cell phone handy."

"Thank you, ma'am."

"No problem. Glad to help. And by the way, if nobody is home, I'll give you a call anyway, then check again tomorrow. They're right in the middle of harvest now, so they won't have gone far."

"Thank you again."

In a moment, the fax of Stacie's photogenic face was etherized across the continent. Estelle sat quietly for a moment, lost in thought. A large figure appeared in her office doorway, and she looked up to see Bill Gastner regarding her. A grin spread across his broad face. "I saw your car here, and wondered if the chow was still on back at the house."

"Of course it is, Padrino." She glanced at the clock. Four fifty-six in Posadas meant almost seven in upstate New York. Stacie Stewart would be exhausted from her stress, from her travels. And she'd get even more of a kick when she saw the Sheriff's Department car swing into the winery driveway.

"You know, I wondered why you were spending so much time with a broken kid up in Albuquerque when you had a homicide on your hands. The *politicos* have actually been calling *me*, trying to get a hint about what the hell was going on."

"Revenge is the most natural motive in the world. When I found out that Arthur hadn't gone to the hospital with his brother and mom, it wasn't rocket science to figure out what his agenda might be. He didn't come to us to report the beating. He went back to the school to take care of things himself. His one big magic moment. I almost got sidetracked."

Gastner raised an eyebrow.

"What Stacie Stewart did—just dropping everything and running—put a shadow over her. It just complicated things. I never thought that she was the shooter—the crime was just too brutal and cold. There was rage there that didn't make sense for her. She wouldn't have done it. Maybe her husband. But his behavior didn't fit either. So," she held up her hands in surrender, "I had no better course than to go talk to Efrin. See what he knew, what he might have seen. I guess that panicked Arthur. He thought he'd already been fingered."

"It's a good thing most criminals are blabby," Gastner said.

"Yes. In a way I guess I admire him. Not for shooting Scott, of course. But when he knew it was all over, he wanted to protect his brother after all. Efrin has talent, Padrino. Even Arthur knows that, and tried to protect him. To him, the threat to Christina Prescott wasn't even real. His revolver wasn't loaded."

Gastner nodded. "He's a lucky boy, then. Lucky that our esteemed sheriff has ice water running through his veins." He looked pointedly at his watch. "See you at home?"

"Yes. The Mass of Celebration is tomorrow at ten in Tres Santos, by the way. Are you going to make that?"

"If they can stand a heathen in the crowd, sure. The more interesting question is, are you?"

She looked heavenward and offered a heartfelt, expressive shrug. "I've given up planning. But I think, yes. And I have a proposal for you."

"Uh oh."

She reached out and took his right hand in both of hers. "How would you like an all-expenses paid trip to Missouri?"

He frowned, one eyebrow creeping upward.

"I can't let the two kids drive back to school by themselves." She lowered her voice. "I just can't do that."

"So…"

"Look, Angie is eighteen. She can do what she wants. But no. Not Francisco."

"And your proposal is…?"

"You drive my car with Francisco, and I'll ride back with Angie. That way, we have the chance to talk about all kinds of things. If she won't go for it, I'll drive Francisco myself. But he loves to talk with you, and he'll keep you awake."

"I'm not about to drive nonstop to Leister," Gastner said. "Francis needs a little vacation, anyway. Volunteer him."

"He can't. I already asked him. He's got…well, he just can't. That's the way it is."

"Bobby can spring you loose right now?"

"Sure. There's the phone if he needs anything." She gave his hand an additional squeeze. "We can leave Sunday afternoon and stay the night in Amarillo, or someplace like that. On to Leister on Monday. You and I turn around and come home Tuesday and Wednesday."

The crow's-feet at the corners of his eyes deepened. "Gosh, what fun."

"Better than worry," Estelle said. "If something happened to them, I couldn't live with that."

"And what if Angie says no…no chaperone riding shotgun with her?"

"Then so be it. Then Francisco and I will drive back in my car. But that's not going to happen."

"It's not?"

"No. I can be persuasive, Padrino. And no matter which way it goes, I will be able to spend some uninterrupted time with my son. Win, win. And right now, that's all I'm in the mood for."

Chapter Thirty-eight

By seven p.m. New Mexico time, or nine o'clock in New York state, the phone had remained blissfully silent. At 7:02, just as Francisco was making himself comfortable at the piano and Angie Trevino was uncasing the bizarre electronic cello, Estelle's phone vibrated. She fished it out, and saw that it was Todd Stewart's cell.

"Hold that thought," she said to Francisco, who was in the middle of introducing *Teresa's Century,* a concerto in B-flat for flute and piano.

"Ma, you got to throw that thing in the disposal," the boy said, almost good-naturedly. Earlier, he had accepted her ultimatum about the trip back to Missouri without argument. For her part, Angie had only nodded without comment.

"The disposal would be a good place for it, but homicides change all the rules," she offered as her only excuse. She stepped out onto the back patio and slid the door closed behind her.

"Guzman."

"Undersheriff, this is Todd Stewart? I finally made contact. Stacie said that you called some sheriff back in New York? Near where her sister lives?"

"Yes. Sheriff Sharon Naylor."

"Well, thank God Stacie's all right. I finally got through to her. Look, she says that she's going to visit her sis for a little while. She wouldn't say how long."

"She called you?"

"Yes. I have her new cell phone number, if you need it."

"Yes, I *do* need it." She jotted down the number as Stewart dictated. "She didn't say whether or not she was coming home?"

A silence followed that. "No. She didn't say. She *wouldn't* say."

Through the closed door, she could hear the surprisingly mellow sound of the cello being tuned in sync with the piano. The tiny amplifier, no larger than a soccer ball, produced sound of startling clarity.

"You asked?"

"Yes."

"She didn't answer the question?"

"No. She started crying. God." He sighed deeply. "I guess it's better knowing where she is than not, but...I don't know. She said that she didn't want me flying back there."

"Did she tell you why she ran?"

"No. She just kept saying, 'I have some things to straighten out.' And then I asked her how she could just up and leave Ginger like that, and that set her off again. Hell, Estelle, I don't know. She said that she was planning to call you, though. Apparently the sheriff told her she needed to do that first thing. Is it true?"

"Is what true?"

"Is all this tied in somehow with that murder at the school?"

"I don't know how it's related, Mr. Stewart, but my guess is that Stacie knows *something* about the circumstances of Scott's murder. That makes her a valuable witness. We think that she was at the school sometime after the game. We're not sure, but it's likely. I don't think that she actually witnessed the killing. But she might have been at the scene at some point, and can fill in some details. It might make a difference in how the murder suspect offers a plea."

"My God. She's not a suspect..."

"No. We have that person in custody."

"Thank God for that. Is it someone I know?"

"I doubt it. The killing was unrelated to any relationship Stacie might have had with Clint Scott."

"Relationship?" Stewart almost couldn't finish the word, then he said in a half-mumble, "I suppose I'm a little naive."

Just a little, Estelle thought. "When she does call, or when I reach her, we'll see what she has to say for herself."

"You'll let me know?"

"Absolutely."

"Call me anytime. Anytime."

"I'll do that."

"I guess I should say 'thanks,' but I'm not feeling all that thankful at the moment, Sheriff."

"Your daughter is safe and snug at home, and now you know where your wife is. That's a start."

"I guess."

Back inside, the tiny audience looked at her expectantly, but she made an "it's-nothing" gesture and sat on the fireplace hearth, settling her left hand on her mother's right. Her husband sat to Teresa's left, taking care of that hand.

"I need to go to bed," Teresa whispered.

"Just this," her daughter said.

"A quick eleven minutes," Francisco offered. Estelle noticed that Angela Trevino had settled heavy manuscript paper on her slender, portable music stand. Dressed in a simple, sheer black dress with a silver-and-turquoise belt, Angie looked ready for the concert hall. She sat in one of the antique bentwood straight chairs from Teresa Reyes' home in Mexico, and the modern cello offered a startling contrast.

True to form, the music rack in front of Francisco was bare. So gentle they were hard to hear, he stroked the four perfect fifths of the cello's tuning, letting the high A linger for a moment while Angie made some small adjustments to her instrument.

"We spent almost all afternoon tuning this beast." Francisco played a four-octave arpeggio and then nodded at his brother, Carlos. "Me and the man." He looked across the piano toward Angie. She nodded. *Teresa's Century* began with a single D in the treble, a note that grew from nothing until it swelled with power, a solo note so mellow and rich, one could become lost in it—and of such duration that it seemed impossible that a single bow stroke could play it.

Estelle slipped her hand into her pocket, found the tiny button, and turned off her cell phone. She closed her eyes and let the music carry her back to rural Mexico.

Chapter Thirty-nine

At nine-fifty that night, the ringtone on Estelle's cell phone joined with the little instrument's vibrating dance. Too exhausted to sleep, she had joined Bill Gastner and the rest of the family on the patio, letting the soft night humors wash away the drama of the day.

The displayed number carried the familiar area code for Pinnacle County, New York.

"This is Undersheriff Guzman," she said. For a moment there was no response. When it came, her caller's voice was husky, but the impatience came through clearly.

"Hi. This is Stacie Stewart. The sheriff here said that I should call you."

"Ah, good evening." Estelle rose from the patio table and walked back inside to the quiet of the living room. "I'm pleased that you called, Stacie."

"What did you need?"

"There are some good people who are worried about you."

After what could have been a sigh, Stacie's tone was flat. "I'm sure they'll get over it."

Estelle paused. The last thing she wanted to hear was the click of disconnection. "You heard about Clint Scott?"

"I talked with Todd not too long ago. He said that someone killed Clint. I don't believe that."

"I'm afraid that it's true. A young man is accused in the killing, Stacie. He's admitted to it. At this point, it appears that his actions are unrelated to any relationship there may have been between you and the victim. But some events occurred that evening that you might be able to help us with."

"I can't imagine what."

"After the volleyball game, did you return to the school?"

"Yes."

"To see Scott?

"Yes."

"Was that a usual place for you two to meet?"

Stacie hesitated. "We'd met at school after a game once or twice before."

"And this time?"

"This time I was going to tell him face-to-face that we weren't going to see each other anymore."

"Did you see him? Did you tell him that?"

"I didn't have the chance." She paused and Estelle let her think uninterrupted.

"Someone killed him? Is what my husband said really true?" Hesitation cracked her voice, but her self-control was remarkable. "I was thinking that was just a really bad joke. That maybe he'd found out about us."

"No joke, Stacie. At the school, and not long after you were there."

"How do you know that? How do you know when I was there?"

"You were seen." Estelle could hear the young woman suck in a long, shuddering breath. Apparently she was having difficulty being as stone-cold as she had first sounded. "Tell me what happened."

"All right, look. As I approached the school, I saw two guys doing something. One of them was up on a ladder. And then all of a sudden, Clint comes charging out of the back door of the school. I don't know. He must have heard them or something. Maybe he could see them out that little slit window on the side."

"Had Mr. Scott left the back door open for you?"

"Yes. He said he would do that."

"Had he done that before for you?"

Silence for the count of ten, and then Stacie said, "That's no one's business but ours."

"In a case like this one…" Estelle started, then changed course. "We have a homicide here, Stacie. Any details that are related to the incident are important. So Coach Scott bursts out through the door…then what?"

"He yelled at the two kids. I couldn't understand what he was saying. I think they were tagging the building."

"How far away were you at this time?"

"I guess twenty-five yards or so. As soon as I saw Clint, I stopped. He didn't see me."

"He was yelling, and you couldn't understand him?"

"Well, they were all three yelling at once, kinda. He swatted one of them away, and then somehow the ladder went down. The kid was way up high on it, and he went flying, all tangled up. He hit the ground so hard. And then this other kid…it was hard to really see…but it looked like he had a gun. And I'm thinking, whoa, no. I'm not going to get in the middle of this."

"What did you do?"

"I ducked away. I should have done something, but I didn't. I mean, no one knew I was there. So I just…left. I mean, I looked back just as Clint pitched the ladder into the back of the little truck they had there. I heard him say like, 'Take your junk with you,' or something like that. I was on the other side of the faculty parking lot when I heard the truck tear off."

"Do you know what happened after that? Later that night?"

"Todd told me, but I still don't believe it. Nobody is going to do something like that to Clint Scott."

"And you didn't think it would be reasonable for you to contact us as a possible important witness?"

"Is that why you called the sheriff here?"

"Yes. We don't just let these things go, Stacie."

"Okay, so I was there. All right. I was there. But I didn't see what happened later. That's all there is to it. I'm sorry for Clint. You probably don't believe me, but I am."

"You two were close for quite some time, then."

Stacie scoffed. "Close. That's good."

"The volleyball game video shows you sitting right behind Clint Scott, sometimes your elbow on his shoulder, appearing to enjoy yourself. Now you're telling me that you were already thinking then, right at that moment, that you were going to break it off with him? "

"That's exactly what I was thinking…like for the past ten years, thinking. Or trying to think. Look, I'm not altogether proud of what I've done over the years. I first…" She broke off and cleared her throat. "Look. Have you ever been addicted to something like heroin?"

"No."

"Then you don't understand. That's what my relationship with Clint Scott was like, from day one. I've come to realize that now. When I'm away from him, I can think it through, I can say 'never again.' I can do all those things that therapists say I should do. But then when I'm close to him, my God, he's like a drug to me. I can't get enough of him."

"Why not just marry him? You've said that this went on for years, Stacie. Why not be done with it and marry the guy?"

"It's kinda pointless to speak ill of him now, don't you think?"

"We deal in motives, Stacie. The why of it all."

"The why. Well, the why is that, other than the sex, marrying Clint Scott would be like marrying the fancy electronic scoreboard down at the end of the gym."

"Ah. That sort."

"Yes. That sort."

"So, at the game this week, you were thinking of breaking it off."

"I was. Yes. I could see that it was going to become more and more awkward, especially as Ginger grows up. You know, Posadas is a small town, Sheriff. Todd doesn't know, I can't ever let him know… No doubt about it, I had to end it."

She tried an uncomfortable laugh. "Go cold turkey. So I agreed to meet with him at school, in the office. We knew no one would be there." She scoffed again. "I mean, it's not exactly the first time, right? I'm sure some friendly folks have filled you in on that. But, yes, I was going to go and tell him that it was over, once and for all."

"Did he know that was on your mind?"

"I don't think so. Clint was Clint, you know? I'm sure he wanted a repeat performance, something to cap his victorious evening. So, yes, maybe I was a little forward, a little too friendly, at the game. I wanted to make sure that he waited at the school for me. And, yes, I suppose he thought that I had other intentions." She pronounced the word carefully, as if afraid she might leave out a syllable. "I wanted the time to make things clear to him."

"After the graffiti incident, after the two young men drove away, why didn't you go inside the school right then?"

"That wouldn't be too smart, would it? He's just had an argument with some jerks, he's confiscated a gun, so he's armed… what, I'm going to go in there to announce that the party's over? I don't think so."

"The party?"

"Look, it's no secret that Clint and I…that we…look, you talked to Dana, I guess. She would have told you."

"What would she have told me?"

A thin laugh greeted that. "You're so much the cop, Estelle." The use of her first name surprised the undersheriff. "I hope you're happy with Dr. Guzman and those two perfect little kids of yours."

"This isn't about me, Stacie."

The phone shifted, and Estelle heard the rustle of tissue. "Look, I'm sorry. I had no cause to say that," Stacie said finally. "You know, Todd and I went to that concert a year or two ago that your son gave at the school. Him and the kid who played the flute? It was beautiful."

"Thank you. Did you have reason to fear Clint Scott? Did you have reason to think that the gun he'd confiscated from the two young men somehow put you in danger?"

"Well, duh. Yes, I suppose I was a little bit afraid of him. I knew he had a quick temper, and I could see that he would be already worked up. And now with a gun? Like I said, not good timing for an ultimatum."

"And the next day, that's what you did. You just left, un-announced."

"I knew that the eastbound Trailways bus stopped at the Posadas Motel once a day, and I had already planned to be on it."

"Leaving daughter and husband. Even the dog."

"Yes." Her voice sounded dull. "Todd will cope. Especially if he has our daughter with him."

"Stacie, why did you leave your daughter and the puppy in your car at the store? Why not at home? At the bank with your husband…anything but that."

"I just thought…I don't know what I thought, except I did not want a confrontation with Todd. I asked Dana to take me to the motel from the store. You know, it was right around noon, and sometimes Todd comes home for lunch. I didn't want any confrontations. I didn't want any complications. That's why even the dog went along. Ginger has a fit if her puppy isn't with her. And who knows what that little turd would tear up if I left him alone in the house."

"You're not all that fond of him."

"I hate that dog. Todd thinks he's great, but he doesn't have to deal with him day in, day out. He's like a little, high-powered rat."

"You weren't surprised when Clint didn't telephone you the next day?"

"I just thought, 'Oh well, that's the way it's going to be.' I'd catch the bus, and then Dana could just go right back and pick up Ginger. Just a couple of minutes. The store is only a block or two from Dana's house, so it seemed easy. And I didn't want to argue with anybody about my leaving. I didn't want…Todd would have made a scene. With Dana taking Ginger, I'd have half a day head start."

"What did you expect Clint Scott to do? I mean, you didn't

know what the circumstances would be later that evening, but you must have had thoughts that he would be upset with you."

A long pause followed. "Like I told you, I had no idea what happened after I saw him with the two kids. By the time I got to the school, I was having second thoughts anyway. And even though he's such a self-absorbed guy, he can be a charmer. I didn't want to give him a chance to change my mind." She laughed without much enthusiasm. "That's the way he is. It's like addiction, you know? You can say all the right things, but when it comes right down to it? When I'm face-to-face with him? Not so easy."

"Self-absorbed? What's that mean, Stacie?"

"His way or the highway sort of thing. I had come to understand that, after being with him altogether too long. I guess I'm a slow learner, Sheriff. I don't know why. Every time I looked at Ginger, it was a reminder."

"You and Clint had been in this affair since when?"

"What difference does that make? And affair? I hate that word. Scott called it recreation. What, since the year after I graduated. That's how long I've known him. I went to college, and we saw each other now and again. And, yeah, some recreation. Then I got that job in Lubbock, and that helped. I put blinders on for those years. Came close a couple of times, 'cause there's always plenty of guys out there looking for recreation, you know what I mean?"

"Sure."

"Then I came back to Posadas, 'cause my dad was sick and my mom was having a rough time with it. I met Todd at a bank Christmas party. I went there to clean up some account mess that was driving my mom crazy. Todd seemed like such a nice guy. Not demanding, just…what…? Cozy. Good looking and cozy. And I'm thinking, maybe this is it. I walked right into a good job with the electric company, and I'm thinking, finally…"

"And then Ginger came along."

"Yes, she did."

"She was Scott's child?" Estelle's blunt question prompted a brief hesitation.

"Yes."

"Did he know it?"

"Scott? As I said, he was self-absorbed. So I don't think so. I didn't tell him."

"Does Todd know?"

"No. And he won't…ever. Unless you tell him. But she reminds me of Clint every day. The same laugh. The same eyes. I had to get away from that for a while. You won't tell Todd…please."

"That's not our job, Stacie. In summary, what interests us is that you were near the scene that night of what later became a homicide…Thursday night after the game. You saw the confrontation. You left immediately, without ever talking to, or confronting Scott. And that's essentially it."

"Yes."

"There is not sufficient cause to extradite you back to New Mexico, at least not at this time. You might have been charged with a misdemeanor for leaving your child in the car, but that's all. If there is no plea bargain for the young man who killed Scott, if there's a trial, you may be subpoenaed as a witness. You understand that?"

"Yes. I guess so."

"I need to ask you to do something for me. And then we'll see what happens."

"Well, that depends."

"I need you to write up a detailed deposition about what happened that night after the game. What you saw, what you heard. We need to know why you were coming back to the school. You can just say that you needed to talk with Coach Scott for personal reasons. We need descriptions as best you remember of the two young men. And especially what you remember about the confrontation. Then take the deposition down to the Sheriff's Office, have it notarized, and fax it to me on their letterhead. That may be enough. Do you understand what I'm asking you to do?"

"Sure."

"We'll take it from there. And Stacie…if you change your phone again, let me know. No more vanishing acts."

"I like it here," she said simply. "Is Ginger all right?"

"As far as I know. Your husband met with a rep from Children, Youth and Family, and he has custody now."

Stacie took a deep breath, but said nothing.

"Things build up, sometimes. It's what you do now that matters, Stacie. I need that deposition as soon as you can. Tomorrow morning would be perfect."

"I'll do that."

"You'll keep in touch with your husband?"

"I don't know what to say to him. He needs to give me time to think."

"I'm sure he'll do that."

"And I really don't want him coming to New York."

"Then you'd best talk to him." *And no, I'm not going to negotiate for you,* Estelle wanted to add. Instead she settled for an almost curt, "Thanks for making this call, Stacie. The best of luck to you."

◇◇◇

Estelle left her cell phone on the kitchen counter and headed toward the patio. As she reached for the door, she heard the round of laughter, and saw Angie Trevino's hand lightly pat Bill Gastner on the forearm. *What a nice fit,* Estelle thought.

"Troubles?" Francis asked as she stepped out onto the flagstones.

"Everything is fine," she said.

"You've had an amazing weekend," Angie said. "Who would have thought that in such a small town…?"

"We have our moments." Estelle reached out and circled an arm around the waiter as Carlos delivered a slice of key lime pie and a condensation-decorated glass of iced tea.

"You should write a book about the cases," Angie pursued.

"Not a chance. That's Padrino's job. He's the one with the encyclopedia of entertaining war stories."

"Nah," Gastner gruffed. "People make mistakes, you know. It all starts with some little thing, something that by itself seems of little consequence. And then, the big slide down that long, slippery slope. Sometimes we catch 'em before they hit bottom, and sometimes we don't." He nodded at the remains of Estelle's pie and then beckoned toward Carlos. "You have any more of that?"

To receive a free catalog of Poisoned Pen Press titles, please provide your name, address, and email address in one of the following ways:

Phone: 1-800-421-3976
Facsimile: 1-480-949-1707
Email: info@poisonedpenpress.com
Website: www.poisonedpenpress.com

Poisoned Pen Press
6962 E. First Ave. Ste 103
Scottsdale, AZ 85251